Complicit

NICCI FRENCH

PENGUIN BOOKS

PENGUIN BOOKS

Published by the Penguin Group
Penguin Books Ltd, 80 Strand, London WC2R ORL, England
Penguin Group (USA) Inc., 375 Hudson Street, New York, New York 10014, USA
Penguin Group (Canada), 90 Eglinton Avenue East, Suite 700, Toronto, Ontario, Canada M4P 2Y3
(a division of Pearson Penguin Canada Inc.)
Penguin Ireland. 25 St Stephen's Green, Dublin 2, Ireland (a division of Penguin Books Ltd)
Penguin Group (Australia), 250 Camberwell Road,
Camberwell, Victoria 3124, Australia (a division of Pearson Australia Group Pvy Ltd)
Penguin Books India Pvt Ltd, 11 Community Centre, Panchsheel Park, New Delhi – 110 017, India
Penguin Group (NZ), 67 Apollo Drive, Rosedale, Auckland 0632, New Zealand
(a division of Pearson New Zealand Ltd)
Penguin Books (South Africa) (Pty) Ltd. 24 Sturdee Avenue, Rosebank, Johannesburg 2196,
South Africa

Penguin Books Ltd, Registered Offices: 80 Strand, London WC2R ORL, England

www.penguin.com

First published by Michael Joseph 2009
Published in Penguin Books 2010

1

Typeset by Palimpsest Book Production Limited, Falkirk, Stirlingshire
Printed in England by Clays Ltd, St Ives plc

ISBN: 978-0-141-04074-5

www.greenpenguin.co.uk

MIX
Paper from
responsible sources
FSC
www.fsc.org   FSC™ C018179

Penguin Books is committed to a sustainable
future for our business, our readers and our
planet. This book is made from paper certified
by the Forest Stewardship Council.

PENGUIN BOOKS

Complicit

Nicci French is the pseudonym for the writing partnership of journalists Nicci Gerrard and Sean French. The couple are married and live in Suffolk.

There are eleven other bestselling novels by Nicci French: *The Memory Game, The Safe House, Killing Me Softly, Beneath the Skin, The Red Room, Land of the Living, Secret Smile, Catch Me When I Fall, Losing You, Until It's Over* and *What to do When Someone Dies,* all published by Penguin.

To Jakob, Marika, Kersti, Claes, Tobias, Torkel and Mattias

After

I turned around and checked the door of the flat. It was closed. That wasn't enough. What if somebody arrived suddenly? What if they had a key? I pulled my sleeve over my hand so that I wouldn't touch it directly and, awkwardly through the cloth, grasped the bolt and slid it across as quietly as I could. The lights were all on, but the curtains still half open. I sidled round the wall until I reached the window, looking out to make sure nobody was standing in the dark street beneath before I closed them.

Starting at the door, I gazed around the room, dispassionately, like a camera, moving my attention from object to object. There was a framed photograph on the wall. I had never seen it properly before. Now I realized that it was a swarm of blurry orange butterflies. On the small table were a phone (what if it rang?) and a bowl with a small bunch of keys in it. Whose were they? His, probably. I needed to think about that. There was a comfy brown suede chair with the guitar case leaned against it. The guitar lay on the floor beside it, smashed through its centre, strings dangling in the splintered wood. I glanced away to the TV that I'd never seen switched on and to the big striped sofa where we had – No, don't. Don't remember. My scarf was draped across one arm where I had left it a couple of days earlier.

I picked it up and wrapped it around my neck, where the violet bruise throbbed like a nasty memory. There was a bookshelf. The books, some of which had been scattered onto the floor, were all Liza's, about art, design, a bit of travel. Liza was far from here, a thousand miles away. On some of the shelves were objects and curios, little sculptures and pieces of pottery. A miniature brass Buddha, a green bottle with a silver stopper. Liza used to bring them back from abroad. There was a low cupboard along the far wall and, on top of it, a mini-stereo with a wire rack barely half full of CDs. They were Liza's too – all except one. I walked across and, with care, using my fingers like tweezers, picked up the Hank Williams CD I had brought the previous week. I opened the case. It was empty. Covering my hand with my sleeve again, I pressed the button on the CD player and the tray opened. There it was. I pushed my little finger into the hole, removed it and returned it to the case. I put it on top of the stereo. I'd need to look for a plastic bag.

A pine table that Liza used for working stood against the right-hand wall. The mail that had arrived in the weeks she'd been away was no longer in a pile but spread out messily on the surface, and a few envelopes were on the carpet. On the table, there was also a silver laptop, its lid closed, the power cable coiled neatly on top, a funny little green plastic tortoise for keeping pens and a tin box full of paperclips and rubber bands. The chair that was usually beside it had fallen over. A vase lay next to it, its red tulips and water spilled out on the carpet, darkening it from the colour of pale barley to that of piss.

Next to that the body lay face down on the rug, arms splayed. It was the arms that showed he was dead, even more than the dark stain that had spread from under his head – really dark, more black than red. I thought of his open eyes staring down into the roughness of the rug, his wide mouth misshapen against the wool. I looked at the hands, stretched out, as if reaching for something.

Before

Those hands. When I first felt them on my face, stroking the skin at the back of my neck, running through my hair, they were softer than I'd expected. Kinder. I felt almost as if he was a blind man learning about my body by touch. He ran his fingers down my naked spine and I felt that I was being played; unfamiliar bass sounds were released from me as he pressed the keys of my vertebrae, strung me out in a pleasure that was close to pain.

After

I couldn't help it. I knelt down beside him for a minute and put one finger into his slightly curled hand, still warm and soft to the touch, and let it rest there for a moment. In spite of everything, he had been mine for a while. He had looked at me as if I was the most beautiful woman in the world, the most precious to him, and I had comforted him. That's not so far from love.

I stood up again and moved around the room, checking things without being sure what I was checking for. I opened the table drawer, crouched and peered under the sofa, lifted the cushion on the armchair. My leather satchel, the scuffed brown one I had carried as a schoolgirl and used again now that I was back at school as a teacher: it should be here. I knew I had left it on the arm of the chair, its strap unbuckled.

I went into the kitchen, placing my feet carefully on the tiles, heel to toe, so that I wouldn't make any noise. There was the usual mess: unwashed mugs and plates, crumbs on the table, a slop of coffee on the hob, an opened packet of biscuits. I stood quite still. Something was wrong; something did not make sense. I opened each cupboard and looked inside. I pulled out each drawer, wincing as it scraped and squeaked, as the cutlery rattled. Where was my apron, the one I'd brought over when I'd cooked us a meal just a few days ago because for once I was wearing a dress that I would mind staining? Where was my favourite – my only – recipe book, with my name written inside the front cover? 'To Bonnie, with love from Mum.' For a moment I stood quite still, baffled, and with an ominous ache in my chest. The tap was dripping very slightly. Outside, I could hear small gusts of wind in the tree at the back and, in the distance, the cars rumbling along the main road, the shake of a lorry that I could feel in my feet.

I tiptoed into the bedroom. The curtains were closed and the bed was unmade. I could almost make out the shape of his body, our bodies, still there. Clothes were piled for washing in a heap to one side of the door. I couldn't see my shirt, the one he had ripped off and tossed aside, although I knew where it had been lying. I remembered the way he had looked at me then, a gaze that made me want to cover my nakedness. I couldn't see my old T-shirt and flannel shorts, the ones I wear at night if it's cool. I pulled open each of the chest's drawers. A few of Liza's clothes were there, the ones she hadn't wanted to take with her, and some of his, but none of mine, and no satchel either. I sat on the bed and closed my eyes for a few seconds, and in the darkness I thought I could feel him there beside me. Would I always live with this or would it fade and dwindle?

There was only one toothbrush in the bathroom. It was mine. His was gone. I took it. My deodorant was missing but his was there. My razor was missing but his was there. My small tub of body lotion was missing. I stared at myself in the small mirror above the basin. Dark eyes in a small white face. Dry lips. The bruise flowering on my neck, half hidden by the scarf.

I returned to the living room. He seemed more massive than before, deader somehow. How quickly does a body become cold? How quickly does red blood turn sticky? If I touched him again, would he feel hard, a corpse now, not a man? Out of the corner of my eye, I thought I saw his hand move, and I had to stare at it to convince myself that it was impossible.

I was standing on something and when I looked down I saw it was the wedding invitation. I stooped and picked it up, folded it in half and then half again, and pushed it with the toothbrush I was still holding into the pocket of my jeans.

Before

'Cheers.' I raised my glass of cold white wine and clinked it against theirs. 'Here's to the holidays.'

'Liza and I aren't on holiday, remember,' Danielle said. 'Only teachers get six whole weeks.'

'Only teachers deserve six whole weeks. Here's to the summer, then.'

I took a sip and leaned back luxuriously. It was evening but the air was still soft and warm. I needed the summer — the late mornings, the hot, light-filled days, the time away from classes of teenagers making tentative scrapes and whistles on their violins and recorders, the staff room where we were no longer allowed to smoke but drank too many cups of coffee instead, the evenings marking homework and trying to sort out my life, paper by paper, bill by troubling bill.

'What are you going to do with all the time you've got?'

'Sleep. See films. Eat chocolate. Get fit. Swim. Catch up with friends. Decorate my flat at last.'

Several months ago I had moved out of a two-bedroom flat I had loved into one of the smaller, darker, dingier one-bedroom flats that Camden Town had to offer, with thin walls, flaking window frames, a fridge that leaked and a radiator that spluttered and only got warm when it felt like it. My project was to do it up. I had romantic ideas of rescuing beautiful pieces of furniture from skips and wielding a brush to work miracles with whitewash, but first I had to scrape away layers of paint and paper, pull up the patterned carpet, and try to persuade overworked friends to take a look at the electrics and the suspicious brown stain spreading on the ceiling.

'So I'm at home this year,' I said. I turned to Danielle. 'I guess you're going away after the wedding.'

'Honeymoon in Italy,' she said, and gave a small, triumphant smile. I felt a stab of irritation. Danielle seemed to think that her approaching marriage meant that she had achieved a moral ascendancy over Liza and me. We had been at university together, part of the great student democracy of mess and heartbreak and growing up, but now she behaved as though she had pulled ahead of us in a race we hadn't even known we were in, and was looking down on us with a mixture of superiority and pity: Liza, the drunken hoarse-voiced partygoer, and me, the flat-chested school teacher with bleached hair and a string of unfortunate relationships behind me. She was even starting to look different. Her dirty-blonde hair had been expertly layered, styled and flounced; her fingernails were painted a pearly pink (all the better to show off the single diamond); she wore a light summer skirt and looked pretty and unthreatening, as if she were trying to tone down her sexuality in order to become the sweet, blushing bride. I was half expecting her to squeeze my hand and tell me not to worry, that my time would come.

'September the twelfth, isn't it?' Liza poured herself another very large glass of wine and took a deep slurp, smacking her lips with gusto. I gazed at her with affection: one of the buttons on her very tight shirt had come undone, and her mane of auburn hair fell in a muss over her flushed face. 'We'll have to think what wedding present to get you. Something unusual.'

'There's only one thing I want from both of you,' Danielle said, leaning forward so I could see tiny drops of perspiration above her upper lip. For a moment, I thought she must have a wedding list and that I would have to buy an electric kettle or half a silver teaspoon. 'I want you to play at the party.'

'What?' Liza and I spoke at the same time, an identical note of incredulity and dismay in our voices.

'I've been dying to ask you. Honestly, it would mean so much to me. And to Jed.'

'You mean, play music?' I said stupidly.

'I've never forgotten the evening when you played at that uni fund-raiser. Gorgeous. It made me cry. It was one of the happiest evenings of my life.'

'Not of mine,' I said, which was an understatement. 'Anyway, Danielle, we haven't played together for – well, probably not since that evening.'

'Definitely not since that evening,' said Liza, with a snort. She'd been the singer and even then, nearly a decade ago, her voice had been hoarse from smoking. I couldn't imagine what it would be like now – something like a rook with twigs in its mouth. 'I don't know where half of them have gone.'

'And don't want to know,' I added.

'Ray's in Australia.'

'You can get together again,' said Danielle. 'Just this once. It would be fun. Nostalgic.'

'I don't know about that.'

'For my sake?' she said winsomely. She didn't seem to understand that we had no intention of playing at her wedding. 'You only get married once.'

8

'It's impossible,' said Liza, happily. She waved her hands in the air exuberantly. 'I've got my sabbatical and you won't see me for dust. I'm away for four whole weeks in Thailand and Vietnam. I get back just a couple of days before your wedding. Even if we could persuade the others, which we couldn't, I wouldn't be around to rehearse. Neither would most of them. It's summer, after all.'

'Oh,' said Danielle. She looked as if she might weep, her cherished plans gone awry. Then she brightened again, propped her small chin on her hand and directed her words at me. 'But you're here, Bonnie. All summer. Doing your flat up.'

I don't know how it was that I said yes, when I really meant no no no *no*. On no account. I don't know how I allowed my lovely six weeks of pottering about between bouts of decorating to be invaded. But I was a fool, and I did.

After

I didn't know what to do next, and although I understood that every second might matter, that time was running out, I simply stood in the living room, not looking at where he lay face down in the puddle of his own blood. I tried to think, but there were spaces in my brain where thoughts should have been. At one point, I put my hand on the bolt ready to leave, to run into the road and breathe in the night air, but I stopped myself. I wiped the bolt clean with my sleeve, rubbing at the smudge, imagining the spirals of my fingerprints disappearing. I couldn't leave. I had things to do. Tasks. I swallowed hard. I breathed, in and out, as deeply as I could. It was difficult. My breath jammed in my windpipe so that for a moment I thought I would suffocate. I imagined my body falling, coming to rest beside his on the floor, my eyes staring into the tufts of carpet, my hand over his.

I got a plastic bag from the cupboard under the kitchen sink and put in my CD, the toothbrush and the wedding invitation. I started in the bedroom, where most of his things were. I had to do this right. I had only one chance. I found his passport in the drawer of the bedside table, as well as a packet of condoms, and I took both of these and dropped them into the bag. What else? I went into the bathroom and took his razor, his deodorant and his empty sponge bag. His jacket was hanging on the back of a chair in the living room. I felt in the pockets and found his wallet. I thumbed through it. There was a credit card, a debit card, a tatty paper driving licence, a twenty-pound note (that I'd lent him), a small photograph of a woman I didn't recognize, a passport-sized photograph of him. His glowing eyes, his sudden smile, his hands on my body. Even now, with his body dead on the floor, my skin tingled with the memory. I dropped the wallet into the plastic bag. What else? He owned so little. 'You,' I heard him say, as clear as if he was by my side. 'I possessed you, Bonnie.' And I felt clammy and cold all at once, goosebumps on my skin and sweat on my forehead as if I was going to be sick. I pressed my fingers against my temples to stop the pounding.

As I stood there like that, I heard the phone, not the flat

phone, not my mobile, which I had turned off anyway. So that was what I'd forgotten. His mobile. I knew where it would be and the muffled sound of the ringing tone confirmed it. I waited until it stopped, then made myself go back to the body and squat beside it. With half-closed eyes I pushed my hand under it and felt for the rectangle shape. I wriggled my fingers down into the pocket and drew out the mobile. I didn't put it into the bag, though. I turned it off without looking at who had called him and slid it into my pocket.

I looked down at him. At it, huge on the floor. Now what? Because I knew that I couldn't do this alone.

Before

Keeping a class of teenagers under control is a bit like conducting an orchestra, except that it's an orchestra made up of some kind of feral, man-eating beast. It's one of those animals that can smell your fear; it can see it in your eyes, sense it in the shortness of your breath, the acceleration of your heartbeat. And then it goes for you. But it doesn't kill you immediately. It's like a crocodile or a shark that grabs you and plays with you for a while. There were teachers who arrived with confidence and qualifications and thick skin, but just one thing would go wrong and you'd find them crying in the toilets. And when things got really out of control, there was only one thing to be done: send for Miss Hurst.

Miss Hurst was Sonia, who had become my best friend at the school and then perhaps my best friend out of the school as well. We hadn't known each other long, but we had got on from the moment we first met in the staff toilets on the first day of term. She wasn't naturally sociable or extrovert – some of the other teachers felt she held herself aloof – and her wholehearted friendship was like a gift she had conferred on me. She had long dark hair and she was larger than me, taller and more imposing, I guess, but her authority wasn't about her physical presence, so far as I could tell. I hadn't properly seen her in action because kids didn't mess around in my lessons. In fact, it wasn't really possible for them to do so: shouting and singing and dancing and moving were what you were meant to do in my classes. Her control didn't have much to do with discipline and nothing whatever to do with threats of punishment, although her contempt, which could be withering, felt a bit like a blow-torch to your ego. She was just so obviously capable. Her subject was chemistry, and obviously you'd trust her to put two chemicals together without blowing the school up – but you also assumed she'd know how to fix a car or pull out a splinter or tie a bow-tie, and she knew how to manipulate that strangest of organisms, a roomful of hormonal teenagers. Just before the end of term, she had put in her application to be the new deputy head, and although she was young for the post, I felt certain she'd be successful: if Sonia was around, you felt safer.

So, she seemed a natural person to call on. She used to play the violin, rather badly, in the school orchestra, but she could sing. She had a good ear and the right husky sort of voice. She wasn't conventionally beautiful, but she was better than that. She had presence: when she was in a room you wanted to look at her, and when she was in a group you wanted to please her. She held herself well, she was confident without being irritatingly arrogant, and if she could stand in front of a class, she could sing a few old country songs at a wedding.

I lured her to my flat under false pretences. I fed her on bagel chips and white wine and asked her advice about colour schemes and light fittings. She had strong opinions, of course, much stronger than any of mine. I inquired casually whether she was going away for the summer. She wasn't; she didn't have the money for it. I took a breath.

'No,' she said. 'Absolutely not.'

I filled her glass.

'You're tempted, aren't you?' I said.

'The idea is completely ridiculous.'

'Can't you imagine yourself standing in front of the musicians, like Nina Simone or Patsy Cline?'

'What musicians?'

Yes, I thought. She's going to do it.

'So far just me,' I said. 'I mean, actually confirmed.' I felt obliged to add, 'The first two people I asked turned me down flat.'

'Who else was in the group? Anyone I know?'

'Amos, of course. That's when we met.'

'Amos?' Was I imagining it, or did Sonia flush? I looked away, not wanting to see, not wanting to acknowledge the suspicion that had been growing for several weeks now

– that she was interested in him. Why did this make me feel so panicky? After all, they were both free, no betrayal would be involved, everyone had behaved honourably. I hated to think that I wanted to be separate from Amos yet still have him hanker after me. When she spoke next, her voice was determinedly casual. 'Is he taking part in this?'

I hesitated. 'I haven't asked him. Yet.'

'And it won't be awkward?'

'Why would it be? It was perfectly amicable, after all.'

Sonia smiled at me, the moment of awkwardness gone. 'Breakups are never amicable,' she said. They're catastrophes – or they're amicable for one person and not for the other. When it's amicable it's only because neither of them was committed in the first place.'

I took a sip, more than a sip, of wine and felt it sting my gums. There was a familiar ache in my chest when I thought about Amos – not pain, but the memory of pain, which has lodged itself in your bones and become part of who you are. 'Well,' I said lightly, 'we managed to remain friends, kind of, whatever that means about our relationship in the first place.' All those high hopes and buoyant plans for the future that hadn't exploded in some climactic break-up but had gradually withered and died, leaving behind a long-drawn-out dejection, a disappointment in us, in myself. All those months when we both knew but couldn't admit that the journey we had set out on together was petering out and that one day soon our paths would separate. In some ways I would have preferred Sonia's catastrophe to the gradual rusting and corrosion we had experienced with a sense of helpless regret.

'Who actually ended it?'

'It wasn't like that.'

'Someone must have said the words.'

'Probably it was me. But only because he didn't have the courage.'

'Was he very upset?'

'I don't know. I was – but you know that. You saw some of it.'

'Yes,' said Sonia. 'Sad, drunk evenings.' We grinned at each other ruefully. It seemed a long time ago now; long enough for Sonia to be thinking of taking my place.

I gave a little shiver. 'You got me through. You and Sally.'

'And whisky.' Sonia always deflected sentimentality.

'And whisky, true. Whisky, beer, coffee, music. Speaking of which ...'

'Will Amos want to play in a band with you?'

'I haven't asked. I don't know.'

Sonia looked at me intently, then gave a nod. 'You waited until the third glass of wine before asking me, didn't you?'

'The second, I think.'

'The third, definitely,' Sonia said, taking a sip as if to confirm it. 'On the minus side, you've only heard me in the choir.'

'And that karaoke night last year.'

'Was that me?'

'One of the best versions of "I Will Survive" I've ever heard.'

'On the plus side, I don't know any of the people who'll be in the audience. Does it matter if you make a fool of yourself in front of people who don't know you?'

'It's like a tree falling in the forest.'

I took my mobile out of my bag and turned it on, punched in the first three digits of the number. Then I changed my mind and turned it off again, dropping it back into the bag as if it might burn my fingers. I had read articles in newspapers about how experts can tell not just whom you called on your phone, but precisely where the call was made from. People were caught out like that, alibis broken.

I couldn't use the landline, and I couldn't use his mobile, wedged into my pocket. For a brief moment, I thought of giving up and simply dialling 999, weeping to the impersonal voice at the other end. Thoughts hissed in my brain and I tried to separate them out, think each through. I picked up the keys from the bowl, checking to make sure the flat key was among them. Then – through my sleeve again – I unbolted the door and opened it, giving his body a last swift glance before stepping out onto the landing and closing the door behind me. It gave an agonizing click as I pulled it shut. What if someone saw me? I knew that the family next door were away on holiday, because we had been watering their plants for them – or, rather, I had. The young man who lived upstairs was around, although not during the day and usually not until very late in the evening, and today was Friday, the beginning of the weekend. But perhaps he was ill and lying in bed just above me. Or perhaps he was on his way home right now. He could be turning off Kentish Town Road at this very moment and walking up the little dogleg lane, hand already in his pocket fumbling for the keys. Maybe I'd meet him as I opened the front door. I couldn't move. I stood on the landing, straining for any sound. I took a deep breath and walked purposefully towards the entrance, trying not to break into a run.

Now I was on the unlit street and no one else was there. Even though the pain in my ribs knifed through me, I started to jog past the small garage opposite, but it was closed for the night, only the sign advertising MOTs and bodywork repairs flapping idly in the wind. Round the bend, and still it was dark and empty, and at last I was out on the main road, the blessed relief of lorries and cars and motorbikes thundering past, people I didn't know on the pavement, alone or in laughing huddles, walking slowly because it was summer and the night air was soft and warm. I didn't know which way to turn for a phone box because I'd never needed one before now. Maybe they would all be boarded up and useless, the dead receiver dangling from its cable. I turned left and went under the railway bridge, striding quickly until at last I saw a red telephone box. Inside it smelled of piss. There was graffiti on the glass and a solitary sticker advertising the services of Mischa, who specialized in massages. I needed change, and fumbled uselessly in my purse for a coin, my fingers thick and clumsy. I dialled the number. Let her be in, let her be in. She was.

'Bonnie? Are you all right?'

'I need your help. Right now. It's something big.'

'Tell me.'

Hearing her voice calmed me. 'I can't, not on the phone. You have to come.'

She didn't ask unnecessary questions, just said: 'All right. Are you at home?'

I thought of telling her to come to Liza's flat, but then I remembered she wouldn't know where that was. Also, I realized it would be better to take her there, rather than having her turn up like a normal person. So we arranged to meet outside the phone box and she said she'd come at once. It wasn't far.

I stood outside the box and stared straight ahead, at the people, the plane trees, the orange streetlights, the smudged charcoal horizon. Everything looked unreal, as if I was gazing at a photograph that was slightly out of focus. I turned on my mobile to check the time, then turned it off again. I walked up and down, just twenty paces one way and twenty back. I didn't want to miss her, though I knew it would take her at least ten minutes, even if she had run out of the house as soon as she put down the phone. I hadn't smoked for several years, but I went into the twenty-four-hour shop on the corner and bought a packet of Silk Cut and a box of matches. I lit a cigarette, inhaled deeply, felt a nauseous dizziness rush through me, spluttered loudly and long. At least it gave me something to do while I waited.

I wondered whether it was wrong to ask her to help me, to ask anyone. I didn't really wonder. Of course it was wrong. Everything was wrong. But what was my alternative? And who else could I ask? Who else could I trust to tell me what to do? I smoked a second cigarette, more successfully this time, and ground out the stub with my heel for an unnecessarily long time.

At last she was there, in a grey cardigan with her long black hair tied back.

'Thank God,' I said.

Sonia took my arm. 'You're trembling. What's happened?'

'You have to come with me.'

We didn't talk as I led her down the lane. She was walking more slowly than I was, and I had to stop to urge her on. I kept expecting to see someone, although Liza's flat stood at the dead end of the road, just in front of the railway line, and people hardly ever went down there. Sometimes a group of teenagers would be hanging around, up to something out of view of the main road, but now there was nobody. I unlocked the street door but when I reached the door to the flat I stopped.

'Bonnie?'

'I didn't know who else to turn to,' I said. 'Please don't make a sound.'

I unlocked and opened the door and Sonia and I stepped inside. I shut it behind us and drew the bolt.

Sonia managed somehow to stay silent. I didn't even hear an intake of breath. She stood just inside the room, the body spread out in front of her, and stared at it. Her arms hung loosely by her sides, her chin was jutted forward slightly, her feet were planted slightly apart as if she was scared she might topple, and her face was blank. It was as if someone had taken a damp cloth and wiped away all traces of emotion and thought. I didn't speak or move either. I waited. All I could hear was the sound of my breathing.

At last she shifted her position slightly and spoke in a whisper. 'It's . . .'

'Yes.'

'He's dead.'

'Yes.'

She looked around the room as if she was expecting

someone else to be standing there. I could see her taking in each separate item: the smashed guitar, the upturned vase and heap of tulips, the chair lying on its side. Her gaze returned to the body. She hadn't looked at me yet, her eyes darting everywhere but towards me. 'I don't understand.'

'I'm so sorry.'

'Sorry?'

'That it was you I called.'

Finally she turned to me. Her eyes flickered. She dropped them from my face to the bruise on my neck.

'Were you and he . . . ?'

'Involved?' I said. 'Kind of.'

She gave a long, deep sigh, as if she had been holding her breath since she stepped over the threshold. Her voice came out in a soft wail. 'Why am I here?'

Before

'I don't know, Bonnie.'

'That means you might?'

'I hardly touch the guitar nowadays.'

'That doesn't matter!'

'Are you going to tell me it's like riding a bicycle?'

'Would that persuade you?'

Neal gave me a smile, which made him look more like the man I remembered from university. We hadn't seen each other for nearly ten years and even then I hadn't known him well. He had been a friend of Andy's and had been hauled in to play bass guitar, reasonably competently. In fact, that was how I used to think of him – as competent, practical. His hair was darker than I'd thought, but not long as it had been then when it had fallen to his shoulders. He had filled out, was no longer the skinny young man everyone in the band had liked because he was always ready to help out, fix things when they broke, ferry things when they needed ferrying. Liza had taken a bit of a shine to him in those days; maybe she had even made a drunken pass. But it had come to nothing, and after university he had slipped out of our lives. I hadn't really thought about him since.

We were sitting in the small garden of his tiny house in Stoke Newington. I'd told him, when I'd found his number in the phone book and rung, that I could meet him outside his workplace, but apparently he worked from home, supplying garden sheds to people who didn't want to move but needed more room. I had an example of the shed in front of me, at the bottom of the garden. He had erected it himself and apparently it served as his office and a demonstration to interested clients of what they could get for their money. It was really just a simple extra room or a large version of a child's playhouse, with a pitched roof, two windows, a door, and enough space inside for a sofa, a desk and a bookcase.

It was mid-morning, and we were drinking coffee in the warm sunlight. Clematis was climbing one wall and the flower-beds were crammed with plants. A bee buzzed above my head. I took a sip of coffee, leaned back in my chair and sighed. 'This is good,' I said. 'I'm not surprised you work from home.'

'It's not always like this.'

'I've got a flat that's about as big as your shed, but not nearly as nice. Maybe I should get one to live in.'

He laughed. I saw a faint scar slanting from the corner of his left eye. His eyebrows were thick and dark. I found myself wondering if anyone lived with him in his little house, helped him water his flowers and do the accounts.

'All right,' Neal said.

'Sorry?'

'I'll do it.'

'You will?'

'I'm not going away until the end of September this year. It'll brighten up my summer.'

We looked at each other. Both of us were smiling.

After

We were speaking in frantic hoarse whispers.

'I didn't know what else to do.'

'Oh, shit.'

'I called you because I trust you.'

'For what?' Sonia's eyes returned to the body, darted away again; went to my face and then away, as if she couldn't quite bring herself to look at me full on. I saw she was clenching and unclenching her fists.

'I don't know. I didn't know what else to do. Sonia? I need help. I can't –' I stopped, swallowed hard. 'Oh, God, oh, God,' I said. 'I just had to have someone else here.' My words came out in a gabble of sound and I couldn't tell if Sonia could actually understand them.

Sonia still wasn't looking at me properly. Her face was stretched into a sour kind of grimace, her mouth slightly open, and she was wiping her forehead with the back of her hand. 'Before you say anything else, Bonnie, let me say this just once. You should call the police. Whatever's happened here –'

'You don't understand.'

'Fucking right I don't. Fucking right.' Sonia rarely swears; even now it sounded wrong, as if a stranger was speaking out of her.

'I can't explain,' I said. I was trying to focus on her face but it kept blurring, as if I was very tired or very drunk.

'This is a nightmare. Jesus.'

'I know.'

'Why am I here?'

'I didn't know what to do,' I said wretchedly. 'And I couldn't be alone with –' We looked towards the body, and away again. 'With him.'

Sonia put her hand in front of her mouth as if to stop herself making a sound. She muttered something under her breath. Her face was pale and I could see beads of sweat on her forehead.

'You were lovers?'

'What?' Even now I couldn't say it.

'I said: you were *lovers*?'

Blood pounded in my head. I could feel myself turning hot and red with such shame I felt I'd scorch and burn up with it. 'None of that matters now.'

23

'You stupid, stupid, stupid idiot. Oh, Bonnie! Why?' She gestured blindly towards the body.

'There's nothing I can say.'

'This is so, so . . .' Sonia trailed off. Again, she put a hand over her mouth as if to stop unwanted words spilling out of her. 'We're standing here talking quite calmly,' she said, 'and all the time – *this*.' She gestured with her hand, blindly. Her face wrinkled for a moment.

'I know. I know.' My words seemed to fill the room. I realized I was shouting and dropped my voice to a whisper. 'I *know*.'

'Know what? What do you know?' She put a hand on my arm. Her fingers pressed painfully into my flesh.

'Don't.'

'Why are you showing me this? What are you doing?'

'I didn't –'

'Don't say you didn't know what to do again!'

'Sorry.'

'He's dead. *Dead*. And you and he – Christ, Bonnie, what have you done?'

'I don't know.'

'What makes you think I won't just call the police myself?'

I shrugged. A sudden weariness came over me, so heavy that I almost lay down under the sheer grey mass of it and closed my eyes. 'You could,' I said, 'and I know you're right. It's probably the only sane thing to do.'

At last Sonia looked at me properly, with an intense, almost fierce gaze. Her cheeks were flushed and her eyes bright. She seemed almost unreal. 'I need to think,' she said.

'I shouldn't have called you. It was wrong. Everything's

wrong. Oh, God, everything's so wrong. How did it all turn out like this?'

'Be quiet. Just don't say anything.'

Suddenly I could no longer stand up. I sat down on the floor, my back to the body, wrapped my arms around my legs and pulled up my knees so they were pressing into my eye sockets. I tried to make myself as small as possible. Curled up into myself, I could hear my heart beat. I waited. My neck throbbed, my ribs throbbed and, around me, the room seemed to throb. At last I lifted my head on the wobbly stem of my neck. Sonia walked to the window and stood by the tiny strip of half-light between the closed curtains, looking out onto the shabby, silent little street. She was frowning, her eyes narrowed as if in intense thought; her lower lip was trapped between her teeth and I could see her chest rise and fall with her breathing. At last she turned back to the room and stared down at the body. Something in her appearance seemed to have changed. She stood straighter, and when she spoke, her voice was clearer. It was as if a fog had lifted.

'OK,' she said, as if she had come to a hard decision. 'You turned to me for help.'

'Yes,' I said, in a whisper from the floor.

'And you won't call the police?'

'I can't.'

'You say you trust me. That's where we're going to start from. Trust.' She was speaking very slowly and clearly, enunciating her words with exaggerated precision as if she was talking to a small child or a foreigner with only the most basic grasp of the English language, but I knew that she was actually talking to herself, going through the jumble of thoughts in her head and trying to order them. 'So, I trust you as well. You're my friend. I'm not going to ask you what happened here, though it seems pretty bloody obvious. If you want to tell me about it, save it for later.'

I nodded. I would never want to tell anybody about it, not ever.

'I have a horrible feeling that I'm going to regret this, but I won't go to the police. That's the first thing.'

'Thank you.'

'I won't do anything you don't want me to do. But what I don't understand is what I *am* supposed to be doing. Bonnie?'

'It's – I don't know how to say it.'

'You didn't just get me to come over here to give you a hug?'

'No.'

'Why didn't you run away?'

'I thought –' I stopped. I couldn't really remember what I'd thought.

'Bonnie.' Sonia's voice was sharp, calling me to attention. 'Why am I here? What do you want me to do?'

It was my turn to pause for a long time.

'I said I called you because I didn't know what to do and I thought you'd somehow be able to tell me. But that's not quite true. I do know what to do – or, at least, one thing I could do. You're the only person I felt I could turn to, but by doing that I think I've done something terrible to you. So I just want to say this: say the word and you can walk out of here and I'll wait until you're safely away and then I'll call the police. I'll have to. Because, you see, what I've been thinking of needs someone else. I can't do it alone.'

Sonia looked at the body lying out of sight behind me, and this time she didn't glance away. She was like someone standing on the edge of an abyss and staring down into it, unable to drag herself away from the horror.

'So what do you want from me?'

'I want –' I took a deep breath, and then the words came out in a blurt, sounding even more absurd and impossible than I'd imagined. 'I need you to help me get rid of the body.'

Sonia gave a gasp and took a step backwards so she was almost against the door. 'Get rid of it?' she said weakly. I noted that she was saying 'it' not 'he', as if she was trying to forget that here was a man she had once known, had not long ago talked to, argued and laughed with. 'Are you serious?'

'If we got rid of it, maybe nobody would look. Not for a long time at least.'

'You are serious? You think that you and me – No, Bonnie. No. You don't know what you're saying.'

'I couldn't do it on my own,' I said. 'I tried to think of a way but I couldn't.'

'This is crazy. Look at him. He's big. We can't just – I mean, how?' She gave a small, high laugh that stopped as abruptly as it had started, though the harsh sound seemed to hang in the room. 'You've been watching too many films.'

'It's the only thing I can think of.'

'It's mad – and it would be horrible. I feel sick even thinking about it. Have you allowed yourself to imagine what it would be like? He's dead. He'll be starting to go hard or something soon.'

27

'Oh, no! Don't.'

'What? Don't talk about it? If you can't even bear to talk about it, how will you actually do it? That's what happens, isn't it? Everything starts to change.'

'Oh, God.'

'You don't want to touch him. The dead aren't like the living.'

'I have to, Sonia.'

'It's a crime, don't forget. Maybe that doesn't mean so much to you, not now, but for me . . .' She stopped and swallowed hard. 'Covering it up, blocking the investigation. We could go to prison for a long, long time. I could, I mean. Have you thought about that?'

She stood over me, her face blazing, and my head sank back onto my knees.

'You're right and this was unforgivable,' I mumbled. 'Get out of here this minute, and I'm terribly sorry I ever rang you. I mean it. Go.'

'Get up, Bonnie.'

'What?'

'Stand up. I can't talk to you while you're crouching on the floor like that.'

I stumbled upright. The room seemed to sway around me. 'I feel drunk,' I said. 'Or as if I've got flu.'

'You really thought we could just get rid of it?'

'No,' I said. 'You were right and you should go.'

'How? I mean, how on earth would we even get his body out of this flat without being seen? And then what?'

'I don't know.'

'When does Liza get back?'

'September. But we can't just leave his body here for her

to discover.' For the briefest second I allowed myself to think of decomposition and decay, of his body seeping and crumbling into the carpet. My stomach turned and I whimpered.

'So?'

'I don't know,' I said. 'The only thing I've thought about is getting rid of it. Making it go away.'

'Yes, that,' said Sonia, grimly, pulling back her mouth again. She almost looked as though she was smiling. But she wasn't.

'Which is why I knew I needed someone. You. I needed you.'

'Did you think about how you – we – would do it?'

'I just thought about putting it somewhere where it would never be found.'

'Brilliant. Like where?'

'Like really, really deep woodland where nobody ever goes.'

'For God's sake, Bonnie, this is England,' said Sonia. 'There aren't deep woodlands where nobody goes. And if there were, how would you – how would we – get it there? I can tell you that, wherever you put it, someone walking their dog would find it. When you read in the papers about bodies being found, that's what happens. A man walking his dog.'

'Couldn't we bury it somewhere?'

'Where? That's got all the problems of finding somewhere to dump the body without being seen, and then when you're there you have to dig a huge hole, deep enough so it doesn't get dug up by scavengers. There's a reason why they make graves six feet deep. And, wherever you do it, it shows for a long time. It's not just a matter of going to Hampstead Heath after midnight.'

'What about burning?' I asked, a bit wildly.

'It's not like an old newspaper.' She made a gesture of repugnance. 'The human body is a difficult thing to burn.'

'They do it in crematoriums.'

'Yes,' said Sonia. 'With an industrial-strength furnace that can heat up to a thousand degrees. And even then it doesn't destroy everything. It's not something you can do in your back garden.'

I had a horrible flashback of cremating my guinea pig when I was small and the smell that had filled our garden. I put my hands over my face, feeling sick. 'What then?' I said. 'What can we do? We can't hide it and we can't bury it and we can't burn it. You're not going to suggest cutting it up, are you? I can't, Sonia. I'd prefer to die myself than do that.' In fact, the thought of dying seemed inviting right now, to close my eyes on all this.

'No, I'm not,' said Sonia. 'I've dissected animals and I'm just not going there.'

'People do go missing, though,' I said. 'Some bodies are never found.'

'Not very often, except in films. Not unless you're the Mafia and you can bury a body in concrete and build a motorway on top of it. This is not an easy thing to do.'

My mind wasn't working properly. Everything seemed to be shifting in and out of focus. His body, sprawled on the floor, seemed to fill my field of vision. Everywhere I looked, I saw it. 'You're right,' I said. 'I can't do this. I don't know why I ever thought I could. Oh, God. Let's just get out of here as quickly as we can.' And I clutched her arm as if to pull her from the room.

But Sonia drew back. 'Wait,' she said.

'We just leave,' I said. 'It's like you were never here.'

She turned to me, her expression calm and almost tender. I could feel her taking charge of the situation and myself letting her – and, after all, wasn't that why I had turned to her? So that someone else could sort out the ghastly, catastrophic mess?

'We can't bury it,' she said. 'We can't burn it, we can't just dump it. What's left?'

'Water,' I said. 'People are buried at sea, aren't they? You see it in war films. They wrap them in a sail with weights.'

'You've got a boat, have you?'

'No.'

'You know anyone who's got a boat?'

I thought for a moment. 'Probably,' I said. 'Friends of friends. I don't think any of them would lend me one and let me take it out to sea on my own, though. Also, I don't know much about marinas but I imagine they're pretty crowded in the summer.'

'It doesn't have to be the sea,' said Sonia.

'Where, then?'

'I don't know.'

'It's no use.'

'I don't know *yet*. It's the best idea so far. Water. A lake or a reservoir or a river. There's a reservoir I've been to once; it's quite near here. That might be the best place. There would definitely be no one around. First we need to sort things out.' She walked over to the body and peered down at it almost dispassionately. 'Why does it look so different from someone who's just asleep?'

I'd seen him asleep and I'd seen him dead and I was trying not to think of the difference.

'The blood's all on the rug,' said Sonia, 'so I don't think we need to do very much cleaning.'

She seemed to decide something and walked out of the room. I heard cupboard doors opening and closing. When she came back in she was wearing pink washing-up gloves. She threw a packet to me and I caught it. It was another packet of gloves, yellow this time.

I ripped it open and pulled them on. Sonia picked up an ornament from the table and contemplated it. It was made of dull grey metal, of a vaguely abstract design, and showed a big figure and a small figure linked together. It probably symbolized something like friendship or parenthood.

'By picking this up,' said Sonia, 'and moving it, I'm interfering with a crime scene. I don't know what the exact charge would be – interfering with an investigation, conspiracy to pervert the course of justice, something like that. If it blows up, we go to prison for years, lose everything. Are you really up for this?'

'Are *you*? You're the one I brought into it.'

Sonia walked across the room and put the ornament on a shelf, placing it just so, like a conscientious housewife.

Before

'You mean it?'

'Don't get too excited, Joakim,' I said drily. 'It's not going to make you rich and famous.'

'A professional band.'

'I wouldn't go that far.'

'Playing a proper gig at last – not just some poxy school dance full of fourteen-year-old girls wearing too much makeup.' His voice was scornful as only a just-eighteen-year-old voice can be.

'It's a wedding, that's all. I don't even know how many people will be there. And it's not your kind of music, Joakim. It's more country and blues.'

'I love country music,' he said. 'It's authentic. Lucinda Williams. Steve Earle. Teddy Thompson. Who else is in the band?'

'So far, there's you on violin, a man called Neal Fenton who was in the original band for a bit – he's the bass guitarist – and Sonia Hurst is the singer. Well, you know her, of course.'

'Sonia Hurst?'

'Yes.'

'The chemistry teacher?'

'That's right.'

'Singing in your band?'

'Yup.'

'Weird,' said Joakim. 'Me playing a gig with Miss Hurst and Miss Graham.'

'You've left school now. You'd better call us Bonnie and Sonia.'

'What'll you play? Piano?'

'Probably I'll just fill in the gaps. It depends on who else we get.'

Until June, when he had taken his music A level, Joakim had been my student. I had first met him when he was fifteen, small for his age with cropped hair and the aggressive posture of someone who wants to be older, taller and cooler. Over the summer between GCSEs and sixth form, he had grown six inches and looked pale, malnourished and ungainly, with puny tufts of beard on his chin and spots on his forehead. But then, six months later, he had filled out and let his dark blond hair grow long, had taken to smoking roll-ups and wearing skinny black jeans. Suddenly he was a young man, languid and determinedly casual, damping down his natural intensity under his laid-back manner, his style a mixture of the romantic and the world-weary. I had witnessed all of his rapid incarnations and it was hard for me not to catch glimpses of the young Joakim, so anxious to belong, so cockily insecure. I had also witnessed his progress as a musician. It seemed to me – perhaps because it was true for myself as well – that it was in playing music he felt least self-conscious and most at home with himself. I spend a lot of my time in a cacophony of sound, screeching and puffing and banging, but Joakim could really play: the flute well, the electric guitar loudly, the violin with outstanding intonation and feeling.

It was this that made me ask him to join us – and that

I'd known he was at a loose end this summer, waiting for his exam results and for the next stage of his life to begin, pretending not to care, biting his nails. He touched me, I suppose, and I wanted him to be all right.

The wedding was weeks away, it was a beautiful summer's day and I was on holiday. I knew I should make a start on my flat, which even on a day like today felt dark, almost subterranean, but not right now. Instead I called Sally and asked her if she fancied a picnic.

'That would be completely and utterly fantastic,' she said, with a fervour that took me by surprise. 'I'm going stir-crazy with Lola.'

Sally was my oldest friend. We had known each other since we were seven, and sometimes I was surprised we had managed to stay in touch over the years. We were almost like sisters. We squabbled and fell out, occasionally took each other for granted and every so often resented each other (me, that she was so settled, and her, that I was so free), but we were inextricably bound together. Lola was her eighteen-month-old daughter: a tiny, plump, fierce child with dimpled knees, hair like sticky candy floss, a voice like an electric drill and a will of iron that often reduced Sally to tears of power-less frustration. I noticed that she had stopped saying she and Richard wanted four children in quick succession.

'You bring Lola and some bread for the ducks. I'll buy us a ready-made picnic. We can meet in Regent's Park.'

We sat on the already-bleached grass and ate cheese rolls while Lola ran around, tripped over, yelled loudly and unconvincingly, her mouth seeming to take up her entire face, followed a squirrel, calling to it to stop and eat her bread, then abruptly crawled onto Sally's lap and fell asleep, her thumb thrust into her mouth and her four fingers spread over her smeared face. Sally gave a sigh of relief and lay back on the grass as well, Lola across her.

'I'm exhausted after an hour,' I said. 'I don't know how you manage.'

'"Manage" is the wrong word,' she said. '"Manage" sounds neat and organized. Look at me – do I look neat and organized?'

'You look great.'

'I look tired, I look frazzled, I look fat, I look like my hair needs cutting and my legs need waxing and my nails need painting.'

'You've been reading too many glossy magazines,' I said. 'The ones that tell you how to be a size eight three days after giving birth.'

'You know, one of the books I read before having Lola had a section on what you need to take with you into hospital – things like a rubber ring to sit on in case you have to have stitches, and a spray bottle for your partner to squirt into your face when you're in labour, though if Richard had done that to me I would have punched him. And one of the essential items was your makeup bag so you could make yourself look fresh and attractive for your husband.'

'That's awful.'

'No – what's awful is that I did. I took in my makeup and even put on some bloody mascara before I had visitors. Can you imagine? You've just brought a whole new life into the world, this miracle, and you have to think about how you look. You wouldn't do that, though.'

'Only because I don't usually wear makeup much anyway.'

'There you are, then.'

'Where?'

'I dunno, really.' She yawned. I could see down her pink throat. She looked like a cat – a large, tired, slightly shabby cat.

'We should go away somewhere for a weekend,' I said.

'Bliss. But what would I do with Lola?'

'We'd take her.'

'No, we would not. If we went away together, I want to drink and I want to sleep. Two things I can't really do with her around.'

'Leave her with Richard, then.'

She snorted. 'As if. Tell me something about the big wide world.'

'I'm getting a band together.'

'What?' She hooted with laughter and Lola shifted on her lap.

'Hang on, it's not as if I've never played an instrument before.'

'How come I didn't know about this?'

'Well, it's only been a couple of days. I haven't seen you.'

'You should have told me.'

'I'm telling you now.'

'Yeah. Sorry. I think I kind of rely on you to give me some vicarious excitement. What kind of band?'

'A folksy, bluegrassy, this-and-that, amateur and not-very-good kind of band that can play at a friend's wedding in the middle of September and then not be a band any longer.'

'Disband the band.'

'Right.'

'Maybe you'll be spotted, be offered a record deal.'

'Hardly. We'll get together for rehearsals once or twice a week, play three or four numbers that no one will pay any attention to and that will be the end of that.'

'Maybe I could join.' She sounded wistful.

'Do you play anything?' I knew she didn't, of course – we'd been in a recorder class together when we were eleven, but that was about it.

'I could shake a tambourine.'

'No tambourines, no triangles, no maracas.'

'Who's in it?'

'Me, Sonia, a pupil – or, rather, an ex-pupil – called Joakim, and this guy who was in our original uni band.'

'Which one?'

'His name's Neal. I'm not sure you actually met him. I didn't know him that well. Dark hair, quite good-looking, a bit shy.'

'He sounds nice.'

'And I was wondering if I should invite Amos.'

'Amos!'

'You think I shouldn't?'

'Well. I mean, why would you?'

'I don't know. He'd be offended if I didn't.'

'So what? Amos being offended is no longer your worry, is it?'

'I guess not. And, anyway, maybe it's too soon. I know it was mutual, sort of, but we were together for ages.'

Sally shifted her position on the grass and gave a great yawn. 'Sorry. I *am* interested. It's just this time of day.'

'Amos thinks we should stay good friends, but it isn't that simple. You can't just go from being lovers who think they might be together for ever to being on civilized good terms. Or I can't, at least. I think it's different for him. Maybe Sonia's right and that's because it didn't mean so much to him, but I think it did. Or maybe I just want to think it did. All that time has to have meant something.' I paused. 'Sally?'

A tiny snore bubbled from her lips. She was asleep. I looked at her, lying flung out on the grass, one arm over her face and the other on Lola's bunched-up body. Her chestnut hair needed washing; there were stains on her dress, purple smudges under her eyes. I put the remains of our picnic into the bag and stood up to drop it into the rubbish bin.

After

Sonia knelt by his body. She hesitated for a moment, then straightened him out with her pink-gloved hands. She took his arms, one after the other, and laid them so they were lying straight by his sides. Her face had become expressionless again. I could only tell that she was distressed by the slight tightening of her mouth and the way, every so often, she gave a small blink as if to clear her vision.

'You have to help me, Bonnie,' she said.

'What shall I do?' To show I was co-operating I took off my thin jacket and hung it over the back of the chair. My knees were trembling and I almost tripped as I turned back to her. My body seemed to have a mind of its own – twitching hands, wobbling legs and a faint buzzing in my ears.

'We'll roll him up in the rug.'

I wanted to say I couldn't do this. I couldn't kneel down and touch him, manipulate his cooling limbs, bundle him up like a piece of garbage. I couldn't. I had lain by this body, held it, kissed it, and I couldn't.

'We have to pull it to one end of the rug and then roll,' Sonia was saying. 'Bonnie? Look, if we're going to do this . . . this . . .' Her voice cracked. 'We have to do it now or not at all.'

'You're right.'

'Take the shoulders.'

I made myself kneel by the body. A few inches from my knee, the pooled blood was dark, almost black.

'When I say, try to shift it up.'

'Yes.'

A dead body is heavy. It won't be shifted. His soft hair. I used to run my fingers through it. I could hear his murmur of pleasure, the way he said my name, like a groan. But it was matted with blood now.

'We're going to have to roll it over,' said Sonia. 'Move it that way.'

I will see his face, his beautiful face. Will his eyes be open, will they stare up at me?

'Yes,' I said. 'Yes.'

'Ready?'

'Ready.'

There he was. His eyes were open and they looked up past me to the ceiling. His face was pale, almost grey, like putty. I couldn't help myself. I peeled off one glove and put out a hand to touch him for a last time, to close those unseeing eyes.

'No.' Sonia's voice stopped me. 'Don't do it, Bonnie. He's dead. It's all over. Now it's a corpse, and we're getting rid of it. If you start letting yourself feel everything, we won't be able to go through with this. Remember later – feel whatever it is you have to feel later. Not now.'

I lifted my eyes to her face, which was stern and handsome. 'You're right,' I said. 'What do we do now?'

'When we're ready we have to get it out of here and into his car. Where are the keys? You have got them, haven't you?'

'In my pocket, with the one for the flat.'

We squatted at either end of the body and lifted the end flap of the rug over it. Now I couldn't see his face any more. Straining with the effort, we rolled the body over in the rug. It rose and fell with a muffled thump. My ribs ached, and sharp stabs of pain shot through me. I had a sudden memory of rolling up a tent when I was a teenager, trying to make it tight and even. But bodies are unwieldy things. Through the rug I could feel his shape. The bulk of his shoulders. Don't feel. Don't remember. Don't even think. Just act.

Before

The phone rang just as a friend who had popped by was telling me he thought I could simply knock down the wall between the small kitchen and sitting room, making one not-so-small room. It was Joakim, still awkward with my transition from teacher to human being. He asked me if I'd found a drummer. I told him we might have to make do without. He gave an awkward cough. 'There's someone I know.'

'Yes?'

'My dad. He's keen.' There was a pause. 'Not good, but very keen.'

After

The body was hidden from sight but, if anything, that made it worse. Before it had been a horrible mess, perhaps even a tragedy of some sort. Now it looked like what it was, which was a crime.

'What next?' I said.

'We carry it out to the car.'

'Won't he be very heavy?'

'We have to.'

'Couldn't we just leave him in the street somewhere? It might look as if he was mugged.'

Sonia sighed, as if I were failing to live up to her expectations. 'We've got to do what we said we'd do,' she said. 'The best chance is for it to seem as if he's gone away. If he's found dead tonight, there'll be a huge inquiry straight away. It'll all fall apart.'

At that moment there was a sound so unexpected that

for a few seconds I couldn't make out what it was. It was as if my brain was refusing to accept it. I had to think hard and then I realized. It was a doorbell. The doorbell of the flat. It rang again. We looked at each other. I was certain that the same questions must have been in both of our minds. Who was it? Had they heard anything? And, most important of all, more important than anything else in the world: did they have a key? My brain was working slowly. I couldn't make sense of it. First I thought: No, they can't have a key or why would they be ringing the bell? But then I thought: Some people leave a key somewhere, under a flowerpot. I'd done it myself sometimes. Was it possible Liza had done that and not told me?

There was another question I tried not to ask myself. What if there was a key and the person let themselves in? What then? To that question I couldn't even imagine an answer. I looked down at the bundle on the floor, then up again at Sonia. She just gave a shrug. Of reassurance? Helplessness? I started to hiss something in a frantic whisper but she shook her head and put a finger to her lips.

There was a silence and we waited, keeping absolutely still. I tried to hear steps from outside but I couldn't make anything out. All I could hear was my heart, the blood rushing and pounding through my body and, beside me, Sonia's breathing – small, shallow gasps that made me realize she was as scared as I was. The phone rang. It had to be the person outside. Maybe they'd had some sort of arrangement. Was there an answering-machine? I hadn't thought of that. The phone rang and rang. It felt as if someone was punching me on a bruise, over and over. Finally it stopped. We waited and waited, much longer than was necessary. I didn't trust myself to speak and it was Sonia who broke the silence. When she spoke it was still in little more than a whisper.

'I think they've gone.'

'Will they come back, though?' My chest hurt, as if I'd run a long distance.

'How should I know?'

'I feel a bit sick,' I said.

'Are you actually going to be sick?'

'I don't know. Maybe.'

'Try to breathe deeply.'

'We mustn't do anything until the middle of the night – I mean about getting him out.'

Sonia gave me an exasperated look as if I were one of her more stupid pupils. 'Does anybody else have a key for the flat?'

'Liza gave one to me, which I gave to him, but I've taken it back now,' I said. 'And she said she was going to leave one with the man who lives upstairs, in case of emergencies.'

'No one else?'

'I don't think so,' I said. 'But you know how it is – keys get copied. He might have given them to other people as well.'

'We should be all right.'

'It's just if someone came in . . .'

'At least it would be simple.'

'Simple?' I said. 'What would we say?'

'I don't know,' she said. 'It wouldn't matter much, though.'

There was another silence.

'Let's agree to take him to this reservoir you went to once,' I said.

'Langley reservoir.'

'Right. And we'll open the windows, take off the hand-brake and push the car off the edge. Yes? But then what?'

'Then we go home.'

'But how? We won't have the car.'

'We'll walk.'

'It might be miles to the nearest station.'

'Have you got a better idea?'

'No.'

'Anyway, that's the least of our problems at the moment. Let's get to that bit and then think about it.'

'OK. You're right.'

'We can leave in about half an hour.'

Before

Guy Siegel was a solicitor in a large and respectable firm, but when I called at his house he was dressed in jeans and an expensively distressed sweatshirt. As he passed me a bottle of beer it felt more as if he was the one who was a musician. He didn't hand me a glass. It was all very rock and roll.

'You probably wouldn't believe it,' he said, 'but in my last couple of years at school I played in a punk band. Well, really we were a *post*-punk band. It probably seems like ancient history to you.'

'It's a bit before my time.'

'Come on through,' he said. 'Ancient history. We were

called Sick Joke. You know, I had a fantasy that we'd be signed up and go on the road and . . . Well, I'd probably better not say exactly what my fantasy was. But you don't get a house like this working in a post-punk band.'

I looked around at the rugs and vast sofas, the tastefully abstract paintings on the wall. 'I guess not,' I said.

'Joakim's like me,' he said. 'He's got a fantasy of working as a musician.'

'He's good,' I said. 'But I told you that at the parents' evening. If you're half as good as him, you'll be fine for us.'

Guy swigged his beer. 'I'm a bit more than half as good, I reckon. You need a drummer?'

'Yes, we do.'

'You wouldn't mind having a father and son in the group?'

'If it's all right with you two.'

'You don't want me to audition?'

'I trust Joakim. And you too, of course.'

'I've got my own drum kit.'

'So much the better.'

He took another swallow from his bottle and looked at me appraisingly. 'As I said, Joakim's got this fantasy of working as a musician, just like I did. It's ridiculous, of course.'

I didn't say anything.

'Don't you agree?'

'I'm a music teacher,' I said, 'so I don't think I'm the right person to say that playing music is a fantasy.'

'I don't think Joakim's got any interest in being a *teacher*.' Guy said this as if it were even worse than being a musician. 'He wants to play live. What do you think about that?'

'What do you want me to say? He's good. One of the best I've taught.'

'He looks up to you. He respects you. Playing like this is all good fun, now that he's finished his exams, but I'd be grateful if you'd talk to him about the realities of being a musician.'

'This is just a one-off performance at a friend's wedding. We're not touring America.'

'But if he asks.'

'I really don't give career advice. However, we're a pretty motley collection. I don't think there's much chance that we'll seduce Joakim with our glamorous rock-and-roll life-style. Anyway, you'll be there to keep an eye on him. Is that why you want to sign up?'

'Not at all,' Guy said. 'I've spent too long playing along to Led Zep records. It'll be good to play with some real people.'

After

I crept out of the door again and onto the lane. It was entirely dark now, just a few stars blinking above me and the dull orange glow of London all around. The lights were out in the flat above, but still, the person who lived there might return at any moment. Even thinking of that made my heart lurch. The shapes on the road became hunched figures that were watching me. I unlocked his car, opened the boot in readiness and returned to the flat.

'All clear,' I said to Sonia.

Without saying anything more, we knelt beside him. I took his feet and Sonia his shoulders.

'One, two, three *and* . . .' she mouthed.

We heaved and managed to lift him a few inches. His body sagged between us. An arm broke free of the rug and I let out a squeal before I could help myself. 'He's so heavy,' I said.

'Drag him,' said Sonia. 'Until we get to the front door.'

We bumped him along the floor, sometimes summoning enough strength to give him a heave that carried him a foot or two along. The rug he was wrapped in stuck on the carpet but slid more easily when we got to bare boards. There were shooting pains in my ribs. My head banged and my neck throbbed and I could feel sweat running off me. Beside me, Sonia grunted and gasped.

At last we were at the front door. I pushed it open and stepped outside. The lane was empty and silent. The garage sign banged faintly in the breeze. I nodded at Sonia.

We half lifted the body. The rug came loose again and his hand dragged on the ground. Those hands, strong and warm: once they had stroked my face, cupped my chin. I tried to stop myself thinking of it. I staggered and couldn't keep a grip and he thumped onto the tarmac. I gave a cry as if we were hurting him.

'Sorry,' I whimpered.

'Just a couple of yards now.'

Stooping, buckling at the knees, we shuffled the last few feet to the car. We shouldered the bundle upwards, not speaking but panting with the effort. The rug slipped further. I could see his hair. Soft hair. But the boot was too small and he was too big. He didn't fit. We had to push it – the corpse, the body, him, the man I had . . . had what? Not loved, unless love can be violent, hopeless and dark, with its end written into its beginning. We had to push and twist his body, shoving it into the space. As if he was a thing – but he was a thing. He was dead. Nothing was left except memory and loss. I heard his head bang on the metal. My shirt was sticking to my back; it hurt to breathe. Sonia stood upright, her face pale in the darkness, and pulled the boot shut.

We drove in silence, me at the wheel and Sonia studying the road atlas we'd found in the car, giving me terse directions. Police cars came at me out of alleys and parked on blind corners; lights flashed blue and sirens wailed in the night. In the rear-view mirror, I saw eyes watching me. I sat up quite straight, pinned my gaze on the road ahead. Our heavy load dragged at my mind. The car was a coffin, a little tin coffin. London dwindled, and at last the headlights were picking out hedges, fields and trees, and finally a tarmac track. The gates were locked and for a moment we nearly gave up – I nearly gave up, putting my head on the steering-wheel and saying over and over again, 'It doesn't matter, it's all over.' Sonia remained calm. She examined the map and directed me round to the other side where there was another entrance. Glinting black waters of the reservoir, sailing boats lined up on the shore, rattling and tinkling in the small breaths of wind.

Before

'I don't know if it's a good idea,' I said to Amos.

We were sitting outside one of those London pubs that used to be a down-at-heel dive, filled with smoke and the smell of stale beer, but had reinvented itself and was now a gastro-pub, serving things like seared scallops on a bed of lentils, or blue-cheese and poached-pear salad – which was what I was eating. Amos had a steak sandwich. The sun poured down from a clear blue sky. We'd done this so many times before – sat outside a pub talking, making plans.

'Why not?'

'Because.' I made a vague gesture with my hands. If he didn't know, I wasn't going to say.

'You mean because we used to go out together and now we've split up?'

'We didn't go out together. We lived together. For years.'

He looked at me. I couldn't make out his expression: it seemed both scrutinizing and beseeching. 'It was fun, wasn't it?'

'Fun? You mean, living together?'

'We had fun.'

'Sometimes,' I replied. Fun, fights, tears, regrets, and a slow, depressing ending. I looked at him: thin, with dark intense eyes and a beaky nose, a shock of dark brown hair. I used to tell him he looked like Bob Dylan – Bob Dylan *circa* 1966. That was when I still loved him.

'We're friends, aren't we?' He sounded like a small boy.

'It's not quite as easy as that.'

'That's up to us.' He took my hand. I pulled it away. 'Who else is going to play?'

'Neal – remember him? Then a boy from school and his rich father. Don't make that face. Oh, and Sonia,' I added, as if she was an afterthought.

'Sonia?'

'Yes. She's going to sing.'

'I can imagine her voice,' he said. 'Velvety.'

'Hmm. I don't quite understand why you're so keen to play in this band, Amos.'

He shrugged. 'It'll be a hoot. And I'm at a loose end.'

'No holiday plans, then?'

'I'm too busy trying to pay off my mortgage to take a holiday this year,' he said. 'Or next.'

Ten months ago, Amos and I had bought a flat together just off the Finchley Road. It was lovely, with tall rooms and big windows and white walls, a balcony for plants. The day we had moved in, a glorious late-September day, we had lain on the carpet together, in the unfurnished, echoing room, and held hands, staring up at the freshly painted ceiling and giggling with happiness and surprise at being so grown-up, so together as a couple because, after all, we weren't really adults when we met, but footloose and penniless students. When I had left him, or he had left me, or maybe we really had left each other, he had had to buy me out, money I had used to put down as a deposit on my depressing hole in Camden.

'You could always sell it,' I said unsympathetically. 'But OK, Amos. Come and play your guitar.'

'It'll be like the old days.'

'It will not be like the old days.'

At that moment, a stocky figure came up to us. 'Bonnie?' I tried to place him.

'It's Frank. We studied music together years ago.'

'Sorry. Wrong context, you know.'

He took a seat beside us.

'I'd have recognized you anywhere,' he said. 'You still look about twelve.'

'Thank you.'

'What are you up to nowadays?'

'I teach music at a school near here,' I said.

He wrinkled his nose sympathetically. 'A teacher?'

'Yes.' I looked at him with dislike, willing him to go away.

'She's got a band, though,' Amos put in.

'I haven't!'

'You've got a band? What kind of band? What's it called?'

'I haven't got a band and it hasn't got a name. I'm putting something together for a one-off thing, a friend's wedding.'

'I'm going to be the guitarist,' said Amos.

'It's just an amateur thing, then,' said Frank, dismissively. 'I thought you meant something serious.'

'What's so good about being serious?' said a voice behind me. I turned in my chair and squinted up to see who was speaking. A tall man with soft brown hair in a wing over his forehead, grey eyes with crows' marks around them, wide white smile, crumpled shirt.

'This is Hayden,' said Frank, then added, as if he couldn't help himself. 'He plays in a real band.'

Hayden studied Frank for a moment, His smile disappeared and his face seemed thinner, older, colder. 'You're a bit of a tosser, aren't you?' he said softly. 'I play music, that's all.'

Frank blushed a deep, unbecoming red. It seeped into his hairline. Even his ears turned red. I almost felt sorry for him. He muttered something about getting a drink and left. Hayden remained. 'What do you play?' he asked me.

'Oh, this and that. Piano. Violin.'

'She plays everything,' said Amos, proudly. He was behaving as if I was his girlfriend again. 'She only has to pick up an instrument to know how to play it.'

Hayden ignored him and concentrated on me. 'What's your name?'

'Bonnie.'

'Hello, Bonnie.'

He held out his hand and I took it. 'Hi,' I said. Then: 'This is Amos.'

Hayden nodded at him. 'Sorry about Frank,' he said. 'Can I get you a drink?'

'No,' said Amos.

'Yes,' I said. 'A spicy tomato juice, please.'

'One spicy tomato juice coming up – oh, except I don't seem to have any change on me.'

I laughed and stood up. 'I'll get it,' I said. 'What are you having?'

'A lager, I think. I'll come with you.'

We left Amos scowling at the table and stood at the bar. Several people recognized Hayden, calling out in greeting. There was an ease about him, a casual familiarity.

'What kind of music will you be playing in this band?'

'I'm not sure yet – maybe a bit bluegrassy, and country stuff, folk.'

'Patsy Cline, Hank Williams, that kind of thing?'

'Yes! Exactly.'

'I love that. Soulful, spine-tingling music.'

'Me too.'

Our drinks arrived and we carried them back to the table. Amos was looking sulky. 'I noticed you didn't get one for me,' he said.

'You said you didn't want one.'

'I thought this was going to be just you and me,' he muttered, and Hayden raised his eyebrows.

'Sorry, am I interrupting something?'

'No,' I said.

'Is there a vacancy?' asked Hayden.

'Vacancy?' Amos leaned forward pugnaciously.

'In your band, Bonnie. I'd like to be involved – if you need any help.'

'We don't need anyone else,' said Amos. 'We're full.'

Hayden ignored him. 'Bonnie?'

'You're probably out of our league.'

'I don't know what that means,' he said. He stared at me as if I was a puzzle he was trying to solve. 'What about it?'

'Are you serious? You don't even know me.'

'No, but this way I will.'

Later that day I went with Neal to a little street market in Stoke Newington, near his house. Stalls had been set up under striped awnings, selling local honey, organic vegetables, burgers and sausages in soft white rolls, and also beaded cushions, incense sticks, strings of beads – things whose bright charm fades as soon as you get them home.

It was another warm evening and there were swallows among the plane trees.

When Neal had rung me, he had been awkward, blurting out the invitation, and now he was shy. We wandered among the stalls. I bought us both a glass of white wine that came from an English vineyard and tasted pale and flowery, and he bought a tub of black-bean salad that we shared.

'You know,' he said, as we stood and watched a man walk by on impossibly tall stilts, 'I used to be a bit scared of you.'

'Of me? Why?'

'You had that boyfriend – what was his name?'

'Eliot?'

'That's the one – with a shaved head.'

'Yeah.'

'You both used to seem so confident and cool.'

I laughed.

'No, really. I used to look at you with your weird clothes and think you were this hip couple.'

'So when did you discover the truth and stop being scared of me?'

'I didn't. I was terrified of ringing you up.'

I smiled and put my arm through his. 'Well, I'm very glad you did. You know what I want now?'

'What?'

'One of those enormous chocolate brownies.'

'This is all wrong,' Sonia said.

'Wrong? How wrong?'

'It's not the way I remembered it.'

'What does that mean?'

'Look.' She gestured out of the window at the shallow gravel shore where boats were turned turtle and lay under their tarpaulins in a long line.

'Yes?'

'Bonnie.' She spoke with a stern patience. 'How are we going to push a car into this? I thought there was a place that went down steeply so we could simply let off the hand-brake and roll it.'

'What shall we do?' I heard the wildness in my voice.

'Hang on.'

She got out of the car and I joined her. Our feet crunched over the gravel and we stood by the water's edge, where little ripples ran over the stones.

'That's what I was remembering.' Sonia pointed to her left. I could just make out the steep concrete sides of the reservoir wall.

'We can't get the car there.'

'That's right.'

'So it's no good.'

'We have to think of something else.'

'What?'

'Give me a moment.'

'We could drive the car somewhere else. Push it off a cliff.'

'Which cliff?'

'I don't know. Cornwall? They have cliffs in Cornwall, don't they?'

'You want us to drive to Cornwall?'

'It's an idea anyway.'

'It'll be light by the time we get there.'

'We could drive there, find somewhere, wait until night-time and then do it.'

'I don't think that sounds like a good idea at all.'

'What, then?'

'We have to do this now, Bonnie. And here.'

'We can't. You've just said so. If we tried, it would just get stuck with the water up to its sills and then where would we be?'

'We can't push the car in. Maybe that would be riskier anyway.'

'Riskier than what?'

'Than just putting it in the water.'

'You mean the body?'

Sonia crouched down, twitched the tarpaulin off one of the boats and craned to peer underneath. 'There's a pair of oars.'

'I don't like this.'

'We could put it in the boat, row out and push it in there.'

'You think?'

'We'd have to weigh it down first.' She looked around. 'There are stones and bits of rubble.'

I sat down on the shore. The inky water glinted and slapped and a sharp breeze stung my cheeks. I put my head on my knees and wrapped my arms around my legs. If I could make myself very, very small, perhaps I could disappear. 'I'm not sure I can do this.'

'It's too late for that, Bonnie,' Sonia said, with a hissing urgency. 'If you can't do it for yourself, you're going to have to do it for me. You got me into this.'

'You're right.' I stood up again. 'Sorry. Tell me what to do.'

I walked along the shore, picking up rubble and large stones, then returned to Sonia who had turned over a small boat. 'Help me drag this to the shore,' she said.

Together we pulled it along the shingle until its bow was nosing the water.

'Now the body.'

Pulling it out of the boot was even harder than getting it in. We had to haul it by the arms. The rug slid off and there was no way of escaping him: how the head bumped and lolled, the legs splayed, the weight of him. I kept my eyes half shut, or sometimes closed them entirely, pulling and jerking blindly. At last he tumbled out and lay at our feet. Without saying anything, Sonia and I took an arm each and dragged him over the gravel.

'How are we going to get it in?'

'If we lean the boat over, we can roll it in, I think.'

We tipped it onto its side, then stood on the rim to keep it steady and manoeuvred the body until it was draped half over the edge, head in the bottom and legs still on the shore. The body slithered and then collapsed inside. He was face down now. I couldn't see his eyes any more, just the side of his head and his bloodily matted hair, the havoc of his splayed limbs. Bile rose in my throat and I turned away.

'The rocks,' said Sonia.

I handed her a piece of rubble, then reached for another and another and another. I tried not to look at her. Finally she stood up. 'That should do it,' she said.

I put the oars into the rowlocks, then we both took off our shoes, rolled up our trousers and pushed the boat out. It was hard at first for it was heavy now and the bottom scratched against the gravel. We waded forward, up to our calves in the cool water, trying to force it along. My jeans were wet and water splashed up onto my shirt. Then I felt the boat floating free in the water and we clambered in at the back. It rocked violently.

'One oar each,' said Sonia.

We sat side by side with the dead bulk of him between us, his arms reaching out, his legs twisted over each other, and rowed in a clumsy and hopeless way, out of synch with each other. The boat seemed scarcely to move. It bobbed and wavered along the shore and only bit by bit did we make any headway out into the open water. It was very quiet: the only sounds were our laboured breathing and the splash of our oars. There was a half-moon, low in the sky, leaving a messy reflection on the surface of the water. But it was dark enough so that we wouldn't be visible from the shore.

'This must be all right,' said Sonia at last. 'It should be deep here.'

'How do we do it?'

'We push it over the edge, head first, maybe.'

I looked at her in the moonlight. Locks of her hair had escaped and lay across her face, which was pale and set in an expression of determination, and I knew that I had to do this. I nodded.

'Pull it around a bit,' said Sonia. 'I'll try to keep the boat steady.'

She sat on the other side of the boat and put her feet against the body, pushing it away from her. I took the shoulders and tugged. The boat rocked violently. I set my teeth and jerked him forward some more. The boat heeled, water sloshing over the edge, and Sonia inadvertently cried out in alarm as I dived towards the middle to keep us from slithering into the water. I fell on top of him, huddled for a moment with my head on his shoulder.

'You'll have us in,' Sonia gasped.

'It's not working. I can't shift him enough.'

'Ease him over the back.'

Together we pulled him up the boat. Now his arms were hanging over the stern. We tugged some more and now his bashed head was there too. The boat heaved from side to side. What if it tipped over? There was an obscene bumping as we got his shoulders over. The back of the boat was dangerously low in the water and the bow reared up. Without a word, we heaved and jerked him some more. I could feel his soft belly under my fingers, the waistband of his jeans rough against my knuckles. Now his head was in the water, his hair floating like seaweed on the surface. One more push and he was slithering in, going down like a diver in search of treasure, like a drowning man, his clothes catching brief bubbles of air, his arms curling back against his body, his legs sliding through the dark, rippling surface. And suddenly the boat was steady in the water again. Its heavy load was gone. He was gone. There was nothing to show he had ever been there. I leaned over the edge of the boat and was sick, violently retching up all the contents of my stomach. After, I scooped up a handful of water and washed my face.

Then I sat down at my oar again and we rowed back. It was much easier without him. We clambered out, dragged the boat up the shore, removed the oars from the rowlocks and turned the boat turtle once more, stowing the oars underneath and replacing the heavy tarpaulin. Sonia found our shoes and we put them on, standing in the dim moonlight with the waters making a faint lapping sound behind us.

After several moments Sonia put a hand on my shoulder. 'Let's go back,' she said.

'Back?'

'Home.'

'Yes,' I said. 'Home.'

'We have to get rid of the rug. I saw some huge bins on our way – we can just push it into one.'

She put her hand on the small of my back and pushed me onto the path.

'What about his car?' I said suddenly.

'What about it?'

'What do we do with it?'

'You're right. I didn't think.'

'Let's just leave it somewhere in the middle of London, throw away the keys.'

'If we leave it, someone will report it. The police will be called to tow it away. You always see it happening.'

'We don't have a choice.'

We walked slowly back to the car. The half-moon was high in the sky now and reflected in the water. I thought of him out there, lying on the bottom for the fish to nibble at.

'I know,' Sonia said. 'We'll drive it to Stansted.'

'The airport? Why?'

'We can just leave it in the long-stay car park. In most places cars get towed away after a few days, but people park cars there for weeks. Months, even.'

'You think?' I said doubtfully. I couldn't work out if the idea was brilliant or crazy.

'I can't think of anything else. Can you?'

'I can't think of anything at all.'

I got into the car and turned the key in the ignition, then looked at her sitting beside me, so upright, fastening her seat-belt and pushing stray locks of hair behind her ears. 'Do you want to know what happened?' I asked.

'Do you want to tell me?'

'Not yet.'

'Then wait.'

'Sonia.'

'Yes?'

'You can't tell anyone about this, ever.'

'I know.'

'Absolutely no one.'

She knew who I was talking about.

Before

I've never really had secrets. When I was at school I had friends who lived in their own families like spies. They led double lives, concealing sexual activity, dubious friends, cigarettes, drugs, laziness, delinquency, in some cases outright criminality. It seemed such hard work. There was so much to remember, so much to conceal. And all it took was a word at the wrong time, something left in the open, a lie that didn't quite fit and everything would be exposed.

I didn't see the point. I didn't exactly rub my parents' noses in my teenage behaviour, but if they asked a question, I answered it with the truth, if not necessarily the whole truth. I didn't have secret lives, I didn't have secret friends, I didn't have secret admirers. I never kept a secret diary or, in fact, a diary of any kind. I never drank in secret or smoked in secret.

But I did have one secret, which, perhaps, on deeper consideration, was the reason I had agreed to Danielle's ridiculous and irritating suggestion. It was a secret love, a secret passion, a secret obsession, which I kept in a case in the cupboard and only brought out when nobody was around. It was a Deering Senator five-string banjo.

Most of my memories of the gig that Danielle had seen were of what was wrong with it. It was under-rehearsed. One of the main musicians had dropped out at the last minute. We all knew it was the end of our college life and that lots of the people there wouldn't meet again for years, if ever. But for me the occasion hadn't lived up to all the emotion, and Danielle had just projected onto our performance emotions that weren't there. Above all, we were lacking a banjo. How can you play bluegrass music without a banjo? You can't.

It wasn't until years later, when I was in Denmark Street to buy some sheet music, that I glanced at the windows of electric guitars and basses and there it was, nestled in the corner, looking at me like a pathetic little puppy begging me to buy it. It cost more money than I had in the bank so I went into the shop and beat the price down to all the money I had and walked away in such a state of shock that I forgot to buy the sheet music I had come for. I took it home like an adopted waif to join the family of instruments I already had, the electric keyboard, the fiddle, the guitar, the recorder I only played at school and the flute I hadn't touched for years.

I suspected that for most people the banjo seemed a comical instrument, the sort of thing that would be played by a man wearing a red-and-white-striped jacket and a straw boater, singing slightly saucy novelty tunes. To ordinary people it probably even looked comical, its round body like a child's drawing of a guitar and its metallic brittle tone lacking the warmth and colour of a guitar. It wasn't like that at all for me. I can't put it into words, not really. Music has always been a refuge for me. Probably what made me turn to it in the first place was that when I was a child we had a piano in a spare room, an old one that was battered and out of tune. When my parents started shouting at each other, I would go to that back room and play for hours and hours, losing myself in the strange songbooks and piles of sheet music they'd inherited along with the piano from some old aunt. That was what music had always been to me. Somewhere I could escape to, where there weren't words, where you didn't have to be clever.

Maybe that was the problem with Amos and me. Amos definitely fell into the clever category. He didn't respect my intelligence, that was for sure. And I suppose I didn't respect his musicianship. Amos loved music. He certainly loved listening to it. He could play, after a fashion – he did his grades when he was at school and all that – but it was never natural to him. For him, playing music was always a frustration. He could never translate what he heard in his head. He had a characteristic tense expression when he played, which at first made me laugh and then didn't. I tried to teach him, in our early days together, manipulating his arms and neck as he crouched over the keyboard, attempting unsuccessfully to get him to loosen up, to let himself go. But I stopped that. Amos had a very developed sense of his own dignity.

I wouldn't dare say this to anyone, but to me every instrument spoke with its own tone of voice. The banjo may seem shallow and silly to other people but to me it talked of something old and melancholy and neglected. Gradually, in the weeks after I had bought it I took it out of its case and tried to get it to speak with some kind of fluency. But I had never played it in front of anybody, not once. When Danielle asked me, I felt it, deep down, as a challenge.

I couldn't think where we should play. My own flat was too small and the walls were dangerously thin. I mentioned the problem to Sally and she said we could come round to her house. I protested feebly, mentioning her child, her neighbours, the trouble and noise, her husband, but she absolutely insisted. 'You'll be doing me a favour,' she said. 'I feel I'm becoming more and more cut off from the world. I'd love to have people around.'

I was a little concerned to hear someone actually pleading with me to have a band rehearsal in their home, but I was too relieved to push the point much further. We decided on Sunday afternoon and then I rang everybody about it. It seemed alarmingly easy.

I arrived at Sally's home in Stoke Newington ten minutes early but I still wasn't the first.

'Hayden's already here,' she said, as she opened the door.

'Oh, I'm sorry.'

'No, it's fine,' she said. 'He's playing with Lola.'

That wasn't completely accurate. He was lying back on the sofa in the living room and Lola was clambering up his rangy frame, as if he was a piece of apparatus in an adventure playground. Her foot, in a grubby green sock, was firmly on his neck and one hand was flat against his stomach. He looked as if he was asleep, but when she toppled sideways as if she was going to fall head first onto the stripped-pine floor, he extended an arm and rescued her. She shrieked with laughter.

'Lola, leave the poor man alone,' said Sally, happily. 'Bonnie's here, Hayden.'

'I know,' he said. 'You'll excuse me if I don't get up right now.' He gave a groan. 'Careful where you put your knee, young lady.'

Lola glared at me briefly and went back to prodding Hayden.

'Can I get you anything?' said Sally. 'Hayden's had coffee and cake and some biscuits. I'm just making him some tea.'

'Fine,' I said. 'Lovely.' I left the room and went in and out of the house, bringing my electric keyboard, my guitar and the banjo. Hayden didn't offer to help or even say anything. He sat up, balancing Lola on one knee, and sipped the mug of tea Sally had brought him, his grey eyes watching me over the rim so that I felt suddenly self-conscious.

'I brought a keyboard,' I said. 'But I'm not sure if we're going to need one and I'm rather hoping we don't. This is just a first get-together. It'll all be very casual.'

He didn't say anything, just looked at me with an enigmatic smile playing on his lips. I felt that he was, in some curious way, making up his mind about me, which of course made me talk more.

'Really,' I said. 'You should treat this as an audition of us. You might well decide that it isn't worth your trouble, and if you do then it will be absolutely fine to —'

At which point, thank the Lord, the bell finally rang. I gestured helplessly and went to answer it. It was Joakim and Guy, who was battling with his equipment. 'I didn't bring the full kit,' he said. 'I didn't know what you wanted.'

He struggled through, followed by Joakim, who shrugged at me helplessly. I turned to close the door and almost shut it on Amos, who didn't look amused. 'I assumed I'm playing guitar,' he said.

'It's all very casual,' I said.

'It doesn't matter how casual it is. You still have to play an instrument.'

Neal arrived with his bass and amp, then Sonia, and suddenly it was like a party. Sally dashed around taking orders and bringing mugs of tea and coffee and trays of biscuits, cake and sandwiches.

'Where's Richard?' I asked her.

'He plays football on Sundays,' she said.

'He does know about this?' I asked, suddenly anxious.

'Of course he does. Why shouldn't he?'

I'd had a horrible flashback to being about fifteen and having someone's father come back unexpectedly to discover something happening that wasn't meant to be. Meanwhile the party seemed to be showing no signs of turning into a rehearsal. Lola was running around screaming with what appeared to be happiness but might at any moment turn into a full-blown tantrum. Hayden had not yet got up from the sofa but he seemed entirely unconcerned about not knowing anyone. He was like a planet: sometimes a person would gravitate towards him and say something I couldn't hear. I had the impression that everyone in the room was intensely aware of him, even when their back was turned to him and they were talking to someone else.

'Who is he?' said Joakim, close to my ear.

'I met him through a friend.'

'What's he play?'

'He's brought a guitar, so I suppose . . .'

'Is he any good?' This was from Amos.

'I don't know.'

Amos looked around suspiciously. 'There seem to be too many guitarists.'

'I thought we could mix and match a bit. It's all very casual.'

'You keep saying that,' said Amos, 'but we're going to be playing in public. We don't want to make fools of ourselves.'

'It'll only be in front of Danielle's friends and family. That's not really making fools of ourselves.'

'Aren't you going to start? I've got to be away by five.'

'That'll be no problem.'

'You're supposed to be in charge,' he said. 'You need to

assert yourself from the beginning. Come on, now.' He clapped his hands in a way that made me feel glad we'd split up and irritated that I'd let him into the band. There was certainly one too many guitars; he was right about that.

'Quiet,' he continued. 'Bonnie's got something to say.'

There was an ominous silence. I coughed. This was ridiculous. I was used to dealing with thirty hormonal teenagers. I could handle this.

'I'm grateful you all came,' I said, 'and grateful to Sally for letting us play here.' I looked around but Sally had gone. I'd last seen her running out of the room in pursuit of Lola. 'This is mainly a chance for us to meet up and get to know each other. I thought we could start by having a go with something simple.'

'Have you got any music?' said Amos.

'We need to talk about what we want to play. Maybe some of you have suggestions. But my first idea is that we could try a tune. I mean a very basic tune that I could play and then everyone can have a go at it on their own instrument. If it works, then it's a fun thing to dance to and it can go on pretty much indefinitely.'

There was much bustle as people took instruments out of cases and tuned them. Guy knocked one of his cymbals over. Neal switched on his amp, which resulted in feedback that virtually shook the house. I looked at Hayden. He hadn't taken his guitar out of its case. In fact, he hadn't noticeably moved. Was he contemptuous? Amused? Bored? Had he finally realized what he'd got himself into? Well, I'd warned him.

With trepidation, I took out my banjo. It was crazy but

I would hardly have felt less nervous if I'd removed my shirt and bra. The sight of it was greeted with a murmur of surprise.

'What the hell's that?' said Amos.

'Are you actually going to play it?' asked Neal, grinning.

But Hayden finally stood up and came over to me. He lifted the banjo out of my hands and cradled it as if it were a newborn baby. Then he ran his hands over the strings, releasing a high, delicate sound. He smiled at me. 'Good,' he said, and returned to the sofa.

'I'm going to play a tune called "Nashville Blues". Sorry, Sonia, there are no words to this one.'

'That's a relief,' she said, to general laughter.

'Guy,' I continued, 'you follow me. You'll just need brushes. And you, Neal, as well. It should be easy enough for you. Then, when we're done, maybe someone else can pick up the tune and we'll see how it goes.' I fitted the picks onto my fingers and fiddled a bit with the tuning. Then I looked at Neal and Guy. 'Listen to a few bars and then follow me. OK?'

One of the things I love about the banjo is that the first note of a tune sound tentative and when you get going it sounds as if a clockwork motor has started and two people are playing at once. As I got into the tune I saw a slow smile coming over Sonia's face and she began to nod in time. When I got to the end I went into a vamp. Then I looked around. 'Anybody?' I said.

Before anyone else could do anything, Amos stepped forward with his guitar and started to play. It sounded awful, so awful that after a few bars it became literally impossible for anyone to continue and we all ground to a halt in such disarray that everybody was laughing. Amos turned bright red.

'Well, that was interesting,' I said. 'And brave. Let's start again.' I looked around. 'Joakim. You have a go.'

I played through the tune, then looked at him and nodded. He started to play, frowning with concentration, glancing at me. It was all right, not bad, but then he pulled a face, stopped and shook his head. 'I can't,' he said, almost with a scowl. 'Sorry. I just can't.'

'It was good,' said Hayden, from the other side of the room. He stepped forward and took the fiddle and bow from Joakim's hands. They looked tiny in his grip. 'You did this, yes?' He played the first notes just as Joakim had played them, glanced at me and nodded. I played the tune once more and looked at him. He smiled and played Joakim's notes once more – then something mad happened. For a moment we weren't in a sitting room in Stoke Newington, we were in the Deep South on J. J. Cale's back porch with Ry Cooder and Earl Scruggs and God knew who else. As he played, Neal and Guy clung on, like fallen riders with a foot caught in a stirrup. He glanced at me in the way you do when you play together, keeping in time, signalling tiny shifts with your eyes. When he stopped, there was more laughter, but of a different kind.

'That was amazing,' Joakim stammered. His cheeks had flushed.

'You did it,' said Hayden, handing him back the fiddle. 'You just need to let go.'

Amos was smiling as well. But not with his eyes.

After

We drove to Stansted in silence. It was three in the morning and the roads were practically deserted. Each time there were headlights in my rear-view mirror my mouth dried and my heart raced at the thought that it might be the police. This was what it must be like to be a criminal, I thought. But, of course, I *was* a criminal now. During the last few hours I had crossed a line into a different world.

At one point, Sonia ordered me to stop in front of a row of terraced houses. She got out of the car and dropped the plastic bag full of everything I'd collected in the flat into a dustbin that was standing on the pavement. She pushed it deep inside and wiped her hands on her trousers before climbing back into the car. I drove on. Later, we stopped at another bin and got rid of the rug.

'Stop,' said Sonia suddenly, as we reached the signs to the long-stay car park. I pulled over.

'What is it?'

'There are cameras at the barrier. When you take your ticket to get in, you're staring into one.'

'Then we can't go there.'

'Yes, we can.' She opened the glove compartment and fished out a pair of sunglasses. 'Put them on.'

'But –'

'Now your scarf. Tie it over your head. Oh, let me.' She wrapped it tightly around and nearly throttled me with the knot. 'Nobody would recognize you now.'

'What about you?'

'I'll lie on the floor. Let's go.'

She lay down in the back of the car and I drove into the car park. I took the ticket, the barrier rose and signs directed us to Zone G.

'Hang on!' Sonia said, from the floor. 'Wait!'

'What?'

'Pull over. This is stupid. It's not just at the entrance there are cameras – they're everywhere. We haven't thought this through properly. I must have been mad.'

'What do you want to do?'

'On the train, as well. We can't get the train back into London. We should never have come here.'

'But we have. Do you want me to turn round and leave?'

'I don't know.' For the first time she seemed confused. 'What do you think?'

'What do I think?'

'Yes. Come on.'

'Where are there cameras?'

'Everywhere! On the shuttle – aren't there? I can't remember, but I bet there are. And in the airport. And in the station. And on the train. Everywhere we go, there'll be photographs of us.'

'Oh,' I said. My brain was working very slowly. I squeezed the steering-wheel and stared at the rows upon rows of gleaming empty cars stretching in all directions. 'So, how about if you get out here and go on alone? And I'll leave the car in Zone G and then –' I stopped.

'Yes?' Sonia hissed from the floor. 'Then what?'

'Then we can meet up at the taxi rank.'

'Taxi?'

'If I, in my sunglasses and scarf, leave the car here, and you get on the shuttle first and wait at the rank, I'll follow a little later and we can catch a cab together. That way, nobody can connect us to the car.'

There was a silence.

'Sonia?'

'I'm thinking.'

'We can't go on sitting here.'

'So we go separately and meet up again?'

'Yes.'

'All right.'

'I'll wait at the rank outside the airport.'

'OK.'

'Hang on – I haven't got any money. We'll have to get the driver to drop me off at the flat so that I can pick up my card and he can drive us to a cashpoint to get the money.'

'Right.'

'If I've got enough in my account to cover it.'

'What if you haven't?'

'I'm sure I have,' I said, without conviction.

As soon as we arrived at Zone G, Sonia climbed over to the passenger seat, opened the door and slid out. I saw her in my mirror walking rapidly away towards the shuttle stop. The car park was full and I had to drive up and down the rows before I found a gap. It felt very strange to be doing this alone. My body felt boneless and alien; my heart felt huge and pulpy. My breath was coming in short gasps. I reversed and then I started to tremble so much that I had to stop and make myself breathe slowly. What if I bumped into another car, set off an alarm?

Very slowly, I reversed into the space, pulled on the hand-brake, switched off the headlights, turned the key, got out. It was nearly dawn. There was a stripe of paler sky on the horizon and the shapes of trees were beginning to emerge. I shivered, suddenly cold. I pulled off the sunglasses and left them on the passenger seat; took the scarf off my head and wound it around my neck, over the bruise, instead. I sat in the car and waited for the first shuttle bus to arrive and leave, taking Sonia away. Not until another car had arrived did I get out and walk over to the stop.

I got onto the bus at the far end, away from the driver, so that he wouldn't get a good look at me. At first it was just me and a middle-aged man in a suit, puffy-faced with tiredness. Then, a few minutes later, the bus stopped and we were joined by a family of five, towing enormous suit-cases on wheels and squabbling. I was very conscious that I didn't look like someone about to go on holiday or to a business meeting. I had no luggage; I was wearing light clothes and didn't even have a jacket. Surely I stood out, looked outrageously suspicious. I stuck my hands into my pockets, stared straight ahead, tried to appear nonchalant. I wished my hair wasn't so short and spiky; I wished I'd taken the stud out of my nose and wasn't wearing ripped jeans that were sodden around the hem and a damp T-shirt.

When we arrived at the terminal, I let everyone out of the bus before me. I was overwhelmingly tired and, as I stepped into the jostling crowds, felt as though I was under water. Everything was happening to someone else, someone who wasn't me, who hadn't done the things I had just done.

I waited for a couple of minutes, then went to join the

queue for taxis. There weren't many people in it yet – night flights were only just now arriving – and Sonia was the third in line. I went and stood beside her and she gave me a brief nod.

'The centre of London,' I said to the driver, when we climbed into the cab. I gave him Sonia's address.

'We can drop you off and then go to mine.' I leaned forward and said, through the partition: 'Is it all right if, when we get to my flat, you wait for me while I run and get my card, and then we go together while I get money out?'

He gave a shrug. 'As long as I get the money,' he replied.

'I know,' I said. I was looking at the meter that clicked forward every few seconds. I already owed him £5.60 and we hadn't left the airport.

'How come you've gone on holiday without your card?'

'We weren't on holiday,' I said. 'We were meeting some-one.'

I wanted to be as vague as possible. And uninteresting. I didn't want him to remember us. I sat back in my seat. Sonia had her hands clasped in her lap and her eyes were closed, but I could tell she wasn't asleep. I opened my mouth to say something to her, but closed it again. After all, what was there to say? The night was behind us now. I closed my eyes too, and let the journey jolt through me. When I opened them again, we were turning into Sonia's road.

Forty-five minutes later, I had paid the driver a hundred pounds and was in my nasty little flat, gritty with tiredness, buzzing with anxiety.

Before

We clinked glasses. Neal's arm was almost touching mine on the table, and I could feel his warmth beside me. If I put my hand behind his head, fingers tangling in his dark curls, pulled him towards me and kissed him, I knew he would kiss me back. He would look at me with his crinkle-eyed smile, say my name as if he was learning it. Maybe we would go into the bedroom and he would unzip my very short green dress (three pounds from the local Oxfam shop) and lift it over my head, and we would be late for the rehearsal and everybody would guess, and Neal would be embarrassed but he would be happy, very happy. I knew that. A little shiver of apprehension went through me.

'Cheers,' I said.

'Cheers.' He didn't smile but shifted imperceptibly in his seat so that our arms touched. For a second everything hung in the balance, but then my mobile rang and it was Sally, sounding busy and excited and also rather bossy, asking me to buy some lemonade on the way over because she had decided to make us some Pimm's, just weak ones. It was such a lovely summer evening and Lola was at her mother's for once so she needed to celebrate.

'We should go,' I said to Neal, and held out my hand to pull him to his feet. We stood for a moment, hand in hand, smiling at each other. Then he lifted my hand to his lips and kissed the back, and when he let it go I touched his

face very gently with the tips of my fingers. We could wait.
I had all summer before me.

Walking towards Sally's house, he said: 'For a long while
there was someone else.'

'Yes?'

'We lived together for almost three years.' He wasn't
looking at me but straight ahead.

'In your house?'

'Yes.'

'I thought it looked as if a woman had lived there.'

'She was good at things like that.'

'So what happened?' I knew that this was a form of
confession, something he needed to tell me before we
went any further. I felt a twinge of apprehension at his
solemnity. 'Why did it end?'

'She died.'

'Oh!' This was so utterly unexpected – not a story of
another messy break-up but something altogether more
heartbreaking – that for a moment I was quite lost for
words. 'God, Neal,' I managed. 'I'm incredibly sorry. How?
Had she been ill?'

'A head-on collision.'

'That's – that's awful. When did it happen?'

'Two years ago. More. It was in February, icy roads. It
wasn't anyone's fault.'

'What a sad thing,' I said. I didn't know what words to
use. I wondered if I should stop and hug him or something,
but he kept on walking, eyes ahead.

'It's all right now,' he said, adding: 'There hasn't been
anyone since.' He gave an odd laugh. 'I didn't know how.'

'I see.' And I did see. It was as if I was stepping into the shoes of a dead woman. This wasn't going to be just a carefree summer affair with Neal but an undertaking. As we walked, I felt a heaviness settle on me, like a warning.

Perhaps the Pimm's hadn't been such a good idea after all. It certainly wasn't weak. Hayden drank a large amount, which seemed to have no effect on him, but he also kept topping up Joakim's glass, which Joakim gulped eagerly while Guy glared at him. Richard came home from work to find six strangers (and me) making a horrible noise in the living room, which, although quite big, was certainly not large enough for an oversized bluegrass band. Sally was lying flung out on the sofa, her cheeks flushed.

'What's happening?' he hissed angrily to her.

She giggled and rolled her eyes at me.

'Is there anything to eat?' Richard asked her.

'Why don't you go and have a look?'

'We're going,' I said to Richard. 'Sorry. We should have left before now. It didn't go very well.'

'It wasn't so bad,' said Amos, a bit aggressively, I thought.

'It wasn't so good,' said Hayden, as Richard left the room and started banging pots and pans in the kitchen. He was sitting on the floor with his knees up and had hardly touched his guitar all evening. He looked tired, maybe a bit downcast.

'At least some of us make an effort.'

'You should try and keep to the rhythm,' said Hayden, in a kindly tone. 'Joakim's got the right idea. See if you can copy him a bit more.'

Amos's entire body tensed. Sonia stepped forward and laid a hand on his arm. 'I thought you did fine,' she said softly.

'It was OK for a first attempt,' said Neal. He was standing at my side. My fingers brushed his.

Hayden shrugged. 'Yeah, well, you're not really in the band to make music, are you? We're not all blind.'

'Hayden,' said Sally, from the sofa, 'shut up and have another drink.'

'Sometimes drink doesn't make you drunk,' he said. 'I think I should go.'

There was a small silence after he'd left. Amos looked at me. 'Are you going to tell him, or shall I?'

'Tell him what?'

'That he's out of the band.'

'Come on, Amos. He's the best player we've got!'

'And he knows it,' said Sonia. 'Maybe he's too good for us.'

'How can you be too good?' Sally sat up rather unsteadily on the sofa. Her hair was mussed.

I couldn't quite believe that she was getting involved in a discussion of who did and didn't belong in our band. I wanted to tell her to shut up but that wouldn't have been right in her house. 'We're lucky to have him,' I said. 'The group feels different when he's in it.'

'He's great.' Joakim's voice was impassioned and slightly slurred from the Pimm's. 'He can really play. If he leaves so do we – right, Dad?'

'Don't be stupid,' said Guy.

I could see that an argument was about to start. I held up my hands. 'I'll go round and talk to him. I don't think he quite knows the effect he has on people.'

'He knows,' said Amos. 'He's got it in for me. It makes me play badly as well. My fingers turn to thumbs when I feel him staring at me. And he does it deliberately.'

'Bonnie's right,' said Neal. 'He just says whatever comes into his mind.'

'Like a child,' said Sonia, a bit contemptuously.

I pulled on my jacket and picked up my banjo. I'd had enough of this. 'I'll explain things to him. Maybe he'll just solve the problem by leaving.'

I cast a glance back at them all as I went: Neal looking rueful, Amos smouldering and Sonia having her usual calming effect on him, Joakim red with angry excitement, Guy austere and Sally very definitely drunk. It was a relief to get out of there.

After

It was nearly seven in the morning. The sky was a pale turquoise, with just a few thin streaks of cloud on the horizon. It was Saturday, 22 August. In a few hours I was supposed to be at a rehearsal. I stood in the kitchen and closed my eyes. Don't think, don't feel, don't remember. I drank a glass of cold water, then another. The pain in my ribs and the pain in my neck seemed to be connected and my whole body throbbed. The keys to the car and the flat lay on the kitchen slab and I stared at them for a moment. What should I do with them? With thick fingers, I separated them, put the flat key on my own ring and held the car key in my fingers, twiddling it. I opened the lid of the swing bin, then changed my mind. In one of the mugs? No, anyone might find it there. In the bread bin, the teapot, the empty biscuit tin, the porcelain jug I used for flowers, the drawer stuffed full of old brochures? In the end, I pushed it deep into the sugar jar. I went into the bathroom, where the tiles I'd prised off lay in a heap by the bath, and peeled off my clothes. I would have peeled off my skin as well, if I could have. I had a shower that started off scalding but gradually ran tepid, and scrubbed myself all over, though I avoided my neck. I washed my hair twice. When I rubbed the fogged-up mirror I saw that my bruise was spreading, like a stain.

I realized I was hollow with hunger, but the thought of anything to eat made me want to gag, so I climbed onto my bed, still wrapped in my towel. The strips of wallpaper that were hanging off the wall looked like skin. I pulled the duvet over my head so I wouldn't have to see them. Images flickered past me and I couldn't stop them. His eyes, his mouth, his hand reaching out towards me, his body splayed in the boat like a beached fish, his dead, unblinking eyes and his body sinking under the surface of the water. The phone rang and I heard a voice leaving a message. Sally. I had to ring her as soon as possible. Then my mother. Then Sonia. My mobile buzzed. I heard the ping of texts arriving. Hours passed. Perhaps I slept. Perhaps I dreamed that none of it had happened, but then I woke and knew all over again that it was true.

Before

He just held open the door. He didn't seem at all surprised to see me. I stepped over a pile of unopened letters and into a small hot kitchen-cum-living room that was strewn with clothes, books, sheet music, empty bottles, tipped-up mugs. On the small table there was a pan of burned rice. He picked it up as if he didn't know what it was or how it had got there. 'Don't worry about the mess,' Hayden said, putting the pan on a chair.

'I wasn't. How long have you been here?'

'Just a week or so. It belongs to a friend. Or, at least, a friend's renting it, I think. I'm looking for something more permanent. Beer?'

'All right.'

He pulled the tab off a can and waited until the spume had sunk back into its hole before handing it over. I took a gulp. I already felt slightly muzzy from the wine I'd had with Neal, then Sally's Pimm's. Hayden, on the other hand, appeared stone-cold sober although I'd seen how much he had drunk. He took a can for himself, then settled into a sagging armchair and pulled off his shoes and socks, wriggling his toes luxuriously.

'That's better.' He tipped the can back and I watched him. 'I could make us something to eat,' he said. 'Or you could, which might be better. A fry-up, if Leo's left stuff in the fridge.'

'I don't cook,' I said, and perched myself on the sofa opposite him.

'Really?'

'Really.'

'Why?'

'Do you cook?'

'Not much.'

'There you are, then.'

'But I'm good at eating what other people cook.'

It was true. He ate anything he was offered, as if he was permanently hungry and nothing could ever fill him.

'I came to ask you something.'

'Let me guess. You want me to be nicer to that guy. What's he called?'

'Amos.' I knew he remembered.

'Yeah. Him.'

'You're upsetting him.'

'I think he's upsetting himself, Bonnie. You and him?'

'That's not the point.'

'He's still half in love with you, or certainly doesn't want anyone else to be, and he's trying too hard to impress you, Sonia too. It's a bit complicated, like a tightrope act, and he's wobbling all over the place. Poor guy.'

'That's not really the point.'

'One of the lessons in life is that the more you care the less you impress.'

'How cruel.'

'Cruel but true.'

'I don't think so.'

He stared at me for a moment. 'You don't care much what people think of you, do you? And look at the result.'

'I care as much as anyone.'

'And then there's Neal, of course,' he continued, as if I hadn't spoken.

'I came here to talk about the band.'

'If we're not going to have a fry-up, at least let's have some crisps. I think there are some in that cupboard.'

Before I could think what I was doing, I'd stood up and was obediently searching among the jumble to find them. I tossed the packet over to him.

'Don't you want some?'

'I'm a vegetarian.'

'Smoky bacon flavour doesn't mean there's bacon in them.'

'You're sowing discord.'

'That sounds Biblical.' He pulled open the bag but didn't eat.

'What's the point of humiliating people?'

'I don't mean to.' A look of puzzlement crossed his face. 'But it was such a horrible noise in there, and Amos doesn't really care about music. He just wants to look good, to make an impression. Suddenly I couldn't be arsed. Do you want a cigarette?'

'I don't smoke.'

'You don't smoke, you don't eat meat. What do you do?'

'Please will you be more tactful.'

'The young guy's OK.'

'Joakim. I know.'

'And you, of course.'

I felt absurdly pleased by that, then immediately annoyed with myself for being pleased. For some reason, I got up from the sofa and stood opposite him to speak, and then felt stupid for doing that, while he lay back in his chair and smiled at me as though I was some comic act he was taking pleasure in watching.

'I want to know if you'll help me,' I said, very formally. 'It's just a stupid thing. I know we're not very good. I know it's not important or glamorous or challenging, and there's no reason that you should be involved at all.'

'Except, of course,' he said, 'there is a reason.'

'You should leave if you can't be part of the joint effort. That's fine, I'd understand. I just won't have you upsetting everyone for the fun of it.'

'I can't leave.'

'What do you mean?' It was suddenly hard to speak.

'You know what I mean.'

He still didn't move, and neither did I. We stared at each other. My heart was beating painfully in my chest; my body felt loose and hot. I couldn't drop my eyes but I didn't know how long I could go on standing in front of him.

'No,' I managed at last. I thought of Neal. I fixed his image in my mind. I remembered his smile. 'I don't.'

He reached out a hand and took mine. I let him. I let him pull me to him. 'Look at you,' he said. 'Prickly Bonnie Graham.'

'I'm not,' I said.

'One of a kind.'

I could say I didn't mean it to happen. I could say I forgot myself – what does that mean anyway, to forget yourself, to lose yourself? I did feel lost, adrift on a tide of desire that took me so much by surprise it was as if I'd been punched in the stomach, all the wind knocked out of me, and I sank to my knees beside the sofa with what sounded like a sob. I could say that I didn't mean it, it wasn't me, it just happened, but it was me who took his face, a stranger's face, unfamiliar, between my hands and held it for what felt like ages so that I was conscious of time passing, of cars outside, people's voices. And then at last he was kissing me and I was kissing him. I knew that this was what I had come for and I knew he had been waiting for me.

'No,' I said, as he lifted me onto the sofa, but I didn't mean it. I know I didn't mean it, because when he said, 'Bonnie?' I said, 'Yes. Yes.'

After

I lay in bed and stared at the light that was now glowing behind the curtain, projecting its stripes onto the carpet. What was the plan? There wasn't exactly a plan. There was nothing more to be done. Nothing except to go over and over things, to work out where we had made a mistake because there was always a mistake. Were we really sure that nobody had seen us? Were we really sure we hadn't left some sort of trace behind? Had it been the right place to dispose of a body? How long would it be before they found the car? Neither of us had any idea what the procedures in the car park were. People go away on holiday for two weeks, maybe three or four. The car park empties and refills like a tide going in and out. What procedure do they have for spotting an abandoned car? Is it possible that we left something in it? Would it be a clever idea to go back to the car park after a week or two and drive it to another zone? I could check at the same time whether we had left something. Or would that be stupid?

You read about criminals returning to the scene of the crime. It's almost like a proverb. Is it a certain fascination, pulling you back like gravity? Or perhaps it's simply the nagging feeling you get when you have to keep going home to check you didn't leave the gas on or the window open. I knew this was a form of madness because I was trying to remember the things I'd forgotten. What were the gaps? What were the objects that were just outside my range of vision? And what about my things? What about my satchel? Where had it gone?

If only I could be certain that this was the best it would ever get. That nothing more would happen, nothing would be discovered. I'd just have the rest of my life to try to think of the mistakes I might have made, and not to think of the terrible things I had done.

Before

I felt weak and unsteady as if I had gone a day without food. The bare boards seemed to sway under my feet as I walked to the bathroom. The water from the shower head was hardly more than a trickle. Everything felt just slightly askew and strange, the way it does when you've arrived in a foreign city and you're noticing life in a way you don't when you're at home. I aimed the shower at my face, trying not to get my hair too wet, then gave up and found some shampoo on the end of the bath and washed it. My body felt tender and bruised but what did I feel? What did I feel in my head? What did I feel in my heart? I pressed my hand against my breast and closed my eyes. What had I done?

I'd seen Hayden at Sally's house, noticed how, with his long body and his air of total acceptance, he had occupied the space. If there was food, he had eaten it, if there was a sofa, he had sat on it – sat on it so conclusively and definitively that there was no room for anyone else. He seemed to live in a perpetual present, the past forgotten or denied, the future unimagined and ignored, cause and effect irrelevant to him. What had happened between us existed in that world of disconnected moments, with no context and no meaning. Was that how I should think of it? Pick up my clothes and leave as dawn broke and the birds began to sing, pretend when we next met that we were strangers?

With Amos, sex had been a natural part of our life, sewn into the fabric of things. We spent time together: we went to movies, concerts, pubs and clubs, we met friends, we ate out and we ate in, we went for walks, we hugged, held hands, made love. But this: I didn't know what it was. It was as if I was a piece of food, a rare and lovely delicacy that Hayden had found, wanted, picked up and eaten with great care and discerning pleasure – something intimate yet also impersonal.

I found a towel and sat on the edge of the bath, drying myself carefully, even under my feet, and tried to think what I was feeling, feel what I was thinking. I wasn't sure of the difference. With Amos it had been clear: sometimes good, sometimes not so good, sometimes tender, sometimes more passionate, sometimes something a bit wrong that we could discuss. But what about this? How had it been for me? I couldn't tell. I didn't even know if I wished it hadn't happened or if I was glad it had. It had felt new, like something I had never done before. Somehow the safety net had been taken away.

When I went back into the room wrapped in the towel, Hayden's head was turned towards me but it was still too dark for me to see if his eyes were open. He didn't speak or move.

I had to kneel on the floor and search under a chair and the sofa for my clothes. It was difficult to find them among all the other mess. My tights were scrunched up with my knickers trapped inside them. My bra and dress were by the end of the sofa. My shoes had been tossed in random directions. I pulled them all together into one pile and then, quite slowly, put them on, facing Hayden. Now his hands were behind his head and I could feel that he was watching me. I imagined him unblinking and expressionless and, in the darkness, felt more exposed than I had ever been before. As I pulled my clothes on, I thought of him peeling them off me with deliberate care, as if I was precious and might break.

When I was done I walked across to the sofa and sat beside him.

'I'm going,' I said.

'It's not light yet.'

'It's just a few minutes' walk.'

'Stay awhile. Nobody should be alone in the small hours.'

'Is that right?'

'Naked in the dark and nowhere to hide.' He shifted. 'Please, lie down beside me for a bit.'

So I climbed back onto the sofa and held his naked body against my clothed one and ran my hands down his back and my fingers through his hair and over his face. His cheeks were wet.

'Don't worry,' I said ridiculously, pulling him closer. 'Don't be upset. It'll be all right. Everything will be all right.'

'Don't,' he said.

'Don't what?'

'Don't get involved with me. I'm no good for anyone. I'll let you down.'

'Who's involved?' I aimed for lightness.

'I'm warning you, Bonnie. You really, really shouldn't.'

We lay like that until light showed between the curtains. His breathing deepened into sleep, but I was fully awake and I watched him for a long time, the way his eyes flickered with dreams and the way his face softened and slackened. Then I woke him, or half woke him because he barely opened his eyes, although he was smiling, and I turned him towards me and unbuttoned my shirt and we both slid together under dark waters, drowsy and full of slow, strong desire. Afterwards, I got up very quietly and left, shutting the door firmly behind me.

What time was it? I sat up and peered at the digital clock, whose green numbers glowed dimly in the light filtering through the flimsy curtains. I wanted it to be dark, the room full of coolness and shadow, but it was two o'clock in the afternoon and heat pressed against the windows. I felt sweaty, in need of another shower. The phone rang again and I heard Sonia's voice. Something about the rehearsal. A shiver ran through me: in one hour we had a rehearsal. We would all be there, except him. But his absence would be like the black hole in the centre of the room, sucking everyone into it. Everyone would know; everyone would look at me. I would have to pretend that I didn't know where he was. Exchange no glances with Sonia. Act out bewilderment, resignation, irritation. A room full of lies, so many people caught up in this terrible charade. Meet their eyes. Shrug. Smile. Play the banjo. Cover up the silence where his music should have been.

I climbed out of bed, pulled on an ancient pair of stripy cotton trousers, which were loose enough not to rub my sore skin, and a long white shirt, a bit like a nightshirt, with a high collar that I buttoned to the top to hide my throat, and long sleeves. I wanted to cover myself up and this outfit, which made me look like a cross between a waiter and a prisoner, was the best I could do. I damped down my hair and brushed it until it lay flat on my head. Now I looked a bit like an adolescent boy after a binge.

The rehearsal was in a different house today: a friend who'd rather grudgingly agreed to have his Saturday afternoon invaded. I took a last glance at myself in the mirror to make sure that there wasn't some mysterious sign of guilt written all over me, picked up my banjo case and left.

Before

I heard Neal on my mobile's voicemail as I walked the mile and a half back to my flat in the early hours of the morning, stars fading from the clear sky, the moon just above the rooftops. 'If you don't get back too late from sorting Hayden out, maybe we could meet up. I could take you out for dinner. Let me know.' His tone was warm, eager. We had an agreement.

'Bonnie.' Neal's voice on my answering-machine at home. 'Call me when you get this. I'd really like to see you. Don't worry about how late it is.' There was a pause, then his voice stumbled: 'I can't sleep anyway. I'm thinking of you.'

Neal was courteous, helpful and somewhat shy. The woman he had loved had died in a car crash. He found it hard to show his feelings. Now, however, he was showing his feelings to me. He was happy because of what he knew was about to happen between us. And I had left him this evening, gone to Hayden's and had sex with him.

Did I still want something to happen with Neal? Did I

want anything else to happen with Hayden? I sat on the edge of my bed, kicked off my shoes and rubbed my aching feet. What had I done and why had I done it? I didn't know. I didn't know anything at all. My body ached and felt strange to me, as if what had taken place with Hayden had changed it in some way. Even thinking of him sent a loose tremor of desire through me.

I would ring Neal tomorrow – except, of course, today had long ago turned into tomorrow. I would tell him – what? That I was ill, I had the flu, That's what I'd do. I'd put everything off for a day or two, hide from him and myself.

After

Alone in my friend's house, I put the bottle of wine I had brought for him on his kitchen table and went into the living room to wait. I sat on the armchair, then stood up again to walk around, examining the books on the shelves, the photos on the mantelpiece. It was five past three. Someone should have arrived by now. Had I got the arrangement wrong?

At ten past three the doorbell rang and it was Sonia. She was wearing a floor-length black skirt with a pale yellow T-shirt, and her dark hair was piled up. She was fresh and clean and strong and full of comfort. I had no idea what to do, what to say, how to behave. I wanted to burst into tears and be hugged by her and at the same time I wanted her to act as if nothing had happened, so that last night could just become a dream of mine, shrivelling in the light of day.

She looked at me appraisingly. She gave me a little nod. 'Good,' she said. 'I was afraid you wouldn't turn up.'

'I nearly didn't.'

'Is anyone else here yet?'

We stood in the room like hosts waiting for a party to start. There was no conversation that wouldn't seem artificial. I had the clutching sense of a friendship coming to an end because what she had done for me was so huge, a favour that overshadowed everything else.

'Sonia,' I began, and the doorbell rang again, three short jabs of sound.

It was a hot day but Joakim was wearing a thick hoodie, whose sleeves came over his hands. He was carrying his violin tucked under one arm and his face was chalky. There were purplish smudges under his eyes. He grunted some sort of greeting.

'Not with your dad?' I said.

He grunted something else.

'You look a bit rough,' Sonia said cheerfully.

'I feel crap,' Joakim said. He flung himself onto the sofa. 'Where is everyone? I thought I'd be the last to arrive.' He huddled against the cushions like an animal retreating into a burrow.

'You need some strong coffee,' I said.

I went into the kitchen, and when the doorbell rang again, I stayed there, leaving Sonia to answer. I heard murmurs but couldn't tell who had arrived until I carried Joakim's coffee into the living room. It was Guy, in what passed for casual wear – ironed denims and a short-sleeved blue shirt. He hauled in his drum kit, nodded at me curtly, then turned his attention to Joakim. 'Where the bloody hell were you?'

Joakim shrugged. 'Out.'

'And you couldn't have rung us? Your mother was frantic.'

'I'm eighteen. Jesus!'

'You still live with us and while you do – What's the matter?'

'I feel a bit sick.'

'Oh, for God's sake.'

'The loo's through there,' I said, pointing, and Joakim lurched to his feet.

Someone hammered at the door, ignoring the bell, and this time I went to answer. I turned away from Neal so that I didn't have to meet his eyes. My voice came out in a croak. I didn't know how my legs were holding me steady.

'Sorry I'm late,' he said.

I didn't reply, wanting to tell him to go away, leave me alone. I felt I couldn't have him near me, looking at me with his dark, comprehending eyes.

'Am I the last?'

'No. We're still waiting.' Then I did look at him and he looked back at me and for a moment we stood in the middle of the room gazing at each other. A small tic started up just under my left eye – surely everyone could see it dancing above my cheek, a sign of my guilt. 'Waiting for Hayden and Amos,' I said – made myself say. The words came out too loudly into the silence that had suddenly fallen. Sonia came over and put a hand on my shoulder. Gradually the room steadied. I dropped my eyes. My face pulsed. Joakim stumbled back into the room, paler than ever.

'Maybe you should go home,' Sonia said to him.

'No.' Guy's voice was sharp. 'He promised to be here. A promise is a promise.'

'The boy's ill.'

'My son is hung-over.'

'We've all been there,' Neal said sympathetically to Joakim, who had slumped back on the sofa.

'Where are they?' Guy checked his watch and gave a deep, exasperated sigh. 'For God's sake, why can't we all arrive when we're meant to for once? Everyone's time is precious.'

'Maybe we should start without them,' I said.

'What's the point?'

'We can tune up, at least,' I said, and went over to my banjo case. I saw Amos through the front window, walking slowly down the road towards the house. He was carrying his guitar on his back, like a rucksack, and his hands were thrust into his pockets. His head was bowed and he was frowning slightly, as if he was deep in thought. I fumbled with the lock on the case. Why didn't everyone notice? How could they not know? The bell rang and Neal went to answer.

I heard my own voice say, 'So where's Hayden got to this time?'

Before

'How's it all going?' asked Liza.

'What do you mean?' I asked.

She laughed and tucked her legs under her. She was

wearing a very purple all-in-one suit, rather like a vast, wrinkled Babygro, and had her hair in plaits, one of which she kept putting into her mouth and sucking. 'It's just one of those routine questions. You know, when you meet someone and you say, "How are you?" and they say, "Fine."'

'Yes, I know that.'

'So: how's it all going?'

I was sitting on her big stripy sofa that made it impossible to sit up straight. On the wall opposite there was a lovely picture, an orange blur on a bright blue background. Liza herself was a mess, but her flat was so well ordered: all the curios and knick-knacks that she had brought back from the countries she'd visited were placed tidily on shelves; probably she had spent hours deciding where each one should go. There were thriving plants on the window-sills and the mantelpiece, their green foliage a reminder of soft rain and cool forests. I thought of the mad disorder and dust of my flat and felt tired at the effort that lay ahead. Bloody Amos.

'You want a glass of wine?'

'I'd better not.'

'I'm having one.'

Liza walked through to the kitchen and came back with a bottle, two glasses and a large bag of pistachio nuts. 'I insist,' she said.

'Just a bit.'

She poured more than just a bit into both glasses and handed me one. 'What I really meant was, how is the music going?' She deftly shelled several pistachios and popped them into her mouth. 'Are you nearly ready for the wedding?'

I took a gulp of wine. 'We've only got together a couple of times. It's not until the middle of September.'

'It's brave of you to take it on. I didn't think you would.'

'I've got this habit of acting without thinking,' I said, 'and by the time I discover why I shouldn't have done something, it's too late.'

'You've got the old gang together?'

'Not really.'

'Who then?'

'Neal's doing it. And Amos and Sonia. I've roped in a pupil of mine. Well, an ex-pupil. And his father. And this other guy.'

'Oh, yes, I've heard about him already,' said Liza.

'News travels fast! Who told you?'

'Amos, as a matter of fact. A real musician. What's he called?'

The mention of him set something off in me, a sense memory. Suddenly I could smell him, feel the texture of his skin, his hair. 'Hayden. Hayden Booth. I think he just found himself with some free time.'

'Bit of a handful, though.'

'What do you mean?'

'A real musician playing with a group of amateurs. It sounds like a recipe for conflict.'

'There's not going to be any conflict. Except the normal kind.' I forced a smile. 'Honestly, it's a bit crazy. I just hope we can fake it on the night.'

There was a pause. Liza took a gulp of her wine and threw a few nuts after it. 'I don't just want to gossip about musicians, pleasurable as it is. You know I said I was going away?'

'India.'

'Close,' said Liza. 'Well, not very close. Thailand and Vietnam. Anyway, that's irrelevant. What I wanted to say, or to ask, is that since, according to research I've conducted, you live closer to me than anybody else I know, I just wondered whether you could pop in every day, or every other day – every day would be much better – and water the plants, check the place isn't burning down. Please, please, please, please. I'd be so grateful. I'd do anything for you in return.'

'That's fine,' I said. 'No problem at all.'

'If you know anyone who'd like to stay here, that would be fine too.'

'I'll have a think.'

'I'd have sorted it out myself but I never got around to it. Well, it's an option. You'll have the key.'

'Just show me where the plants are and I'll do it.'

'And maybe stack any mail up there.' She gestured to the pine table against the wall. On its surface stood a vase of flowers and a green tortoise pen-holder.

'OK, will do.'

'You could stay here yourself.'

'I do actually have my own flat.'

'You could stay here while it's being done up.'

'I'm doing it up myself.'

'That's what I meant.'

'Liza, it'll be fine. Your plants will be loved and cared for.'

'That'll do for today,' I said.

'You reckon?' said Amos.

'Is something wrong with that?'

'I don't think we got it right.'

'Maybe we're not in the right mood,' I said.

'It doesn't work without Hayden,' said Joakim. 'That song's built around his part.'

'Where the bloody hell is he?' said Guy. 'Did he say anything to you, Bonnie?'

I hadn't prepared myself properly for this. How much was I supposed to know? How angry was I supposed to be? I was the one who organized the rehearsals, who made sure everyone was available. Should I be baffled? Did I need to act hurt?

'No,' I said. 'I suppose something came up.'

'Maybe he just forgot,' said Amos. 'I don't think we're particularly high on his list of priorities.'

'Could be.'

'If he's got some other project,' said Guy, 'it would be worth finding out and then we can get someone to replace him.'

'Nobody can replace him,' said Joakim.

'Anybody can be replaced.'

'We'd have to start again.'

'We don't have to think about that now,' I said. 'I'll ring him and find out what's going on.'

'Do it now,' said Amos.

'OK.'

'I mean right now.'

I took out my mobile and scrolled down to a number that I knew wasn't operational and would never be operational again. I made a call to a phone that was now scattered in pieces in various parts of north London.

'Hayden,' I said. Was my voice trembling? This felt worse than almost anything, nearly worse than when the body had slid beneath the surface of the water. 'Hayden. It's Bonnie here, but where are you? We missed you at the rehearsal. Give me a call, OK?'

I snapped the phone shut.

'Well, that's not much use,' said Guy.

'He'll call back,' I said.

'You should have been more assertive,' said Amos.

As the instruments were put away, Sonia and I collected the mugs and took them through to the kitchen to wash up. I turned on the tap and faced her. She didn't respond and I didn't trust myself to speak. Then I felt a presence behind me, eyes burning into my back, and looked around. It was Neal.

'How are you doing?' he said quietly, leaning towards me.

I took a step backwards. 'I'm fine,' I said. 'What about you? Are you all right?'

'I'm rather tired,' he said, and he did look it, as if his skin was stretched tighter than usual. In spite of everything, I felt a spasm of guilty tenderness pass through me. He gave a small shrug. 'I couldn't sleep.'

'Ah,' I said uselessly.

'It wasn't the best rehearsal, was it?'

I looked at Sonia, who said bravely: 'Things will get better, when Hayden's back.'

'Yes. Of course.' Neal gave me an intense stare. 'But remember, as Guy said, nobody's irreplaceable.'

Neal left before anyone else and I watched him lope down the road, his head bowed. Then Guy and Joakim went off together, Joakim pasty and sullen, Guy still grim. Sonia asked if I wanted to go for a drink with her and Amos, but – unable to meet her eyes – I said I couldn't. Sally rang me and said she'd love it if I could come round for an hour or so to look after Lola while she popped out on an errand. I told her I couldn't: there was something I needed to do, and it was true. It had been sitting in my brain like an itch through the afternoon, growing more and more ungovernable as the rehearsal went on, so that by the end I thought I'd have to make an excuse to the rest of them and rush from the house.

I made myself wait until everyone had gone and then I double-locked the front door and posted the key back into the house. I walked, half jogging, to the Underground, pain jolting through my body with each step, then had to wait for twelve minutes on the platform, pacing up and down with impatience, before the next train arrived.

When I got to Kentish Town I tried to behave normally but I couldn't suppress a sense that people were watching me, that eyes were following every move I made. Perhaps I wasn't behaving normally. I went into a chemist's and bought a pack of plastic gloves. We had thrown away the ones we'd used before.

I turned down the little lane, casting glances over my shoulder to make sure nobody I knew was near me. The garage was open today, a car on the courtyard raised on a ramp with a man in a dirty vest lying underneath it. I strode past and made it to the front door. It was impossible to tell if the young man on the first floor was in or not, and I slid the key into the lock and turned it carefully, trying to make no sound as I pushed the door open and stepped into the communal hall. Quiet and empty. This time yesterday nothing had happened. But twelve hours ago, Sonia and I had been pushing Hayden's body into the dark waters of the reservoir and watching the waters close over him. I extracted a pair of gloves from the packet and pulled them on with a snap.

The door to Liza's flat swung open with a creak that made me wince, and I stepped inside, closing the door slowly behind me. For a moment I thought he would be there, his arms flung out, the dark blood. But there was just a space, a great nothing. He was gone.

The idea that I had left something behind had been buzzing in my head: did I actually take the scarf? (Of course I had – I'd wrapped it around my head at the airport.) Did I really pick up the Hank Williams CD? (I knew I had, but what if I hadn't?) Had I wiped the door handles properly? What had I forgotten, what detail had I overlooked? And above all of this, under it all, where was my satchel? Why hadn't I found it? Perhaps in my terror I hadn't looked properly. That must be the answer. It was bound to be somewhere, under the bed or at the back of a cupboard, and I had to get it before someone else found it. Yet I remembered where I'd left it, carelessly on the floor by the sofa. I could *see* it.

Sonia and I had wiped away our fingerprints yesterday evening. Why had we done that? It was just an act of paranoid stupidity. In fact, if anyone ever checked, it would seem very suspicious indeed if I hadn't left fingerprints everywhere. After all, I was Liza's friend: I had spent many hours in this flat and, what was more, I had watered her plants and collected her mail for the first few days of her holiday. I paced around the room, putting my hands on shelves, on the little table and the backs of chairs, conscious that I wasn't making matters any better but unable to stop myself.

We had cleared up the spilled tulips and righted the chair, but we had left the mail scattered on the carpet, so I gathered it up and put it in a neat pile on the table. Hayden's beloved guitar was still lying on the floor, with its smashed body. I picked it up and cradled it in my arms for a moment. I could see his face as he played it, the way he lost himself in music, his face both dreamy and rapt. Perhaps, I thought, that had been his true face – not charming and boisterous, not angry or contemptuous or watchful, but peacefully self-forgetful, in a world where he had nothing to prove and nothing to lose.

I put the guitar in its case and zipped it up, then started to look for the satchel again. I searched everywhere I had searched before. I searched places I knew it couldn't be (under the bedclothes, and I couldn't prevent myself from putting my head on the pillow where his had been, smelling his smell); in the bathroom cupboard that housed the boiler; under the sink where Liza kept cleaning stuff – and, anyway, we'd been through that yesterday when we were scrubbing away evidence. It wasn't anywhere. I sat on the sofa and put my throbbing head into my sweating hands. What now?

I had to leave and never come back. Even as I thought

this I heard noises above me, someone's footfall in the upstairs flat, and then I saw the red light flashing on the answering-machine. What messages had been left on it? Was my voice there, for instance? I couldn't think – and neither could I work out if it mattered or not. I stood up slowly, like an old woman, and shuffled towards the door. Then stopped: there was something I'd forgotten, after all. In the kitchen I filled the miniature watering can and went from plant to plant, letting small streams of water trickle onto the drying soil of Liza's plants until it was moist and spongy. I had a memory – so sharp I felt that if I turned quickly enough he would be there – of standing with this can in my hand and Hayden taking it from me, putting it down on the kitchen surface, pulling me towards him by my belt, never smiling but just gazing at me as if he was about to say something urgent. He didn't speak, though. He wasn't one for fine words, really – neither of us was. He had once promised to write a song for me, but he never had.

I emptied the last of the water out of the can and put it back in its place with a tiny click. Then I took a final look around – at the bed where we'd lain together, the sofa where I had pushed him back and kissed him hard on his lovely mouth, the floor where his body had ended up – and left as quietly as I'd come.

Before

Hayden didn't call me and I didn't call him. Neal rang several times and I made excuses. I waited, uneasy with a dread that settled in my stomach. I waited and hated myself for waiting. I made a half-hearted start on my flat – which mostly involved pulling things out of drawers and off shelves and then not sorting them. When a group of friends invited me to go to a new three-day music festival in the Dales with them, I looked around my flat, with its half-peeled walls and boxes full of chipped plates, assorted glasses and unwanted gadgets, and didn't hesitate.

I sent a text to everyone in the band saying the rehearsal that week was cancelled and I'd be in touch about the next one. The only person who seemed bothered was Sally, who seemed to love having us play in her house. I realized with a pang how lonely and Lola-centred her life had become. I packed boots and shorts, a sleeping-bag and a mouldy little two-man tent that let in rain, and met them at the station. My spirits rose and my despondency dropped away.

For three hot, grubby, sleep-deprived and music-filled days I didn't think of Neal, or Hayden, or paint colours, or upcoming weddings. I ate noodles and tofu burgers and cheese crackers and drank warm beer and bad coffee and danced and lay in the sun, burning my shoulders and the tip of my nose. It was summer. I was on holiday. I was going to enjoy myself.

When I got home, I felt full of new energy. I threw away almost all my clothes, and painted the wooden floor of my bedroom white, though streaks kept showing through and it didn't look the way I'd expected. I threw away old magazines, bags I never used, shoes I didn't wear, pens that didn't work, music I didn't play, food I would never cook, photos I didn't want to look at, letters that reminded me of times I wanted to forget. I went out and bought several pots of paint. I didn't know if the energy coursing through me was euphoria or rage. I thought of getting a tattoo done – a small one on my shoulder, maybe – but I'm scared of needles. Then the phone rang and it was Neal. He wasn't reproachful, he simply said would I please, please come round. I imagined his handsome face: those wide-set eyes and the way he smiled when he saw me.

'All right,' I said. 'I'll come now.'

In the hallway he kissed my shoulder and my mouth. In the living room he took off my shoes, untying the laces carefully and placing them neatly side by side. On the way up the stairs, he put a warm hand on my back to guide me. In the bedroom he unbuttoned my shirt and then, holding my chin in his hand so I couldn't look away, he said, 'Why didn't I see how lovely you were all those years ago?'

But as he laid me on the bed, I said, 'Neal, there's something.'

'What?'

'You mustn't get involved with me.' I heard Hayden's voice as I spoke. 'Really you mustn't.'

'Whatever you say.' He thought I was joking, and I didn't know yet whether he was right or not. My thoughts clouded under the intensity of his gaze and the heat of his touch. Sometimes it's hard to tell the difference between being desired and being desiring. I took his face in my hands, kissed him and heard him sigh.

When I woke at dawn, a thick golden light shining in through the open window, I turned and looked at him sleeping, his lips puffing slightly with each deep breath. I laid my hand on his hip. I told myself I would forget about Hayden, just as he had already forgotten about me. What had happened was a bizarre but meaningless slip, a wrong turn that I had quickly corrected. No one would ever have to know.

After

I woke with a start and lay, for a moment, rigid under my sheet and covered with sweat, my heart beating too fast. I tried to shake myself free of my dream, but it had been about Hayden, his face disappearing under the water, gaping head and eyes still open. I sat up and breathed deeply, in and out, shuddering, feeling the sweat dry on my forehead until I was cold and clammy. What had I done? *What had I done?* I crept out of bed in the darkness, made it to the bathroom and threw up in the toilet. I washed my face and cleaned my teeth, then lay down again, waiting for dawn.

The doorbell rang and I blundered out of bed, pulled

on a towelling robe over my T-shirt and knickers and ran down to the communal hall.

'Bonnie Graham?'

'Yes.'

'Special delivery.'

I signed the form he held out on a clipboard and then he handed over a squashy parcel wrapped in brown paper, my name written across it in bold capitals.

I put it on the table and made myself a cup of tea, then discovered I didn't have any milk. I sipped it anyway, and started to open the parcel. But halfway through, I stopped: what was this? I sat still, staring at the package, then took a deep breath and ripped off the last of the paper. There it was.

My satchel. The satchel I'd been searching for in Liza's flat. The one I'd left there. I licked my dry lips and put out a hand to touch it. There was no doubt about it. This was my satchel. It had been in Liza's flat. Someone had found it there and sent it back to me. Why? Who? Was it a message? A warning? Also, it seemed fatter than I remembered, as if it was stuffed full of things.

The buckles were securely fastened, although I knew I had left them undone. I unfastened them now, but hesitated before opening the satchel. Then I thought: What could be worse than I've already seen?

I opened it and just found my own belongings: the book I had been reading, a few unopened bills I had stuffed in there and forgotten about, a magazine, my small diary, a purse containing a five-pound note and a handful of coins, a few pens without their tops and a piece of sheet music. But it was odder than that, because my apron was in there too, rolled up neatly, and my cookery book, my T-shirt and flannel shorts, the shirt he'd ripped off me and I'd left lying on the floor. I lifted it out and held it up, pressing it against my face to see if I could smell him on it. Deodorant, razor, body lotion. Everything I had left behind. Also, at the bottom, a small velvet bag that contained, when I undid the drawstring around its neck and eased it open, a thin silver necklace I didn't recognize. I slipped its cool smoothness between my fingers.

Who could have done this and what did it mean? I looked at the handwriting on the brown paper, but there was no clue in the neat block capitals. Nor was there any address written on the back. I screwed up the paper and pushed it deep into the bin, then stared at my satchel again, its scuffed brown leather and tarnished buckles. I put the necklace round my sore neck, closed my throbbing eyes and pressed the tips of my fingers against the lids.

Before

I thought I knew most of the live music venues in north London but I'd never heard of the Long Fiddler. Hayden told me it was on Kilburn High Road but I had to check online to find the exact address. When I arrived, I realized it wasn't really a music venue at all, just a pub with a platform at one end. Hayden was already there, standing at the bar with two men. When I approached, he raised his hand in casual greeting.

'I'll catch you in a minute,' he said. A few days ago we had made love and he'd wept in my arms. Now he was behaving as if I was a friendly acquaintance.

I bought myself a beer and a packet of crisps and sat at a table just far enough from the stage and off to one side that I wouldn't be in Hayden's direct eye line. I checked the texts on my mobile: there was one from Neal asking me to ring him, one from Joakim asking when the next rehearsal was, one from Liza yet again reminding me about her plants. I rummaged through my satchel. It was full of pieces of schoolwork but nothing to read, so I couldn't help watching the group at the bar.

One of the men was dressed in leather boots, jeans and a sort of work jacket topped off with a black Stetson. He had a greying, straggly goatee. It was the get-up necessary either for roping a steer or playing in a bar band. The other was wearing a brown suede jacket and jeans. He seemed more tentative, slightly ill at ease. I couldn't make out what was being said but there were raised voices. It didn't sound as if things were going well.

Hayden wasn't saying much but he had a hard, sarcastic expression on his face. At one point I saw him jabbing a finger at Suede Man, but Suede Man didn't respond. He had a bottle of beer next to him on the bar and he had his fingers around it, tipping it this way and that, as if he was conducting an experiment into how far he could tip it before it toppled over.

I drank my beer, wondering why on earth I had come. I thought perhaps I'd stand up and leave, sidle out while Hayden was looking the other way. He had called me just an hour or so ago to ask if I wanted to come and I had refused.

'Whatever,' he had said, like a teenager in one of my classes. 'I just thought you might like to hear the kind of music I play.'

He was right. I did want to, so I was here against all my better instincts, watching him in his world, telling myself I'd stay for a couple of songs and leave.

Finally, Suede Man took a call on his mobile and Hayden and the goatee man walked across and sat at my table. Hayden introduced him as Nat the bassist, who barely acknowledged my presence but turned instead to Hayden. 'You could have been a bit more polite.'

'I'm sorry,' said Hayden. 'Have I derailed our career? Did I offend Colonel Tom Parker? Has he put his chequebook away?'

Suede Man was still talking on the phone.

'If it's relevant,' I said, 'he can probably hear what you're saying.'

Hayden shrugged.

'The guy has come to see us,' said Nat. 'They're talking about a contract.'

'Oh, please,' said Hayden. 'He's the assistant to the assistant to the assistant.'

'He's here. That's what fucking matters.'

'They're dicking us around.'

'Nat looked at me, then at Hayden. 'They're talking about a record,' he said. 'You know, a cash advance might be useful. Especially for you.'

Hayden took a long, slow drink of his beer. 'You'll get your money,' he said.

'I'm sorry,' I said. 'Do you want me to leave you to it?'

'You know when bands break up?' said Hayden. 'They

always talk about creative differences. What they really mean is arguments about money.'

'By arguments,' said Nat, 'what Hayden means is some-one taking money that's due to the whole group and spending it.'

'When couples break up they argue about custody of the children,' said Hayden. 'With bands it's custody of the money.'

I thought of Amos. 'Couples can argue about custody of the money as well.'

'There's no argument about who got custody of the money,' said Nat.

Hayden laughed. 'It's not as if there was much in the first place.'

'I came to see you guys play,' I said.

'We're just warming up,' said Hayden. 'Getting ourselves in the mood.'

I bought a round of drinks, then Nat bought one and the room started to fill up, without ever being in danger of getting really full. The other musician, Ralph, arrived with his guitar. He was wearing a checked shirt, canvas trousers and trainers with no laces. 'Is he here?' he asked, as he sat down at the table with a pint.

Nat nodded at Suede Man, who was now tapping away at his BlackBerry. 'He seemed pretty keen, but Hayden sorted him out.'

Ralph seemed gloomily unsurprised and just gulped some beer. 'Are we ready?' he asked.

They got up and edged their way through the tables. Most of the audience seemed to be people they knew. A couple of men stood up and said hello. A woman gave a shriek and ran across and put her arms around Hayden. I felt a sharp stab of something that felt like jealousy, but that was ridiculous. How could I be jealous? He didn't put his arms around her, just a hand on the small of her back, as if to steady her, and for a moment it was as if his hand was on me, not her, and desire snaked through me. This was why I had come. Because even when I wasn't thinking about Hayden, was refusing to consider him, I was conscious of him.

My body held the memory of him: the night I had spent with him returned to me in sudden flashes – I could be listening to music or eating a sandwich or standing at a bus stop and suddenly I would feel his lips pressed against my shoulder or his hands on me. Even as I acknowledged this, another text arrived and, of course, it was from Neal. It just said: 'Thinking of you.' He was thinking of me and I was trying not to think of Hayden and Hayden was – well, what? He was impenetrable to me.

The three of them took to the stage without any introduction. Nat went to the side and unpacked not the bass guitar I'd been expecting but a battered old double bass. As they arranged the chairs, altered the mike stands and generally sorted themselves out. I saw a change in them. Around the table they had been edgy, scratchy, sniping, but on stage there was an easy familiarity between them. They had the intimacy that only people who have played music together have. They tuned up quickly, Hayden gave a nod and then, without any introduction, they were away.

This was what I had been waiting for. I knew Hayden. The cliché would be that I had 'been intimate' with him.

I'd been naked with him, I knew his smell and his taste, he had been inside me, I knew the sound he made when he came. We had talked a bit. I had seen him play. And yet I didn't really feel I knew him at all. He was a musician, but even when I'd seen him at our rehearsals he was constrained, like a huge winged seabird on land. With people like Amos and Neal, he couldn't be much else. What I wanted was to see him in the air, flying free.

The change was immediate. They started with a country song I didn't know, and at once I understood that I was in safe hands. They communicated with the occasional glance and nod but mainly you could see that they just trusted each other, like acrobats who know that their partner will always be there to catch them, so that they didn't even need to look round. Nat was a real presence on the bass, slapping away, enjoying himself, grinning across at Ralph. They were definitely the support. Hayden was up at the front, slightly in a world of his own, eyes mostly half closed. But, even so, he understood that they were behind him, filling in the gaps. The first song finished and there was a burst of applause, shouts, even a few whoops. Hayden's face relaxed into a smile. He even looked slightly shy.

I glanced at Suede Man, who was doing something with his BlackBerry, then back at the stage and my eyes briefly locked with Hayden's. He gave me a small slow smile, which sent a peculiar sort of pubescent thrill through me. Having the lead singer in a band smile at you. Singling you out.

When the band struck up the second song I felt an odd twinge of desire for something and it took me a few moments to identify it. It was the longing for a cigarette. It felt wrong somehow to be sitting in a bar, drinking beer, and not have a cigarette between my fingers.

Song followed song and in between there were bits of banter, jokes that sounded like private ones with old friends, raising laughs from particular tables. They played a few of their own songs. I noticed that Ralph wasn't quite as good as the other two. Did this mean that he was a stand-in? Or perhaps he was a founding member of the band, someone Hayden was never quite able to get rid of. He looked the part, though. I could imagine them on a poster.

But mainly I just enjoyed watching Hayden. When you saw him in a normal house, he was gangly and unkempt. Here on stage he had an odd arresting grace, cradling his guitar in an embrace, his long fingers drooped over the strings. He held the audience. But then, gradually, I began to think of something else as well.

Years and years ago when I was a teenager I had played tennis. I even had a coach – he was in his mid-twenties, more than six feet tall, and had long hair and, of course, I had a crush on him. He taught at a local club. Just occasionally when he was with us he would let go with a proper forehand and the ball would rocket past about a millimetre over the net. It was the most powerful, sexy thing I'd ever seen in my life, so when I heard he was playing in a match against another club I went to watch. Suddenly there he was, playing at full power, serving, running up to the net, and he didn't win. He wasn't humiliated, he didn't behave badly – he didn't throw his racket around or argue with the umpire or refuse to shake hands at the end – but he didn't win. I suddenly realized, aged thirteen or what-ever I was, that my coach was good but he wasn't that good, and the player who had beaten him was better but he wasn't that good either.

I suppose music isn't like that entirely. But, even so, after the seventh or eighth song I had something like the same feeling. Hayden was very good. He was much better than Neal. He was much, much better than Amos. Perhaps he was even better than very good. He was an outstanding guitar player and he had a captivating voice, husky but at moments genuinely lovely. And it wasn't that there was something you could point to that was missing. He was better as a musician than my tennis coach was as a tennis player, but still, he wasn't going to play at Wimbledon. It wasn't about winning – music isn't like success – it was just the extra unpredictable element that hits you in the pit of your stomach, or makes the hairs on your neck stand up, or wherever music gets to when it bypasses your brain and gives you something you could never have imagined was missing. When music's that special it answers a question you've never even thought of asking and Hayden wasn't going to do that. He wasn't quite there. So what? He was good. Wasn't that enough?

They played for just over an hour and then, as an encore, did a song that several people in the crowd seemed to recognize. While they were playing it I looked across at Suede Man but he had gone. The song finished and they were done, the spell was broken and the stage wasn't a stage any more, just a raised platform with some carpet over it. He was surrounded immediately by a group of people clapping him on the back, hugging him. A tall young woman kissed his lips.

It took ages to get free of them but finally we were outside on Kilburn High Road, still warm, though it was after eleven and the breeze was fresh and cool. I hailed a taxi. He seemed to assume he was coming back to my place. Did he also assume we'd fall into bed, because we happened to find ourselves together at the end of the day? If so, I told myself, he was going to be surprised. I was not going to be taken for granted. However, my flat was on his way: I would just give him a cup of coffee and send him home. Definitely. Then I'd call Neal.

On the journey he didn't seem to want to talk much. I knew the feeling. Sometimes after performing you need to wind down and you don't want to put everything into words. It feels like a betrayal of the experience.

When we came into the chaos of my flat, he leaned his guitar case carefully against the sofa. He looked suddenly defenceless, like a small child. 'I don't know what to do with myself,' he said, half smiling and yet serious. 'I'm all empty inside, Bonnie.'

A terrible tenderness for him engulfed me, leaving me breathless. I let my satchel drop to the floor. 'Come here,' I said.

I pulled his jacket off. Under his shirt, his body felt warm and damp. I leaned into him. He smelled of beer, yeasty and good. His lips pressed the top of my head, his arms closed around me. I could feel his heart beating and shut my eyes. Usually a hug makes you feel safe, protected and comforted. But it wasn't like that with Hayden — it was never like that. It felt vertiginous, as though we were clinging together at the edge of some precipice and could topple over it at any moment.

At last we pulled apart. He sighed and rubbed his eyes as if he was coming out of a dream. 'What did you think? Honestly.'

'It was really good,' I said. 'Great. I loved it.'

He frowned at me intently. 'Come on, Bonnie.'

'There were some fabulous songs,' I said. 'And you and Nat worked really well together.'

'You didn't like it.'

'I did. I really did. I think you're wonderful on stage.'

'Don't be a coward.'

'I liked it, Hayden. A lot.' My voice sounded thin and unconvincing.

'Who the fuck do you think you are?'

'What?'

Suddenly I felt a thump on my back as I was stopped by the wall, and at the same time I had the sensation of being inside a firework, coloured sparks flying off in different directions. I wondered what had happened, and then I realized and almost had to say it to myself: I've been hit.

Hayden had hit me.

For several seconds, we stood there in absolute silence, him with his hand still raised and me leaning against the wall. We stared at each other, and it was as if I was seeing into some deep and hidden part of him, and I couldn't draw away or utter a word.

Then he collapsed, like a piece of paper that's just been set alight and is suddenly losing its shape. His face crumpled, his body folded up, and he was kneeling on the floor, beside himself.

'I didn't mean . . . Your poor face.'

I touched my cheek, wincing. It felt pulpy and sore, and my fingers came away wet with blood. Hayden put a hand out as if to take mine and I jerked to one side violently. 'Don't you dare touch me.'

He scrambled to his feet. I barely recognized his face, which was wild with grief.

'I warned you. Nobody should get involved with me,' he said. 'Nobody. I hurt what I love.' He repeated the words with a kind of howl that sounded as though it was tearing the back of his throat. 'I hurt what I love.'

'This isn't some crappy song,' I said. 'You hit me.'

'You're right to hate me.'

'Hate you? Just fuck off. Now.'

'Please.'

'Now.'

Hayden lowered himself onto the sofa and put his head in his hands, rocking backwards and forwards slightly.

'Stop it,' I said. I went over and stood beside him.

'Please please please please please,' he was whimpering.

'Enough now.'

And I laid my hand very lightly on the top of his head.

He became abruptly silent, then leaned forward and buried his face in my stomach, putting his arms around me as he wept with renewed force. The sobs that were convulsing him shook through me as well. At last he stopped and lifted his face. It was wet, gleaming, terribly beautiful. 'Does it hurt much?' he whispered.

'I don't know.'

He touched my cheek with two fingers. 'Christ, Bonnie.'

He led me to the bathroom. A bruise was flowering on my left cheekbone; I could see it darkening as I watched. My nose throbbed and I could taste blood in my mouth. Hayden soaked cotton wool in warm water and dabbed at the injury very carefully, biting his lip when I gasped at the stinging pain.

'Now we've got to put a cold compress on it,' he said. 'To stop the swelling.'

'I can do that for myself.'

But I let him sit me down in my dank little kitchen and rummage in the freezer compartment of the fridge. He snapped several chunks of ice from their bendy plastic tray and wrapped them in a rather grubby tea-towel, which he held to my cheek. His eyes were puffy and his face still stained with tears.

'Something awful came over me,' he said.

'You felt humiliated by me,' I said. 'That's what came over you. I didn't praise you enough, or act like one of your groupies, or say that you were a genius.'

'I can't remember,' he said. 'It's this horrible roaring blank and then I was standing there looking at you with your bruised cheek.'

'Very convenient. It wasn't really you.'

'No. No. I know. It was me. Something in me. That's what's so scary.'

If Hayden had made any excuse at all or tried to explain it, tried to convince me that there was some kind of rationality behind the burst of violence and rage, I would have pushed him out of the door and never seen him again. Or that's what I tell myself, because I can't bear to think it might not be true. But he didn't. He sat beside me holding the ice cubes against my skin, looking so defeated, and it was as if I had seen someone that no one else ever had. Could it really be that this was the moment at which I properly fell for Hayden, when he had lashed out at me and then wept?

'I'm hungry,' I said, after a while. It was true. All at once I felt hollow inside.

Hayden took away the compress. 'How about if I get us something? A curry? There's an Indian down the road.'

'Sure.' There was a pause as he stood uncertainly beside me. 'My wallet's in my bag.' I gestured towards the satchel by the sofa.

Later, we sat together and ate ravenously out of the tin-foil containers, not speaking. Then I had a shower, standing under the nozzle and letting the tepid water stream over my bruised face and tired body. When I came back into the living room in my dressing-gown, Hayden was fast asleep, a tiny rumbling snore escaping from his half-open mouth. He seemed entirely at rest. I watched him for a long time, and I don't know what I was thinking or what I was feeling. It was as if I was under water, moving slowly through an unfamiliar element, and the world I knew was far away.

I went into my bedroom, pulled my sleeping-bag out of the cupboard and unzipped it, laying it over him where he slept and making sure the zip wasn't against his skin. Then I went back to my own room, shut the door firmly and climbed into my bed. My face throbbed and I felt utterly drained and depleted. Yet several times in the night I woke, thinking of Hayden on the other side of the wall, sleeping like a helpless baby. And in the early morning I went to him and took him in my arms to comfort him for having hurt me.

After

'You're not dressed properly for this, Bonnie. You can't demolish a kitchen in your pyjamas.'

I had forgotten that Sally was coming round to help me with the flat this morning. She stood in the doorway, dressed for the part in tatty old jeans with split knees and an over-sized T-shirt that had a picture of a bear on the front. Her hair was tied up in a scarf.

'I'll get dressed,' I said, trying to hide my dismay at seeing her. 'After coffee – you want coffee, right?'

'Yes. I'm so tired I could fall asleep standing up.'

'Is Lola not sleeping?'

'Yes. And stuff. You know when you lie in bed and thoughts churn round and round in your head?'

'Yes, I do,' I said. 'What have you been fretting about?'

'Oh, life,' she said vaguely. 'Small-hours panics.'

At any other time I would have encouraged her to tell me about them, but not now, not this morning. 'Is Richard looking after Lola?'

'As if,' said Sally. 'My mum's got her for a few hours. It'll give her a chance to get to know her granddaughter. It's the first time she's spent real time with her.'

'You should be off having fun, going to an exhibition, drinking coffee. I mean, really drinking coffee, in a café, not working like this.'

'No, you're wrong, Bonnie. This is just what I need. I can spend a morning being a normal person, not having to feed her or try to get her to go to sleep or, when she's finally gone to sleep, lean over her to hear that she's still breathing. Did I tell you I still do that?'

'No.'

'Nobody ever warned me about motherhood. They told me about how awful childbirth was, but not about what it's like to love your baby so much that you're their prisoner. This is a great relief for me. Just being normal. I'll go and make that coffee while you're getting dressed.'

As I rooted through a bin-bag for something old to wear, I already felt weary and fragile. I'd been having trouble keeping down any food, especially since the satchel had been delivered, and felt permanently queasy, my legs reedy and weak. I went into the kitchen where Sally was making coffee, and tried to smile at her while I endured the sensation that I was having an internal haemorrhage.

'This is so good for me,' she said, as she handed me the mug, and I felt ashamed of my impulse to throw her out of the house and slam the door behind her. She'd been so hospitable to the band as well. I told myself to be polite, to make an effort, to say something nice.

I needn't have bothered because I didn't have much of a chance to say anything at all. Sally was behaving like someone who had been released after years of solitary confinement, as she often did when we spent any time alone together, away from her sleep-deprived, child-clogged routines. She talked and talked and talked. She talked about the frustrations of her home life, of course, which seemed sharper than normal – not just the usual anxiety about being a stay-at-home mother while Richard worked, which had unbalanced their relationship in a way that she hadn't expected – but now with something close to panic or even a kind of fear, I thought. I asked her why she didn't go back to work, return their marriage to the equality it had had before, but she shook her head violently. 'That's not it,' she said. 'You don't understand.'

'What don't I understand?'

'This isn't about not working. It's about – about not being me. Anyway, I don't want to leave Lola. It would be like ripping my heart out.'

'But you're always wanting to leave her!'

'No. Not like that. Just – you know, moments of flight.'

'Are things getting worse between you and Richard?' I asked. I was trying to behave in the way I would have done a few weeks ago; I was trying to remember how to be myself, the self I seemed to have temporarily mislaid in all the madness and horror. 'You can always tell me.'

'Huh,' she said. She seemed about to say more, but visibly stopped herself and started marching around the flat, interrogating me about my plans for redecoration. Apart from ripping out old kitchen units, which I had no idea how to do, painting and putting up a few shelves, I didn't have any, but that was fine because all of a sudden Sally had lots, most of them not particularly helpful. She wandered around commenting on cracks in the plaster, rapping on walls. I didn't mind now. I didn't feel like talking or even thinking, and it was restful to sip my milky coffee and let my mind go blank while Sally had ideas that I wouldn't be able to carry out in a million years. The milky coffee tasted like some sort of baby food but it was warm and probably had useful vitamins and minerals in it.

When Sally briskly announced that we had better get on, I was almost disappointed. 'So what do we start with?' she said.

'Painting this wall,' I said. 'That's really all I had in mind for today. One wall would make me feel better.'

Sally looked at it doubtfully. 'Doesn't it need an undercoat?'

'My idea was that we just keep painting until we can't see any of the colour underneath.'

'Strictly speaking, you ought to fill that big crack.' She ran her fingernail down it.

'The paint will fill it in,' I said. 'A bit. This is only temporary. If I ever have any money, I'll do it properly. In fact, if I ever have any money, I'll move.'

'You'll meet someone soon,' said Sally, out of the blue, her words sliding under my guard like a knife between my ribs. 'I predict it. You'll meet someone and fall in love again.' She added, a bit wistfully, 'Men adore you.'

I stared at her, stricken, and couldn't speak.

'Oh, Bonnie, don't look at me like that! I didn't mean anything,' she said.

'It's fine,' I managed.

'Me and my big mouth.'

'It's all right.'

'Is it because of Amos?'

'No. No.'

'Come here. Hang on, give me your mug – you're spilling the dregs.'

As she took it from me, Sally suddenly looked at me, apparently surprised and confused at the same time. Our eyes met, and she blushed a deep crimson. She went back into the kitchen with the mugs, and I heard the tap running. It didn't take long to wash two mugs, but it gave me time to collect my feelings. In my one attempt at professionalism, I spread an old sheet under the wall we were going to paint. Not that the carpet deserved much protection: it might have looked better with splashes of paint on it. I took the sheet away again. When Sally came back she seemed distracted.

'I've got these brushes,' I said, aiming for cheerfulness. 'You can have the big one or the little one.'

She didn't hear me.

'I said –'

'Sorry,' she said. 'This sounds stupid. I couldn't help noticing your neck.'

I flinched. I had almost forgotten about the bruise, which had faded to a dirty yellow now, and was a bit puffy. 'It's nothing,' I said. I couldn't think of a single good reason why I would have a bruise on my neck. 'An accident.'

'No. It's not that,' she said, and blinked several times. 'I don't mean to sound rude, but you wouldn't mind telling me where you got that necklace, would you?'

Twisting uncomfortably, I peered down at it. Why on earth had I put it on? My mind went fuzzy. 'I don't know,' I said. 'I just picked it up somewhere.'

'Would you mind if I looked at it more closely?'

'Is there a problem?' I heard myself say. What was up? Had I made some sort of mistake?

'No, no, not at all. I'd just like to look at it.'

'If you want,' I said, and unclipped it. I gave it to her, draped over my palm. She took it and examined it closely.

'You think it's worth something?' I said, making a feeble attempt at a joke.

'This is a bit embarrassing,' said Sally, 'but I think it's mine.'

The air seemed suddenly cold. 'You *think*?'

'I mean I'm sure it is. It was a present when we were on holiday in Turkey. From Richard.'

I tried to force my brain to think. It was like starting a rusted-up machine. The necklace had come in the satchel from Liza's flat. How could it possibly belong to Sally?

'Are you sure?' I said. 'They can sometimes look alike.'

'It's the one I always wear,' said Sally. She held it up. 'There's a new clasp here, where the old one broke. I got it replaced. It doesn't quite match.'

There was a silence as we looked at each other. What was going on? Was Sally accusing me of having stolen her necklace? No. She was as hesitant as I was. And when she spoke her words came in a rush: 'It's an easy thing to do,' she said. 'It must have happened when you were rehearsing. I must have taken it off – to do the cleaning or something like that. It gets caught. You know how it is. And you just saw it and put it on automatically, the way you do.'

That was all rubbish. You don't put on other people's necklaces by mistake in the middle of a music rehearsal. She was making excuses for me. Almost apologizing to me. And, anyway, I knew I hadn't picked it up at her house.

'It's the sort of mistake anybody could make,' she said, almost babbling. 'You pick up the wrong thing, put it on automatically. I was wondering what had happened to it. Richard would have found it really strange if he'd seen you wearing it. That would have been funny.'

Her expression showed that she didn't find it funny at all. Now I knew. Sally had left the necklace at Liza's flat. Sally and Hayden. I looked at her. Her cheeks were red. She knew. And now she also knew that I knew. She must do. And what else did she know about me? What did she suspect about me? What did she suspect about Hayden? What did she think had become of him?

'Yes,' I said slowly. 'What a stupid thing to do. I must have picked it up without thinking. You need to watch me. Next thing I'll be forgetting my own head. Ha ha. Lucky you saw it. Well, let's do some painting.'

I prised the lid off the tin of paint with a screwdriver. It looked like white, or sort of white, but the colour was called 'String'. We started slapping it on. Sally seemed to have lost her eagerness to talk.

Sally and Hayden. Hayden and Sally. Was it possible to be jealous of a dead man, to feel retrospectively betrayed by someone whose body I'd just got rid of? After all, it wasn't as if I'd had any illusions about him. If there was music being played, he would join in. If food was put in front of him, he'd eat it with a hunger that was never satisfied. And it was the same with women. A desperate woman, lonely, neglected, bored. He would make her feel better, special again, alive again. He would run his hands over her body and tell her she was beautiful, and she would become beautiful. I tried not to picture them in bed together, naked bodies entangled, his familiar smell. The way he smiled, a smile that started slowly and seemed to spread over his entire face, warming it. For a moment I stopped, dripping paintbrush in hand, ambushed by the loss I felt.

I went back to my task, slapping almost-white paint over the dreary beige surface. When had it happened? Where had I been when it was going on? Was it when I was at that music festival? It must have been, yes – but had he moved into Liza's flat by then? I couldn't remember. My brain was clogged with sludge. What deceptions had been necessary? I tried to remember what, if anything, Sally had said to me about Hayden or Hayden to me about Sally. Anyway, this was stupidly, wickedly wrong – what right did I have to feel betrayed? What right on so many levels?

And what did Sally know? Did she know about us? She must, unless she was forcing herself not to.

There was something satisfying about the glutinous texture of the paint, the squelching sound as I pushed the brush into it and twirled it so that it didn't drip. I would almost have liked to push my hands into the tin and smear the paint onto the walls.

Hayden with Sally and Hayden with me. But, of course, throbbing behind all those questions there was something else, something much more important, the ocean under the rippling waves. The necklace had been left in Liza's flat. It must have been on the bedside table. Perhaps it was like a superstition: before committing adultery, Sally might have thought it appropriate to remove the necklace her husband had bought her. The feel of it on her neck while she was wrapped around Hayden might have put her off. So it was lying on the bedside table where somebody had seen it and thought it was mine and sent it to me. What for? Was it a warning? A kind of statement? I know you've been there.

I know you left something of yourself there. You can't escape. Nobody escapes.

Meanwhile Sally and I were beside each other painting. It was grotesque. I made myself break the silence. 'How's it going?' I said.

'I'm not sure this is going to cover the colour underneath,' she said.

'It'll do.'

Before

Neal arrived with a bottle of white wine, cold, with little drops of condensation on it, and with a smile so eager and confident it was like a knife being pushed into me. I looked at him standing on the doorstep, his hair brushed into uncharacteristic neatness. He was wearing a lovely linen shirt that he must have ironed before he left his house.

'Hello, Neal,' I said. I felt like a murderer, waiting to deal the fatal blow.

'What happened?'

I touched my fingers lightly to my swollen cheek. 'I fell over.'

'You look like you've been in a boxing ring.'

'It looks worse than it feels,' I said untruthfully.

'Where did you fall?'

'Does it matter?' I said. I hadn't prepared the follow-up line. I tried to think of something plausible. 'In the bathroom. Standing on the rim of the bath trying to reach something off the top shelf. My foot slipped and I just crashed down. I hit my face on the edge.'

'Ouch,' Neal said sympathetically. 'When?'

'Yesterday evening.'

'It looks pretty fresh. I tried to call you then but there was no reply.'

'I was probably lying on my bed holding ice to my cheek,' I said. It was only half a lie.

'I thought we could go for a picnic,' he said. 'If you feel up to it, of course. It's a lovely day.' And he kissed me on my mouth, very gently so as not to hurt me. I felt his lips smiling slightly against mine and drew away.

'Let's go inside,' I said.

In the kitchen, I put the table between us. 'Tea or coffee?' I asked, playing for time.

'Neither,' he replied. There was the faintest frown on his face now, a tremor of anxiety passing through him.

I filled the kettle and turned it on, my back to him so I wouldn't have to see his face. 'I've been thinking,' I said.

'That doesn't sound good.' He was trying to keep his voice unconcerned.

'You and me,' I said.

'It's been ages since I felt like this,' he intervened, trying to cut off what he knew I was about to say. 'You know that.'

'I've done you wrong.' I winced – the line sounded as if it was lifted from a corny country-and-western song, yet it was what I felt. I had done him wrong.

'I closed down so I wouldn't get hurt.'

'I'm not ready,' I said hopelessly.

'What does that mean?'

'It happened too fast, at a strange time in my own life.'

'I don't want to rush you.'

'I think we should just be friends.' I felt ashamed even as I was uttering the glib words.

'What happened? I don't understand.'

I turned to him, made myself look him in the eye. 'Nothing happened, Neal. I thought things over.'

'I read it all wrong.' He rubbed a hand over his face as if there were cobwebs on it. 'I thought you felt the same as me.'

'It was lovely, Neal, but I'm not someone you want to have a committed relationship with.'

'But I do want to,' he said. He wasn't giving way. He wasn't letting me off the hook.

'It's no good.'

'Is there someone else?'

'That's not it.'

Something in his expression had changed as he stared at me. 'There is,' he said. 'And your face. It wasn't an accident, was it? Someone hit you.'

'That's enough,' I said. At last he had given me an excuse to get angry and kick him out and I seized it. 'You should go now.'

Neal walked round the table and stood a few inches from me. He lifted his hand and touched my bruised face. 'You can't get rid of me that easily, Bonnie.'

'You need to go.'

'It's not over,' he said.

'I'm not just jerking you around.'

'It can't be over. I won't let it be. I'll wait for you to change your mind.'

I felt a prickle of unease on my skin. 'You didn't hear what I said.'

'I heard you. I just didn't believe you.'

Hayden arrived an hour later. I opened the door and pulled him inside. We didn't speak. He pressed his lips to my bruise, then undid the buttons on my shirt. I knelt on the floor and untied his shoelaces. When I looked up at him, there was such hunger on his face that I almost cried out. We had sex standing against the wall just inside the door, both of us still dressed, and then we went into the bedroom. He took off my clothes very slowly and stared at me as though I were miraculous, touched me as though I were breakable. We lay together on my bed for hours, sometimes holding each other and sometimes simply gazing. I felt as though I were looking deep inside him, at a place people rarely got to see.

When the light outside the window started to soften and then thicken, we got up and showered, and went out to a tapas bar a few minutes from the flat. We ordered potato croquettes, mild green chillies, broad beans with mint, slices of thick omelette and salty cheese, and washed them down with a jug of cheap red wine. I was ravenously greedy, eating with my fingers and swallowing the wine in loose gulps.

We walked back to the flat, wrapped up in each other. He held me tight. I didn't care what happened after. Nothing mattered any more. Only this.

'What I want to know is, where the fuck is Hayden?' Amos was pacing about the room with his guitar. His face was red, with heat or anger I couldn't tell. 'It's getting beyond a joke.'

It was oppressively hot that Wednesday evening when we gathered for our rehearsal in my long-suffering friend's house. He was there this time, but had retired to his bedroom. I had wanted to cancel but Joakim reminded me fiercely that it was only just over a fortnight until 12 September and the wedding. We were certainly a ragged little group, not at all ready to perform.

'I'm sure he'll turn up,' I said. 'He's only a bit late.'

Guy checked his watch again. 'Nearly half an hour. Something's up.'

'What do you mean?' Sonia sounded very calm, genuinely interested in what he had to say.

'Have you heard from him, Bonnie? Did he ever answer your message?'

'No.' That at least was true.

'It's not good enough.'

'You know what he's like,' I said. 'He's probably gone off with his band.'

'He's not with his band.' We turned to Joakim. 'I went to one of their gigs a couple of days ago. He wasn't there. They had a crap evening, I can tell you,' he added with relish. 'Without Hayden, they're nothing.'

'I don't know why you're not more worried.' This was

Sonia again. I stared at her with incredulity. 'I mean, how long's it been?'

'Only a week,' I said. Then, through the fog of my thoughts, I grasped what she was doing: my normal, natural reaction should be anxiety. 'Actually, maybe that's quite a long time,' I added.

'It certainly is, for people who take their responsibilities seriously!' Amos's voice rose. Sonia laid a hand on his shoulder, and I could see how she soothed him. The tension left him and he smiled gratefully at her, and she smiled back, and I thought: They're having a love affair, or if they aren't they will be soon. More than that, they'd be good for each other – or, at least, Sonia would be good for Amos, calming his intemperate nature, not minding his irritability. She'd look after him, because that was what she was good at and what she took pleasure in doing. I hadn't been like that with Amos, and with Hayden there had been nothing rational or patient about us. We'd been heading for a wall together. But still: my ex-partner, the man I had thought I would maybe live with for ever – or, at least, as near to for ever as someone like me could imagine – and my closest friend. Closer than ever now. My accomplice, bound to me by guilt and secrecy. The thought shot through me: Has she told him? As if she sensed my concern, Sonia turned her head and gave me a quick, private smile.

'Wherever Hayden's got to, we should carry on as if he isn't coming back,' I said. 'We can do it without him. Joakim can play guitar. The rest of us can fill in the gaps.'

'No,' said Joakim. He was almost frantic, his thin face flushed with excitement. 'We can't just go on without him as if it's no big deal.'

'Jo . . .' began Guy, as if he were a small child, and Joakim swung round.

'You're pleased, aren't you? He showed you up and he made me question my life in a way you didn't like. You don't *want* him to come back, do you?'

'Don't be childish.' But Guy was clearly aghast, and a horribly awkward silence filled the room.

'Let's take the second song,' I said brightly.

'Joakim's right, we should probably do something,' Guy said, making an obvious effort to stay calm.

'What do you think?' Sonia turned to Neal, who was hunched on a chair with a hand over his face as if he were nursing toothache.

'Like Bonnie said, we should assume he's not coming back and get on without him.'

'Crap,' said Joakim. 'Fucking crap.'

'Joakim!'

'He'll just have gone off somewhere,' continued Neal. His voice was low and dull and we had to strain to hear what he was saying. 'That's who he is. He picks people up and drops them, uses them and uses them up. Let's get this over with so we can put it all behind us. Hayden's gone, scarpered. Right?'

'You're not in a very jolly mood,' said Amos, pugnaciously. 'What's up?'

'Second song, you say, Bonnie?' asked Sonia.

'We should check his flat,' said Joakim.

'He's right,' said Sonia.

'I agree,' I made myself say, against all my instincts. 'Something might have happened.'

'Where is it, though? I thought he was just staying on friends' floors at the moment.'

'Bonnie knows,' said Amos, helpfully. 'It's Liza's flat and Bonnie arranged it. Hayden was staying there while Liza's travelling – right, Bonnie?'

'Yes,' I said. 'I tried ringing him there as well. There was no answer.'

'We'll just go and have a look, then,' said Joakim. He wasn't going to give up. 'What's the address?'

'Now?'

'When else?'

'We don't have a key,' Sonia objected. 'We can't just break in.'

'No, certainly not,' I agreed. I had the key on my key-ring, which was in my bag, a few feet from me. I almost thought it would start flashing some message into the room.

'Why can't we?' said Joakim. 'He might be ill.'

'Tell you what.' Guy was talking to his son, trying to make amends for something. 'Let's do this sensibly.' He turned to me. 'Liza gave you a key, right?'

'Which I gave to Hayden.'

'Did she say anything about leaving a spare with a neighbour or anything?'

'Um, I'm not sure.'

'I'll bet she did,' said Joakim.

'Why don't we contact this Liza and ask her if anyone has a spare key? Just tell her Hayden's away and we need to water the plants.'

'Contact her?' I said stupidly.

'Text her,' said Joakim.

'She's on the other side of the world. I don't want her to be worried about her flat and lost keys.'

'What are we going to do, then?'

I took a deep breath and said what I would have said if I hadn't been the woman who had dragged Hayden's body out of the flat in a rug. 'We should go round there and check things are OK.'

'Right!' Joakim was on his feet and almost heading for the door.

'*After* the rehearsal, Joakim,' I said, and he subsided. 'Now let's practise. Second song.'

Sonia had a lovely voice. It had never been trained and it wasn't perfect by any means but it was strong, slightly husky, and had a plangent tone that suited the music. Also, she had a kind of charisma, the same quality that kept thirty fifteen-year-olds bent over chemistry formulae. Now she sang about her sweetheart, while Neal barely held the tune, Joakim played tempestuously, and Guy lost the beat. She managed to hold the group together as if all she was thinking about was the music.

'Great,' I said, at the end. 'That was the best yet.'

'Shall we go, then?' said Joakim, putting away his violin, and snapping the clasps of the case.

'OK.' I tried to sound unconcerned. 'No time like the present.'

Before

'I've spoken to Liza, and you can stay here for the next couple of weeks as long as you water her plants,' I said to Hayden.

'Sure.'

'I mean, really water them. Every day. Keep them alive. She's very attached to them. They're like her surrogate children.'

'Right.'

'And don't make a terrible mess.'

'You sound like someone's mother.'

'Only because you're like a child.'

'Am I?'

'Yes. Here's the key.' He pocketed it. 'She's left a spare with the man upstairs.'

'Why couldn't he have watered the plants?'

'Because she doesn't trust him to. Don't you want to stay here?'

'Of course I do. It's great. I'll water the plants and vacuum the floor, and I'll buy her a thank-you present before I leave.'

'Odd little road,' said Guy, as we turned into the lane leading to Liza's flat. 'It feels like something forgotten about.
They could build some flats here.'

'That's what Liza's scared of,' I said. 'There are only a
couple of houses in it, and this garage.' It was deserted, its
shutters closed and its iron sign flapping at the hinges. It
was nearly nine o'clock and the light was softening, giving
even the scrubland a ghostly air and making the rather dingy
little lane almost picturesque. 'It's the one at the end that
backs onto the railway line.'

I could scarcely believe that I was standing at the front
door once more. I pressed the bell and waited.

'He's obviously not going to answer,' said Joakim. 'Ring
the other bell.'

I pressed it reluctantly, praying that no one would answer.

'I don't think anyone's here,' I said, after a few seconds.

'Hang on.' Joakim pressed the bell several times, leaning
on it as if that would make the sound louder. 'I think I can
hear someone.'

Sure enough, footsteps were coming rapidly towards the
door.

The man who opened it was young and dark-skinned,
with huge glasses and a fringe. I had seen him before, but
he didn't seem to remember me. 'Hello,' I said. 'Sorry to
trouble you.'

'Yes?'

'I'm a friend of Liza's.'

'Liza's away.'

'I know.'

'Have you got a key to her flat?' Joakim broke in eagerly.

The young man transferred his gaze from me to him. 'I'm sorry?'

'We urgently need to get into the flat. Have you got a key?'

'If I had a key, why should I let you in?'

'*Have* you?'

'My son isn't explaining himself very well,' said Guy. 'A friend of ours has been staying in the flat and we're worried about him. We want to check that he's all right.'

'A friend?'

'Hayden,' said Joakim. 'Hayden Booth. He might be ill. He might need our help. He's not answering the phone or coming to rehearsals. You have to let us in.'

'Do you have the key?' asked Guy.

'How do I know you're who you say you are?'

'My name is Guy Siegel,' said Guy, in a ridiculously pompous tone. 'I'm a solicitor.'

'Solicitor? What's he done, this friend of yours?'

'No, that just happens to be my job. We simply want to make sure everything's OK.'

'Bonnie is Liza's friend,' said Joakim.

'Oh, are you Bonnie? Why didn't you say?'

'Sorry?'

'You're the one Liza left to water her plants. She told me about you. So you knew I'd got the key in the first place.'

'Did I?'

'She said she'd told you.'

'Oh. Well. I must have forgotten.'

'Can we have the key, then?' Joakim was practically hopping from foot to foot, as if he thought Hayden needed to be rescued at once.

'Sure. Wait a minute.' He ran up the stairs and reappeared almost immediately. 'Here you are. Just pop it back when you're done.'

But Joakim hadn't finished. 'Have you see Hayden recently?'

'I dunno. Has he gone? He was definitely here a few days ago. I think his girlfriend was staying for a bit.'

'I didn't know he had a girlfriend. Did you, Bonnie?'

'Let's go and take a look,' I said, turning towards Liza's flat entrance so they wouldn't see my cheeks burning.

'When was that exactly?' asked Joakim, still not moving.

'Let's think. Five days ago? A week? More? I don't know. I wasn't really paying attention.' A worried expression crossed his face.

'It's fine. Thanks for your help,' I said. 'Come on, you two.'

I put the key into the lock, pushed open the door and stepped inside. For a moment, like the last time, I half expected Hayden's rotting body to be lying on the floor, blood puddling around his head and his arm outflung, his fingers curled. The burning in my chest made breathing painful.

'Hello,' called Guy, stepping into the room after me. 'Hello? Hayden? Are you here?'

'Hayden,' echoed Joakim. 'Hello.'

I couldn't make myself shout his name. After all I'd done, it would only have been a small moment of hypocrisy but it wasn't possible. I just waited, or pretended to wait.

'No one's here,' I said.

'Let's have a look around, then,' Guy said.

'Look for what?' I said, and then, at the very moment I was saying the words, I really did see something.

'Maybe there's a clue to show where he's gone so we can call him up and shout at him.'

'What?' I said stupidly. I hadn't been able to pay any attention to what he was saying because there, quite casually draped over the back of the chair by the wall, was my light grey cotton jacket. I was overwhelmed by a sort of madness. This was what madness must be like, when there seems to be no fit, no proper cause and effect, between the inner and the outer world. I could make no sense of what was happening. Possessions of mine from this flat had been delivered to me in a package and now this piece of clothing was here to incriminate me. Who was doing this to me? What was the point?

It took me a few more long seconds to remember that I was the person who had left the jacket there. I made myself concentrate and I could clearly remember taking it off before I helped Sonia clear up. And then, if it's possible to remember an absence, I could now remember not putting on the jacket when we left – or, rather, I couldn't remember putting it on, and I definitely hadn't been wearing it for the rest of that night. Yet I had returned to the flat since that awful evening and still failed to see it. Was I asking to be caught?

Guy and Joakim were wandering around what was really a theatre set that Sonia and I had created. Guy looked at the mail on the floor inside the door and flicked through it. 'There's nothing here for him,' he said.

'I don't think he's the kind of guy who gets much mail,' said Joakim.

'Everybody gets mail,' said Guy.

I wanted to say something but I couldn't think of anything normal and noncommittal.

'I don't get mail,' said Joakim.

'I meant all adults – but maybe Hayden doesn't count as an adult.'

I had to force myself not to look. Instead I pretended to examine objects I had arranged.

'The kitchen,' I said suddenly.

'What?' said Guy.

'Do you think it might be worth checking out?' I said. 'People keep lists there. To-do lists. Attached to the fridge with a magnet.'

It sounded incredibly feeble and Guy seemed doubtful. I made myself speak in a lighter tone. 'You could check out what he keeps in his fridge at the same time.'

Even using the present tense took an effort. 'Keeps' not 'kept'. As far as Joakim and Guy were concerned, Hayden was somewhere at this moment doing something. Perhaps he was just about to walk through the door. They were able to feel irritated or puzzled by him in the way you can't feel about people once they're dead. You can hate them or love them, you can mourn them, but you can't be irritated by them, you can't resent them. Guy looked very irritated indeed, muttering to himself as he made his way, slightly reluctantly, towards the kitchen. Joakim followed, probably out of a genuine interest to see what Hayden had in his fridge.

I crossed the room and snatched the jacket off the chair. I looked around desperately. I didn't have a bag with me and my mind wasn't working clearly enough. I simply couldn't decide whether trying to hide it was a foolish risk. I heard some noises from the other room. For lack of any other idea, I slipped the jacket on. I heard voices, getting louder. They were coming back. All that mattered was the first couple of seconds. I'd heard of experiments – if you were distracted, it was amazing what you didn't notice. On the mantelpiece was a slim black vase, elegant, expensive and fragile. I took it in my hands and as they came into the room I let it fall. It shattered on the stone fireplace. 'Shit,' I said.

The two ran forward.

'What the hell was that?' said Guy.

'It was a vase,' I said. 'Oh, God, that was so clumsy. I feel awful.'

Guy gave a grim smile. 'Not to worry. If we dispose of the bits, it can safely be blamed on Hayden.'

'That sounds terrible.'

The two of them cheerfully mocked my incompetence as they found a dustpan and brush and swept up the pieces. They didn't say a thing about the jacket. The diversion had worked. It was also because they were men, of course. If Sally had been with me, a hundred broken vases wouldn't have stopped her asking where the jacket had suddenly appeared from.

'So, are we done?' I said, when the fragments of what was probably a family heirloom of Liza's had been tipped into an old shopping bag.

'I guess so,' said Joakim, disconsolately, glancing at his father.

Guy was still looking around discontentedly. I was feeling physically sick as I thought about what I'd done and what I'd almost allowed to happen. Sonia and I had re-arranged the flat, adjusted furniture, removed evidence and then I had left my jacket on the back of a chair for anyone to find. If I'd done that, what else had I forgotten about? The fact was that there were just so many things that needed arranging, concocting, concealing, lying about, and I only needed to get one wrong. It was a matter of concentration, but what was the activity of mind that would allow me to find the things I had forgotten or omitted? It would stay like that for the rest of my life unless it all went wrong and everything was exposed. The prospect of discovery suddenly seemed almost restful.

'You didn't find anything in the kitchen?' I said, trying to control the tension in my voice.

'You know the funny thing?' said Guy.

'No,' I said. 'What?'

'The point about Hayden is that he's a wild, spontaneous musician, right? He suddenly doesn't turn up at a rehearsal and doesn't trouble to inform us, and we're supposed to think he's left town, he's back on the road, that he got some gig he couldn't turn down.'

'I don't know.'

'Did he really live here?'

'What do you mean?'

'Of course he did. There's a case in the corner of the room that's clearly his, and I saw some shirts hanging in the wardrobe, among this Liza's clothes. There were a couple of beers in the fridge – but it doesn't look like the sort of place a rock-and-roller just walked out of. There's no milk gone off in the fridge, no screwed-up shirts tossed in the corner, no old newspapers.'

I made myself not reply, just concentrated on keeping my breathing steady. What was his point?

'You know what I think?'

I shook my head, not trusting myself to speak.

'I don't think this was sudden at all. I think he was planning to leave well in advance. The fact that he didn't tell us was just his way of saying a big "fuck you" to us.'

'Dad,' began Joakim, in an angry, protesting tone.

'He just thought we were a bunch of amateurs and he wanted to make sure we knew it. Doesn't that sound like him?'

I saw Joakim's expression of hurt and betrayal. 'It might,' I said.

'There's one way to find out,' said Guy.

'What?'

He didn't answer, but began rummaging in the drawers of the little table.

'What are you doing?'

'Searching,' he said mysteriously.

'What for?'

'Well, where's his passport, for instance?'

'Why do you want his passport?'

'I don't. But I want to see if it's here, because if it isn't it means he's taken it with him, and if he's taken it with him, he's gone off somewhere. End of story. Where else would he have kept it?'

I followed Guy as he pulled open drawers, lifted up papers, even pushed his hand into Hayden's jackets and trousers.

'No passport,' he said triumphantly, to Joakim. 'No passport, no wallet, no phone. Face it, he's done a runner.'

'He wouldn't do that.'

'*And*,' continued Guy, as he went into the bathroom, 'no toothbrush, no razor. He's gone, son.' His face softened at Joakim's stricken expression. 'Sorry,' he said.

'You're not sorry. You're glad. You thought he was a bad influence on me.'

'We had our differences. But I'm sorry it ended like this,' said Guy. 'I know what you felt about him.' He put a hand on Joakim's shoulder, but Joakim wrenched himself free and half ran back into the living room.

'We ought to go,' I said, following him. 'He's not coming back here.'

'He left his guitar,' said Joakim, pointing at the case propped against the sofa.

'Is that his?' I asked stupidly.

'He would never have left that. He loved it.'

Joakim knelt down, opened the case and drew it out. He stared at its splintered body and broken strings, touching them gently with his fingers as if they were flesh and he could heal them. 'It's wrecked,' he said at last. 'Who did that?'

'He did, of course,' Guy said. 'Who else?'

'No. You don't understand. That would be like punching someone he loved.'

'Yes? People do that all the time.'

'We have to go,' I repeated. My skin was prickling with dread. I felt I couldn't stay another minute in this place, that if we didn't leave very soon, I was going to say or do something terrible.

I pulled the door shut behind us and went up the next flight of stairs to hand back the key.

'Any luck?' the young man asked.

'He seems to have moved on.'

'It's probably not relevant, but I did hear strange noises coming from the flat.'

'Oh?'

'I don't know when, though. I just thought it was him and his girlfriend.'

'It probably was.'

Before

There was daytime, when I scraped off wallpaper, met friends, sat in the park plugged into my music, or shopped. There was night-time, when I lay in the darkness with Hayden, the headlights from cars striping the ceiling of the bedroom where we clung to each other, inflicting pleasure. These were different worlds and it seemed as if there was no connection between them. Feeling glazed and unreal, I would look at myself in the mirror and scarcely recognize myself. Sometimes I was scared, but not scared enough to stop.

'I nearly went out with Neal.'

I was sitting in Sonia's car, and she was driving me to her sister's house in a village in Hertfordshire, where we were going to have lunch and then pick strawberries at a pick-your-own farm nearby. It was Sonia's idea – it wasn't the kind of thing I would ever have thought of doing. She said she was going to make jam for all her friends this year.

'I know,' she said.

'You know?'

'I guessed.'

'Was it so obvious?'

'Yes. To me, anyway. The way he stares at you, follows you with his eyes. So why didn't you?'

'I didn't feel right about it,' I said. I wanted to talk to Sonia but not mention Hayden; wanted to tell her without telling her; wanted her advice without her knowing what she was advising me about.

'He's nice.'

'Too nice, maybe. Too eager. He's the kind of guy you always call when you want something fixed.'

'Is that such a bad thing?'

'You know what I mean.'

'You mean there's something in you that's drawn to men who aren't nice, sensitive, respectful, gentle like Neal?'

'It's not how I want to be.' It was easier to have this kind of conversation in the car, with both of us gazing ahead at the road. 'Why is it so hard to talk about?'

'Is it just Neal that's prompted this?'

'Kind of.' I watched the hedges, fields, cows standing peacefully together at the fence. 'My father used to hit my mother. Did I ever tell you that?' I knew I hadn't – I never told anyone. Just saying the words out loud made me feel slightly dizzy.

Sonia gave me a quick glance. I felt my fading bruise ache and a flush spread over me. 'No, you didn't,' she replied softly. 'But I'm glad you have now.'

'I tell you things I thought I'd never be able to tell anyone.'

'Thank you.' Her voice was grave, comforting.

'You won't tell anyone?'

'You don't even need to ask that.'

'Not even Amos?'

'Not even Amos. It's your secret, not mine.'

'Yes.'

'So you're scared of repeating the pattern.'

'I guess. Yes.'

'And do you?'

'Maybe.' I thought of his fist on my face. 'I don't want to.'

'Yet I don't think you're the submissive type,' she said. 'In fact, I'd say that you're the one who is usually in control.'

It was my turn to look at her. 'Have you been talking to Amos about me?'

'No.'

'Sonia?'

'He's mentioned you. Obviously. You were with each other for a long time. You're his history – he can't not talk about it to me. I'm sure you can understand that. Though of course it's strange.'

'You and Amos …' I paused, waiting for her to fill in the gap, and when she didn't, I finished: 'Are you properly together now?'

'Do you mind?'

'Why should I?'

'We don't need to play games. Amos and I …'

'If you and Amos are together, I'm very pleased for you.' Was I? It wasn't that I wanted Amos myself, but there was something strange about one of my closest friends being with my long-term partner. Something almost incestuous.

'And you really mean that?'

'Really,' I said, meeting her sceptical gaze. 'I'm glad. Just don't talk to each other about me, that's all. I mean, do. Of course you will. Just don't tell me about it.'

At the end of Sally's road I stopped. 'I'll go first. You wait for a couple of minutes.'

'Why?'

'So no one knows.'

'Knows what?'

I smiled at him and kissed his lips. 'Nothing.'

They were all there, waiting.

'Where've you been?' asked Amos. 'You're supposed to be the group leader.'

'That makes us sound like the Brownies.'

'Where's Hayden?' asked Joakim.

'Shut up about Hayden,' said Guy, turning on him. His neck had gone puce.

'But what –'

'Just shut it.'

Sally burst out of the kitchen bearing a cake. She had done something to her hair and was wearing lipstick. As she came towards me I smelled her perfume. 'Where's Hayden?' she said.

'Here I am,' said Hayden, entering the room. 'Hi, every-one. Were you waiting for me? Sally, you look very nice today. Why, hello, Bonnie!' He gave an exaggerated start of surprise. 'How are you today?' His slow grin undressed me in front of everyone.

'Let's get on,' I turned away from him. Neal was look-ing at Hayden and then at me. It was as though I could actually see the knowledge enter him like a poison. He knew. And, as our eyes locked, I could see that he realized I had understood this.

'Who wants cake?' asked Sally, brightly. 'Coffee and walnut. Bonnie?'

'Not just now.'

'I'll have some,' said Hayden. He took a large piece and put half of it into his mouth, chewing and then swallowing it as everyone watched him. He licked his fingers.

'Neal?'

'No.' His voice was soft and tired. I turned away so I wouldn't have to see his face but I sensed his eyes on me.

'What have you done to your face?' Amos asked.

'It's nothing,' I said lightly.

'You should see the other guy,' Neal said. It was meant as a joke but it came out too loud and harsh. There was a silence.

'I fell against the bathtub,' I said. 'It hardly even hurts any more.'

'It's yellow.'

'Thank you.'

'Shall we start?' Joakim was tuning his fiddle. Its pure high notes hung in the room.

'Ready, Sonia?' I asked.

She nodded and let her arms fall to her sides, palms turned slightly outwards in her singing position.

'Sonia's going to show us how "It Had To Be You" should be sung,' I said.

'She has a voice like smoke and velvet,' said Hayden.

'Why, how nice of you, Hayden,' Sonia said ironically.

'Very sexy.'

I could feel Amos bristling in the corner. The room seemed clammy. Out of the window I could see Richard and Lola in the garden. He was dead-heading the roses and she was squatting on the ground, peering intently at the soil. It looked so cool and clean out there, away from the hot, thick air inside. My hands were damp and little drops of sweat ran down my chest. I wanted to be somewhere far away, somewhere green and peaceful and empty of squabbling people.

'On the count of three,' I said. 'Let's channel some Billie Holiday.'

After

The phone rang loudly beside me, jolting me from crowded dreams. Still only half awake, I put out a hand, found the phone and brought it to my ear. 'Yes?' I said.

'Bonnie, it's me. Sally.'

'What time is it?'

'Just before seven o'clock.'

'What's wrong? Is Lola OK?'

'I've phoned the police.'

'Why?'

'I told them I wanted to report Hayden missing.'

'Why?'

'Because he's missing.'

I tried to think clearly and make myself react as an ordinary person would. 'Not missing in a phone-the-police way, Sally. We checked his flat. He's probably just moved on.'

'I've done it now. I can't undo it. Will you come with me?'

I couldn't come up with a convincing excuse to get out of it. Perhaps it would be useful to be there and hear what Sally had to say. After I'd hung up, I tried to think. My brain felt like a wheel turning uselessly in mud, deeper and deeper. Sally had gone to the police. What did that mean? Would they start investigating Hayden's disappearance or simply dismiss her worries as the hysterical suspicions of an infatuated woman? Would they want to talk to people? To us? To me? And what would I say? Would they go to the flat and look for clues? If I'd managed to leave my jacket there, hung casually over the back of the chair, what else had I left, overlooked, forgotten, mismanaged, slipped up on? Were my fingerprints on everything? Had he told people about us? I thought I'd covered everything up but I suddenly realized I was absurdly deluded. Clues would surface that I couldn't even imagine. Single strands of hair could be enough to convict someone. My hair would be on his pillow, my sweat on his towels, on his sheets, my fingerprints on his mugs and glasses, my image on a CCTV camera somewhere. Maybe there'd been a lens pointed at us when we'd slid Hayden's body into the reservoir's dark waters. You can't go unnoticed. I'd stand in a line-up and someone I'd never seen before would point their finger and say: 'Her. She's the one. Yes. Without a doubt.'

I told myself to calm down. What could they discover? As long as Sonia didn't say anything, nothing could incriminate me. Could I trust Sonia, though? Surely I could. She was my friend. And, anyway, if she told anyone, she'd be incriminating herself as well as me. But someone else knew something. They had to, or why would they have sent my satchel back to me? My satchel full of all the things I'd left in the flat, and the necklace belonging to Sally. What did it mean? Something was happening and I didn't know what it was. Things were waiting to ambush me, nasty surprises lurking round corners and behind doors.

I put on a pair of denim shorts and a stripy top. I looked androgynous and undeveloped, like a teenage boy just before he hits the spotty adolescent phase, or one of those rag dolls with flaxen hair and floppy legs. I studied myself in the mirror. What had Hayden seen when he had stared at me so intently? Who had he seen? Why had he wanted me so urgently?

I drank two cups of black coffee and poured myself a bowl of cornflakes before discovering the milk had gone off. I felt suddenly and violently hungry but there was nothing else to eat, except a tin of sweetcorn in the cupboard. I opened that and had a couple of large spoonfuls, but it wasn't a very satisfying breakfast and, anyway, hungry as I was, I also felt sick.

Sally, when she arrived, was dressed as though for a job interview in black trousers that were too tight for her, a black tailored jacket and a white shirt. Her hair was tied up and she wore small gold studs in her ears.

'You look smart.'

She grimaced. 'You must think I'm an idiot.'

'Not at all. Come in. I can offer you coffee without milk, or tea, also without milk.'

'Coffee, please.'

We sat at my little table and she burbled about a broken

night, then stopped abruptly, tears welling up in her eyes. 'This is a farce. You know, don't you?'

'Know what?' Of course I knew, but knowing wasn't the same as hearing it spoken.

'About Hayden.'

'Tell me,' I said, straining to keep my voice steady. I felt my features harden into a parody of a normal expression.

'It's why I went to the police. He can't just have disappeared. I don't believe it. He wouldn't do that. He would have said something to me, I know he would.' But she made the statement sound like a question, then gave a small, tearful laugh. 'I'm not being very coherent, am I? Sorry. It's just so – I'm all over the place, if you really want to know. Do you have a tissue?'

I went to the bathroom and returned with a toilet roll that I handed over.

'I wanted to tell you before. I knew you wouldn't be judgmental. But I felt – I felt so ashamed. And so happy too. Alive for the first time in ages. He made me feel alive.'

'Hayden did?'

'Yes. Sorry. We had a – a thing together. Maybe you knew about it anyway – at the time, I mean. I thought it might be obvious.'

'Not until the necklace.'

'The thing is, he was so nice to me. Stupid word. "Nice" isn't a word to use about someone like him. From the very first moment I met him, he made me feel special, as if he really saw me – not Sally the housewife, not Sally the mother, but *me*. He said I was gorgeous. Do you know how long it is since someone told me that? You know, when you have a kid, you just disappear. Richard goes to work in the morning and comes back in the evening and he's tired and I'm tired and we don't really talk about anything except arrangements, and I can't remember the last time we had sex. And all my friends – even you, Bonnie, and it's not your fault – you're out there in the world, falling in love and having fun and earning money, and it feels as if all that's over for me. I've been going around down in the dumps, with greasy hair and stained jumpers and bags under my eyes, and suddenly this man comes along and makes me feel wanted again. Do you know what I mean?'

'Yes.' But I didn't want to think about it, or imagine the two of them together. I'd go mad if I thought about that.

'I love Lola and I wouldn't be without her. And I love Richard too. In a way. But we don't notice each other any more. Then along comes Hayden. You know what he's like.'

I made an indeterminate noise and gulped some coffee, though I already felt jittery with too much caffeine.

'He ate my cakes and drank my tea and told me I was lovely – that I *looked* lovely. He laughed at things I said, and took Lola off my hands, and asked me questions about myself as if he really wanted to know the answer, and it was like being a teenager again – you know, butter-flies in my stomach. Before he came along, I just wanted to sleep all the time. I was so tired I felt I could sleep for days on end and still be tired. Suddenly I felt full of energy, fizzing.'

'So you had an affair.' My voice sounded dry as dead leaves.

'You couldn't really call it that.' Sally's voice wobbled. 'That makes it sound important. It was only twice. And it wasn't even as if it ended – nothing happened, he still smiled at me and touched my hand and behaved as if I was special, he just didn't do anything about it any more.'

'When did all this happen?' I wanted to know if we had overlapped.

But Sally didn't answer. Instead, she said earnestly, 'I think he's a damaged person. Something must have hurt him once and now he's – Well . . . I don't blame him. I think it did mean something to him. I'm sure it did. It must have. Maybe he stopped because he didn't want to wreck my marriage.' She gave a gulpy hiccup and dabbed her eyes again. 'I thought I could help him, give him love and make him feel better about himself. Don't laugh.'

'I wasn't. What about Richard?'

'You mean, does he know? I was so terrified of him finding out. I thought someone might put two and two together and tell him or something – and the weird thing was, I gave myself away. I told on myself. I just found myself saying it. It had got so grim between us and he knew something was wrong and he was horrible about Hayden anyway, called him a – Well, never mind that. He definitely suspected something. That's why he refused to let the band play in the house again – though he didn't suspect I'd been unfaithful. He doesn't think of me sexually any more, so I guess he couldn't imagine anyone else thinking of me like that either. Maybe I wanted to hurt him, shock him out of his bloody complacency, or maybe I thought that telling him would make him look at me properly for once.' She gave a sharp laugh. 'It's certainly done that.'

'How did he take it?'

She gave a little shiver. 'Let's just say he wasn't calm about it. He kept saying he didn't know how I could do something like that to Lola. Oh, God. I wasn't doing anything to Lola. I love Lola and I'd never harm her and if I thought – The thing is, though, he's not completely blind, Richard. He knows, he half knows, that it wasn't just my fault. If we'd been getting on better, it wouldn't have happened. I was so *lonely*, Bonnie.'

I put my hand over hers. 'You should have told me before.'

'You always seem so in control of things. You wouldn't have a husband who treated you like you were there to keep the house clean and put meals on the table. No one would just fuck you a couple of times when they first met you and leave you without even bothering to tell you he was leaving.'

'That's just what I seem like on the outside,' I said. 'From the inside it doesn't feel like that.'

'What happened with Hayden – it was so important to me, and important to Richard as well. Maybe it's even ruined our marriage, although I don't think either of us wants that. But now I think maybe it meant nothing to Hayden. Just one of those things. He'll forget about me soon enough – perhaps he already has.'

I recognized everything she had said. In a way, her story had been my story – except she was now trying to return to her husband, retracing her footsteps to where she had been before she'd met Hayden. But I had crossed a line and was in another country, one from which there was no coming back. My old life, as it had been before Hayden pulled me into his arms and kissed me, seemed far away, safe and luminous with the soft allure of something irrevocably lost. It wasn't just my old life that was lost, but my old self. I could never be that woman again, I thought. I had done something that couldn't be confessed and forgiven.

'We should talk properly about what happened,' I said, 'and what's going to happen with you and Richard now. But you're about to go to a police station, so tell me why you've reported him missing.'

'I got scared.'

'Scared?'

'It sounds stupid. I know he's just wandered off to the next bit of his life. I don't think he has the kind of continuity that you or I have. It's just one thing, and then the next thing, and nothing adds up. As a matter of fact, I think even when he was with me there was someone else, although he never said so. I just got this sense. I think that's why he didn't come back after the second time. But I was thinking – I was thinking what he said to me once.'

'What?'

'That he was worthless. That I shouldn't get involved with someone like him.'

'He said that?' The very words he'd used with me, and I'd repeated to Neal.

'Yes.'

'You think he might have killed himself.'

'No! Yes. I don't know. I don't really think he'd do that but once I started wondering I couldn't just leave it. I went round there, you know – I phoned him on his mobile and on his landline, and went to where he was staying and rang the bell. I felt sure he was there, knowing it was me and not wanting to see me. It was horrible.'

But it was me, I thought – me and Sonia with Hayden's

dead body, listening to you, willing you to go away. My skin prickled at the memory.

'So?' I prompted her.

'I told Richard yesterday that I was going to report it to the police and even he thought it might be sensible.' She looked at me with her reddened eyes. 'Did I do right, Bonnie?'

'You did what you had to.'

'I've realized I don't actually know anything about him. I don't know where he grew up, who his parents are, his friends, anything.'

I didn't know much either. Just odd fragments he'd let slip. Once he'd said he loved elephants because they never made any noise when they walked but were silent and delicate, and that when any of their family died, they mourned them; when I'd asked him how he knew, he told me he'd once spent some time in Africa. The idea of Hayden in some game park looking at elephants and lions through binoculars was so ridiculous it had made me laugh. He had mentioned women, of course – that one's spirit, that one's madness – but never by name or in specific detail. He talked about them as if they were fantasies or dreams or myths. He had talked about bands, festivals, odd gigs in obscure pubs, but with no date, no location. I knew he had grown up somewhere in the West Country, that his father had been hopeless and his mother sad, that he had hated school, wherever that school had been. I wondered if that was why women had so adored him. He seemed to have come from nowhere and to carry with him an air of mystery and hurt. We wanted to solve him and we wanted to cure him. For a minute, I saw his face flushed with rage and his fist raised. Stupid, stupid, stupid.

'I'm so glad you know,' Sally was saying.

'I'm glad too.' Did *she* know, though? Did she suspect? Surely, surely she must. And why hadn't she asked me how I'd come to have the necklace? 'I'll come with you to the police.' Because there was nothing else I could do. This was Sally: my secret rival, unwitting whistleblower and oldest friend.

Before

'Sally rang and told me we can't play at her house any more,' I called, into the bathroom.

'That's a pain.' Hayden was in the bath. He'd been there for about an hour. Every so often he would pull out the plug to let out some water, then put it back and turn on the hot tap for a bit. I could barely make him out through the fug.

'She sounded very upset. I think Richard's put his foot down.'

He reached up a big toe and turned on the tap. 'There'll be somewhere else.'

It wasn't the way I expected a police station to be. It – or, at least, the bit of it we were allowed into, just walking off the street – was more like a very downmarket bank, with the police officer sitting on the other side of a plastic grille. You could imagine strange people hearing voices, brandishing weapons, coming in demanding justice or revenge or something they didn't quite understand. Even the police needed protecting.

The officer seemed engrossed in filling out a form and he barely looked up when Sally started to speak. His face was screwed up with concentration, his balding head shining with the effort of it. When Sally said she was there to report a missing person, his head jerked up, but as she gave her meandering account of what had happened and why it was so important, his interest visibly waned.

'So, are we meant to make some sort of statement?' said Sally.

'When was it you last saw him?' said the officer.

'Nine days ago,' said Sally. She turned to me. 'When did any of us see him, Bonnie?'

'The eighteenth, I think. Or something like that.'

'Of *this* month?' said the officer.

'That's right,' said Sally. 'Ten days ago. Almost. He's just vanished without a word. Something's happened to him. I'm sure of it.'

The officer rapped his pen several times on the desk but he didn't write anything down.

'We're not going away,' said Sally. 'Somebody has to look into this.'

The officer turned to me. I made a face that I hoped would demonstrate a vague support of Sally without being too persuasive.

'Please take a seat over there,' said the officer. 'I'll send someone out to see you.'

We sat on a wooden bench opposite posters advising us of our rights and urging us to lock our doors and mark our valuables. A succession of people arrived and made their complaints at the desk about acts of vandalism, petty crime and other grievances that were almost incomprehensible. It was as if they just had to tell their story but it wasn't clear whether they needed a policeman, a doctor, a priest or just someone who would listen. Sometimes the officer wrote something on a form, but mainly he nodded patiently and murmured something we couldn't hear from our side of the waiting room.

Finally there was a buzz. The reinforced door opened and a uniformed policewoman came out and sat next to us. She introduced herself as PC Horton ('but call me Becky') and said she understood we had some concerns.

'Concerns?' said Sally, crossly, and began the story once more – but then she stopped. 'Aren't you going to write any of this down?'

The policewoman leaned forward and placed a hand on her arm. 'Tell me about your concerns first.'

Sally looked suspicious. 'Are you here as some kind of

therapist? Are you going to reassure me or are you going to find Hayden Booth?'

'First we need to be clear about what's happened,' said Becky. She felt like a Becky, rather than a PC Horton. She was being our friend. That seemed to be the point of her. 'Then we'll decide what to do.'

So Sally told the story, as she saw it, of Hayden's appearance and disappearance and how she was sure that something serious must have happened.

'Don't you see?' she said, looking at me, as if for validation. 'He was rehearsing for an upcoming concert and then, without a word, he's gone and nobody knows where he is or what's become of him.'

'Have you made any attempt to find out?'

'Of course. Bonnie here and a couple of other people went round to his flat to check up on him.'

'What did you find?' Becky said, to me.

I felt like an actor who had been pushed on stage suddenly. It wasn't just that I didn't know my lines properly but that I hadn't decided what part I should be playing. It was crucial that I seemed loyal to Sally, that I was backing her up and supporting her. But it was far more crucial that I wasn't so convincing in the role that I persuaded the police to mount a full-on search for Hayden. I ought to have thought about all this but there hadn't been time.

'He didn't show up at a rehearsal and we couldn't reach him, so we went to his flat to see if he'd left something to show where he'd gone.' An idea occurred to me. 'When I say *his* flat, I don't really mean that it's his. He didn't . . .' I corrected myself: 'He doesn't own it. He's not even renting it. A friend of mine's gone away and he was just staying there for a bit.'

'What did you find?'

'Nothing, really. We couldn't find his passport or mobile phone or wallet or anything like that, so we assumed he'd taken them with him.'

'They found his guitar broken,' said Sally. 'Don't you think that's suspicious? He's a working musician and his only guitar is smashed and he's gone.'

'It's not exactly his *only* guitar,' I said.

'It's his favourite, then.'

'Did you contact his employer?' said Becky.

I didn't reply. I left Sally the task of damaging her own argument.

'He doesn't have an employer,' she said. 'He's a musician.'

Becky seemed puzzled by that. 'What kind of musician? Does he have a group or a regular venue where he plays?'

'I don't know,' said Sally. 'I don't think so.'

'How long has he been . . . Well, where he is now?'

'I don't know. A few weeks,' said Sally.

'And where was he before that?'

Sally's face had gone red. She was flustered. 'I don't know. Do you, Bonnie?'

'No,' I said. 'Before he moved into Liza's flat, he was staying on people's floors.'

'Floors?'

'Or sofas. Before that, he was playing somewhere out of London, I think. I don't know where.'

'Perhaps he's gone back there,' said Becky.

'But he hasn't,' said Sally. 'He just hasn't. I know. He wouldn't have just gone. He would have said. Look, I don't understand this. If someone comes and reports a missing person, isn't it your job to go out and find them? That's what you see on TV – lines of people searching forests, dragging lakes.'

I felt a twinge when Sally said that, as if someone had jabbed me with something deep inside.

When Becky spoke, it was in a gentle tone, like a mother soothing a hysterical child. 'The word "missing" can mean different things. If a toddler has been missing for half an hour, it's an emergency. When it's an adult, it's more of a problem. Adults have the right just to leave, if they want. It can be very distressing for their loved ones. We hear terrible stories of husbands abandoning their families. But unless we have reason to believe that a crime has been committed, there's not much we can do.'

'But there is reason to believe it,' said Sally. 'Haven't you heard all I've been saying?'

'This man is some sort of rock musician, is that right?'

'Sort of.'

'I don't know much about this kind of thing, but I understand that people like that have quite irregular lifestyles. They go on tour, they suddenly get jobs, they come and go.'

'He hasn't just gone,' said Sally. 'He's vanished off the face of the earth.'

Becky's expression changed to one of slight suspicion. 'Were you involved in some way with this man?'

I saw Sally's eyes flickering in distress. What was she going to risk?

'We were friends,' she said.

Now there was a long pause. I could see that Becky was weighing this up, wondering whether to tell us to go away.

'If you give me your address, a colleague or I will come round and talk to you again, and see if there's a basis for further inquiry.'

'Thank you,' said Sally. 'That's all I ask.'

'And remember,' said Becky, 'it may be nothing. He'll probably be waiting for you when you get home.'

Before

Sometimes everything is wrong and there's nothing you can do about it. I had no time to arrange anything remotely acceptable so the next rehearsal took place at my flat. There really wasn't space for them in the living room and I had to start by telling everyone that we'd have to play as quietly as possible because I couldn't risk falling out with my new neighbours.

Guy didn't turn up, which wasn't necessarily a bad thing. There wouldn't have been room for him and his drums, and the noise would have been disastrous. I felt acutely self-conscious about Hayden. We'd only got out of bed just before the rehearsal was due to start, and although I had showered and cleaned and scrubbed, I felt they'd be able to smell him on me. And he had such an air of possession: he looked at my stuff, picked up books, left bits of clothing around. Of course, he was like that everywhere. He always seemed to take over any space he occupied but my flat now seemed permeated by him. It must be obvious to everybody.

I thought of telling him to go out and come back but he would have been utterly baffled by the idea or turned it into some kind of impromptu stunt at my expense. Then the bell rang and Joakim arrived. There was a glow about him. Some of it was probably the forbidden excitement of seeing the real-life place where your teacher lives. He was always a bit on edge around Hayden, but no more than I was at that moment.

I didn't particularly like having Amos in my flat. He thumbed through books, seeing whether they were his. 'We need to have a final sort-out,' he said.

'This is not the time,' I said.

He got a diary out and suggested dates until I snapped at him. Then he became huffy. Worst of all was the playing – I'm not sure why. Maybe it was the constraints of space or my strange Hayden-induced state of nervousness and agitation. Sometimes it's like the weather, that jangling feeling when you know a storm is due and you long for it to come and be over with. Sonia wasn't at her best. She was suffering from hay fever and her voice had gone croaky. Not croaky in a sexy way, like Nina Simone, but just squeakily out of tune. She edged her way to the kitchen to make herself a warm drink.

I was trying out a new tune on them, 'Honky Tonk', which I thought might get people moving at the wedding, but it wasn't working out. Neal was in a foul mood. There was a sort of arpeggio pattern he had to play on his bass – it was the rock on which the whole song rested – but he couldn't get it. Three times in a row we started the song, then the bass-line collapsed and the performance with it. People looked at each other awkwardly.

'Don't worry about it,' I said. 'Maybe we should just move on to something else.'

'No,' said Neal, too loudly. 'I've got it. I did it perfectly when I went over it last night. Come on. One, two, three . . .'

We started, and then we stopped again, like a slow-motion car crash. It was almost funny, except that it wasn't funny at all. I heard Neal swearing at himself under his breath and then not under his breath. He started playing it over and over on his own, still getting it wrong. 'I'm sorry,' he said. 'I'm losing it. It's getting worse instead of better.'

'Hang on,' said Hayden.

He put his guitar down and took the bass from Neal, who was too astonished to speak or react.

'Listen,' said Hayden.

He played the bass-line, and it immediately flowed and swung and brought a smile to my face that I instantly suppressed. I hoped Neal hadn't seen it. Hayden carried on playing, apparently oblivious to us all, his eyes closed, a smile on his face, varying it gradually, making it sound even better. Suddenly he seemed to remember where he was and stopped. He handed the bass back to Neal. 'Something like that,' he said.

Neal's eyes were shining with anger. 'Why don't you just play it yourself?' he said.

'I would, but what would *you* play?' said Hayden. Unforgivably.

There was an expression almost of disbelief on Neal's face. Of very angry disbelief.

'That came out sounding worse than it was meant to,' said Hayden. 'I could look the bass part over for you, if you like. Make it a bit simpler.'

I wondered if Neal might hit him. Or just spontaneously combust, like people did in Victorian novels.

'Sure,' he said, in a strangled tone. 'That would be good.'

After

That night I slept heavily and woke late, troubled by the last remnants of a dream I couldn't recall. I lay for a long while under my covers, staring up at the blotchy ceiling and reminding myself of where I was. It was a hot, still day, the sky a flat, electric blue, the sun like a blowtorch. The leaves on the trees outside my flat were a dark, dirty green and the grass in the small square up the road was bleached yellow. It was hard to be anything but listless in such heat. Late August, the dying days of summer.

When I got up to look outside, I could see the neighbour-but-one's dog lying stretched out in the patch of garden, and in the house opposite a tiny naked child stood pressed against the upstairs window, as if the glass was cooling her hot pink body. I told myself I should be painting the bath-room, or pulling more of the wallpaper off my bedroom walls, which already looked flayed. But it was too hot. I shouldn't be here, in this poky flat, with my heart jumping in my chest at every sound, my stomach lurching. I should have gone away this summer, gone to a Greek island. For a moment I imagined myself sitting on a boat, a sea breeze on my face, dangling my feet in the clear turquoise water, with some impossibly beautiful whitewashed village behind me. Drinking ouzo, dancing, swimming, walking on white sand, being free – not here, not trapped by what I'd done and trying to inch myself along with my lies and half-truths and fears.

When a police officer rang and said they wanted to come and see me, I almost broke down on the phone and confessed. It would have been a relief. Instead I arranged to see them in my flat at two o'clock that afternoon. They wouldn't take up much time, said the officer.

I immediately rang Sonia. I hadn't talked properly to her since that terrible evening. We had exchanged glances, laid comforting hands on each other's shoulders, given each other reassuring or warning smiles, but said not a word about what we had done. It lay between us like a deep crevice. I said we needed to meet.

'Not now,' she said. 'I'm on my way to see Amos.'

I told her about Sally and the police.

'I know,' she said. 'I got a call from them, and so did Amos. Sally gave them various names. But it'll just be a formality.'

'We have to make sure we get our stories straight.'

'Bonnie.' Her voice became stern. 'We don't have a story. Just keep it simple and keep it short.'

'You don't think we should meet?'

'There's no need.'

I paced around the flat. I pulled a few more shreds off the wall. I took a door off a cupboard that was fixed to the wall but which I intended to remove once I'd bought proper tools – no more cupboards, I decided, just open shelves and hanging rails. I drank tepid coffee, found cheap rails on the Internet and ordered three, which was far too many. There was nowhere I could put them. I rifled through the clothes in my wardrobe, wondering what to wear for my police interview. Nothing seemed suitable. What would be suitable, anyway? I practised answers in my mind. 'No, I didn't really know much about him . . .' 'Yes, I found him a place to live, as a favour to my friend . . .' 'No, he never said anything about going . . .' 'When did I last see him? Let me think. It must have been the last rehearsal. Do you need the date?' 'I think he just moved on. He was like that . . .' I had to seem helpful, rueful, not really worried.

The phone rang, breaking into my reflections and start-ling me. It was Neal.

'Hi,' I said, my skin prickling with dread. 'Everything OK?'

There was silence at the other end. Then he said: 'Do you want to talk?'

'No. No, I don't.'

'I just thought you might.'

'I don't think that would help. But if you need to say something, then say it. Though when things have been said, they can't be unsaid.'

'You have a fucking nerve, Bonnie Graham.'

'Is this about the police wanting to interview us?'

'Of course it's about the police. What do you think?'

I thought of Sonia's advice. 'Just keep it simple. It'll be fine.'

'Oh, will it? Is there anything you want me to tell them – or not tell them?'

I sighed. 'No, Neal,' I said slowly. 'There's nothing I want you to say.'

'You're quite sure?'

'Yes.'

'If you need me –'

'Thank you. But I'm fine.'

After he had gone, my legs felt weak beneath me and my hands were shaking so much that at first I couldn't even turn on the tap. I splashed water over my face and neck and drank two glasses. Then I sat at the kitchen table, put my head in my hands and waited.

Becky Horton came, with a male police officer. From the first moment he was clearly bored, just wanting to get it over. It made me feel better. They refused coffee.

'We won't take up much of your time,' said Becky, comfortably.

'I'm sure there's no need to be concerned,' I said. 'He'll turn up in Newcastle or Cardiff or somewhere, playing in some weird dive.' I had to shut up: in a minute I'd be telling them everything, just to fill the silence.

'Why Newcastle?' said the male officer, suddenly interested.

'That was just a random city,' I said.

'Random?'

'I said Cardiff too.'

In the end I only told them what I'd said the previous day with Sally: that I'd last seen Hayden about nine days ago, that I had checked his flat two days ago and found signs of his disappearance, that I had no idea of where he could be but wasn't really worried.

'How well did you know Mr Booth?' said Becky.

'Not well. I met him by chance. He was playing in our band.'

'You didn't see him socially?'

I paused for a moment. I didn't want to be caught lying. 'Just in the way that you do when you're playing in a band,' I said. That could cover quite a lot.

'Did you know any of his friends?'

'No,' I said.

Before

I wasn't drunk enough, or they were too drunk, or both. Things that seemed hilarious to them didn't seem funny at all to me – particularly when they got on to remembering all the different places they'd trashed in their time on the road. Nat and Ralph were there – the two I'd seen that night at the Long Fiddler – and so too were a couple more people Hayden had played and toured with.

'Remember when you set fire to the waste-bin?' said Jan – I think his name was Jan: he was tall and thin and bendy, with straggly blond hair and pale blue eyes. He was wearing mud-encrusted boots that were resting on Liza's nice table between the tin-foil curry containers.

'And you tried to put it out with a bottle of whisky?' That was Mick, who had a scar that puckered his lip, and dark red hair.

There were roars of laughter. Jan reached for another can of beer, missed and sent it flying to the floor, where it lay leaking its pale liquid over the carpet while he simply picked up another.

'Remember that flat in Dublin?' said Ralph, setting up another quiver of hilarity around the room.

'Or those cockroaches that fell on our faces when we were sleeping?'

I picked the can up and pushed Jan's feet off the table. He barely noticed. I stomped off to the kitchen to get a cloth. Tales of vomit, broken glass, excess drugs and cute women floated through to me and I stood there scowling and feeling like a nagging wife, worrying about the stains on the rug, the marks on the table, the fragile black vase on the mantelpiece, all of Liza's precious knick-knacks.

When I came back into the room, Hayden was giggling like a teenager, his eyes watering and his shoulders heaving. He had the best giggle of any man I'd ever met, hiccupy and infectious. He'd drunk a large amount of whisky and beer, and his body had a floppy looseness about it.

'I think I'm going to make a move,' I said, as his mirth subsided.

He grasped my wrist. 'Don't go.'

'No, really.'

'Please. You can't leave. This lot will be off soon.'

'Will we?' asked Nat.

'Bonnie?'

'Invite us over, then throw us out when you've found something better to do.' This was from Jan.

I stared at him for a moment but he didn't seem bothered. 'Now I really am going to go,' I said coolly.

'Don't mind them. They're just oafs,' said Hayden. He stood up, with some difficulty, and wound his arms around me, leaning against me. I felt the weight and heat of his body, his breath against my cheek. There was a group jeer.

'Piss off,' said Hayden. He kissed my jaw but I pulled away from him. I could feel the atmosphere in the room curdling.

'Remember that time with Hayden and the tabby cat?' Mick was attempting to return the group to its previous boozy nostalgia.

'Remember the time with Hayden and the mysteriously disappearing money?' said Jan. 'That was fun.'

Hayden held my hand. He rotated my thumb ring slowly, not looking at Jan and appearing not even to hear him.

'Not now, mate,' said Mick, quietly.

'It's all right for you to say that. You didn't lose any money. You don't have a sodding debt to pay off.'

Hayden went on playing with my ring.

'Aren't you going to say anything?'

At that Hayden looked at him. He didn't seem in the slightest bit drunk any more. His voice was contemptuous. 'What do you want me to say? If you want to be safe, go and train as an accountant. You're a musician. Of a kind.'

'Now then,' said Mick.

'Your self-pity makes me sick.' Hayden's voice was horribly amiable. He put my hand against his face and held it there.

Jan's face became mottled with anger. 'You took the advance – our advance – and spent it. Sounds like theft to me.'

'Have you ever heard of expenses?'

'You mean you pissed it away.'

Hayden shrugged. 'I did what was best for the band,' he said. 'Get over it.'

'What? Losing my money and my girl to you? That's your advice, is it?'

'It worked all right for me.'

It seemed to me that Hayden was asking to be attacked. Certainly, he didn't move when Jan hurled himself across the room, and when Jan's fist hit him in the stomach he merely gave an approving grunt. I held on to Jan's arm but he shook me off and hit Hayden twice more, once on his head and then, clumsily, his neck, before Mick and Nat dragged him away. Hayden sat back and smiled at me, a very sweet smile that frightened me. There were tears in his eyes.

'Leave now,' I said to the four men, and they shuffled out, leaving the flat like a demolition site. I turned to Hayden. 'You're an idiot.'

'Yes,' he said.

'Did you steal the money?'

'Of course not.'

'But you spent it?'

'It went. The way money does.' He rubbed his face and when he took his hand away the smile was gone and he just looked tired. 'If you're telling me I'm hopeless, of course I am. I told you at the beginning not to get involved with me.'

'And I told you I'm not involved.'

'No?'

'No. This is my summer interlude.'

He gave a soft laugh. 'You think?'

I woke up with a start. What was it? Was someone in the flat? I listened for a few seconds. A car drove past. I heard voices but they were far away, out in the street somewhere. No. It wasn't that. Something in my dream, but not just a dream, something important. Suddenly it came to me out of the dark. The key to Hayden's car. Why had I kept it? It was unbelievably stupid. That it was in a clever place made it even more stupid. If the police searched my flat and found it just lying around, I could pretend, just about pretend, that during our affair Hayden had lent me a spare car key. But if they found the key in the bottom of a jar of sugar, there could be no possible innocent explanation. And they probably would find it. I was a panicky, amateur hider and they were professional finders. They knew the kind of places where idiots like me hid things, and if they didn't know they'd find them anyway, because when they really wanted to find something, they ripped everything apart.

Not that it was a particularly brilliant hiding-place. What if someone who came to the flat suddenly did something that needed lots of sugar, like making lemonade or baking a cake, emptied the jar and found the key? It sounded stupid, but what would I actually say?

I got up, ran to the kitchen and plunged my hand into the jar. I suddenly thought: What if it isn't there? But, of course, it was. I placed it on the table and sat and stared at it. It was like a talisman, representing my contact with Hayden, my guilt. It almost exuded energy, so that I hardly dared touch it. Instead I thought about it so intensely that I almost felt dizzy. What I needed to do was throw it, and the flat key I still had, away somewhere they would never be found. Why on earth hadn't I done that in the first place? Why? I tried to interpret the motives of this other person, the earlier me, who had abandoned the car. There must have been a reason, even if I hadn't articulated it to myself at the time.

I forced myself to think about this, even though it was in the past and all I really wanted was to shut it away. Yes, there had been a reason for keeping the key. If I had thrown it away, I would have lost my last chance of doing anything to the car. If I had remembered a mistake I had made, something I had left behind, there would have been nothing I could do about it. Now the car and its location wormed their way into my thoughts. Was leaving it there really such a great idea? If the police started to search for his car, wouldn't an airport car park be one of the first places they'd look? It wasn't as if they'd have to check all those thousands of vehicles one by one. They'd probably just have to type the registration number into a database. They'd be able to find the exact time the car had arrived there, which would give them the time of Hayden's disappearance. They could start asking for alibis. Was it really likely that we hadn't left some traces in the car? Even if we hadn't, the photograph of us entering the car park would show a woman driving. There were too many weaknesses. I made myself think and think and, with a sickening lurch, realized where my thoughts were taking me. I was like a person with vertigo who was making herself walk to the edge of a very steep cliff and lean over as far as possible to stare down into the depths.

I washed and dressed, but it was too early to go out. I needed to wait until the shops opened, and I wanted to get to the airport when there were lots of people around. The key lay in front of me, burning a hole in the table, as I drank cup after cup of coffee and hunted through the phone book until I found what I needed. I tore a corner off a newspaper and wrote the address down.

It was eight thirty when I finally left the flat. First I went to a cash machine and withdrew £300. I was now £233 overdrawn: how would I pay my mortgage next week, or buy food? I walked up the high street until I reached a shop I vaguely remembered but had never been into before. It sold strange clothes at unbelievably cheap prices. I bought a garish pair of maroon slacks for five pounds, a horrible sweatshirt that bore the slogan Spalsboro Sports Club and a picture of an eagle for two pounds, and a pair of cotton gloves for two pounds fifty. I went back to the flat, put them on and faced myself in the mirror. I looked strange. I looked poor. But it didn't matter. All I needed was the cash and the key.

I went out to Stansted on the train, surrounded by people with luggage, heading off on holiday. I stared out of the window at the canals, the vast construction projects, the scrubland that eventually gave way to a brief moment of countryside. I felt another sudden stab of horror. The car-park ticket. What had we done with it? I was almost sure we'd left it in the car. I thought of ringing Sonia, then decided not to. I'd probably have to tell her what I'd done, but I'd leave it till afterwards. Was it in the car? What would I do if it wasn't? I'd just have to leave the car, go back to Plan A, and worry about it for the rest of my life.

When I got out of the terminal building, ready to catch the shuttle to the long-term car park, I realized I needed to know which zone to get to. There were twenty-six, one for each letter. I had parked there before and I'd always remember the letter by connecting it with something I knew, a name, a place, a pet. But I hadn't done that this time. I hadn't thought I'd be coming back. I ran through the alphabet in my mind. The letters all seemed neutral. A, B, C, D, E, F, G . . . That was it. G for God. All-knowing, all-powerful, non-existing. At least, that was what I hoped. I got on the bus.

When I reached the car I found the ticket in the glove compartment. Everything went easily. I had to go into the office to pay £80.20 but the girl behind the counter barely looked at me and there was no camera when I drove out of the barrier. They're not bothered about you when you leave, just so long as you've paid.

When I got to London, I turned off into Walthamstow towards the address I'd written down. It was perfect. The SupaShine Twenty-Four-Seven Car Cleaning Service was located on what must previously have been a petrol station or a car showroom. As I pulled in, I saw a large group of overalled young men hard at work with hoses and sponges on a row of cars. I removed my gloves, because they made me look insane. I got out and an extremely fat man holding a clipboard came up to me. 'You want standard wash and leather?' he said.

'What else do you do?'

He pointed up at the sign on the wall.

'What's the Interior Valet?' I asked.

He sniffed. 'Vacuum and shampoo all carpets, including boot carpet. Clean every surface, remove rubbish, clean the ashtrays.'

He peered at the car dubiously. It was absolutely filthy.

'What about the exterior?' he said.

That didn't matter so much but I didn't want him to remember me and he had probably never in his entire life been asked to clean the inside of a car and not the outside. 'And the exterior as well,' I said. 'Of course.'

He walked over and looked more closely at Hayden's shoddy old Rover with its rusting sills and balding tyres. 'It's usually company cars that have the Executive,' he said.

'I borrowed it,' I said. 'I promised to have it washed before I gave it back.'

'That'll be ninety pounds,' he said, with a shrug.

'A bargain,' I said, and counted the money out.

'It'll take about half an hour,' he said. 'We've got a waiting room.'

'I'm fine,' I said.

For the next half-hour I stood in the warm morning sunshine in a part of London I had never visited and watched the men doing what Sonia and I should have done, which was to scour every surface, vacuum-clean and remove a surprising amount of clutter, some of which may have been things that we – more probably I – had dropped by mistake. Better still I heard the men talking to each other in a language, or languages, I didn't understand. I knew this type of place. They employed recent immigrants, low wages, no questions asked, high turnover. Nobody would remember me. Nobody would even still be here should any questions be asked. Nobody would remember the woman from the non-existent Spalsboro Sports Club.

I put my gloves back on and drove away, but only went a few hundred yards before turning left onto a busy road full of down-at-heel Internet cafés, shops selling cheap umbrellas, greengrocers with tubs containing fruit I couldn't name, a seedy taxidermist's, a barber, a shop selling canaries, budgerigars and hamsters in cages that were stacked up in the window, and another offering hardware. It was a poor and crowded area – perfect for my purposes. I pulled up behind a white van delivering fizzy drinks, checked that I had left nothing on the seats to incriminate me, turned off the engine but left the key in the ignition, got out and strolled away, trying to look nonchalant. Now someone just had to steal it. Surely that wouldn't take long.

I had planned to go straight home, but I suddenly found I was so tired and so dizzy with a sensation that might have been hunger or might have been fear that I could barely put one foot in front of the other. I stumbled down the street until I came to a café with two tables by the window and a counter full of doughnuts and pastries. I ordered a cup of tea and a blueberry muffin and sat at a table. The tea was tepid and stewed and I had to drink it in hasty sips; the muffin had seen better days. It was like sawdust in my mouth, but nevertheless I could feel its sweetness giving me energy.

Outside the window life was going on. Women pulling toddlers passed by, teenagers in a gaggle, solitary men – some walking slowly and others with a quick and purposeful stride. There were a lot of cars, barely moving on the traffic-clogged road. Motorbikes and lorries too. And – I blinked but there could be no mistaking it – a tow-truck with a rusty old Rover on it. Hayden's Rover. The Rover I had left with the key in the ignition to be stolen. How had that happened? It had taken them less than half an hour to tow away the car I'd left to be stolen. Had I parked it on a red line? Surely not. Now, instead of Hayden's car getting its number plate ripped off and being driven around London by a thief, it had been taken away by the traffic police. Had I ruined anything? And then I thought: Maybe not. Maybe I had found a good way of getting rid of the car. Or was it a disaster? I didn't know and there was nothing I could do about it. It was too late.

An hour later, I was back at home. I took my crazy clothes off and put real ones on, then walked around Camden, depositing the slacks, the sweatshirt and the two gloves in four different litter-bins. Then, with great unwill-ingness, I rang Sonia and told her I needed to meet her and, yes, it was urgent and, no, there was nothing to worry about and, yes, it should just be me and her, so she told me about a pub along the road from where she lived. I met her there and bought two glasses of wine, and we went outside on the pavement into the sunshine and I told her everything I had done. When I had finished, Sonia was silent.

'Well?' I said.

'You idiot,' she said loudly.

'Sonia,' I hissed. A couple were sitting at one of the picnic tables out on the pavement and the man looked at us.

'You stupid, stupid idiot,' she repeated, but this time in a furious whisper. 'What the hell were you playing at?'

'I thought it was too risky to leave it in the car park,' I said. 'We might have left some trace. We should have washed it first, washed away any clues. We were bound to have left something. Fibres, I don't know. And they would have found it soon, just standing there.'

'How do you know?' said Sonia. The effort to keep her voice down seemed painful. 'How can you possibly know?'

'They must have some way of checking after a couple of weeks,' I said. 'Otherwise people would go and dump cars in airport car parks all the time.'

'What if you'd had a breakdown?' said Sonia. 'Or an accident? Or been caught by a speed camera? Or been stopped by police?'

'It seems mad . . .'

'So you've just handed Hayden's car to the police? That was your plan?'

'It wasn't what I had in mind but it's not really the police,' I said. 'I've had cars towed away a couple of times. They take them to the pound.'

'Yes?' said Sonia angrily. 'And then?'

'I've been thinking about that. I suppose it'll just stand there,' I said. 'And I suppose they'll send out a letter and then another, but as he had no permanent address, who knows how long it will take them to trace it back? And even if the police do discover it, so what? What's suspicious? And now it's not tied to the time of Hayden's disappearance.'

Sonia took a sip of wine, then a large gulp. 'Something's wrong,' she said. 'You'll have been caught on a CCTV camera or something.'

'It was the right thing to do,' I said.

'There are cameras everywhere. Remember – surveillance society?'

'Yes,' I said. 'But I thought I needed to get it scrubbed down. At least I've done that.'

'We made a plan,' said Sonia. 'I haven't said this before but I'm saying it now. You brought me into this. I helped you. We made a plan. You can't just wake up in the night, have a bright idea, change everything and only tell me about it after.'

'The plan was wrong.'

'It wasn't. Or if it was, it wasn't as wrong as undoing it and making another wrong one. If they'd found the car, they'd have assumed he'd left the country. What will they think now?'

'I don't know,' I said unhappily. 'It doesn't matter. They probably won't think anything. Does anyone really care, apart from us?' And then I remembered my bag arriving in the post and the adrenalin of terror sloshed through me again. 'Hardly anyone.'

Before

'Miss Graham! Miss Graham! I did it!'

I looked at the slip of paper and then at her. She had a grin splitting her face in half and two fat tears rolling down her cheeks. I put my arms around her and kissed her. 'That's fantastic, Maud,' I said. 'And well deserved.'

'I can't believe it. I'm so happy. I'm so happy.' And she

was off, running across the grass to a group of girls who were hugging each other, squealing and taking photographs with their mobiles. I looked around me at all the young people walking into the school with their faces set in tense apprehension, or coming out with their envelopes in their hands, my ex-students, in groups or alone.

I hate results days at school. However many get the grades they need, there are always some whose hopes are dashed. The worst is collecting GCSEs – that would be next week – when large groups of students, who haven't worked, whom you've known from their first day at the school and will probably leave with few qualifications, gather for this ritual public humiliation. But even today, collecting A levels, felt brutal enough. Looking around the scattered crowds, I could tell immediately which ones had done badly: not just Amy, weeping onto the shoulder of her best friend, but Steven Lowe, laughing and shrugging, pretending he didn't care and fooling no one, a shy young man called Rob, who looked as if he had been punched in the stomach and was having trouble standing upright, Lorrie and Frank, sucking desperately at cigarettes.

Along with nine other teachers, I had been there since half past eight and it was now ten o'clock. Generally, the day got worse before it ended: the students who expected to do well usually turned up first thing. Others came later, dragging their heels, acting indifference, putting off the moment of bitter and anticipated truth.

Then I saw a figure I knew, slouching nonchalantly along with his hands in the pockets of his jeans and a cigarette hanging from his lower lip. Joakim spotted me and lifted his hand but didn't stop and I watched him as he sauntered towards the table where his envelope was lying. His neck and shoulders were stiff, but then I watched them relax. That was the nearest he got to expressing relief or gladness. He rolled the piece of paper loosely into a hollow tube, stopped for a few seconds to talk to a mate, let a girl with blonde pigtails cover him with lipstick kisses, shook the hand of Joe Robbins, the school head, then turned to go.

'OK?' I said to him, as he passed.

'All right.' A smile quivered on his mouth. He handed the printout to me to read.

'Terrific,' I said, putting my hand on his arm and seeing his cheeks glow with pleasure. 'You should be very proud of yourself.'

'Thanks.'

'Go and celebrate,' I said, as a boy hollered at him to join them. 'I'll see you this evening.'

'You will?'

'Our dry run – at the barbecue. You're the one who arranged it.'

'Oh, that.'

'You'll be there?'

'Sure. I'd be going to the party anyway. It's a celebrate-or-drown-your-sorrows thing. Our gig can just be a little break in the drinking.'

By the time we started to play, it was threatening rain. A hot wind shook fat drops from the sky. There must have been at least 150 young people there, most of whom were already drunk when they arrived – and if they weren't, they quickly proceeded to become so, swilling back cans of beer, smoking joints and eating burned sausages or grey burgers. I saw a boy I had taught several years ago vomit into the shrubbery, groaning and weeping as he did so. Nobody really took much notice of our music, except to cheer and cat-call Joakim. Many of them knew Sonia and me, at least by sight, and there was a comical double-take when they saw us standing there. But they quickly forgot about us and all of the old hierarchies. The ex-school captain took a year-twelve girl behind the shed where he seemed to believe they were invisible. The leader of the school council threw a stone at the cat. The band played on.

'Did you hear about Joakim's results?' said Guy in the break, a look of barely restrained smugness on his face. 'Did he tell you?'

'I know. Fantastic.'

'He's a star,' added Sonia.

'It's a relief as much as anything.'

Hayden had taken himself off to a group of teenagers, including Joakim, who were gathered at the end of the garden. Ripples of their laughter drifted over to where we stood. They were passing round a thick joint and I saw Guy glance at them, then away.

'He's going to Edinburgh, isn't he?' I asked, to distract him.

'Yes. Less than six weeks. His mother will miss him.'

'What about you?'

'Me?'

'Won't you miss him?'

'It's different for a father,' said Guy. I opened my mouth

to argue, then shut it again.'Anyway, we've been squabbling so much lately it'll be good for us both to get a bit of distance. He's itching to leave home. I said,' he raised his voice for his son and Hayden, who were making their way down the garden towards us, 'that you're itching to leave home.'

'I wouldn't say that, exactly.' Joakim cast a pleading look at Hayden.

'I don't blame you,' said Guy.'Maybe I've been a bit hard on you lately.'

'Nah.' Joakim shuffled his feet.

'I was saying to Bonnie and Sonia that your mother will miss you. But so will I.'

'Oh, but you don't need to say goodbye just yet,' said Hayden, buoyantly.

'Six weeks.'

'Six weeks, six months,' said Hayden.'Who knows in this crazy old world?'

'What?'

'It's about Edinburgh, Dad.'

'What about Edinburgh?'

'I've been thinking I might take a gap year after all.'

'What for?'

'I think we should play the next set now,' Amos interrupted.

Guy ignored him.'When was this decided?'

'I've been thinking about it for ages.'

'But you know what you want to do. Go to university.'

'What about the university of life?' This was Hayden.

'Is this your doing?' said Guy.

'We've talked about it,' said Hayden, with a slow smile,

as if he was enjoying the effect this was having on Guy.

'Have you even asked Edinburgh if they'll defer your entry?' asked Sonia.

'I've only just decided,' said Joakim.

'Decided?' said Guy, his voice rising.

'You should talk about this afterwards,' I said. 'Privately.'

'Maybe I'll make it and not have to go anywhere,' said Joakim, talking to his father over me. 'I don't know anything. I'm starting from zero.'

'Make it?' Guy's voice was a croak. 'What do you mean, make it?'

'Hayden said he'll help me.'

Hayden lifted his hands modestly. 'I'll do what I can. Joakim has definite promise.'

'You stay out of this,' said Guy. 'Don't do this, Jo. Please. Don't just throw everything away.'

'It's my life,' said Joakim.

'Is that what you want? To be some ageing failure sleeping on other people's floors and sponging off friends of friends, waiting to *make it*?'

'Enough,' said Sonia. 'Now we're going to play.'

'I don't feel like it,' muttered Joakim.

I leaned towards him. 'You want to make it as a musician, Joakim? The first thing you have to do is learn a bit of professionalism. Play now, we'll talk later.'

'I'm ready.' Hayden picked up his guitar.

'You've got a lot to answer for,' Guy said.

'I've nothing to answer for.' The smile disappeared. Hayden's face became hard with dislike. 'Because I'm free. That's what you can't bear, isn't it?'

The cat a boy had thrown a stone at earlier brushed

against Guy's legs and he kicked it viciously so that it ran away with a high mew of pain.

'Dad!'

'One – and – two – and – three,' I said, and the music filled the garden and the rain began to fall.

Later, Hayden said cheerfully, 'That wasn't too bad. Now, let's go and celebrate.'

'Do you mean have a drink?'

'No. This is for kids. Let's go somewhere adult.'

I had a sense of foreboding: his pupils were dilated and his speech was faintly slurred.

'I'm going home,' said Guy, his voice thick with hostility. 'My wife will be waiting and there are things she and I need to talk about.' For some reason, he always called Celia 'my wife' when Hayden was around, as if he needed to remind himself of his own unassailable stability.

Hayden shrugged. 'As you wish. But one of my mates is throwing a party. We might as well drop in, see what it's like – it isn't far from here. Ten minutes' walk, if that.'

'What kind of party?' asked Amos.

'A grown-up party.' Hayden grinned at him. 'You look a bit anxious.'

'Why should I be anxious?'

'I don't know. Why should you?'

'I'm not.'

'So you're coming?'

'Yes,' said Amos.

'I thought we were going to have a meal together,' said Sonia. I could see that she was trying to give him a way out.

'I'm not hungry,' said Amos. 'I had a burger, anyway.'

'You'd better come as well, Sonia,' said Hayden, jovially. 'Keep an eye on him. Make sure he doesn't go wild.'

Sonia looked at him icily. She was the only one among us who ever seemed to quell Hayden, but not tonight. He patted her shoulder and said: 'Is that glare your way of saying yes?'

'I'll come if you want,' said Sonia to Amos, turning her back on Hayden.

'Great. Neal?'

'No,' said Neal.

'No?'

'I'm not in the mood.'

'OK. That's the four of us, then.'

'Your maths is wrong,' I said.

'You, Sonia, Amos and me — I assume young Joakim is staying with his mates.'

'You haven't asked me. You're making assumptions.'

'You'll like it.' He touched the back of my hand. 'You're a party animal.'

'A tired and pissed-off party animal.'

'Please.' He leaned forward and said softly into my ear, 'I need to be with you tonight.'

I was glad that in the dim light no one could see me blush. 'Just for a bit, then.'

'Well.' Neal aimed for a casual tone and missed. 'If you're all going, I might as well join you after all.'

Hayden smiled widely at him. 'Of course,' he said. 'Why not? The more the merrier.'

It was a big party and a tiny house. Every room bulged with people. They overflowed up the staircase and spilled out into the narrow garden. Music pumped loudly; I could feel the walls shake and the floorboards vibrate. As far as I could tell, in the smoky half-darkness, it was a motley collection: some young, even as young as Joakim, and some much older – men with grey hair pulled back into ponytails, women with tattoos on their shoulders and a musky smell. It was like being in a music tent at Glastonbury, except the beer was free, cold and plentiful.

Hayden was swallowed up in the crowd, most of whom seemed to know him. I saw a woman with beautiful red hair throw her arms around his neck. Sonia and Amos went into the garden together; later I saw them sitting on the uncut grass under a small dead tree, sharing a glass of wine and talking to a hugely pregnant woman. Neal stuck to me as I threaded through the rooms in search of a drink and a place I could sit and watch the crowd. When I was a teenager, I used to hate being at a party where I didn't know anyone: that agonizing self-consciousness when you stand in a room full of animated strangers talking to each other, hugging, kissing – what are you supposed to do with yourself? Arrange your face in that I-don't-care look? Spend a large amount of time in the bathroom, while people who genuinely need to be in there rattle the door handle? Walk purposefully around as if you're searching for a friend you know isn't there? I can't remember when I stopped feeling awkward and learned just to sit back and see what happened.

'Where are we going?' Neal said.

'I'm going to sit on the stairs, I think.'

We found a step near the top and I took a gulp of beer from the can I'd found in the bath, which was full of ice cubes. From there, I could see Hayden. If he looked up, he could have seen me too, but he didn't look up. He was focused on whoever was with him: at that particular moment, it was two women and another man, and they were all laughing. I understood that, before long, Hayden and I would part. There was a kind of giddy momentum between us. It was like being on a swing, swooping high, but soon we'd reach the top and curve down again. Then it would be over.

'Is this step free?' a woman with a handsome face and prematurely grey hair asked.

I smiled at her and she sat just below Neal and me and leaned her head back so it was resting against my knee, as if we were old friends.

'I'm Bonnie,' I said. 'This is Neal. And we know nobody.'

'I'm Sarah. If you don't know anyone, how come you're here?'

'Hayden brought us along.'

'Hayden?'

'That's right.'

'I didn't know he was here.'

'He's down there.' I nodded in his direction. He'd got hold of a bottle of whisky from somewhere and was pouring it into his glass and the glass of the woman he was talking to.

'So he is. Charming another poor fool.'

'Do you know a lot of the people here?' asked Neal. His voice was unsteady; he seemed mysteriously to have got drunk without drinking anything.

'Not as many as I thought I would, considering it's my party.'

'Oh! You live here, then?'

'Yes. I'm dead tired but someone's in my bed. Two people, actually. Hello, Hayden.'

He was making his way up the stairs, still holding the whisky bottle. The woman he'd been talking to trailed after him, huge kohl-rimmed eyes, and a cigarette jammed between her lips.

'This is Miriam Sylvester,' said Hayden. 'She's a teacher too.'

'Hi.' I raised a hand.

She gave me a curious look. 'You're the friend of Sonia's.'

'You make that sound like a bad thing,' I said, with a laugh. 'I'd thought I wouldn't know anyone at all, but everybody seems to know Hayden and now I meet an old buddy of Sonia's.'

'Well, we worked together in Sheffield.'

'You've got to tell me something embarrassing about her,' I said. 'Something I can use against her one day.'

Miriam took a deep drag on her cigarette. The column of ash grew longer, then delicately dislodged itself and fell at her feet.

'And *Sarah* here,' said Hayden, 'Sarah knows an ex-girl-friend of Amos's.'

I looked at her with new interest. 'You mean Jude?' I said.

'We were at school together,' said Sarah. 'You know her?'

'Bonnie was the girlfriend after,' said Hayden.

'This is insane,' I said. 'Can someone please introduce me to someone who doesn't know everyone I know?'

Miriam lit another cigarette. 'So you know Sonia, do you?' she said, with the irritating glint people have when they know something about you. 'And I know about you.'

'Me?'

'Banjo,' she said triumphantly.

'I'm not ashamed,' I said. 'In fact, I'm unashamed.'

I saw a face I thought I recognized and then realized it belonged to Hayden's quarrelsome friend Nat; he was clearly very drunk and walked with a shuffling, crablike gait through the gradually emptying room. Then I saw Amos and Sonia come in from the garden and I raised a hand to catch their attention. Sonia looked up and grimaced. I beckoned to her but she hesitated, then shook her head, taking Amos's hand and leading him towards the front door. I could guess what she was feeling. In a way it was fun to meet people who knew friends of mine but it felt claustrophobic as well. Lucky Liza, I suddenly thought, travelling far away where she knew nobody. Except that, with my luck, if I climbed Everest I'd probably find a previous girlfriend of Hayden's at the top.

There was another reason to avoid us. I could see from the way Amos was holding himself that he was really quite drunk. I remembered all the stages of Amos's drunkenness: he would be argumentative, just a ratchet or two up from his usual confrontational self; then he would be emotional and confessional, and maybe he would tell Sonia they should get married and have children, lots of children with her hair and his eyes; then depressed; then asleep in his clothes.

Miriam now had her head on Hayden's lap and his hand was resting on her hair, as if she was a small child. Her eyes were closed. He smiled at me and shrugged helplessly, mouthing a word I couldn't make out. I didn't smile back and gradually his smile faded and we stared at each other. Beside me, Neal gave a quiet snore; I felt his head settle on my shoulder. I went on sitting on the stairs with Hayden, sleeping people all around us, and waited.

After

At twenty past seven on Monday morning, a phone call woke me. It was Danielle. She sounded breathless, as if she'd just come in from a run. It must have been obvious she had woken me. 'If it's about the band,' I said, 'you don't need to worry. It's in hand.'

'Well, it *is* about the band, in a way.'

'You don't want us to play after all? That would be fine.' More than fine, *wonderful*.

'No no no. I'm longing for you to play. Especially now.' She sounded excited. 'Though you might not want to.'

'What are you talking about?'

'Hayden Booth,' she said. 'He was playing with you, wasn't he?'

'Oh, you heard? Don't worry. We'll be fine without him.'

'That's a bit hard-hearted, Bonnie.'

I sat up in bed and shifted the receiver to the other ear. 'What do you mean?'

'Haven't you heard?'

I heard my voice asking, 'Heard what?' I heard Danielle telling me that a man's body, found in Langley reservoir last night, had been identified as that of Hayden Booth. She'd heard it on the radio just a few minutes ago.

What would someone say if they knew nothing?

'Oh. God.'

'Isn't it awful?'

'Awful. Yes. It is. Awful. God.' I was thinking: Ring Sonia. What about Neal – did Joakim know yet? Guy? Or Sally. Did poor Sally know?

'I know. I mean, I'd never actually met him, but it's so shocking. Wasn't he one of your best players?'

'He was in a different league.'

'So will you still be able . . . you know?'

'I'll let you know. But we'll be fine.'

'It's only a matter of days away.'

'We'll be there,' I said, raising my voice a little.

'I'm just the messenger, Bonnie.'

Before

He lay in the water on his back with his arms spread out. My day out, my little snippet of a summer holiday. His body moved lazily as small waves rolled under him, gathering to breakers as they reached the shore. I swam towards him. His eyes were shut against the sun but he reached out an arm and pulled me towards him so that we both went under, gasping. I felt his limbs tangling with mine, put out my hands and touched his long wet hair, his cool neck, came up to see his laughing face – a laughing face that turned grave as he pulled me against him and we were hugging, holding each other and trying to tread water, and there was salt stinging our skin and the chilly slap of waves against our flesh and light bouncing off the sea in dazzling arrows. Lips against my shoulder, my eyelids, my mouth, sinking and then rising again and finally making it to shore, where there was no one to be seen or to see, and we lay on the gritty sand, seagulls shrieking and the shush of the waves, fragments of shells digging into us. Then we ran into the water again and washed each other down. He dried me with his shirt and rubbed the sand from between my toes.

Afterwards, Hayden insisted on buying a dozen oysters from the shack along the coast. We sat outside at a scrubbed wooden table and squeezed lemon juice onto the quivering slimes. He ate eleven and I ate one. They were too alive, too slimy, too salty for my taste.

Hayden seemed happy that day, sweet and sunny. I guess he was on holiday too.

After

I tried to ring Sonia but it was hopeless. I could imagine that everybody was ringing everybody else in that gleeful excitement people feel when something really terrible happens – that great pleasure in life: being the bearer of bad news. Have you heard? Have you heard? I texted her: Ring me. I switched on my answering-machine and sat numbly listening as message after message was left. Twice, it was Joakim, in the first sounding dazed and in the second shouting with grief. Then I heard the beep, a hesitation, and Sonia's voice. I ran forward and snatched up the phone.

'Sonia, it's me, I'm here.'

'I got your text.'

'Yes? Well?'

'I've heard.'

I'd known that I needed to talk to her but I hadn't really thought about what I had to say.

'I don't know,' I said. 'This wasn't part of the plan.' There was silence on the line. 'Are you still there?'

'Yes.'

I couldn't tell whether she was frightened or angry or shocked or just being Sonia. 'There'll be an investigation now.'

'Of course there'll be an investigation,' she said. 'A body's been found dumped in a reservoir. It's in the paper. There'll be a murder inquiry.'

I took a deep breath. 'Sonia, I'm so sorry I brought you into this. If you want to go to the police . . .'

'It's too late for anything like that.'

'You're probably right.'

'Just don't try to be clever.'

'That won't be too difficult,' I said.

'I mean it, Bonnie. No more of your brilliant improvisations. We just do nothing, and say as little as possible.'

'I'm scared.'

'Of course you are. But sit tight.'

I put down the phone, and before I could put the answering-machine on, it rang again.

'This is Nat, Hayden's friend. The bassist.' His voice was thick – whether with drink or wretchedness I couldn't tell.

'I know who you are.'

'You heard?'

'Yes.'

'It's fucking awful. We've got to talk.'

'We are talking.'

'I mean face to face. I'll be in Camden Lock in half an hour.'

I reluctantly agreed, and he gave me elaborate instructions on how to find him, which involved locating a falafel stall and a weaver of baskets. Then I switched the answering-machine back on and turned off my mobile. I checked my computer. Thirty-four messages and most weren't trying to sell me things. While I was watching, a thirty-fifth, a thirty-sixth and a thirty-seventh arrived. I looked through them. Four were from Sally. Oh, God, Sally. I switched the computer off and put my head into my hands, trying to block out the world.

Everything was switched off. The door was locked. But still I had the feeling I always got on a day when I was going to play a concert. I'd do things that felt normal but all the time there'd be a bit of me that knew that soon I'd be in front of an audience, that I'd be in a situation where things could go right or wrong and there wasn't very much I could do about it. I made myself a cup of coffee and got dressed in a pair of jeans, a shirt and a sweater that looked casual but not grungy. I was prickly with heat, so I took off the sweater and put on a different shirt. Though I wasn't hungry, I had a piece of hot buttered toast. Then I put on a bit of makeup, just enough to stop me looking entirely strung out. I was about to leave when the bell rang and I opened the door to find two people standing there, a man and a woman, both dressed for business.

They could have been insurance salesmen but I knew, even before they said anything, that they were detectives. They took out their ID cards and showed them to me.

'I'm Detective Inspector Joy Wallis,' the woman said, 'and this is my colleague Detective Inspector Wade. We have some bad news for you.'

'I've heard,' I said. 'Someone rang me.' Was that it? I wondered. Were they just coming to break the news to me? Hardly. I wasn't his wife. 'I was on my way out.'

'We hoped you'd give us a moment,' said the woman.

I led them through. I sat on the only chair and they sat on the only sofa. The frantic mess of the flat made me seem a bit like a madwoman. DI Wallis had a file under her arm and she laid it on the table in front of her. I was tempted to start babbling about how terrible it was, as a normal person would, but I remembered what Sonia had said and forced myself to stay silent.

'It must be a shock,' said DI Wade.

'Yes,' I said. 'A terrible shock.'

She leaned forward and, with one finger, flipped the file open. 'You talked to a colleague of ours,' she said. 'Last week. You expressed anxiety about Mr Booth. In fact, you reported him missing.'

'We didn't exactly report him missing,' I said. 'I went with my friend, Sally Corday, and we were sent away. We were told not to worry.'

'Why were you worried?'

'A group of us are playing a concert soon – on September the twelfth. Hayden was playing with us. Then, suddenly, he didn't turn up. Sally was the most worried. I thought he'd just left.'

'Why did you think that?'

'He's a musician. I thought of him as the sort of person who'd move on if something better came up.'

'Instead somebody killed him.'

'Are you sure?' I asked.

The two detectives looked at each other.

'I'm sorry?' said DI Wallis.

'Could it have been an accident?'

'These are early days,' she said, 'but when someone is found at the bottom of a reservoir weighed down with stones and there's evidence of a severe blow to the head, we start a murder investigation.'

I couldn't stop myself. I needed to know. 'How was the body found,' I said, 'if it was at the bottom of a reservoir?'

'It wasn't very deep although it was in the middle,' she said. 'I understand a fisherman got his line caught.'

I thought of when I was a child and I'd fished with my dad on a holiday in Scotland and the line had snagged on something and broken and we'd forgotten about it.

'That was lucky,' I said.

'A colleague has already talked to your friend Mrs Corday and she said you'd be a good person to talk to about people who knew Hayden Booth.'

'I know a few,' I said. 'Not many.'

DI Wallis paused for a moment and ran her finger gently along the edge of the file. 'Close friend, were you?'

This moment had come too soon. How much did other people know about Hayden and me? What would they tell the police? Meanwhile the phone was ringing and we heard my answering-machine message over and over again.

'The word's getting around,' I said. 'Sorry. This has been a terrible shock. I've only known him a couple of weeks, really. A few weeks. I agreed to play at a friend's wedding and I needed some musicians. I met him through a friend. I can't believe this has happened.'

'I'm very sorry,' said DI Wade. 'This must be difficult for you. But you could be a great help in catching whoever's done this.'

'Of course,' I said. 'Can I make you some tea or coffee?'

They said yes and I was able to bustle around the kitchen and collect my thoughts. I came back with a tray of coffee and biscuits. I got my address book and my mobile phone and my laptop and I read out a few phone numbers, addresses and email addresses of people who knew or might know Hayden, or know someone who had known him, and DI Wade laboriously copied them onto two sheets of paper. It was all very low tech.

'Tell me about him,' said DI Wallis, after the list was complete.

'Tell you what?'

'Anything you like.'

I gave an abbreviated and highly edited version of how I'd met Hayden, how he'd played with us, how I'd met some of his friends. So slowly and laboriously that I almost wanted to help her, DI Wallis leafed through the file page by page until she seemed to find what she wanted. 'My colleague talked to you,' she said.

'Becky something.'

'PC Horton. And you told her you didn't really know his friends?' She looked up at me. 'Is that right?'

I felt my face getting hot. Was I blushing? Police officers

can probably tell when you've got things to conceal. 'I met some other people he'd played with. I don't know if they were his friends exactly.'

'What can you tell us about his personal life?' said DI Wade.

'I don't know what you mean by that,' I said. 'He wasn't really someone who divided his life into compartments. He played music, he hung out, that was basically it.'

'I mean, was he in a relationship?'

'I don't think he was someone who had steady, permanent relationships, if that's what you mean.'

'So he didn't have a girlfriend?'

'Not that I knew of,' I said, which was true, or not exactly a lie. I wouldn't ever have described myself as his girlfriend.

'Can you think of anyone who could have done this?' said DI Wade.

'When you talk to people, you're going to find out that Hayden had a gift for rubbing them up the wrong way. He could be charming and he could be . . . well, difficult.'

'Did *you* find him difficult?'

'I think pretty much everybody did. He wasn't malicious, but he took what he wanted from people and moved on. He pissed quite a few people off. As you'll discover.'

'This wasn't just pissing someone off,' said DI Wade. 'Somebody battered him to death and they went to a lot of trouble to dispose of the body.'

'That's what I've been thinking,' I said. 'I can't make sense of it.'

'Did he have money problems?' asked DI Wallis.

'Of course he did,' I said. 'He was a musician. All musicians are basically broke. Except for Sting and Phil Collins.'

'Was it a source of conflict?'

'A couple of the names I've given you are people he used to play with. As far as I know, they had a bit of a bust-up over some money. They'll tell you about it.'

'A serious bust-up?'

'It's the kind of thing all bands go through. It's always about the money – it doesn't arrive or it goes to the wrong person or gets frittered away. But it was just the normal unpleasant band stuff. This wasn't the Mafia. It wasn't worth killing him over.'

'You wouldn't believe what people would kill over,' said DI Wade. 'It doesn't generally seem worth it.'

'It's such a waste,' I said, into the pause.

DI Wallis flicked through her notes as if she was looking for something. Then she raised her eyes towards me. 'Did you like him?' she said.

'Like?'

'Yes,' she said. 'Did you like him?'

I was completely floored by that simple question. 'That doesn't seem the right word for someone like Hayden,' I said. 'It sounds too normal.' I felt I'd said too much. I'd got too close to telling the truth.

At last I rang Sally, dreading the conversation, but Richard answered. He said she and Lola had gone to stay with her mother for a while. When I asked when she'd be back, he said he didn't know. His voice was heavy. Even listening to it made me feel wretched. I knew why Sally had gone and presumably he knew that I knew, but neither of us said anything.

I called Sally on her mobile but only got her voicemail.

I left a message saying that if she needed to speak to me, I was there. It was the least I could do.

Before

That evening, back from the seaside, we lay in Liza's bed together, our skin burned by the sun. Drowsily we kissed and made love and lay entangled with each other, and I half slept and when I woke he was there, looking at me. Maybe it didn't matter how long this went on. It was the summer. What happened in the summer was like a dream, cut off from before and after, obeying its own impossible rules. I could lose myself in this until September, when work and real life began.

After

I made my way through the market at Camden Lock, pushing through the cartoon-style punks with their huge Mohicans, past the Goths and the tourists. Nat's instructions turned out not to be very accurate and it took me some time to find the meeting-place. When I got there, I couldn't see him at first. Eventually I caught sight of him some distance away. He was leaning on a bollard near the canal. As I approached, I saw that Jan was with him, bent over slightly, the way tall people often are, as if they've spent too much of their lives avoiding low ceilings.

'Where have you been?' Nat said.

'I'm sorry. Some people arrived just as I was leaving. Police.'

'Jesus,' said Nat.

'Why did you want to see me? Was there a reason?'

'A friend of ours has just been pulled out of a reservoir,' said Nat. 'I'd call that some kind of a reason.'

'I didn't mean that.'

Nat fumbled in his jacket and produced a packet of cigarettes and a lighter. He offered me the packet.

'I've given up,' I said.

'It's time to fucking start again.'

He handed a cigarette to Jan and the two of them lit up. I felt an overwhelming urge to join them but instead I jammed my hands into my pockets as if that was a way of avoiding reaching out for a cigarette. 'So?' I said. 'You needed to see me.'

He looked at Jan and then at me. 'Hello?' he said, in a raised voice. 'Hayden's fucking dead. Somebody dumped him in a reservoir.'

'It's a terrible shock,' I said.

'That's right,' said Jan, in an odd, muted voice. It was the first time he had spoken.

'How did you get my phone number?' I asked.

'Hayden gave it to me one time,' said Nat. 'In my notebook I've literally got about thirty different numbers that he gave me at different times where he could be reached, most of them crossed out. Now I guess I can cross them all out. Do you want to go for a walk? I'm cold just standing here.'

'It's a warm summer day,' I said.

'I get cold when I stand around.'

We moved off and made slow progress through the crowd.

'What is it with these punks?' said Jan, fretfully. 'I was a kid when punk happened and people didn't look like that. The real punks didn't look like punks.'

'What do you mean they didn't look like punks?' said Nat.

'Look at the old pictures of the Sex Pistols. They don't look like punk rockers. The uniform came later.'

'We all wear uniforms,' said Nat. He turned to me. '*You* don't. Were you ever part of a tribe?'

'I don't think so,' I said. 'For me it's always just about the music.'

'No wonder you and Hayden got together.'

'We didn't really get together . . .' I began.

'I'm just like those punks,' said Nat. 'What we play – played, should I say? – is a sort of alt-country so I dress like I was born in Texas. I grew up in Norfolk, for fuck's sake. Hayden was never like that. He wouldn't have seen the point.' He stopped. 'We've got to toast him.'

I checked my watch. 'It's ten past twelve.'

'We've got to toast him.'

Jan looked at me and shrugged, and we followed Nat to a pub by the canal. We sat at a table outside and Nat went in. He emerged carrying a tray with three small glasses containing a dark liquid, and three packets of crisps. He

214

sat down and handed them around. 'Bourbon,' he said. He picked up the glass and contemplated it. 'Bonnie. Do you want to say a few words?'

Now there was a long pause because I really, really didn't want to say any words at all. I didn't want to be drinking bourbon at midday with two musicians I hardly knew. 'I don't know what to say,' I said. 'I didn't know Hayden the way you two knew him.'

'That's true,' said Jan, in a tone that made me feel sick.

'Hayden was a great musician,' I said. 'Somehow I don't think it ever quite worked out for him. It shouldn't have ended like this.'

'Of course it shouldn't have fucking ended like this,' said Nat. 'That's not much of a tribute.'

I looked at Jan. 'Can you do any better?'

Jan dabbed his finger into the bourbon and touched his tongue with it. He picked the glass up. 'To the memory of Hayden Booth. He took my money. He fucked up my career. He once stole my girl. But the good thing about Hayden: he'd do something terrible to you, but when he'd done it, it was over. He wouldn't hold a grudge. To Hayden, and short memories.'

'That's not much of a tribute either,' said Nat.

'The last time I saw you together, there was a fight,' I said.

Nat gave a grunt. 'Like the man said, it's only rock-and-roll. I can do better. To Hayden, who walked the walk.'

'He did not walk the fucking walk,' said Jan. 'He talked the fucking talk, but he did not walk the fucking walk.'

'Are we going to have this drink or not?' said Nat.

'I'm just not going to bullshit about the guy.'

'All right, all right. What about this? To Hayden. He died young. Or kind of young. He died young and he left a beautiful corpse. What about that, Bonnie? Will you vouch for that? Did he leave a beautiful corpse?'

Until then it had all been oddly detached. It had been a relief to be with people I didn't know or care about but suddenly the word 'corpse' hit me and I saw his body lying on the floor, and the blood and the unnatural position of it, and even caught a certain smell that I'd entirely forgotten. I made myself nod. 'Yeah,' I said, in hardly more than a whisper. 'I guess he did.'

'Fine,' said Nat. 'To Hayden.'

I lifted the glass and just felt the liquid against my lips but then I opened them and felt the hot stinging on my tongue, tipped the glass and swallowed it all in a gulp. Even before I had properly noticed what was happening, Jan had gone, come back and there was another glass of bourbon in front of me. Rather desperately I tore open a bag of crisps and crammed several into my mouth. The saltiness and sweet spiciness were repulsive and I had to force myself to swallow.

'Why me?' I said. 'Why call me? And why are you both here?'

'What did the police ask you?' said Jan.

'When you rang, I hadn't seen the police.'

'But it was obvious, wasn't it? You're the one he was with. You'd be the first person they'd talk to.'

'I wasn't with him.'

'You were playing with him,' said Nat. 'You found him somewhere to live.'

'I just suggested a place,' I said. 'Somewhere to flat-sit.'

'I saw you together,' said Nat. 'I saw the way he looked at you. He depended on you.'

'He adored you.'

'The police didn't ask anything special. There's a murder inquiry. They just asked the stuff you'd expect.'

Jan picked up his glass, then set it down very gently, without tasting it. 'Which is?' he said.

'Did he have enemies, did he have special friends, did he have money problems – that kind of thing.'

'Did you mention us?'

'Shouldn't I have?'

'Which means you did?'

'If you really want to know, I said that I had very little knowledge of his life, but I did mention the musicians he'd been playing with, which means you. Is there a problem with that?'

'No,' said Nat. 'No problem. So I guess they'll be in touch.'

'I didn't give them your number, if that's what you mean, but I suppose they'll track you down. I mean, that's what they do. What I also said is that they'd find quite a long list of people Hayden had pissed off. They asked me who might be angry with him.'

'Only people who knew him,' said Jan.

'That's roughly what I said.'

There was a pause and I stared at my drink. I definitely couldn't manage any more of it. At the next table there was a group of people who were a wild mixture of tattoos and pink hair, thigh-length boots and tigerskin. What did these people do when they weren't on holiday? Did they work in banks and primary schools?

'What did Hayden say about us?' asked Nat.

'Nothing,' I said. 'Or nothing that I can remember. Why?'

'On the times we met, you must have seen we weren't exactly on the best of terms. We just wanted to say that you shouldn't get the wrong idea.'

In other circumstances I would have found it difficult to stop myself smiling. Not today, though. Today I didn't feel the smallest temptation to smile. 'Is that what you called me about?' I said. 'The two of you came all the way over here and plied me with drink to tell me that you weren't on bad terms with Hayden?'

'No,' said Jan. 'We were on bad terms with him. Or pretty bad terms. As you saw. But there wasn't anything new about it. That's the way things always were with Hayden. With all of us.'

'Fine,' I said. 'I believe you.'

Nat looked suspicious. 'And you didn't ask Hayden what had happened between us?'

'I know what happened between you. At least, I know all I want to know. What I assume happened is that Hayden spent money you were stupid enough to entrust him with. And, no doubt, there were other things as well. I imagine that if there were any moments when success looked at all likely, he probably wasn't much help.'

'To say the least,' said Nat. 'And why do you think that was?'

'You mean why is . . .' I stopped myself. 'Why *was* Hayden like that? Do you want me to say that he was abused as a child? That he had some hidden trauma that made him feel he didn't deserve success?'

'I wouldn't say that,' said Jan. 'I'd say it was that no success could ever be quite enough for him.'

'I wasn't his psychiatrist,' I said.

Jan smiled. 'No,' he said. 'No, you weren't.'

I was sick of this and I just wanted to go, but then I looked at them, two middle-aged, not very successful musicians and I surprised myself by feeling an ache of sympathy for them. 'This will be big,' I said.

'What do you mean?' said Nat.

'The police investigation,' I said. 'Today's the beginning. It's not going to be pleasant for anybody who knew Hayden.'

'Especially the low-life musicians he worked with,' said Jan. 'I mean us. Not you.'

'But that's all right, isn't it?' said Nat. 'Because we all just want the person who did this caught.'

'Obviously,' I said.

'When I first heard, I thought it was a mugger,' said Nat. 'Just a robbery gone wrong. But then I heard about the reservoir. A mugger doesn't weigh you down with stones and throw you into a reservoir.'

'I don't know much about muggers,' I said.

'Just one thing,' said Jan.

'Yes?'

'You said Hayden spent all our money.'

'I just said it. I don't know anything.'

'But he didn't give you any money? For safe-keeping or as a present?'

'To me?' I said.

'It's not just us,' said Jan. 'Hayden owed a lot of people money. A lot of angry people.'

'I don't know where the money went,' I said. 'But I don't remember Hayden spending any. Definitely not on me.' I got up to go.

'You haven't finished your drink,' Nat said.

'You have it,' I said. 'You can toast Hayden again. Sorry, that came out sounding wrong.'

'So you think the police will want to talk to us?'

'I think they'll want to talk to everybody.'

'We won't have much to tell them.'

'Then it won't take long,' I said.

'Do you know how to reach me?' said Nat.

'Am I going to need to reach you?'

He wrote his number on a beer mat and handed it to me. 'You could keep us in touch with what's going on,' he said. 'If there's anything we need to know.'

As I walked home I went over what I'd said to the police. I'd been so stupid. I'd thought I'd been so discreet about Hayden and me, almost invisible, but people had known, perhaps everybody. Soon the police would hear and would want to know why I'd been less than truthful. I would have to think what I was going to say about that.

Before

I knocked briskly on the door that used to be my door and assumed a nonchalant expression.

'Bonnie!'

'Hi. Sorry I'm a bit late.'

'Late?'

'You've forgotten?'

'No – that is, what?'

'I've come to collect my things. We arranged it at the last rehearsal.'

'Was that today?'

'Sunday morning, when you could be sure to be here. Can I come in?' I took a step forward so that I was standing on the threshold.

'I'm not quite ready for you. Sorry. Maybe we could do it another day. There's no real hurry, is there?'

'That's easy for you to say.' I winced at the sharpness in my voice. 'The thing is, I've borrowed Sally's car. There's not that much, and you said you'd put it all in boxes already.' I advanced a few paces more and Amos backed away from me. He looked as though he had just got out of bed, in a baggy and stained pair of shorts and a ragged T-shirt, his face stubbly and his hair standing on end.

'You'd better come up, then,' he said, rubbing his face with the back of his hand as he went up the stairs that led to the flat. I remembered when we'd first seen it together. The estate agent had unlocked the door that Amos was pushing open now and we'd stepped through into the main room, empty of furniture, cool and full of sunlight that shone through the two large windows and lay across the grey carpets in slanted rectangles. I'd fallen in love with it at once, imagined sitting there, listening to music, looking out at the street at the end of a day, leading my life, gradually filling the spaces with memories and clutter. Now I was a stranger again, come to remove the clutter. I glanced around. Everything was slightly unfamiliar. The sofa stood in a different place; there was a low coffee-table that hadn't been there before and on it were several mugs that post-dated me.

'Coffee?' asked Amos, hovering awkwardly, unsure of how to treat me – was I a guest? An intruder?

'That would be good.'

'With or without milk?' He blushed. 'I mean, I know how you used to take it, but you might have changed.'

'It's OK. I haven't. Not with how I take my coffee anyway.'

In the silence there was the sound of a lavatory being flushed, then a tap running.

'I – um – I should have said.'

Muffled footsteps, and the door opened.

'Hello, Bonnie.' Sonia stood in the entrance wearing boxers and a black T-shirt with 'Dyslexics Untie' across the front. Her feet were bare, the nails painted deep red.

'That's my top,' I said.

'I'll wash it and get it back to you.' She smiled at me in a kindly fashion. For some reason I felt wrong-footed by the pair of them, horribly ill-at-ease in this place that had been my home until recently. 'How are you doing?'

'Good. Fine. Great. I'm collecting my stuff. Then I'll be off.'

'No hurry. Let's have coffee and then I'll leave you to it.'

'I'm just going to get it,' said Amos, and hurried into the little kitchen that adjoined the living room, half tripping in his eagerness to get away.

'I didn't know you'd be here.'

'And I didn't know you were coming. But it's all right. Isn't it?'

'It's weird.'

'I know.'

'And you and Amos –' I stopped.

'Yes?'

'That's weird too.'

'You said it was fine.'

'Fine, but weird.'

'Right.'

'I want to run away.'

'I can see it's odd, me being here with Amos and you coming on your own.'

'It's not that,' I said, although of course it was. I felt at a perilous disadvantage.

'You'll find someone soon.'

'I'm sorry?'

The door opened and Amos came in, carrying three mugs of coffee.

'You'll meet someone,' said Sonia. She spoke quietly but she had a clear and carrying voice – she was one of those people whom you could hear in a crowded room.

My cheeks burned. I glared at her to shut her up but she didn't seem to understand. Amos put the mugs carefully down on the coffee-table before giving me a sympathetic look. 'It's true,' he said.

'I don't want to meet someone. I'm quite happy not meeting someone, thank you. It's nice of you to be concerned, Amos, but I'm much happier being on my own, getting my sense of independence back.' I couldn't seem to shut up. 'I'm having a lovely time. A great summer. I just want to take my things.'

'I'll have this, then pop out to get some food, shall I?' Sonia said to Amos.

'Yeah, that'd be best.'

'Stay if you want. You can be our referee.'

'That's precisely what I don't want to be, Bonnie.' Sonia grinned.

'I can see it might be difficult. That's my picture, by the way.' I pointed to the small black-and-white photograph of swans on a river.

'I don't think so,' Amos said. 'We bought it together, I clearly remember.'

'We bought it together with my money.'

'That's not how I recall it.'

'And I don't think you ever liked it.'

'Maybe not, but that's hardly the point. Anyway, I'm coming round to it.'

Sonia sighed and stood up. 'This is not a competition, Amos,' she said evenly. He turned beetroot. 'You don't get to win or lose. You don't like it, so don't hang on to it.' She lifted the photograph off the wall, dusted the glass with the edge of her shirt – my shirt – and put it into my hands. It was a demonstration to me. 'Now, I'll put some clothes on and be out of here. See you, Bonnie.' She leaned down to where I was sitting on the edge of the sofa, put her hands on my tense shoulders and kissed me, first on one cheek, then the other. I breathed in her clean, soapy smell and felt the softness of her thick hair against my cheek. 'Sorry,' she said.

'It's OK.'

'Yes.' Her voice was firm, like a command. 'It is.'

It was better after she had left because we could behave in a childish, petty manner without feeling ashamed of ourselves under her grown-up, considering gaze. I got the glass vase but he kept the wok that neither of us had ever used; I got the four champagne flutes that had been a moving-in present from a friend and he kept the shot glasses. I bartered the patchwork throw for the bathroom mats.

We bickered over books, almost came to blows over a Crosby, Stills and Nash CD. It's extraordinary what you accumulate. I had always thought of myself as someone who travelled light, yet an hour and a half later Sally's car was stuffed with printer ink, DVDs, a pair of speakers, old copies of music magazines, scuffed walking-boots, sheets and pillow-cases, a bean bag, a stool, several cushions, a stand-alone mirror, a cafetière and a chipped teapot, wind chimes, pos-ters, lampshades, pot plants, plates, mugs, a large hammer, a small rusty saw, a bag of buttons, last year's wall calendar, a Christmas-tree stand plus a box of defective Christmas lights. All the debris of life: phone chargers, adaptors, pens, socks, cotton reels, assorted bits of makeup. When they were locked away from me, they had seemed intensely desirable and the thought of them being in Amos's posses-sion had filled me with rage and a self-righteous grievance; now, in the back of the car, they returned to being useless, unwanted, superfluous. I stopped at a skip and threw in several bags, barely checking what was inside them. Then, at the florist in Camden, I bought a large bunch of flowers to go with the vase I'd fought for, and drove home.

After

It was DI Wallis and DI Wade again, but this time it wasn't at my flat but at the police station, and it wasn't an informal chat but a formal interview, with a tape recorder playing.

They didn't smile at me, and they didn't reassure me, and I found that my hands were shaking so much that I had to put them on my lap to hide them. My voice seemed to echo in that small, bare room, which was so brightly lit that I felt every twitch on my face would be noticed by them, that every lie would be amplified. I told myself to say as little as possible, to repeat what I'd said before – but I could no longer remember what I'd said. My story, such as it was, seemed to have been lost in the whirling panic of my mind – or, at least, tiny fragments remained, floating around in a blizzard of thoughts and fears. I was an actress with a scattering of randomly remembered lines and a whole play stretching out before me, a concert musician without music, a child back at school again, facing the nightmare of exams and only a few unassimilated facts bobbing around in the stew of ignorance.

I had spent the morning reading newspapers in the café down the road. I had ordered a pot of coffee, which I had drunk too quickly, burning my lips and increasing the jittery sensation in my limbs, and an almond croissant I scarcely touched because I felt so queasy that I thought even a few sugary flakes might make me throw up. All the papers had stories about Hayden Booth, the gifted musician with a promising future, whose body had been found in a reservoir. Headlines screamed of mystery, tragedy, relatives' sorrow. What relatives? Did he have a mother, a father, brothers and sisters he had never mentioned, maybe little nephews and nieces he'd let clamber over him as Lola had clambered over him? In almost all, there was a photograph of him taken several years ago: he was standing on a stage and holding his guitar, his face half in shadow and

226

his eyes hooded. He looked like someone famous, like someone beautiful. The fact of him took my breath away and I folded my arms around myself and waited until the thudding of my heart subsided and I could see the newsprint clearly again.

I didn't want to read about him but I couldn't stop myself. I scanned every line, waiting for my name to leap out at me, or for some damning fact to hit me, but there was nothing I didn't know, except his age, which was thirty-eight, and the name of his ex-manager, Paul Boland. The stories had been hastily put together the day before, and the police, who were sitting opposite me now, were way ahead of them. They knew, for instance, that I hadn't told them the whole truth.

When I had first sat down, my bare legs hot and sticky against the plastic chair, I had been offered a solicitor. It was my legal right. 'If you don't have one, we can arrange one for you.' DI Wade waited for my reply.

'I don't know. I don't think . . .'

If they were offering me a solicitor, did that mean I was – what was the phrase that was always used? – under suspicion? My first instinct was to say yes. I imagined someone – a silver-haired man in a grey suit, carrying a slim leather briefcase, or a slender, well-groomed woman with high cheekbones and a fine, ironic intelligence – sitting beside me and steering me through the dangerous waters ahead, making everything steady and safe. But, then, what would I tell the solicitor? I realized I would have to lie to them as well, have to attempt to remember the exact story I had already told, and the thought of adding another layer of deception to the tottering edifice made me feel giddy with panic.

'No,' I managed. 'I don't need a solicitor.' I attempted a breezy self-confidence. 'Why would I?'

'Why indeed?' said DI Wade. 'So . . .'

So we began – and began, of course, with the fact that I had known Hayden Booth rather better than I had previously let on.

'You told us . . .' said DI Wade, flicking through his notebook '. . . yes, you said that he didn't have a girlfriend.'

'Yes,' I replied. 'That is, yes, I told you that.'

'Would you like to amend that statement?'

'What do you mean?'

'Do you still want to tell us that he didn't have a girlfriend?'

A deep heat flooded my body. I could feel it passing through me in waves. My face burned. 'He didn't. I mean, that's not the word for it.' They both waited. Joy Wallis bounced her pencil lightly on the surface of the table, tap tap tap. 'It wasn't like that with Hayden.' Silence opened in front of me and I thought for a moment that I would hurl myself into it, blabber everything, get this over with. I swallowed hard and looked up. 'He wasn't the kind of man who had a steady girlfriend.'

'So you said last time.'

'Well, then.'

'You misled us.'

'I didn't understand.'

'Understand what?'

'I don't know.' I tried again. 'I'm sorry. I didn't mean to mislead you. It's true that I wasn't Hayden's girlfriend.'

'How so?' mused DI Wade.

'We weren't in a committed relationship,' I said. 'I had

only known him for a couple of weeks or so, through the band. You know. I told you before.'

'Were you sexually involved with Mr Booth?'

'Yes.'

'So. You weren't his girlfriend but you were sexually involved with him?'

'Yes.'

'You had sex with him.'

'Obviously.'

'How many times?'

'Sorry?'

'Approximately how many times did you have sex with Hayden Booth?'

'Is that relevant?'

'We'll know once you've told us.'

'I'm not sure.'

'Once? Twice? Three times? More?'

'Nearer that, yes.'

'More than three?'

'Yes.'

'How many more?'

'I don't know. A few.'

'Say, six or seven times in less than two weeks and you weren't his girlfriend?'

'No. I wasn't.'

'Was it secret?' This was from Joy Wallis.

'Kind of.'

'Why?'

'It just was. We didn't want people to know. To make assumptions. That kind of thing.'

'Assumptions that you were a couple?'

'Something like that.'

'So nobody knew.'

'I guess Jan and Nat knew. Kind of. The guys in his band. Knew that we had a – thing.'

'This *thing*.' DI Wade spoke the word carefully, as if it was an accurate portrayal of what had been be-tween Hayden and myself. 'Was it still going on when he died?'

'I guess so.'

'Sorry – you guess so?'

'It was.'

'Where did you meet?'

'My flat. His. It belongs to my friend who's away at the moment – but I've told you that.'

'Did you have arguments?' Joy Wallis again. Her voice was softer than DI Wade's and she didn't look at me when she spoke, but down at her notebook, in which, I saw, she was not writing.

I flinched. For a moment, I saw Hayden's fist plunging towards my face. As they looked at me, waiting for my answer, I felt the now-faded bruise on my neck throb, as if to give me away. Surely they must see it, feel it.

'No. We snapped at each other, of course. You know.'

'Not really. Go on.'

'He was a bit of a slob.'

'So you argued about mess?'

'A bit. Maybe.'

'Was he faithful to you?'

'I told you, I wasn't his girlfriend. He didn't need to be faithful.'

'So he wasn't faithful.'

'The word doesn't apply.'

'There were other women?'

I thought of Sally, whom he'd captivated and abandoned. 'I don't know,' I said.

We went round and round the subject. My head was banging in the stifling heat. My hands sweated. And then DI Wade asked: 'Did Mr Booth have a car?'

'Yes.' My voice rasped. I wound my fingers together and tried to make my voice stronger. 'He had a car. I went in it once.' That was in case traces of me remained in spite of the valet cleaning.

'Do you remember the make?'

'Blue. That's all I know. Old and blue.'

'A blue Rover, thirteen years old.' He gave me the registration number as well, reading it out from the file.

'Maybe.'

'Do you know where he kept it?'

'That would be outside Liza's flat, where he was staying.'

'I see.' He leaned back in his chair and put his latticed hands behind his head. 'I'm going to tell you something about that car, Miss Graham. It's not outside his flat now.' I muttered something meaningless. 'It was found in Walthamstow, parked illegally on Fountain Road on the afternoon of Sunday, the thirtieth of August.' He consulted his notebook again. 'It was ticketed at seven minutes past three and the vehicle was removed twenty minutes later.'

There was a pause.

'Someone must have stolen it,' I said.

'The keys were still in the ignition.'

'So?' I said.

'Doesn't that seem strange?'

'Sorry,' I said, 'I don't mean to be rude but what does it matter what it seems to me?'

'Do you know where it was before that?'

'No.'

'It was at Stansted airport, the long-stay car park.'

'What was it doing there?' I said.

'It was left there just after four a.m. on the twenty-second of August . . . The driver was wearing sunglasses and a headscarf. In the middle of the night.'

'Do you think it could have been Hayden?' I asked.

'It doesn't seem very likely. We believe the driver was a woman.'

'Ah,' I said.

'White, quite young.'

I made a noise that came out wrong, a strangled croak.

'On the morning of August the thirtieth the car was driven down the M11 towards London, west onto the North Circular and then immediately off.' Joy Wallis looked down at her file. 'But then the car was simply left, with the key in the ignition, as I said.'

'Sounds weird.'

I heard Sonia's voice in my head: You *idiot*.

'Doesn't that seem strange? Can you think of any explanation why the car should be parked for a week at the airport and then moved?'

'Maybe it was stolen.'

'I think that's extremely unlikely. I've seen the car. There may have been something in the car that needed delivering. Something valuable.'

'Was anything found?' I asked.

'Nothing at all. When did you last see Mr Booth?' asked DI Wade.

'I told you before. It must have been at the rehearsal. The Wednesday, I think. You can check that with the others.'

'And where were you, Bonnie?'

'When?'

'Where were you between the morning of August the twenty-first and the morning of August the twenty-second?'

'That's easy,' I said, 'I was with Neal. Neal Fenton.'

'All day?'

'Yes.'

'And all night?'

'Yes. He's my boyfriend, you see.'

I was kept at the police station for just over six hours. We went over and over my account, and then I was taken into a different room where a woman took my fingerprints and then stuck a cotton bud into my mouth for a DNA sample. Only then was I allowed to leave. I walked out into the sunny, late-afternoon street. I wanted to stop and curl up in a ball on the pavement and howl, but I thought someone might be watching me, so I kept going, trying to impersonate a normal person, an innocent person, until the station was quite out of sight. I took out my mobile and found the number with clumsy fingers.

'Neal. Don't go anywhere. I'm coming round now.'

'I'm about two minutes away. I'm coming round.'

'No, Neal.'

'I've got something to say to you.'

'There isn't any point.'

'Two minutes,' he repeated.

And two minutes later, there he was, standing at the front door.

'What is it?'

'Can I come in?' His expression hardened in comprehension. 'He's there, isn't he?'

I didn't pretend not to know who he was talking about. 'Yes.' I looked at his face, stiff with misery. 'Look, I'm sorry – about everything. Really.'

'What I came to say,' he began, as if he hadn't heard me, 'was that I don't think you know what you're doing.'

'Maybe not.' He started to reply but I interrupted him. 'Or maybe I like not knowing.'

'And when it's over I'll still be there.'

I didn't know what to say. I couldn't work out if this was creepy or touching; probably it was a bit of both. Or perhaps, I thought, this was just what love was like when it wasn't returned – oppressive, inappropriate, with something embarrassing and almost shameful about it.

'Thanks.'

'Right.'

I shifted from foot to foot, feeling hot under his gaze. 'So remember, Bonnie.'

After

When I arrived at Neal's I felt as if we were two fearful, panicking strangers who didn't know how to deal with each other. Neal asked me if I wanted a drink but I refused. I felt dizzy already, with a queasy sense of unreality that made it hard to stand steadily and speak evenly. I just wanted to get this over with and be gone.

'I was just going to have one myself,' he said. 'A glass of wine or a beer.' He looked at his watch. 'It's almost six. Maybe you need something stronger. I've got whisky and there's vodka I bought in Cracow.'

'A glass of water would be fine,' I said. 'Just from the tap.'

He filled two large tumblers and handed me one. I drained it without any effort and still felt thirsty. I passed it back to him. He gave me the other tumbler and I drank half of it. 'Are you all right?' he asked.

'I've been talking to the police,' I said.

'I know.'

'No, they interviewed me again. I've just spent the day with them.'

Neal's expression was completely impassive. 'Is there a problem?'

I took a deep, shuddery breath. 'When I first talked to them, I was a bit evasive about my . . . you know, connection with Hayden.'

'You mean the fact that you were sleeping with him?'

I was tired after my hours of talking to the police, hours of having to think all the time and keep my story consistent. I didn't feel I could manage any more of it. 'They asked me if he had a girlfriend and I said he didn't – because, you know, I *wasn't*, not really – and then they talked to other people who mentioned me, so they thought I was lying and I had a *reason* to be lying, and so they've asked me a lot of questions. They were pretty aggressive about it. I've come straight from the police station.'

'I'm sorry,' said Neal. 'What do you want me to do, Bonnie? I mean, you did have a reason to lie, didn't you?'

The way he phrased his sentence unsettled me. It took me a few moments to reply. 'We haven't talked about what happened. I understand that. Neither of us wanted to. There are some things it's best to leave unsaid. But now there's something important I've got to tell you and I needed to tell you before you talked to anyone else.'

There was a pause. I was on the verge of speaking the words that I had stopped myself uttering for days and days, but I was going to be forced into it now.

'Yes?'

'The police were suspicious,' I said. 'They were particularly interested in the evening of August the twenty-first. They even asked me where I was.'

'I'm sure they did. And what did you say?'

I wanted to sit down, bury my head in my hands, block out the whole loud, violent world. My legs were shaking under me. 'That's why I came here. I said I was with you. I said you were my boyfriend.' I looked closely at Neal, his cold, blank face. 'Do you understand, Neal? I gave you an alibi.'

Neal turned away from me and brought one hand up to his head. I could see him thinking, as if it was an immense physical effort to be wrestled with. Finally he turned back to me. When he spoke it was slowly and deliberately. 'You want me to be your alibi? Is that it?'

'No. Why are you doing this? I *know*, Neal. You know and I know, and the great charade is over at last. You can stop pretending and so can I.'

'What are you trying to say?'

'Neal?' Everything seemed to be happening in a murk of incomprehension. 'Are you listening? I gave you an alibi for the evening Hayden died.'

'You gave *me* an alibi?'

I held up a hand to ward off any words. 'You don't need to say anything. I don't really want to talk about it. I want it all to go away. Just accept it, OK?'

'I think I'm going to regret asking this, but why did you give me an alibi?'

'Oh, come on, Neal, you know why. Don't make this even more difficult.'

'No, Bonnie, I don't know. What the fuck are you trying to say?'

'You want me to say it out loud?'

'Go on.'

I took a deep breath and held his gaze as I finally said the words: 'Because you killed Hayden.'

There. I'd said it. I thought Neal would get emotional,

angry. Perhaps he would break down and cry and tell me he hadn't meant to, it was an accident, a moment of violence that had turned his life into a nightmare. But he simply stared at me, his face slack and wiped of all expression.

'What?'

'You forced me to say it. I wasn't going to.'

'I killed Hayden?'

'Yes.'

'What's all this about?' he said. '*I* didn't kill Hayden.'

'I know you did, Neal. You don't need to continue with this.'

'No. No, Bonnie. This is – well, this is just the most –' He stopped and gave a loud and shocking bark of laughter. 'What the fuck do you think you're doing?'

'Me?'

'Come on, Bonnie.'

'I don't understand,' I said. 'What? *What?*'

'This is just so – Of course you know I didn't kill Hayden, because of course I know who did.'

'What?'

'You heard me.'

'No. But I don't – I don't know what you're doing. Are you trying to send me mad?'

'That's rich, coming from you.'

'Neal. Stop. Stop now. It's over. The lying is over, the pretending is over.'

'Hang on.' Neal held up a hand to silence me. 'Just shut up for a moment.' He stood up and started walking around his room aimlessly, apparently not seeing where he was going. He was like a man I'd once seen climbing out of his car after an accident and reeling across the road, drunk with shock.

'You really didn't kill him?' The force of what he had said hit me. Suddenly it was as if the floor had given way beneath me, and there was nothing to hold on to. I sat down abruptly on the armchair and put a fist against my mouth.

'Stop,' he said. 'Let me think. Why were they interviewing you? What do they have on you?'

'They don't have anything on me,' I said. 'I mean, not as far as I know. But as I said, they think ... I mean, they know I was involved with Hayden. And on that night his car was photographed with a woman in it. So they're suspicious.'

There was another pause.

'Just at the moment,' said Neal, 'I feel like you and I are two people blundering stupidly around in the dark. I don't even know what question to ask. But here's one: what I don't understand is, how or why did Hayden's body end up in a reservoir seventy miles north of London?'

'No. First, I want to get back to the question of killing Hayden. You can tell me. I'm the one person in the world you're safe with.'

He leaned across and grasped me by the shoulders so that it almost hurt. 'Listen, Bonnie, and I'll say it again, loud and clear: I did not kill Hayden.'

'You must have done. I even saw you walking away.'

'I did not. Of course not. And you know it, so stop this now. You're the one person in the world who knows I did not kill Hayden. You've got it the wrong way round.'

'What does that mean? I don't know what you're saying.'

'What does that mean?' he echoed. His face seemed older and softer; he looked almost stupefied, as if he'd been punched and was still reeling. 'You have to answer my question.'

'But why are you even asking it?' I said, or perhaps I shouted it. 'Isn't that what happens with the bodies of people who've been murdered? They get dumped in canals and rivers and reservoirs. And sometimes they get found. I'm not the world's greatest detective, but it seems to me that the only reason you'd be asking that question would be if you'd killed Hayden in his flat and left his body there. In that case you might be quite surprised if the body wasn't found there.'

'No,' said Neal. 'It's not the only reason.'

'I'm not thinking at my clearest,' I said. 'I'm thinking at my least clear. So, tell me, what other explanation could there possibly be?'

'You really want me to tell you?'

'Jesus, let's get this over with. Yes.'

'All right, Bonnie. The charade is over at last. The reason I was surprised when Hayden's body was found in Langley reservoir is because I saw his dead body lying on the floor of his flat.'

'You saw it?'

'Yes.'

'Of course you saw it! It was you –'

'*No*. I didn't kill Hayden.' He stopped as I made a long, low whimper into my cupped hands. 'I came and found his body. That's all.'

'I don't understand. You found his body and you didn't call the police?'

'That's right.'

'Why not?'

'Because I knew you'd done it.'

'What?'

'I knew you'd done it.'

'And how did you know that?'

'I knew he'd hit you again, and I knew you were going to see him. You told me. I couldn't bear it any longer. I felt I'd go mad if he got away with it. So I went to see him first to warn him off, to tell him what would happen if he ever touched you again. I mean touched you like *that*. I had a drink first, to get my nerve up – he always rattled me, Hayden, and I was determined to be the one in control that day; I wasn't going to let him get to me. When I got there, about half an hour after I'd left your flat, the door was open so I walked in. I could see at once what had happened. You'd gone round as soon as we'd all left after that awful rehearsal and you'd got into an argument. Maybe he lashed out at you again. You reached for something, grabbed a bronze ornament, a heavy bronze ornament. One blow would have been enough. It looked to me as if he'd been hit twice. Was the second out of revenge for what he'd done to you? Or was it to finish him off? It sounds terrible, but part of me was pleased. That was my first reaction. I hated him, that's the honest truth. I even hated him enough to want him dead. He'd stolen you from me and then he'd treated you like dirt and me with – what? Amusement, maybe, as if everything was just a big game. I wanted him dead and there he was, dead. And you'd killed him. Then I started to think. You'd killed him and now you'd have to pay for it, and I didn't want that. It wasn't really like a decision, more a realization that this was what I was going to do. I'd make it look more like there'd been a violent scuffle, the kind there would have been if there'd been another man there or a couple of men. I knocked some things over, moved stuff around. Then I went round the flat and took everything I could find that belonged to you. You got your satchel, did you?'

The bag. So it hadn't been a threat. It was from Neal. To help me. I could only stare at him. 'But I didn't kill him.'

He took hold of my forearm in a hard grip. His face looked strange to me, full of shadows and planes. 'It doesn't matter,' he said. 'You don't have to lie to me.'

'I didn't. I swear. I thought *you* did.'

'I wouldn't blame you, Bonnie. I even thought you were right. Then after, when you looked at me as though you hated me . . .'

'I didn't kill him,' I said. 'I was going to see Hayden but I arrived after you did. I found Hayden and I . . . I guess I found what you'd done.'

Neal looked dazed. 'So what did you do?'

'We . . .' I stopped myself.

'Why didn't you just leave?'

'You'd done it for me,' I said. 'It seemed like my fault. I couldn't just leave you to it.'

'But I didn't do it.'

'I didn't know that.'

Neal had the expression of someone hearing bad news followed by even worse news, a boxer at the end of a fight being hit and then hit again. 'Then who did?' he asked in a whisper. 'Who did kill him? Oh, fuck.'

'I don't know. I don't know anything any more. Shit, there's a killer out there. I didn't think of you as a killer, it was just an accident – but this. This is something else.'

'Bonnie, Bonnie, Bonnie.' Neal's voice was a groan.

'When the body wasn't found, I thought I was going completely insane.' He looked at me. 'And that was you?' I didn't reply. 'You thought I'd killed him and you wanted to protect me?'

'I felt responsible.' I leaned forward and put my hand on his.

'You protected me, I protected you. Someone's got away free.'

'Yeah. I know. But the police are going to think it was me. Or you. Or both of us together.'

He put his head into his hands and rocked to and fro slightly. I could hear him muttering. Finally he looked up. 'OK, we have to talk about the alibi. I interfered with a crime scene and you did a hell of a lot more than that. I mean, you haven't killed someone so I guess that's something, but God knows what laws you've broken. And I don't know how long your plan will hold together. The car, his car, what happened to it?'

'It was found in Walthamstow.'

'How did it get to Walthamstow?'

'I left it there.'

'What for?'

'I don't know – I thought it might confuse things.'

'What a brilliant idea,' said Neal.

I don't think he meant it. We gazed at each other and I had the dizzy sensation that I was looking into a mirror. I heard myself laughing, a snorting giggle that didn't sound like me. Neal's face broke into an appalled answering grin, although he had tears in his eyes. I wanted to cry as well but instead this dreadful snickering mirth spilled out. I felt as though I was breaking up with the hilarity and terror of it all, the sheer farcical horror of what we had done.

'And meanwhile,' said Neal, 'there's someone out there who really did do it and one after the other we covered up for them and now they must be wondering what the hell happened and what they ought to be doing about it.'

'Yes, that's true. I hadn't thought.'

'So tell me, Bonnie, what do we do now? Have you got another master plan?'

'Can I try some of that vodka first?'

Before

I put on the Hank Williams CD I'd brought and we sat and drank a glass of the white wine I'd also brought, and Hayden had a smoke, but after the fifth or sixth track about being lonesome or lovesick or divorced or rootless it didn't seem such a good idea. I asked him if he wanted me to put something else on.

'What for?'

'Isn't it a bit depressing? It's just song after song of different kinds of misery. My baby done left me and I'm so lonesome I could cry.'

'If something's that good,' said Hayden, 'it can't be depressing. He's the daddy of us all. Forget Dylan and Buddy Holly. Hank was the first great singer-songwriter. He sang about his own experiences. He went out on the road and lived it and then he wrote beautiful songs about it.'

'And he died when he was about thirty-five,' I said. 'Worn out by it.'

'He was twenty-nine,' he said. 'The same age as Shelley. And a better poet.'

'I always had trouble getting over the tasselled shirts.'

'He died in the back seat of a car on the way to another gig,' said Hayden. 'That's the way to go.' He laughed. 'You don't believe that. It's the woman in you. You think it's sad when someone doesn't die at three score and ten surrounded by their family and household possessions, with a pension plan and lots of money in the bank.'

'Don't pigeonhole me.'

'But it's true, isn't it?'

'Is it so bad to grow old? Is it so bad to have things?' I said.

'You mean the sort of things you argue over when you break up with someone?'

'You're drinking wine I bought for you. You're living in a flat I arranged for you.'

'You're trying to provoke me,' he said, 'but I won't be provoked. Not today.'

'Liza worked for this flat,' I said. 'At the end of the summer after she left college she got a job, and after a year she put down a deposit and bought this, and she's been paying the mortgage ever since.'

'And your point is?' said Hayden. He leaned forward and picked up the little metal sculpture on the coffee-table. 'She probably saw this in a gallery somewhere and paid fifty pounds for it. Or maybe someone gave it to her. And when she's died some relative will look at it and say, "What the fuck can we do with this?" And it'll either be a doorstop or it'll be put on a skip.'

Hayden ground the butt into one of Liza's ashtrays and then he kissed me, but I pushed him away, if only for a moment. I glanced around the room at the pictures, the ornaments, the books. 'When I look around this room I see a woman who loved things, who took pleasure in them, even if they weren't great works of art, even if they'd end up on a skip.'

'Don't pretend you're like that,' he said. 'You know you're better than that.'

'Better? Better, Hayden? You'd rather die in the back of a car with nothing?' I said. 'With nobody to care for you?'

'Why would there be nobody? Being free isn't the same as being lonely.'

I knew Hayden took pleasure in me. Sometimes he even adored me, in his fashion. But I was the woman who was there at that moment. There had been others before and there would be others after. A thought occurred to me that I spoke out loud before I had time to stop myself: 'What if you die in the back of a car and you're not Hank Williams? Does that make a difference?'

He brought his hand up, the one that was still holding the metal sculpture, and touched my shoulder with it, almost playfully, but not quite. 'Careful now,' he said.

'Right. We have to think. I can't think. My brain isn't working. It feels like bits have come loose in my head. Nuts and bolts.'

'That would be the vodka,' I said, holding up the bottle that was now only half full.

'No. The vodka makes things clearer. Or slower or something.'

'I feel a bit distanced from everything myself. Or insulated, maybe. It's quite a relief, actually. As if I'm standing to one side of my life and looking at it as if it was happening to someone else. Which it isn't, I know.'

'We have to think, Bonnie.'

'Yes. What about? I mean, what shall we think about first?'

'I have a question.'

'Another question?'

'I'm not stupid, you know. I mean, I might be in love with you – don't look at me like that, you know I am – and I might be a bit drunk and I might be in shock and I might have done something colossally foolish, but I'm still not stupid.'

'I know you're not.'

'Then tell me.'

'Tell you what?'

'Who were you with?'

'What?'

'Come on, Bonnie. He was a big man. You didn't get his body into the car and then into the reservoir alone.'

I closed my eyes and tried to sort through the jumble of my thoughts. Could I tell Neal about Sonia, or was that a further betrayal of the person who had helped me so unconditionally? 'I don't know what to say.'

'You mean, you don't know whether to tell me?'

'Right.'

'Someone was with you when you found him?'

'Not exactly, no.'

'So you called someone to come and help you?'

'Yes.'

'And you don't want to tell me because – what?'

'Because it doesn't feel like my secret to tell. I promised to keep quiet.'

'It might be a relief to them.'

'I think this person simply wants to put it behind them,' I said carefully. I was having trouble getting the pronouns right. Words would betray me, I thought, trip me up and expose me when I wasn't paying attention to them.

'Don't you think that you and I and this person should get together and talk about what we know and what we should say?'

'I don't know. I don't know what I think.'

'For instance, are we going to the police?'

'The police?'

'The police. For God's sake, someone killed Hayden.'

'Yes. I'm not forgetting that.'

'But it wasn't us.'

'No.'

'Now we know that, do you think we should go to the police?'

'But look at what we've done.'

'We have to think about it, at least.'

'I am thinking,' I said. 'I'm thinking I'll wake up and this will be a dream.'

'We can't even begin to make any decisions about it without this other person. Your third man. Or woman, of course.'

'They did it for me,' I said wretchedly. 'Because I asked them to. How can we go to the police?'

'How well did you cover your tracks?'

'I don't know. I wake up night after night in a cold sweat, remembering things I should have done.'

'You say they're suspicious of you already.'

'I was having sex with him. I lied about that – and a whole lot of other things, of course, but they don't know about that. Not yet, anyway. What shall we do?'

'Do you want something to eat?'

'I don't know. Am I hungry?' I put my hand against my belly. I couldn't remember when I'd last eaten. Days had lost their normal structure, a wheel turning round and round and carrying me along with it, and had broken down into jagged, clockless episodes of fear, guilt, a dazed sense that all the time I'd thought I was running away from everything I was actually running towards it – helter-skelter into the arms of disaster.

'How about a poached egg on a muffin? That's one of my stand-bys.'

'All right.'

I watched him while he cooked, proficient and domestic

in a way that Hayden had never been, and I thought of how it could so easily have been different. I could have stayed with Neal and avoided my head-on collision with Hayden. Maybe he would still be dead, but it would be a story that had happened to somebody else, not to me, not to us. We ate in silence, knives and forks scraping against the china, and afterwards Neal made a pot of strong coffee. I drank two mugs, then said, 'I'll ring them.'

'The third person?'

'Yes.'

Day was turning to night, and Neal's garden was soft with fading light and the blurred chortle of wood-pigeons.

'Sonia, I have something to tell you.' I heard her give a gentle sigh, as if she had been expecting this moment. 'Neal knows what we did.'

'Neal!'

'He doesn't know you were involved, just that someone was.'

'What have you gone and done, Bonnie?' Her voice cracked.

'It's hard to explain on the phone. Everything's changed. Nothing means what I thought it meant. I'd like to see you as soon as possible.'

'Where are you?'

'At his house.'

There was a long silence that I didn't try to break. At last she said, 'I'm coming over.'

'He doesn't have to know it was you.'

'I'm coming over,' she said. 'Give me his address.'

When I went back, Neal looked up from his chair.

'Before you say anything,' he said, 'there's something I need to know.'

'Go on.'

'Did you love him?'

I replied before I had time to stop myself: 'I don't know. But sometimes I miss him so much that I'm not sure how to bear it.'

Before

I followed Hayden up the hill. I could see the muscles in his back working under his thin top. His shoulders were broad and strong. As if he could feel my eyes on him, he turned and his face softened in a slow smile.

People say 'just sex'. They say just sex, just desire, just a physical thing. I don't know what that means. Desire ran through me in a stream; sex transformed me and made me feel alive, every nerve in my body singing with the sheer physical joy of it.

I drew level with him. We didn't touch but the space between us throbbed. My summer days, no before and no after, just now, just him.

After

At first it was awkward, almost embarrassed – as though we couldn't confront the enormity and folly of what we had done and had retreated into a kind of social formality. Nobody seemed to know how to behave: Neal was solemnly pissed, Sonia was coolly impersonal towards him, and I was concentrating on not breaking into wretched fits of giggles again, although my eyes were stinging and my chest ached.

But there was something strangely comforting about being a threesome. I knew it was dangerous. Perhaps it meant the secret would spread out through the cracks. But for the time being, sitting in Neal's cosy house, I felt less afraid, as if the fear had been shared out. I looked at them both – Sonia in her grey soft-cotton trousers and a white T-shirt, her face grave and handsome, Neal, sitting with his head propped on his hand and his fingers pushing his dark hair into comical tufts – and thought about what they had both done for me, or in Neal's case, what he had thought he was doing for me.

When Sonia had arrived, I could almost feel the passion coming off her. It was all the more powerful for being contained. She seemed to pulse with it. 'Tell me,' she said, when I met her at the front door.

I took her into the garden because I wanted to be alone with her when I told her. Through the lighted window I could see Neal sitting in the living room. I told Sonia everything, leaving nothing out: the brief fling with Neal, which she half knew about anyway, the affair with Hayden, the violence and obsession of it, my certainty on discovering the body that Neal had done it, and done it for me. It didn't take long, after all, and when I had finished there was a silence between us.

'I was protecting you,' she said at last.

'I know.'

'You let me think you'd killed him.'

I didn't say anything. She was right, after all.

'You misled me, Bonnie.'

'I didn't want to but I couldn't tell you. You see why, don't you?'

'Maybe.' Her voice was still very controlled. 'So I did all this for Neal? Who I hardly know?'

'I'm sorry, Sonia.'

Her face was closed and inscrutable in the half-light.

'I guess we need to talk,' I said.

'You want to go to the police?'

'I don't know,' I said. '"Want" is the wrong word. But maybe it would be for the best, in all ways – for a start, and this is way the most important, they could concentrate on the real killer. We're in their way. They're suspicious of me. They know I lied to them. It's better if I tell them before they discover it for themselves. Better for all of us, I mean. Neither of you needs to be involved. I can just say I found the body and got rid of it because I panicked.'

Sonia shook her head. 'How are you going to explain doing it all by yourself?'

'I can say I helped.' Neal leaned forward in his chair. 'It's almost true.'

'You're worrying about the lies you've already told and now you're planning more. It'll never work.'

'So what do you suggest we do, Sonia?'

She was silent for a long while, her face heavy with thought. 'Nothing,' she said at last.

'Nothing?'

'I don't want you to tell the police. You keep finding new ways of getting yourself deeper and deeper into the mess. And me with you.'

'This wouldn't be a new way. This would just be the truth. We can't obstruct their investigation. Someone killed Hayden and they need to find out who.'

'Yet you didn't think that when you believed it was Neal.'

'Because I thought Neal had done it by mistake – and for me,' I said miserably.

'It's complicated,' she said. 'And I'm scared.'

I looked at her in consternation: somehow I'd thought Sonia was never scared. She was my rock and I leaned on her, knowing she wouldn't give way.

'I'm so sorry about everything,' I said. 'I wake up every night feeling as though there's a great boulder on my chest that's stopping me breathing. I don't know if I can bear it much longer.'

'I don't want to stop the police finding out who did it, of course I don't, but I don't want to go to prison for you either.'

'You won't have to.'

'You can't know that, Bonnie.'

Neal stood up and went to the window that gave out over his garden. 'Let's try and see this from another angle,' he said. 'I tampered with the evidence and then you two didn't just tamper with it, you got rid of it, including the body.'

'That's not a different angle,' said Sonia. 'That's just restating our position.'

'What did we see?' asked Neal, as if she hadn't spoken.

'We saw Hayden.' I didn't say that I saw him still. He had become my ghost and was haunting me. I woke at night and he would be standing at the bottom of my bed, looking down at me.

'We didn't see the same things.'

'I don't understand.'

'What you saw wasn't what I saw because I messed everything up and made it look different. You didn't see the real crime scene, but the artificial one.'

'You're right.'

'And why is this important?' asked Sonia.

'I don't know, but it feels relevant to me. As if all this time everyone's been looking at the wrong picture.'

'There isn't a picture at all any more,' I said. 'Sonia and I saw to that.'

Before

Once again Guy didn't turn up, and Joakim, when I asked him where he was, mumbled something, avoiding my eyes. Amos wasn't exactly bad. He'd practised, I could see that. He didn't make all that many mistakes. He didn't come in at the wrong moment all that often. But he was playing music as if he were filling out a form, slowly, laboriously. Neal was all thumbs. He really was playing badly. He was obviously angry with Hayden and wanted to make some sort of point, but whatever the point was, it was doing nothing for his music. What made it worse was that Hayden didn't respond. He didn't make sarcastic comments. He didn't point out wrong notes or suggest improvements. He had clearly given up on them and that was the greatest insult. He seemed bored, as if his mind was elsewhere. The only time he was engaged was when he and Joakim retreated into the corner and worked together on a piece that had nothing to do with what the rest of us were doing. I left them to it.

After

Sonia left and I was going to leave but Neal poured me another glass of his vodka. We didn't discuss it any more. I wasn't capable of it. I just needed to go away, preferably to an uninhabited island somewhere, and think about it, get it straight in my head, draw diagrams, make connections, and then I would be able to sort out what I had really done, and when I had that clear, I might start to have ideas about what I should do next. What was the rational thing to do. What was the right thing, if that had a meaning any more after the pile-up of wrong things. As I was drinking this last glass, I saw Neal hovering in a solicitous way and wondered if he thought that this was going to bring us together somehow.

Slowly and laboriously, as if my tongue had doubled in size and didn't properly fit into my mouth, I tried to explain the situation. 'I think I'm a bit drunk,' I said. 'And I'm in a state of shock. I'm not sure if the shock has made the being drunk worse or better. What I'm going to do is lie on the sofa for a bit and if you could just turn the light off, that would be great, and go away. When I've gathered myself together, I'll get off the sofa and walk home.'

He did switch off the light and leave the room, then came back with a blanket, which he laid across me, and left again. I lay in the dark and thought in a maudlin fashion about how I'd got involved with Hayden and not Neal when Neal was clearly a better and more suitable and more decent person in every imaginable way. I almost started crying and then I wondered if I was ever going to sleep, and then I woke with a start and looked at my watch and saw that it was almost six thirty.

I felt terrible, much worse than before. My head ached, my mouth was dry, my brain felt like it had been left out in the rain and had rusted, and my clothes had that irritable, scratchy feel they get when you've slept in them. I couldn't face Neal. I just wanted to escape. I let myself out and walked home. The freshness of the early-morning sunlight and the sight of people heading for work made me feel even more stale and grubby. When I got home, I had a shower, then crawled into bed and pulled the duvet over my head. I didn't have a plan. It was more like a reptilian instinct deep in some primitive area of my brain to sleep for a whole day and then a whole night.

I was having a dream where I was trying to catch a train and I was unable to pack, and when I'd packed I couldn't buy a ticket and I couldn't get to the right platform, and then there was a whistle of the train coming or about to leave, but I couldn't find it and I couldn't find my luggage and, anyway, somewhere along the way I'd lost my ticket and the whistle changed from being a whistle to something I vaguely recognized and then realized was the doorbell. Still half in my dream I hoped someone else could answer the door. My mother, maybe, or Amos. But then I pulled the duvet off my face and remembered that my mother was two hundred miles away and Amos didn't live with me any more. The light hurt. I got up and opened the door and two uniformed officers were standing there.

'Does it have to be now?' I said.

I knew Joy Wallis well by now but there was another detective with her at the police station I hadn't seen before. She introduced him as Detective Chief Inspector James Brook.

'Call me Jim,' he said, as he took his jacket off and draped it over the back of a chair. He was about forty and his hair was cut very short, almost shaved, so it was like grey stubble. He looked at me with a smile. He was on my side, the smile said. We were in this together. It was about helping each other. He made me feel instantly insecure. Joy Wallis sat down further away. It seemed that Brook was in charge today. I imagined that he was one of those detectives who were meant to be good at getting people's trust and persuading them to talk. He reminded me of the guys at college you hear are particularly successful with women. In a way it was a self-fulfilling prophecy. It almost made you want to sleep with them just to see what their secret was. But usually it irritated me – and it irritated me now. If only I hadn't been so tired, my head so fuzzy and generally inoperative . . .

'Are you all right?' said Joy Wallis.

'I had a bit of a bad night.'

'Anything you want to tell us about?'

'What for?' I said. There was a pause. 'Sorry. That came out sounding wrong. I just meant that there isn't anything to talk about.'

Brook leaned back and folded his arms. 'I know these things are difficult,' he said.

Even in my utterly befuddled state, I could see what he was doing. He was trying to get a conversation going in which I would be carried away or led into an area I didn't want to go. Since there was no area in which I *did* want to go and since I was in an utterly confused state, it was clear that the only possible strategy for me was to play dumb.

That wouldn't be too hard. Brook began in the usual way by worrying that maybe I'd be better served if I had legal representation but I just repeated that I didn't want that. He seemed disappointed but also slightly confused. Could it be that my behaviour was the sign of someone who was innocent or stupid or both? Finally he shrugged as if he realized, with regret, that there was nothing more he could do to help me.

'I know what you're going through,' he said, 'being involved in a case like this and having to talk to people like us, all the fuss and the media.'

'I'm not involved,' I said.

Brook looked puzzled. 'Of course you're involved,' he said. 'You were intimate with the victim. Did you think I meant something else?'

'I thought you were accusing me of something,' I said.

Now he looked even more puzzled, like someone on stage acting out bafflement for the spectators at the back.

'What would I be accusing you of?'

I suspected he was trying to get me to do his work for him, to accuse myself of what I thought he might suspect. I just mumbled something. The impulse to spill the truth, to let it flood out of me and be empty and peaceful at last, was almost impossible to resist. Only the thought of Sonia and Neal kept me mute.

'I've been reading through the file,' said Brook. 'I've looked at the witness statements, talked to people. Your Hayden was a difficult man. He clearly had some sort of charisma. At least for women.'

I gritted my teeth so that I couldn't say anything. I wasn't going to volunteer any information, any opinion unless asked point-blank to do so.

'Clearly he had a difficult side to him,' Brook continued. 'He wasn't everybody's cup of tea.'

Still no question.

'As I went through the file,' he said, 'I saw him as someone people had strong feelings about. He was someone you loved or hated, someone you could be angry with. Very angry.' He looked at me. 'Were you ever angry with him?'

Everything in the room seemed slightly strange as if the contours around objects were indistinct. How long had I slept? Two hours? Maybe a bit less? This was what the authorities did to torture people before interrogation. You deprive them of sleep. I'd done it to myself and delivered myself up to the police.

'Why are you asking that?' I said. 'Why are you asking all

of these questions? What's the point? He's dead. What does it matter any more what I felt about him? That's all over. It's over.'

I listened to myself as I talked. I sounded slightly drunk or insane; I sounded like someone about to veer out of control. Brook just smiled sympathetically, nodded.

'It's all about patterns,' he said. 'A detail here and there.' He paused as if waiting for a reply from me, which didn't come. Then his face took on an expression of concern. 'Have you told us everything you know?'

'I don't know what that means,' I said. 'I'll answer any question you put to me.'

'My colleague is correct,' he said. 'You don't look well. Trouble sleeping?'

'Not really,' I said.

He leaned across the table so that he was uncomfortably close. I could see the little laugh lines at the corner of his eyes. I could even see little purple broken veins in his cheeks. 'I've been doing this job for twenty years,' he said. 'And one thing I've learned is that when you tell everything, when you own up and finally tell someone the full story, it's the greatest relief you can imagine. People tell me that afterwards. They thank me. They tell me they feel suddenly clean for the first time in ages and ages.'

I knew he was right. There was nothing I wanted more than to tell the full story in a way I had never told it before, not even to myself. *Would* have. If it had been only me. But I would have been taking Neal and Sonia down with me. And both of them were in that vulnerable position because of what they'd done for me, in their own deluded ways. 'I've answered every question,' I made myself say. 'That's all.'

'You were the one involved with him,' said Brook. 'People say it was quite tempestuous.'

'What people?'

'Two of you, both with a bit of a temper, both with wills of your own. Your relationship had its ups and downs, did it?'

'It wasn't really much of a relationship,' I said.

'Not enough for you?'

I could see he was still trying to suck me into a conversation, perhaps taunt me into saying something reckless that would give me away. I shrugged and didn't reply.

'I could imagine an argument,' he said. 'Almost a fight. He comes for you, you pick up something and hit him with it. If you confessed to that, got a good feminist lawyer, you could walk away with a suspended sentence for manslaughter.'

I didn't reply. Brook's face darkened.

'But if you don't confess, and the case has to be made against you, it starts to look more like premeditated murder.'

'I don't care what it looks like,' I said. 'I didn't kill him. Of course I didn't. Why would I confess?'

'Listen, Ms Graham. You're only a fingerprint or a hair or a fibre away from being charged. And let me tell you that I wouldn't be satisfied with a charge of manslaughter. I'm interested in the lengths that were gone to in disposing of the body. I'm interested in the fact that we can't identify a crime scene. We don't even know where he was killed. I'm especially interested in what happened with the car. I'm interested in why someone would take the car to the airport car park and then that person or maybe another person would drive it away a week later. That's the puzzle we need to solve.' He reached a hand across the table and put it on my forearm. 'Was your boyfriend in trouble?'

'He wasn't my boyfriend. I told you. I was with Neal Fenton. You can ask him.'

'We'll come to your alibi later.' He put the word in quotation marks, staring at me, and I tried to hold his gaze. 'But let's turn to the question of where he was killed.'

My heart was hammering so loudly I felt sure he must be able to hear it.

'The first place to look at was where he was staying – your friend's flat. Let's see: Liza Charles, at present travelling and unreachable.'

I couldn't speak, couldn't even make a small assenting noise.

'We have, of course, done a forensic examination of the place. You'd be amazed by the things you can pick up. One hair, one spot of blood.'

I thought of Hayden's body, face down on Liza's rug. The blood puddling out beside his battered head. But we'd thrown away the rug.

'So what did you find?' I made myself say.

'Well, of course, the difficulty was that he was living there. There are traces of him everywhere. It makes things harder.'

'You mean you found nothing?'

'Oh, no. I wouldn't say that. I'll tell you one thing we discovered.'

'What's that?' I dug my fingers into the soft skin of my palms and waited.

'For a feckless musician who lived on other people's floors, your friend cleaned up very well.'

'Oh.'
'Odd, wouldn't you say?'

Before

'Guy, the rehearsal's over!' I said in surprise, but Guy was already in mid-sentence – he must have started speaking as soon as he'd rung the doorbell.

'– so if you could please let us come in,' he said, with icy courtesy, and, not giving me time to reply, swept past me, leaving me face to face with a tall, thin woman who I imagined usually was calmly elegant but today was brittle with miserable fury.

'Hello,' I said. 'You must be –'

'I'm Guy's wife, Celia. Joakim's mother.'

'Which is why we're here,' said Guy, from the foot of the stairs.

'Hello, Celia,' I said. 'I think we've met at parents' evening.' I held out a hand, but she didn't take it, and I realized that she was holding back tears. 'Please. Come in. It's a bit of a mess – the others have all just gone and I haven't cleared up. And I'm decorating.' I made myself stop babbling.

'He was here, was he?'

'You mean Hayden? Yes.'

'What about Joakim?' asked Celia.

'Yes, he was here as well.'

'Of course he was.' Her mouth tightened as if she'd

sucked a lemon. 'He wouldn't miss a chance of spending time with his beloved Hayden Booth.'

'Celia's a bit upset,' said Guy.

'Yes, I can see that,' I said cautiously. 'Can I offer you anything? Tea? Coffee?'

'I'm not a bit upset. I'm very, very, very upset.'

'I'm sorry,' I said. I sat down in the chair but they remained standing, so I got up again.

'Very,' she said again.

'He has a place at Edinburgh,' said Guy.

'Yes, I know.'

'But he's not going.'

'He's so rude to me.' Celia's voice caught on a sob. 'He treats me as if he had contempt for me.'

'Teenagers ...' I began, without knowing what was going to come next.

'What have I done to deserve that?'

'What I want to know,' said Guy, 'is what you're going to do about it.'

'Me?'

'Yes.'

'I've been there for him his whole life and a few days with this – this sleazeball ...'

'I don't understand, Guy. Obviously I know you're disappointed –'

'You're his teacher.'

'I was his teacher. He left school a couple of months ago.'

'You're his teacher and you roped him into your wretched band, and now this second-rate musician has lured him away from everything he's worked for.'

'It's like a cult. A cult and he's been brainwashed.'

I stayed silent.

'Hayden says this and Hayden does that and I'm going to dress like Hayden and talk like Hayden and lie around all day like Hayden. I'm losing him.'

'Celia, let's try and keep this rational, shall we?'

'That's all very easy for you to say. I'm his mother!'

'I'm his father, you know.'

It was as if I'd blundered into a private argument. Guy seemed to notice my presence once more. 'He's a con-man,' he said. 'And he's conned my son and you're responsible.'

'Joakim is eighteen years old,' I said.

'You don't have any children. How can you be expected to understand? I knew she wouldn't understand.' Celia regarded me with distaste so that all at once I felt acutely conscious of my spiky hair, my nose stud, my ripped shirt.

'I just don't know what you expect me to do about it. Joakim's an adult.'

'He's not an adult. He doesn't know what he's doing – he doesn't understand the consequences.'

'Have you tried talking to him?'

'We're not here to ask your advice about him, thank you,' said Guy. His voice was tight with fury and a small vein ticked in his forehead. 'We're here to say that you have to undo the harm you've done.'

I was getting irritated. 'Don't you think part of the problem is the way you're thinking of your son?'

'No,' he roared. 'I do not think that is the fucking problem. The problem is Hayden Booth. *You* sort this out before I do. Got it?'

I left the police station, walking slowly and unsteadily. I didn't know where I was going and the hot sun bounced on my skull and burned in my eye sockets. I needed to sit down. I needed to eat something. I needed to lie in bed and sleep and sleep and sleep and preferably not wake up for a year when all of this would be over – except, of course, it would never be over, not really. Above all, I needed for this not to have happened. I didn't want to be me, here, now. I thought back to the end of the school term and the feeling I'd had then that summer lay ahead of me, wonderfully empty and full of possibility. I wanted to go back to that time and do it again, and not say yes to Danielle's request, not meet Hayden by rotten random chance, not be this Bonnie Graham – the one reeling down the road from the police station with fear in her mouth – but the Bonnie Graham of before, carefree and untested. Go back, go back – and then I saw his face.

It stared up at me from the newsstand, taking up almost half of the front page under the banner headline: 'Death in the Fast Lane'. It wasn't the picture the papers had used previously. He was quite a few years younger; his hair was long and he had stubble that almost amounted to a beard. He was smiling at whoever was behind the camera and his eyebrows were slightly raised so that he looked sardonic and questioning, as if he was sharing a secret thought with the person facing him. He had looked at me like that, as if he understood me, recognized me. He had looked at Sally like that too. And who else? Hundreds of women, I was sure, who, even as they knew he was unreliable, had fallen for that charm. And then someone had killed him – a stranger, after all, or someone who knew him, someone who hated him, loved him, hated him because they loved him?

I told myself I wouldn't buy the paper, but I found myself counting out the change, taking it and trying to read it as I walked along the street. The caption under the picture told me to turn to page seven, so I stopped in the first café I came to, where I ordered a cappuccino and a slice of carrot cake. I felt I needed a dose of carbohydrate and sugar. Only when I'd eaten half of the cake and finished the coffee did I turn to page seven, and when I did, another photo leaped out at me: of a youthful Hayden with his arm wrapped around a woman who was vivid with happiness. She was slight and had a mane of chestnut hair, a wide, smiling mouth. Underneath the photograph there was a caption. Her name was Hannah Booth.

I closed my eyes for a moment but when I opened them again, there she still was. I liked the look of her. She was someone I could imagine having as a friend in another life. I looked at the caption again. The photo had been taken in 2002, seven years ago. Hayden would have been about thirty then – his face was thinner and softer than the one I had known, perhaps happier. Or perhaps that was simply because he was standing arm-in-arm with his wife. Why was I surprised and why was there a pain in my chest and why did my eyes sting?

I skimmed the story, my eyes jumping from paragraph

to paragraph. Much of the beginning was a rather floridly written repetition of what had been in the papers before – talented and reckless musician, mysterious death, shocked friends, body found in the reservoir, police following up clues. But at the centre was the interview with Hannah Booth, who had spoken to the reporter about her grief ('although I always believed he would die young') at the murder of her estranged husband. 'Estranged' – I seized on the word and let it comfort me a bit, until my eyes lit on another word: 'child'. I felt as though someone had punched me hard in the stomach. Hayden had a child, a son, aged just six and a half, who had last seen 'his daddy' a few months ago. His name was Josiah. Hayden had left Hannah and Josiah four years ago, when his son was just a toddler. Hannah Booth described how their marriage, embarked upon with such hope, had deteriorated. 'I don't think Hayden knew how to be content,' she said. 'He never had that kind of stability. He let his ambitions and his dreams destroy the reality of what we had together. And he hated getting older – he was just a kid at heart. A great, lovable kid. But you can't be married to a child, especially when you become a parent yourself.'

I laid the paper aside for a bit and finished my cappuccino, sipping it slowly through the froth, trying to concentrate only on its milky sweetness. He had told me he never wanted to be a father, and all the time he had been one; he had told me he never wanted to be tied down and all the time he was married. OK, married to a woman he never saw, but married all the same. She had even taken his name. Why hadn't he told me? Then I remembered his hasty, urgent note, my last communication with him – was that what he had wanted to tell me?

When I returned to the story I read about his mother, who said that Hayden had been a naughty boy and a troubled man and, no, she hadn't approved of his lifestyle, but that a parent should never have to bury a child. His sister, three years his senior, who said that he had a lust for life. His great friend Mac, who was absolutely gutted: he had seen Hayden just a week or so before his death and Hayden had seemed excited about life and newly happy. All these people whom I'd never known existed. Of course I'd realized that Hayden had a life of his own, friends, relationships and a complicated history behind him – but never before had I understood what a tiny corner of his existence I had occupied, how very little he had communicated to me. It was as if he could only live in the perpetual present, blotting out all that had gone before and all that would come after.

I closed the paper and folded it so I wouldn't have to see his face. He had a mother and a sister; he had an abandoned wife and son; he had best friends who would miss him; and presumably he had made dozens of enemies along the way, people who would have wished him dead in the way that most of our band had done at one time or another. Even me. There had been times when I had wanted him, if not dead, at least wiped from my consciousness without a trace left behind, so that I could forget not just about him but about the me that I was when I was with him.

I put the newspaper on the table when I left and walked blindly home, with no idea of what I was going to do with myself when I got there.

*

Sally was crying. She lay on my sofa in a crumpled heap, her skirt above her knees, her blouse bunched up at her waist and her hair half over her face, sticking to her wet cheeks. I had never seen her weep like this – or anyone at all, really, except my mother on her worst days. Her body seemed entirely taken over by wretchedness: she gulped and sobbed; tears streamed from her eyes and ran down her face and into her neck; words came out in whimpers and hiccups and she couldn't catch her breath for long enough to make any sense. Her crying was more like uncontrollable retching. She was heaving up her misery. All the while, Lola stood beside her, occasionally reaching out a hand to give an anxious poke at Sally's shoulder or stomach.

She didn't seem distressed, more curious and a bit nervous. 'Mummy?' she said every so often, but Sally would only wail louder. At first I tried to calm her, crouching beside her and putting a hand on her writhing body or wiping away the snot and tears from her cheek, but after a while I gave up and concentrated on Lola instead.

'Do you want a biscuit?' She stared at me. 'Or some juice? No, sorry, I don't have juice. I have milk. I think I have some milk. Or some –' What did someone of Lola's age like? 'You could draw something,' I said. 'Shall I get you a pencil and some paper and you could make a picture for Mummy, to cheer her up?'

Lola went on staring at me. She chewed her fat bottom lip.

'She'll be all right soon,' I continued. 'Everyone cries sometimes. What do you cry about?'

Lola shifted from one leg to another. Her face was scrunched up with effort.

'Do you need a wee?'

She nodded.

'Here.' I took her hot little hand in mine and pulled her towards the bathroom. 'Do you need help?'

She nodded again.

I pulled down her knickers and lifted her onto the toilet. Her legs dangled; she was wearing red shoes with striped laces. We waited. She put a thumb in her mouth and gazed at me pensively. We could hear Sally's loud sobs; there was a certain regularity to them now and I wondered if she was coming to the end of her crying fit at last.

'Done?' I asked.

She nodded her head firmly. Sally's sobs turned into long, shuddering breaths and then there was silence. I lifted Lola down from the toilet, wiped between her legs, pulled up her knickers and then washed her hands under the cold water. When we went back, Sally was sitting up, her skirt pulled down over her knees, her shirt straightened and her hair pushed behind her ears. Her face was puffy and there were red blotches on her cheeks.

'You OK?'

'I think so. Sorry. Lola?' She opened her arms but Lola shrank back against me, her thumb in her mouth again. 'Lola, will you come and give me a hug?' There was a note of panic in her voice.

'I'm going to make a pot of tea,' I said, and left them alone.

I stood in the kitchen and stared out of the window at the blank blue sky, feeling so vastly tired that there was no room for thoughts or emotions any longer. I could hear the murmur of Sally and Lola's voices from the other room.

The kettle boiled, sending up puffs of steam. I poured the water over the teabags and found some shortbread biscuits at the back of the cupboard. I carried them through and sat on the sofa next to Sally. Lola was on her lap, her head on her shoulder and her eyes closing.

'Do I look a wreck?' asked Sally.

'I've seen you better.'

She gave a tired grin. 'You too. You look as if you've been up all night.'

I opened my mouth to say that I had, then stopped myself. I couldn't start unburdening myself to Sally because that might be like easing the first small stone out of the wall.

Lola gave a long, gurgling snore and I could sense her body softening and slumping against Sally, who leaned her chin on her daughter's hair and sighed.

'Hayden?' I asked.

'Oh, Bonnie. Hayden, Richard, the whole sheer fucking fact of it all, if you know what I mean. Which I don't. Bloody life. The mess I've made of everything.'

'I'm sorry about it all,' I said inadequately.

'I've been staying at my mum's for a bit, but it was awful. I couldn't tell her anything – I didn't know how. And then the police called me up and I had to go back to be inter-viewed again. Oh, God, Bonnie, it was horrible.'

'Horrible how?'

'The way they talked to me, asked questions. I told them everything.'

'About you and Hayden?'

'I had to. They were behaving as if they knew anyway, and I suddenly thought how petty and unfeeling I was being, worrying about my stupid little secret getting out, when someone has murdered him. So I told them every-thing – not that there was much to tell. And then they were really interested. They behaved as if I'd done it. And they asked about Richard, if he knew and how he'd reacted and was he the jealous type, and I think they're going to inter-view him now. I know I did a terrible thing and deserve to be punished – but this feels as though the whole world is falling round my head. I slept with another man, but I'm not a monster because of it.' She gave a violent sniff, and I put a hand on her shoulder.

'It's better it's out in the open,' I said. 'Secrets are dangerous.'

'They think I did it.'

'I'm sure that's not true.'

'Or Richard.'

'No – they're just following up all leads.'

'Oh, Bonnie, I don't know what I'd do without you to talk to.'

'If it hadn't been for me, you wouldn't have met Hayden and then none of this would have happened.'

'Something would have, though. I couldn't have gone on the way I was.'

'How are things with Richard now?'

'I don't know. I mean, sometimes he's very sweet to me and sometimes it's as if he can't bring himself to even look at me. As if I'm carrying some terrible disease.'

I nodded.

'Sometimes he cries. Not in front of me, though. In the bathroom, when he thinks I can't hear.'

'Things will get better.'

'Do you think so?' She shivered and kissed the top of Lola's head.

'I don't know.'

'Nor do I.' She rubbed the back of one hand against her forehead. 'He seems a bit mad sometimes.'

'Mad?' Unease settled on me.

'Wildly unpredictable, at least.' She looked down at Lola. 'You know the only good thing to come out of this?'

'What?'

'How I feel about her. I never get impatient with her any more. I just want to be with her and never let go of her. How could I have threatened all of that?'

'These things happen,' I said uselessly. 'They take us unaware.'

Before

Even when you've split up with someone, it takes quite a long time for them to give up the rights they used to have over you. Except that in the case of Amos I strongly believed that he ought to give them all up immediately, especially the right to come to my flat unannounced and walk in as if we were still living together.

'Is this something urgent?' I said. 'Because I was just about to go out.'

'Where?' he said.

'You see, that's the sort of thing you don't get to ask any more,' I said, 'due to us not being together.'

Amos took a piece of paper out of the pocket of his

jeans and unfolded it. 'I'm not blaming you for this,' he said.

'What?'

'Disentangling possessions after two people have been living together is always a complicated business.'

'We did this already, remember?' I said. 'It's done.'

'It's just a few loose ends,' he said. 'I've been jotting them down as I've thought of them.'

'Are you saying I took things I wasn't entitled to?'

'No, no, no,' he said, as if he was trying to calm an over-exuberant puppy. 'It's just that we did it so quickly.'

'What we need is to draw a line,' I said.

He looked at the piece of paper. 'The one-volume Shakespeare,' he said. 'I got it as a prize when I was in the sixth form. You couldn't have taken that by mistake, could you?'

'No, I couldn't,' I said, 'due to it having a big label inside it with your name on, which you kept showing me and telling me about how you won it.'

'Did you take my Steely Dan boxed set?'

'No, I didn't,' I said. 'Due to me being a woman.'

Amos looked hurt. 'Is that one of those things women don't like?'

'Apparently.'

'Oh, well, I may have lent it to someone.' He went back to the list. 'There was a small etching.'

'What of?'

'I can't really remember. It had gone very faint. I think it had a windmill in it and a horse or a donkey. An aunt gave it to me.'

'I don't remember that at all.'

'I had a blue bowl that my mother gave me. I didn't think much of it but apparently it's made by someone famous.'

I was going to say no again and then I felt a jolt. An uneasy jolt. I had an internal flashback of me putting the bowl into a cardboard box. I'd never thought of Amos as the sort of person who would own a decorative bowl. Or perhaps because I had been the only person who had ever got the bowl out of the cupboard and put fruit into it I had assumed that it must have been mine. Unfortunately, the first flashback was followed by a second flashback in which, with great clarity, I saw myself throwing the box onto a skip.

'I haven't got that,' I said, quite truthfully.

'It'll probably turn up,' said Amos. 'Sonia's got this thing about bowls of fruit. She keeps bringing apples and pears and oranges and then there's nowhere suitable to put them. I must say that, for me, fruit should go in the fridge, if you buy it at all. Why put it on the table?'

'Is there anything else?' I asked, keen to move on.

'Those green towels. Were they really yours?'

I thought for a moment. 'Do you know?' I said. 'I'm really not sure whether they're mine or yours. I thought we'd sorted it out, but if you want them, take them. One's hanging over the bath, so you'll probably need to wash it before you use it.'

'And you checked inside the books you took away? Mostly I write my name in mine.'

'Which is why I checked,' I said. 'But if there are any you want, you can take them back.' I thought with a pang of guilt about the bowl. 'In fact, if there's any object at all that you want, take it, but take it now. We've got to draw a line

– we've got to have, you know, like that thing where you can't prosecute Nazi war criminals any more.'

'A statute of limitation.'

'That's right. We had this strange time where we shared our things and we owned things together but it's over.'

Amos folded up his piece of paper and put it back in his pocket. 'You can keep the towels,' he said. 'They've gone a bit rough anyway.'

'Is that it?' I said. 'You came all the way over here about towels you don't want?'

'And the Steely Dan boxed set. You're really sure you haven't got that?'

'Is anything up?' I asked.

Amos didn't seem to be paying attention. He wandered around the room, inspecting the half-painted walls, the books in boxes, the general air of neglect and abandonment. 'You want to get someone in to do this.'

'I was planning to do most of it myself. That's why I didn't go away this summer.'

'It looks as if you're behind schedule.'

'I think I may have taken on a bit too much,' I admitted.

'What happened to us?' he said.

'Amos . . .'

'When I look at this mess here, you trying to make a home for yourself, and me with my stupid piece of paper and us arguing over who bought which paperback book . . .'

'We didn't really argue. We bickered.'

'I can't believe we started there and ended up here. Do you remember the early days? That time we had the plan to cycle along the canal towpath until we reached the countryside but we didn't make it and came back on the train? That was when even the things that didn't work out seemed somehow fine, and then we got to a stage where something was wrong even with the things that did work out. How did we get there – here?'

I'd known almost from the start that this visit wasn't just about a few things he thought I'd taken. 'We've been through all of this,' I said. 'Over and over again. We've moved on now. You're with Sonia. She's a special woman.'

He smiled. 'In a way that you're not?'

'I can quite honestly say that Sonia is special in many ways that I'm not. I should also say that this is exactly the sort of conversation that you and I don't have any more.'

Amos frowned and there was a pause.

'It's not working out,' he said finally.

'What do you mean?' I said. 'I had no idea.'

'What?' said Amos, puzzled. 'No, I don't mean Sonia and me. That's fine. Whether it's a serious thing, whether it'll last, I don't know.'

'Stop,' I said. 'Don't talk to me about that. I don't want to hear. You've no right.'

'Who else have I got to talk to?'

'Not me,' I said. 'Anyone but me.'

He was affronted by that. Did he want to have Sonia and somehow hold on to me as well?

'Anyway, I didn't mean that. I meant the music, the performance.'

'What's your problem?'

'*My* problem?' he said, with a sarcastic laugh. 'I just feel it's my responsibility to point out that things are not going well.'

'Have you been sent?' I said. 'Is that it?'

'Of course they haven't sent me,' said Amos. 'This isn't the mutiny on the fucking *Bounty*. I just thought I should point out some salient truths to you. I mean, what a fucking collection you've brought together. I admit that Joakim's a nice kid, although I can't work out whether he's got a bigger crush on you or on Hayden. You haven't done him any favours by throwing him into this lion's den. But his dad's a complete pain in the arse.'

'He's out of his milieu.'

'I don't even know what he's doing in the group apart from spying on his son and then not turning up when he feels like doing something else, though he's pretty pompous about other people doing the same. Neal's Neal, I suppose, and I'm not sure what he's doing there either, unless your point was to surround yourself with admirers.'

'Fuck off, Amos.' He laughed. 'No, really, I mean it. What's this about? You were the one who wanted to be part of it.'

'And what you thought you were up to letting Hayden loose on everybody, I just don't know.'

'So you don't like him? Big deal. Get over it. You only need to see him a couple more times.'

'I can't understand what you thought you were up to bringing him in. If ever in my life I've met someone who was trouble, it's him.'

'I didn't exactly bring him in. He offered to help out and thank God he did. He's a real musician.'

'He's a real something,' said Amos. 'And I'm not really sure that I do dislike him. Which is pretty incredible of me, because I've never in my entire life met anyone who treated me the way he does. The only comfort is that he treats other people even worse. At least he doesn't play around with me. In fact, if it was just me I'd find it quite interesting watching him at work fucking with people's heads.'

'Which is not what he's doing.'

'Oh, I'm so sorry,' Amos said. 'Am I venturing onto delicate ground?'

'If what you're saying is that you want to drop out, then I can't stop you.'

'What I'm saying is that in my opinion either Hayden goes or it's time to call a halt to this. It's only a wedding. There are other dance bands in the phone book. I think we'd make a better contribution if we clubbed together and bought them a set of wine glasses.'

I didn't immediately retort angrily, which I was tempted to do, because a part of me had been thinking the same thing. I'd embarked on this because I'd thought it would be easy and wouldn't take much time. I'd been wrong on both counts.

'No,' I said. 'It's too late. It's like when you taught me to play poker – you know, when you've put all your money in the pot and you have to stay in just to see how the hand turns out. Do you understand what I mean?'

Amos just shook his head. 'I think I've realized for the first time why things didn't work out with us. I wasn't good enough at music and you weren't good enough at poker.'

After

What I used to do at times like this was lose myself in music, in a place where there were no words, no ideas, no having to be clever. Now music was no longer there for me in that way. It was like a drug that had stopped working. The feel of a guitar or a keyboard wasn't an escape but a sharp reminder of things that had gone terribly wrong.

In normal times, or at least in normally abnormal times, I would have gone out to see friends. But I knew they would want to ask about him, to get my side of the story, to pump me for memories, to share in some of the celebrity of knowing someone who knew a murder victim. I was tormented by the feeling that it would take just one slip, one wrong note, one misjudged response to raise suspicions and everything would unravel. I imagined saying something to someone and they would respond, 'But I thought you said . . .' or 'But how could . . .' or 'But doesn't that mean that . . .' or 'But weren't you . . .' There was one truth hidden by an infinity of lies.

Sally rang and told me she and Richard were going away together to try to sort things out. She kept crying so I could hardly hear what she was saying, but I did gather she had been with the police again, and so had Richard. I kept receiving emails and texts from friends. Had I heard about that band he'd been in? Who could have done it? They helpfully sent me links to footage on the Internet of appearances he'd made at festivals in Germany, Holland, Suffolk.

There was a Wikipedia entry on him. It said that his career had been promising, that back in the nineties he had been talked of as a major young talent, but that from the beginning he had been a maverick with a self-destructive streak and that in the end his career hadn't come to much. That was me. I was part of what his career hadn't come to.

What I knew was bad enough, but what was worse was what I didn't know. I felt like a very minor soldier in a big battle, right on the edge, who didn't understand what the struggle was about, or who was winning, or what the tactics were, but just heard occasional explosions from a distance. I had no idea what they meant. Sudden lulls. I had no idea what *they* meant either.

I was almost sure that the police still had no idea of where Hayden had been killed. Did they suspect? Were they combing the flat for evidence? Even if they were, I couldn't think of anything significant they would find. What about his body? Would it just take a hair off my head, a fibre from my sweater? But they knew we'd been together. If I just stonewalled and denied everything, whatever they put to me, surely I'd be safe. But now there were Neal and Sonia as well. We were as strong as the weakest link. The one comfort was that there was no doubt it was me.

I knew that the police had talked to the others. What had they said? Did it matter what they'd said? I had no sense of whether the police were working on a theory or whether they were just interviewing everyone who had had anything to do with Hayden and hoping for the best. I suspected they were a bit dubious about me, but did they actually think I'd killed Hayden? Did they think I was the woman in the car? That I was both? Or one and not the other? And what happened with these inquiries? Did they go on for ever or did they just gradually fade away? I remember hearing or reading, or probably seeing on some TV detective show, that if a murder wasn't solved in the first twenty-four hours, it probably wouldn't be solved at all. Was that true or just an urban legend? After all, I didn't know very much and most of what I thought I did know generally turned out to be wrong whenever I checked it with anyone.

Above it all, or beneath, there was the person, or the people, who had killed Hayden and whose evidence we had covered up. What were they thinking? What had they thought when the body hadn't been found? When it had turned up in a reservoir? Were they doing anything about it or just letting events take their course? Was it someone from his past, someone I'd never heard of? Or was it someone I knew? Was it all just staring me in the face? That question of who could possibly have killed Hayden was the least mysterious of all the questions I asked myself. The answer was, anybody who had known him because, with Hayden, that was about enough to give you a sufficient motive. That was the thing. I could have done it, given the right moment, the right argument, the right heavy object in my hand. What would God say to that? Perhaps the fact, if it was a fact, that I could have done it was as bad as if I actually had done it.

So I sat in my unfinished, indeed barely started, flat and asked myself questions because I didn't want to speak them aloud. I couldn't lose myself in music because music was now part of the problem. And I couldn't lose myself in drink because I couldn't trust what I might do or what I might say.

*

In the end, I couldn't stand the voices scratching in my head. I had to speak to someone or I'd go mad and, of course, the only people I could possibly speak to were my accomplices, my co-conspirators: Sonia and Neal.

Sonia would be with Amos, and if there was anyone I wanted to avoid right now, it was Amos.

So it was that I found myself taking the bus to Stoke Newington and walking along the charming little streets to Neal's house. It was such a beautiful day, the air soft and warm, the sky a deep blue with trails of cloud on the horizon. People looked happy in their light clothes, their faces open in the golden light.

It hadn't occurred to me that he wouldn't be there but when I rang the doorbell there was no reply. I peered in through the letterbox and saw nothing but the strip of floorboard leading to the stairs. And now what should I do with myself, with my knocking heart and the hot dread that snaked through me? I sat on the doorstep and put my head into my hands, closed my eyes because the sun throbbed in my skull.

'Bonnie?'

I looked up, blinking. 'Neal!'

'How long have you been here?'

'A couple of minutes, if that.'

'Are you all right?'

'I think so.' I forced a smile. 'I don't know why I'm here. I didn't want to be alone in my flat. How about you? Are you OK?'

'Me? I – to tell the truth, I can't seem to settle to anything. I'm jittery. That's why I went out – because I couldn't stay in. But then I couldn't stay out either. I had to get back to the house, as if I needed to hide from everyone. God, I'd make a lousy criminal.' His mouth widened into a desperate smile, like a hole in his usually handsome face. 'But I am a criminal, aren't I? I am! Me? Fuck. Who'd have thought it? I'm such a geeky, boring, law-abiding person. I never even break the speed limit, not even when I'm in a hurry.'

'Shall we go inside?'

'I keep thinking I'm going to tell someone. Like the Ancient Mariner. I'm going to stop someone in the street and tell them what I've done.'

'Inside, Neal,' I said.

'Yes. Sorry. Here.' And he fumbled with the key, muttering curses under his breath.

'I'll do it,' I said, taking it from his thick fingers.

I made us a pot of coffee and then some toast and Marmite. We sat in the kitchen and Neal took a gulp of coffee, a giant bite of his toast, and then said – rather indistinctly through the crumbs, 'Are we idiots?'

'What?'

He took another bite; his cheeks bulged. 'They're going to discover, aren't they?'

'No. I don't think that at all.' I understood that although I had come here for a kind of comfort, or at least the companionship of a shared secret, I was going to have to prop Neal up.

'I did it for you.'

'I didn't ask you to,' I said helplessly.

'I know. I know you didn't. You didn't ask me and I didn't ask you – sometimes I feel almost euphoric with what we've done for each other.'

'That's not the way it was.'

'And sometimes I just feel terrified.'

'I know. Me too.'

'Do they know anything?'

'I don't know what they know. I don't think they know he died in the flat. They know about him and me. And I've told them about me and you.'

'Not that there was anything to tell,' he said. 'Just one night.'

'I said we were together. So, as long as we stick to that we're all right.'

'Yes. We were together. Yes.'

'All evening and night.'

'Yes.'

'He was married.'

'What?'

'Hayden was married.'

'He had a wife?'

'A wife and a son.'

He pushed the last of his toast into his mouth. 'What does that mean?'

'Neal, I don't have a fucking clue what anything means. All I know is that Hayden had a whole complicated, messy life and the police are going to be looking at all that as well. He had a wife he'd left behind, a son he hardly ever saw, he had friends he'd betrayed, people he worked with whom he let down. And you're forgetting something.'

'What? What am I forgetting?'

'We didn't do anything to him. I mean, I know we tampered with the evidence.' He snorted wildly at that. 'OK, you tampered with evidence and me and Sonia – well,

I don't know what you'd call it. But we didn't kill or harm him at all. That's a different kind of guilt. Someone out there killed him.'

'And we cleared up for them.'

'Yes.'

'What must they be thinking?'

'Well, what were you thinking when the body disappeared?'

'I was thinking – well, I was thinking: Oh, fuck, oh, Christ, is this a dream, a nightmare, oh, my God, am I mad? I was – I was – I don't know – It was just surreal and I swear to God I've never been through anything like that in my life, nothing even approaching it, when there was nobody I could talk to about it.' He pulled at his hair.

'Exactly. That's probably what they're thinking as well, whoever they are.'

'Do you think it was anyone we know?'

'Probably not. Maybe it was just a stranger. Maybe we'll never know – nobody will ever know.'

'And then what?' He pushed away his mug and plate, laid his head on the table and started to cry. His shoulders shook and whimpers escaped from him.

I leaned across and put my hand on his back. 'Don't cry,' I said. 'Neal, don't, please. It's going to be all right. You didn't kill him. You just tried to help me. You did it for good motives. We both did. We did it for each other and we're going to get each other through this. Don't cry.'

I looked at him lying across the table, his body shaking with wretchedness, and I wished it was me who was collapsed like that, and someone else was sitting with their hand on my back telling me it would be OK. For a moment

I saw Hayden, his face open, crinkles round his smiling eyes, and he was saying, 'But you're a tough cookie, Bonnie.' And I was. I wouldn't cry and be comforted, not yet anyway, and not by Neal.

The phone rang and he jerked upright, his face tear-stained.

'You don't need to answer,' I said.

But he was already reaching out. 'Yes?' His face tightened. There were corrugated lines scoring his forehead. 'Yes, that's me. Yes. Um, I think that would be all right. OK, I'll be there.' He put the phone down.

'The police?' I said.

He nodded.

'When?'

'An hour.'

'You know what you're going to say?'

'I think so.'

'We're an item. We were together.'

'OK.'

'The whole time.'

'Yes.'

'Everything else, everything that happened around Hayden, you just tell the truth. You can say you didn't like him, you can say you know we'd had a fling and of course you felt a bit jealous, you can talk about the tensions in the band. You don't need to conceal anything except what happened on that one evening. All right?'

'I'm a terrible liar.'

Before

After Amos had left, I looked around the flat, seeing it as other people must when they came into it for the first time. It wasn't a pretty sight. The reason I hadn't gone away, apart from not having any money, was to decorate it and make it more habitable, but all I'd succeeded in doing was to make it look as if a deranged person lived there. I'd emptied half the cupboards into boxes, but then emptied the boxes back onto surfaces or simply onto available floor space in order to find things. I'd painted parts of walls but then given up. I'd started pulling away wallpaper and then got distracted. In the kitchen, I'd ripped up a few of the vile green lino tiles to reveal unlovely wooden boards beneath. The problem, I decided now, was that I hadn't concentrated on one room at a time. I had been acting on the principle that if I created chaos everywhere I'd have to deal with it, but actually what I'd discovered was that if I created chaos everywhere I simply got used to it.

I went from room to room and realized there was a second problem: I had no real idea of what I wanted. I just knew what I didn't want: this dinginess, this pokiness, these flat kitchen units, this grubby beige carpet, this plastic bathtub. The bedroom had patterned wallpaper that probably dated back to the sixties, a worn green carpet that hadn't been properly fitted around the radiator and the general appearance of a room into which a motley collection of things picked up in a second-hand shop had been crammed

– which was pretty much the truth. Nothing went with anything else. I would start here.

I managed to pull the wardrobe out of the room, although for ten minutes it got stuck in the doorway, wedged at an impossible angle, and I only wrenched it free by taking a chunk out of the plaster and leaving a nasty scar along the wall. I pulled the chest of drawers out as well, discovering lots of objects behind it – pens, an old phone charger I'd been fruitlessly looking for, a scratched CD of folk music. Now, in order to get from the bedroom to the rest of the flat, I had to practically clamber over the chest and squeeze past the wardrobe. This I did, to retrieve the scraper that was in the kitchen. I spent the next two hours scraping and tugging off the wallpaper. After about ten minutes, I began to wish I had simply painted over it several times until the pattern was obscured, but by then it was too late to stop. Also I wished I'd thought about the mess I was going to create. Scraps of paper lay everywhere; flecks scattered the room like dandruff. My bed, which I had failed to cover, was littered with shreds and scabs of it. Underneath the pattern there was another, less geometric and more flowery. How far should I go down in this archaeological project? When would a plain wall appear?

I was hot, sweaty, dirty, thirsty. My scalp itched and my eyes watered. I opened the window wide and sounds from the street filtered in. People talking, laughter that floated in the warm air, birdsong and traffic. I laid down the scraper, clambered over the chest of drawers and escaped.

After

She stood just outside the door and I stood just inside, and we stared at each other for a moment. I knew at once who she was, even though she was different from the photograph, older, of course, but also less vivid, thinner and more finely drawn. I saw she had eyes that were almost green and there were grey threads in the auburn hair she wore brushed behind her ears. She had on cream cotton trousers, a thin brown shirt and espadrilles, and looked cool and clean and in control. I wondered if she had thought about what to wear to meet me, whether she had stood in front of her wardrobe considering how she should present herself to her dead husband's lover. Certainly I wished I'd known she was coming so that at least I wasn't dressed only in an oversized man's shirt that was, I realized, with a rush of horror, one that had belonged to Hayden. Maybe she had given it to him one Christmas. I did up the top button and said, 'You're Hannah Booth.'

'That's right. I was married to Hayden. And you're Bonnie Graham.'

'Yes.'

'I've been told you knew my husband.'

'Yes.' I hesitated, then said, 'Will you come in? It's a mess. Everything's everywhere.'

'That's all right,' she said. She gave me a cautious smile. 'I don't care about that.'

I took her through to the kitchen and offered her tea.

When she sat down and laid her thin hands on the table I saw that she wasn't wearing a wedding ring.

'I'm so sorry about Hayden,' I said.

'Thank you.'

'I read that interview with you.'

'Oh, that. I don't think I said any of the things they quoted. I just said I was shocked.'

'How did you know?'

'About you? I spoke to Nat and he told me you and Hayden seemed . . .' She paused and made a wry grimace. '. . . close to each other. Whatever that meant with Hayden.' She leaned forward. 'I'm not here to judge you. That's not what this is about. We weren't living together and hadn't been for years. Of course there were other women. Probably dozens of them. Even when he was with me.'

'So what is it about?'

She looked down at her hands, then plaited her fingers together. 'I suppose I just wanted to see what you're like.'

'Well, here I am. My hair needs washing and I'm usually better dressed.'

'You're not what I expected.'

'I don't know what that means.'

'I wanted to find out what he'd become since leaving me and Joe. I'm not jealous of you, it's not that at all – I didn't want him back. You couldn't even say that I still loved him or felt anything much for him at all, except anger perhaps, and even that wasn't very strong any more. Now everything's been stirred up. You knew him when he died and I didn't really know him at all any more.'

'I think you've got the wrong idea of how close we were. It was just a summer fling, really. No strings attached.'

'Hayden was good at that,' she said.

I realized she was dangerous: she made me feel as though I could confide in her and, indeed, I had an almost over-whelming urge to do just that. I sat up straighter. 'What do you want me to tell you?'

'I don't know. Sorry. It's probably been as bad for you as for me. Were you very fond of him?'

'He hit me.' I hadn't known I was going to say the words, and as soon as I spoke them, they seemed to swell and fill the room. My face glowed with shame and I felt utterly exposed.

'You poor thing,' said Hannah. She gazed at me with what almost seemed like yearning. Her eyes were bright with tears.

I shrank back from her sympathy. 'Only twice.'

'You must have hated him.' Her voice was low and soft.

'I didn't hate him,' I said. 'I was shocked.'

'It wasn't anything to do with you,' she said. 'It was him.'

'When he was with you, did he . . . ?'

'No. But he had this anger beneath the surface. He could be like a little boy – I don't mean in a good way. He had tantrums. Like Joe, when he was two.' She paused and then said: 'And he was a real stirrer, wasn't he?'

'What do you mean?'

'He liked making mischief, setting the cat among the pigeons and then sitting back to see what would happen.'

I thought of Hayden with the band, deftly touching off insecurities and playing on exposed nerves. 'Yes,' I said.

'Maybe it killed him.'

'Maybe.'

'The police think it was some drug thing.'

'Do they?'

'It would make sense but, then, anything would make sense, really. He made so many enemies. I used to tell him he went out of his way to make them – as if it was a sign of his authenticity or something. Bloody musicians.'

'Are you a musician?' I asked.

'I'm tone deaf. I never even learned to play the recorder. I'm a speech therapist. It could never have worked, could it – a part-time, tone-deaf speech therapist married to a feckless, charming singer who thought commitment was some kind of fatal compromise?'

There was a pause.

'Don't tell anyone, will you?'

'Tell them what?'

'That he hit me.'

'Who would I tell?' She looked at me curiously. 'Is something troubling you?'

Her voice was insidious and all of a sudden I felt she was my enemy – or perhaps that was just another sign that I was going mad.

Before

If I could have chosen who I did not want to see as I practically ran from my flat, the list would be, in no particular order of preference: Neal, Amos, Guy, Joakim, probably Hayden and Sonia as well. Oh, and Danielle, the person responsible for creating the mess of the band in the first place. She saw me from a distance, so we walked towards each other with our smiles fixed in idiot grins and her hand that wasn't carrying shopping bags raised as if I would lose sight of her if she dropped it for a second. She wore a pale blue shift and sandals and looked polished and buffed and blonder than ever. Her lips were glossy, her teeth were white, her legs were smooth and tanned, and I wanted to kick her in the shins as I reached her.

'What a lovely coincidence.' She touched her lips to my cheek and I caught the waft of her perfume.

'Yes,' I said, through gritted teeth.

'You look hot – and what's that in your hair?'

'I am hot and it's wallpaper.' I ran my fingers through my hair and bits fell out. 'I'm in the middle of decorating and I just needed to escape for a few minutes.'

I felt her eyes on my grubby skin and the sweat marks under my armpits.

'Let me buy you a cold drink. I could do with one myself. How about in here? It looks cool enough.'

She bought me a tall glass of old-fashioned lemonade and herself a ginger beer and we sat in a dark corner away from the sunlight, which slanted through the café window.

'How's it all going?' I asked her.

'Frantic! You wouldn't believe the things you have to get done before you marry. I have these lists and no sooner have I crossed one thing off than I remember another. It's like the Forth Bridge.'

'I'm sure.'

'Not long to go now. But it's me who should be asking you how it's going. How is it?'

'You mean ...?'

'The music, of course. I hope you don't think I've been neglecting you.'

'No. I don't.'

'Maybe I could come and listen to you all some time, get a feeling for what's going to happen on the day.'

'I think it would be better as a surprise.'

'Yes, perhaps that would be more exciting. I can't tell you how grateful I am. It'll be wonderful, I'm sure.'

'I wish I shared your confidence.'

'Don't be so modest, Bonnie.' She frowned. 'You have all been practising, haven't you?'

'Oh, yes.'

'So you'll be ready?'

I thought of our frayed sessions, the arguments and walk-outs, the unpredictable sounds we made. 'Yes, we will,' I said firmly.

'Of course, I shouldn't even ask. You're a professional. How many sets – is that what you call it? – will you be playing?'

'Just six or seven songs,' I said.

'Only six?'

'Six is enough, Danielle, believe me.'

'Well, you're the boss.'

'Yes.'

'It's lucky I bumped into you, actually. I was going to ring you to ask you something.'

'Ask away.'

'It's about what you'll be wearing.'

'Wearing?' I looked at her blankly.

'Yes. When you play.'

'I don't know what you're talking about.'

'For instance, will you all be wearing the same thing?'

'Hang on, Danielle.'

'I was thinking something hillbilly would be good. Loose cotton trousers and braces and hats. Or wouldn't the women like that?'

'What makes you think the men would?'

'You don't think it's a good idea?'

'No, I do not.'

'Maybe something more romantic.'

'Romantic?'

'Long and drifty for the women – you could even wear flowers in your hair.'

'My hair's too short for flowers.'

'And what about light summer suits and hats for the men. Trilbies. Or would that be incongruous? What do you think?'

'You want to know?'

'Of course.'

'We've agreed to play at your wedding. We have not agreed to wear fancy dress.'

'Oh. Well, just let me know in advance, will you?'

'I want to make it quite clear, Danielle, that –'

'Oh, God, is that the time? Must run! I'm so glad we had time for this chat.'

''Bye,' I said to her departing back, the bobbed hair that bounced cheerily as she walked away.

After

It was Joakim who organized the next rehearsal. I could barely face it but he badgered me. He rang me several times and in the end he said we either had to cancel the performance or get together. Which was it going to be? He talked about Hayden and said that the performance would be our tribute to him. It would be what he would have wanted. Part of me found that idea horribly comic. That was what people always said about the dead. They suddenly became an expert in what they 'would have wanted'. I had to restrain myself from shouting down the phone at Joakim. Hayden had had no coherent sense of what he wanted even when he was alive. Now he was lying in a fridge in a morgue somewhere in God knew what condition. He didn't exist any more. What did any of that matter? But I knew that this was my problem, not Joakim's. He was so young, so hopeful. He still thought he could do something for Hayden. He thought that these gestures mattered. He was probably right. I just couldn't see it any more.

Joakim actually rang the school and somehow persuaded the school caretaker, who never listened to anyone, to open up one of the rehearsal rooms. I thought there were rules about procedure and insurance that forbade such things but Joakim managed it. As we arrived, he even brought in a tray of coffee from the place across the road from the school. It almost made me cry. We sipped the coffee and then, nervously, as if we were doing it for the first time, picked up the instruments. Joakim coughed and said he had a couple of ideas. He pulled out a piece of paper on which he'd jotted a few chords. I quickly saw that what he'd done was to strip out some complications that would make 'Nashville Blues' easier to play without Hayden. It must have taken him hours. I made a couple of adjustments and then we started and, really, the result wasn't all that terrible.

When Sonia sang 'It Had To Be You', we started to sound a bit better than not all that terrible. Her voice seemed bereft and world-weary, rather than as if she'd just got up.

An hour later we finished, and as people were gathering their stuff together, I saw that Sonia was huddled with Neal, murmuring something to him, and he was replying in an insistent tone, much louder than hers, although I couldn't make out what he was saying. I glanced across at Guy and Amos. They weren't paying attention. I joined Neal and Sonia.

'What's up?' I said to Neal. 'Is everything OK?'

'I've had an idea.'

'I don't think I can cope with any more ideas.'

'No. This is really important. It came to me like a bolt from the blue. I can't imagine why it didn't occur to us before.'

'Are you talking a bit loudly?'

'I was thinking about you feeling guilty, and wondering whether we should go to the police.'

'This really isn't the place to talk about it. How are you getting home?'

'I've got the car.'

'We'll come with you,' I said.

'I can't,' said Sonia. 'I'm going out with Amos.'

'Make an excuse,' I said.

Sonia leaned in close to me and spoke in a whisper: 'We can't keep going off as a trio,' she said. 'It doesn't look right.'

'I know,' I said. 'But we need to hear what Neal has to say.'

'All right,' she said. 'I'll join you outside. This had better be good, Neal.'

Neal and I waited in his car until Sonia came out and sat in the back seat.

'What did you tell Amos?' I asked.

'You don't need to know. It's OK, though.'

'I just wondered if he was suspicious.'

'I told him it was important and he had to trust me.'

'What's up?' I asked Neal. 'Was it the police?'

'No, don't worry. It wasn't the police. I was completely effective with them. I didn't say anything harmful to us. I didn't say anything that might actually help them to solve the murder, though. Which was what made me think.'

'Think what?'

'Hang on. I'll take this short-cut. Let's wait till we get home. We need paper.'

'What?'

'Paper. And pens.'

'Are we going to play a game?' said Sonia, ominously. 'A parlour game?'

Neal pulled up outside his house and got out, unlocked the front door and pushed it open. We walked in after him. Sonia made coffee, and when she eventually sat down it was as if we were beginning a meeting.

'Well?' I said.

'I've been thinking,' he said.

'You already told us that.' Sonia stared at him over the rim of her mug. I could practically hear her crackle with impatience.

'Here's the thing. We've all done the wrong thing for the right motive. Yes?'

'Go on.'

'Now, the only thing we should really feel bad about is if we're concealing something from the police . . .'

'Well, of course we're bloody concealing something from the police!'

'Hold on, you didn't let me get to the end of the sentence. If we're concealing something from the police that would help them in their investigation – in other words, help them find out who killed Hayden. Yes?'

'How does this help us, Neal?'

'We can do something.'

'Do something?' said Sonia.

'What we did was to destroy evidence and dispose of a body. But, listen, there were three different crime scenes, or was it four? On top of each other. There was the original one when Hayden was killed. Maybe the killer did something to that, but that was the one I found. I thought you'd done it, Bonnie, so I altered it to make it look as if there'd been a violent scuffle and it wouldn't seem as if you'd done it. Or something – actually, I wasn't thinking straight. Then you . . .' he looked across at Sonia '. . . then you, with Sonia, tried to make it look as if a crime hadn't been committed there at all. That was pretty stupid, but from what I understand it worked to a certain extent, in that the police still don't know where the murder happened. My point is that we could be like archaeologists. We could peel away the layers and get to the original murder scene.'

'You mean go to the flat?'

'No, that would be way too dangerous. The police don't know the murder was committed there, but they know he was staying there. If they stumbled on the three of us there, it would be . . . well, not easy to explain. But we could reconstruct it in our heads.'

Sonia looked dubious. 'I don't really see how this is going to work,' she said.

Neal got up and rummaged through a drawer for pens. Then he tore some pages off a notepad and passed a couple each to me and Sonia.

'What are we meant to do?' asked Sonia. 'Draw a diagram?'

'That would be too hard. Anyway, I don't know what would be on it. We should all start by writing down every object we can remember from the flat, every single thing. And when we've got the list we can try to place where they were and then we can see if what you remember fits with what I remember and . . . and . . .'

'And then what?' I said.

'We can reconstruct the scene.'

'And then?'

'I don't know.' Neal rubbed his eyes and, for a moment, looked despondent. 'We can't tell. But if we get a list of as many objects as possible and place them, some pattern might emerge. If I could tell before we'd done it, what would be the point of doing it?'

'I'm not sure it's going to be productive,' Sonia said.

'It's something.'

'You really think we can re-create the scene from memory?' I asked.

Neal banged on the table. 'What's the point of arguing about whether or not we think we can do it? Let's have a fucking go at it.'

I turned to Sonia. 'You're good at games like this.'

'Shut up, everybody,' Neal said, 'and start writing.'

I picked up my pen and stared at the blank piece of paper on the table. I smoothed it with my fingers as if that would help. For a moment, my mind was as blank as the page. I closed my eyes and tried to make myself see it, to put myself back in the room. It took a particular, painful effort because I had spent weeks making it a part of my mind I would never visit again. The struggle was almost physical, as if I was pulling at a stuck old door to a room I hadn't entered for a long time. But the door came open with a jolt and I was there. It was blurry and fragmentary, though, and I could only make out a few objects. I started to write. There were the CDs, including the Hank Williams one that I had retrieved. There was a green plastic tortoise thing for keeping pens in. That had been on the table. There had been a little tin of paperclips next to it. There had been a cushion on the chair and a vase with tulips in it tipped over. There was the wedding invite, which I had also taken and got rid of. There had been the broken guitar and some books on the floor. My scarf. The scene seemed to go further into the distance the more I tried to see it.

It reminded me of being in an exam room when I was seventeen years old, spying on the people around me, who seemed to be writing more than I was, and with more concentration. It was certainly like that now. Neal was writing steadily. I couldn't read the words but he had done much more than I had. Sonia too. As I had thought, she was much better than I was at this sort of thing. Not that it really mattered. I couldn't seriously imagine that anything would come of this. That hadn't really been the point. The point, I knew, was to make us feel better about what we'd done. A plaster on a gaping wound.

I had stopped writing. That was like an exam too, those awful last minutes when I had nothing more to say and stared at the clock waiting for the end, wondering whether I should check my work once more.

'Are you done?' I said. 'I can't think of anything else.'

'Hang on,' said Neal, still scribbling energetically.

Sonia had also stopped writing.

'Can I have a look?' I said, and she passed her paper across to me.

As I suspected, she had done miles better than I had. She had remembered the phone and the bowl with keys in, which didn't really count. All flats have phones and bowls with keys in, don't they? She'd mentioned the guitar case. And I'd forgotten the little brass Buddha and the green bottle and the laptop, and there were various sculptures, which I remembered now. And the mail on the floor. Sonia was amazing. As I read through her list the room really started to take shape again in my mind.

'I'm done,' said Neal.

'Now what?'

'Now we need to go through the objects and work out where they were. Then you can try to remember which ones you moved and we can work our way back to where everything was when you walked in and found the body. Let me have a look at yours.'

I passed the two lists to Neal and he ran his finger down each one, item by item, like a small child who has just learned to read. 'Jesus,' he said. 'Sonia's way better at this than you are.'

'I didn't know it was a competition,' I said.

Neal held our two lists, one in each hand, and studied them intently, first one then the other. He tossed them onto the table and leaned back, staring at the ceiling. His chair rocked. I worried for a moment that he might tip over and do himself a mischief. Finally he let it down with a bump. 'I don't even know why we're doing this.'

'It was your idea.'

'It was a stupid one.'

Before

Hayden was crying in my arms. He was crying like a baby cries, he was crying the way he made love and the way he ate and the way he laughed – with abandonment and a lack of self-consciousness that astonished and moved me. I held him against me and I felt how emotion was making his entire body quake. He gulped and groaned and bit by bit he calmed down until at last he was lying still and heavy, like a dead man. I stroked his damp hair and bent to kiss his shoulder.

'Do you want to tell me?' I asked at last.

He sat up and used the hem of my shirt to wipe his cheeks. 'That's better,' he said, as if he'd had a long drink of water after great thirst.

'Hayden?'

'Mm?'

'What was that about?'

'I'm hungry.'

'Hayden?'

'You were going to cook me that meal, weren't you? You even brought your mother's old cookbook with you. You've never cooked for me before. I like firsts.'

'You might not like this one.' I stood up and put on the apron I'd also brought – I was wearing a pale grey sleeveless dress I'd picked up on a market stall that morning and didn't want to ruin it with my incompetence. 'Sea bass with spices I've failed to buy so we'll have to do without, and rice. OK? Don't you want to talk about it?'

'I want to eat. I'm ravenous.'

After

The phone rang and rang. In my dreams, it was the sound of bells. I was trying to walk up a hill towards a small grey church but was hardly able to move. I realized I was in a wedding dress, but one that was ripped, badly fitting and covered with mud, and I was trying to reach Hayden, who

307

was standing near the entrance with water streaming from his hair and a rug around his shoulders. He was smiling at me, or maybe grimacing, but however hard I tried, I couldn't reach him. My legs dragged. The bells became louder and more insistent, pealing out. I forced myself up out of the sheets and reached for the phone, fumbling in the darkness and still half tangled in the dream. I barely knew where I was, who I was. I found it and lifted it, jabbing at the buttons to answer, but the sound continued and I realized it wasn't the phone after all. Someone was ringing the doorbell.

I stumbled out of bed and went to the front door, which I opened. Everything seemed unreal. Neal's face, looking at me through the gap, seemed unreal, something from long ago.

'We've got to talk,' he said.

'What time is it?' I felt jet-lagged – perhaps I'd slept for many hours and it was the next day, but it was dark outside, or as dark as it ever gets in London, not even a band of light on the horizon.

'I don't know. Let me in.'

I stood back, suddenly aware that I was wearing just an old singlet over some knickers.

'Wait here,' I said in the kitchen, and went into my bedroom for jogging pants and an old top that covered me properly.

'I had to see you,' said Neal, as I came back into the kitchen and sat down opposite him.

'You only just saw me. Remember?'

'I've been thinking.'

'You should have been sleeping instead.'

'I was sleeping, and then I woke with a jerk. Do you ever do that?'

'Yes.'

'And it occurred to me.'

'What did? Hang on.' I stood up and opened the fridge. 'I need something to calm me down.' I pulled out a carton of milk. 'Do you want some hot chocolate?'

'No.'

'Whisky?'

'No. I need to keep a clear head. So do you.'

I poured the milk into a mug and drank it cold. 'That's better,' I said. 'Now. Why do I need a clear head?'

'Look.' He handed me a piece of paper. 'Talk me through this,' he said.

'Am I still dreaming, or didn't we already do this earlier?'

'Go on, look,' he insisted.

'This is Sonia's list.'

'I want to check that our memories coincide on this.'

I started to read the list out loud. 'Really, it's all pretty straightforward. Sonia's got more things because she's got a bigger brain than I have. But I've no problem with any of it. I only have a problem with you waking me in the middle of the night to go over it again. Because I'm tired, Neal, I'm so tired that I feel as if everything's fraying inside me.'

Neal leaned forward with his elbows on the table, rubbing his head with his hand as if there were an itch deep inside that he couldn't get at. 'What about those two sculptures?'

'I remember them,' I said.

'But they weren't on your list. I've got that here. Look.' He leaned down and pulled the sheet of paper out of the canvas bag he'd brought with him, waved it at me as if he was trying to attract my attention.

'I remember them *now*,' I said. 'They went out of my mind when I was trying to think of things. I'm really amazed I got as much as I did. What is this?'

'Describe them to me,' said Neal.

I looked back at the list and made myself concentrate.

'One of them was a sort of grey-metal abstract thing. It was like two figures with something over them, a cloud or an umbrella.'

'What about the other?'

I looked again at Sonia's mention of it. That was harder to remember but it was vaguely familiar.

'It was a kind of rough-textured vase. Was it bronze? It had a sort of greenish tinge, like old metal statues. And I hate to say this, but I've got a feeling that it had breastlike protrusions. I suspect it was meant to echo the female body.'

'That's very precise,' said Neal. 'Why didn't you put it on your list?'

'I told you,' I said. 'It was like the other sculpture. I didn't put it down because I didn't remember it.'

Neal nodded his head slowly, many times. I gazed at him, wondering if he'd finally gone mad. There was a new glitter in his eyes, a sense of contained excitement.

'It's not like the other sculpture,' he said.

'What do you mean?' I said.

'It's not like the other sculpture,' he said. 'You didn't remember the first sculpture because you forgot it.'

'Well, exactly.'

'But you didn't remember the second sculpture because it wasn't there.'

I looked down at Sonia's list, written in her neat, bold hand. This made no sense to me.

'What do you mean it wasn't there? How do you know it wasn't there? Of course it was there. Sonia remembered it. I remember it now – kind of. I've described it to you. Are you all right?'

Neal leaned down again and opened the flap on the bag at his feet. He removed a bulky object and placed it on the table.

'It wasn't there,' he said, 'because it's here.'

'Here?' I said stupidly.

'Look.'

I looked. A vase in the shape of a female body. Ugly. Who'd want to put flowers in that?

'I don't understand,' I said. My tongue felt thick in my mouth; I shaped the words with difficulty. 'I don't understand what you're saying.'

'I took it away.'

There was no doubt about it. That was the vase. The vase with tits.

'Why? What's it doing here now?'

'It's the wrong question – not why, *when*.'

'When?' I asked obediently, although I still didn't understand why that was the right question.

'On that evening, Bonnie – on August the twenty-first, the day Hayden was killed – I took it away because I thought it might have been the murder weapon. It was lying there on the carpet in the patch of blood. It's got that funny handle thing on it. I imagined that someone – you, Bonnie, yes, you – during a row might have picked it up, lashed out, caught him on the head, killed him.' He looked at me. 'I know you remember the vase, because you saw it when you were there with Hayden, or maybe when you visited the flat before. And I know why you didn't put it on your list. Maybe because you've got a bad memory or, even more probably, because it wasn't there. Now do you understand?'

'No,' I said. 'No. No.' I wanted to cover my ears with my hands, or curl up in a small, tight ball. 'I don't.'

'Don't you see?' His voice was calm and patient, as if he was trying to explain something to a particularly stupid child. 'You didn't remember it was there. But I remembered it was there. And Sonia remembered it was there, the first time.'

I could hear the words Neal was saying but they were only partially making sense.

'What do you mean, the first time?' I said.

'The first time,' said Neal. 'Earlier in the evening. When she killed Hayden.'

Before

Days often seemed like nights with Hayden, when we would draw the curtains or pull down the blinds, tug the sheets over our heads and explore each other in our own twilight world, the sunlight pouring down unheeded outside and the birds singing in the plane tree by the window. And nights could merge with days, losing all boundaries, because Hayden didn't keep to the same hours as other people and didn't even have an approxima-tion of a structure. He didn't own a clock or a watch, and though he had the time on his mobile, he rarely if ever checked it. He ate when he felt like it, slept when he was tired, had difficulty keeping any appointments, including appointments with the band – the only reason he turned up for rehearsals as frequently as he did was that I was often with him.

For him days and nights, the passage of time itself, the fall and lift of darkness, were like a great river that was carrying him along: sometimes drifting into the shallows, sometimes flung into the fast-moving centre, sometimes wallowing luxuriously in the slow currents, but never striking out with purpose. He would sleep two hours, or seven, or fifteen; eat once or five times in what served as his day; drink wine at eleven in the morning and eat cereal at midnight; make no plans and then triple-book people.

That night, after his weeping fit, he ate my sea bass (burned) and rice (gluey with overcooking) as if he was saving himself from starvation, washing it down with cold tea and tepid wine. Then he said, 'Let's go for a walk.'

'It's nearly two in the morning. I'm dog tired.'

'I need to expend some energy. And it's still warm, warm as day. Look, the moon's nearly full.'

'Where?'

'I dunno, wherever our feet take us. Come on.'

'I need to change into something more sensible.'

'No – just put your shoes on.'

'I need to get my stuff.'

'Leave it here.'

We walked down through Camden, past Regent's Park and into Bloomsbury. There were still a few cars on the roads, and a straggle of pedestrians on their way somewhere

– London is never quite empty, never quite silent or dark – but as we walked over Waterloo Bridge it felt as though we were the only people awake in the whole vast and glittering city. The moon shone on the river and we could hear the small waves smacking against the shore. The clock on Big Ben showed four. Hayden walked fast, not talking. He looked young and purposeful, striding out as if he was heading towards a particular goal. His face in the moon- and lamplight was smooth, quite peaceful. We turned off the bridge and walked eastwards, along the Embankment, under the shadow of empty, monumental buildings. Now there was a faint band of light on the horizon and birds were singing in the trees. He turned and suddenly smiled at me, held out his hand for me to take, and I was filled with a surge of happiness so strong it made my chest ache.

Still we didn't talk. We went back across the river at Blackfriars but with one accord stopped in the middle to look out at the City.

'I think I'm going away quite soon,' Hayden said.

'Oh?'

'Yeah – time to head off.'

'Where?'

I didn't look at him, but down at the water beneath. Beside me, I felt him giving a shrug.

'Somewhere else,' was all he said. 'Something's come up. Anyway, maybe I need a change.'

'What about the wedding?' I forced my voice to remain absolutely neutral.

'Wedding?'

'That we're rehearsing for.'

'I'll probably stay around for that.'

'I see.'

'What do you see, Bonnie?'

'It doesn't matter.'

He took my chin in his hand and forced me to look at him. 'Nothing lasts for ever.'

'No.'

'Come on.'

And we set off again, no longer holding hands, and the light came up and the shutters rose on newsagents and the traffic thickened. We stopped in a working-men's café in Farringdon, and Hayden ate fried eggs on toast and I drank coffee. Before we reached my flat, he left me. He said he had things to see to.

After

'You're being ridiculous,' I said. 'It's not possible.'

'It has to be.'

'Sonia?' I stared at him. 'I don't believe it.'

'She could only have remembered the vase if she'd been there earlier in the evening.'

'Maybe she saw it before.'

'Had she ever been to the flat before?'

'No.' I remembered she had claimed she didn't know where the flat was. I'd met her on Kentish Town Road and shown her the way.

'There you are, then.'

'The fact that she was there earlier doesn't mean she killed him.'

'Why has she lied?'

'Why did you lie? Why did I?'

My brain was working slowly and ponderously. I could feel facts clicking heavily into place; interpretations re-arranging themselves. I had called Sonia to come and help me get rid of the evidence of Neal's crime – but it was her crime. She had come and helped me get rid of her own evidence. Or I had helped her. Together, we had cleared away every clue she had left behind. I stared wildly at Neal.

'It can't be true,' I said. 'It can't be.'

'Let's go and find out.' He stood up, decisive and full of new authority.

'Now?' I said stupidly. 'It's still the middle of the night.'

'Yes, now. What – you want to wait until morning?'

'No – but she'll be with Amos. She said she was going there.'

'So?'

'Well, what about Amos? We can't just – well –' I stopped and put my head into my hands. I felt as though my brain was hissing.

'Ring her mobile. Tell her we have to see her.'

'She'll think we're mad.'

'Unless I'm right. You'll see.'

I picked up my mobile and scrolled down to Sonia's number. 'What shall I say?'

'Tell her we know what happened and we have to see her at once.'

I pressed the dial button and waited. The phone rang and rang. I pictured Sonia curled up next to Amos.

When she answered, her voice was thick with sleep.

'It's Bonnie.'

'What is it?' Now she would be struggling into a sitting position, turning away from Amos so as not to wake him.

'I have to see you.'

'Wait a minute.' Now she would be outside the bedroom, closing the door. 'It's the middle of the night.'

'It's four o'clock. I'm with Neal and we need to see you at once.'

'Why?' Did the tone of her voice shift?

'We know what happened.'

'You want me to come and see you?' Sonia still sounded quite calm. 'The Underground isn't running.'

'We'll drive to you.' I looked at Neal and he nodded his approval. 'Neal's car is here. We'll be waiting outside Amos's flat. Ten minutes.'

'All right. Ten minutes.'

Neal drove and I gave directions, then looked out of the window. It was foggy, although later the sun would burn it away. I thought about Sonia, her competent, practical kindness. I closed my eyes and for a moment let myself feel how very tired I was. Yet I was full of a restless, churning energy that made it difficult to sit still.

And then there she was, standing on the pavement in a belted mac, her hair tied back.

Neal pulled up. She opened the back door and climbed into the car. For a few seconds no one spoke.

'Well?' Sonia said at last.

'Let's drive to the canal,' I said. 'It seems a bit odd to be sitting outside Amos's flat to talk.'

Sonia sat back and folded her hands on her lap. I told Neal where to go in a voice that sounded absurdly formal.

317

The three of us were like awkward acquaintances. It was impossible to say anything at all except the huge unsayable thing that was squashing the air out of the space.

The car stopped. Neal turned off the headlights and the ignition. He coughed loudly and then I coughed as well.

'Spit it out,' said Sonia.

I twisted round to face her, made myself look at her full on. 'Neal found the vase.'

'Vase?'

'The vase you remembered was there, except it wasn't. With breasts.'

'Breasts?'

'Yes. You remembered it but it wasn't there.'

'You got me out of bed for that?'

'The point is that you remembered there was a vase and I didn't remember and then later Neal realized it wasn't possible . . .'

I glanced at Neal. I was making a mess of this.

'You were there before,' Neal cut in. 'That's what Bonnie's trying to say. We know you were. You saw the vase lying on the floor, but later I took it away with me. You were there before Bonnie and before me.'

'But you pretended to be surprised,' I said. 'You pretended you'd never been there.'

She looked calm, far calmer than me or Neal. 'What do you want me to say?' she said.

'You lied,' I said. 'You were there. You knew everything and then – then you let me believe you were shocked but trying to help me.'

'That's not what's important,' said Neal. 'The only thing that matters is that you killed Hayden.'

Sonia closed her eyes. She seemed to be thinking. When she opened them again she looked first at him and then, for a longer moment, at me. She nodded. 'Yes, I did.'

'*And?*' I said. 'You can't just say that. Why did you do it?'

'I should have said this earlier.' Her voice was quiet but still steady. She spoke slowly, as if she was considering each word, making sure it was correct. 'I knew you and Hayden were together. It wasn't a very secret secret. And I knew he'd hit you.'

'What's that got to do with anything?'

'I never really liked him in the first place. On the Friday at the rehearsal, when you had that bruise on your neck and seemed so subdued and unlike yourself, I asked myself what I should do about it. As your close friend. As someone who cared about you, loved you, and hated to see you putting up with treatment you should have reported to the police. In my opinion, he was abusing you.'

'It wasn't like that.'

'It never is. So, immediately after the rehearsal, I went round to see him, to tell him I wouldn't stand by and see him hurting you. Do you really want to hear this?'

'I think we'd better,' said Neal.

'All right. I got to the flat and he let me in. He was a bit drunk, although it was still early. About six, I think. He didn't seem surprised to see me, and he didn't really seem to listen to what I said.' She paused and swallowed. 'He kept smiling at me, as if he was taunting me. It was horrible and it also made me feel scared of him. Then he grabbed hold of me. I didn't know what he was going to do. I thought he might attack me or even try and kiss me or something. I struggled, tried to get away. Things got knocked over, smashed. I could hear this horrible noise around me of things breaking and me shouting – and suddenly everything was out of control and I was very frightened. I reached out and tried to grab something, anything. I found I had the vase in my hand and I swung it at him and it hit him on the head and he staggered and fell over and he must have hit his temple on the corner of the table because he was lying on the floor and not moving. He was dead. I'd killed him.'

'And then I rang you.'

'I'd just got home when you called and asked for my help.'

'That was a bit of a problem for you,' said Neal. He was tapping his fingers against the steering-wheel and frowning.

'It was like a sick joke,' said Sonia.

'Why didn't you tell me?'

'That it was me who'd killed Hayden?'

'Yes. Why did you go through that whole awful pretence?'

'I don't know,' she said. 'I'd done it for you. Maybe I was letting you help me in return.'

I opened my window and let the cool damp air in. 'So Neal thought I'd done it and cleared away evidence. I thought Neal had done it and called you to get rid of the evidence. I thought you thought I'd done it and were doing me a huge, unimaginable favour. And all the time you were the one who'd done it and . . .' But I couldn't continue. My body felt as though it was coming apart. My head rang and my eyes stung and I found that little snorts were coming out of my nostrils.

'Let's get out,' said Sonia. 'Get some fresh air.'

The three of us walked down to the side of the canal. For several minutes none of us spoke.

'What are you going to do now?' asked Sonia, finally.

'You mean, about knowing you killed Hayden?'

'Yes.'

'What should I do? Go to the police?'

'When you thought it was Neal . . .'

'When I thought Neal had done it for me, I cleaned up after him. Now we know it was you, we've already done the cleaning up. There's nothing left to do, is there?'

'I don't know.'

'You should have said.'

'Would it have made it easier?'

'What were you thinking, all this time? What did you think when I called you to help me get rid of the body?'

'I was surprised.'

'Surprised?'

'I'm not very good with words,' said Sonia. Her voice trembled and I realized that, for all her calm, she was deeply shaken. 'What do you want me to say? I was completely shocked, stunned. I don't know. Like an abyss opening up at my feet.'

'Why did you not say anything when you realized what Bonnie and I had both been assuming?' asked Neal. 'When you understood what had been going on?'

'I don't know. It was too late.'

'But you must have thought –'

'*I don't know!*' shouted Sonia. 'Don't you understand? I don't know. I can't say anything else. I don't know. I'm sorry. I did it for you and I don't know why I didn't say.'

'Look at us,' I said. 'Three fools.' I wiped my eyes with my sleeve. 'And three friends,' I added. 'What we've all been through for each other.'

'We did it for you,' said Neal.

Suddenly I felt cold and sober and very weary. 'We'd better hope that the police go on following their red herrings and never find out what happened.'

'And don't arrest the wrong person,' added Neal.

'If they do that, we're going to tell them, do you hear?' I thought of Sally and Richard and clenched my fists at my powerlessness. 'No one else is going to suffer for this. That's a pledge we all have to make. Can I ask you something, Sonia?'

'Of course.'

'Did he die at once?'

She hesitated. 'I think so.'

'Doesn't it haunt you?'

She stared at me. I knew she'd been trying to help me and I knew it had been a mistake, but for a moment, I felt hot with hatred for her. She had killed Hayden. She had been with him when he died. My beautiful Hayden, my love. 'What do you think, Bonnie?' she replied at last.

'All right.'

'We'd better get home,' said Neal.

'Does Amos know?'

'Of course not.'

'You haven't told him?'

'No.'

'Can you manage that?'

Sonia looked at the oily surface of the canal. 'You could,' she said. 'And I can too. Our secret.'

When I got home I was trembling with agitation and distress. I walked from tiny room to room, knocking against boxes full of tattered books, cracked china, clothes I would probably never wear again. The flat resembled my brain – chaotically disordered and full of things that were unwanted or in the wrong place. Falling apart, unloved, abandoned. I lay on the floor and stared up at the ceiling, thinking, trying to think, trying not to think, trying not to see Hayden's smile as he taunted Sonia, his face as he reached out to take hold of her, his expression as the vase hit his head and he fell, his eyes as the life went out of them. How stupid, how sad and absurd and meaningless, to die like that, for nothing at all.

Before

I lay on the floor of my flat and stared up at the ceiling. Hayden lay beside me, on his stomach, his arm over my belly. The carpet was rough and stung my back; my face stung too, from his stubble. I turned my head and looked at him. His legs were bent; one knee pressed against my thigh. One of his toes was slightly bruised. There was a mole on his lower back and a long, faint scar running across his left shoulder-blade. His hair fell in a scruffy wing across his face and his eyes were closed.

'I can tell you're looking at me,' he mumbled, without opening his eyes.

'How?'

'I can feel you.'

'I left my bag in your flat and my stuff.'

'We'll go and get them together. Later.'

'Why did you come back?'

'I wanted to see you. I had to. I couldn't wait. I was sitting in my friend's house and all of a sudden I had to go and find you. I thought you might not be here. You might have gone.'

'Where would I go? You're the one who's leaving.'

'Am I?'

'That's what you said a few hours ago, remember? On Blackfriars Bridge.'

'So I did.'

'I feel strange,' I said, rolling onto my side and curling up slightly, watching him.

'Maybe I won't.'

'Won't leave?'

'Maybe not. I don't know. You've got me all confused.'

'What are you saying?'

His eyes half opened. He put out a hand and ran it through my hair. 'You're a funny creature, Bonnie. Spiky but soft.'

'Hayden.'

'You're hard to leave. Maybe that's why I thought I had to go – because for once I don't want to.'

'Then stay awhile.'

'Perhaps.'

'Is it always you?'

'Me what?'

'You who does the leaving.'

'Probably. I warned you. I told you not to get involved.'

'You've never wanted to stay with someone before?'

He muttered something I couldn't hear.

'Why haven't you?'

'Don't.'

'What?'

'Don't pry.'

I sat up and wrapped my arms around my knees, feeling suddenly chilly. 'Is that how you see it? Any kind of closeness, and you see it as prying, intruding? What makes you think I want you to stay, anyway? Nothing ever advances.'

'What do you want to advance?' He made it sound ludicrous.

'You cry and then won't say why, you tell me things about yourself but the next time we meet it's as if it never happened. You want to go, want to stay – it's all just a whim, nothing to do with me, and it's as if I have no say in it at all.' I stood up. 'I'm going to make us some coffee and then I'm going out.'

He lay on the floor and watched as I pulled on the dressing-gown I'd been wearing when I opened the door to him earlier, knotting the belt firmly.

'Very milky for me,' he said.

'Right.'

I boiled the kettle and scooped coffee powder into the pot, banging mugs loudly on the surface to make some kind of point, and turned as he came into the kitchen, wearing only his jeans.

'Don't be angry, Bonnie.'

'Why not? I like being angry.'

'Don't be angry with me.'

'Of course I'm bloody angry with you.'

'Shall I heat some milk?'

'You're like a small boy. You've never grown up.'

'Is that what you think?' Suddenly he had a cold, sickening smile on his face. I should have stopped there, left the flat at once.

'Yes, I do. Never have children yourself, Hayden, and if you do, God help the poor sods. A child shouldn't have children.'

It was very slow. I had time to think about everything that was happening to me. He swung round, knocking the milk bottle over so that white liquid streamed onto the floor and a puddle formed, spreading between my bare toes. Then he lifted up both his fists. His mouth was drawn back in a horrible grimace, like a horse having a bit forced between its teeth. His arms were strong. I could see his biceps clench. I thought how much taller and stronger he was than me and I imagined the pain I would feel when his fists landed on me. His eyes were wild, the pupils dilated, and I remembered, so vividly it felt as though it was actually happening again, the night my father had punched my mother so hard in the jaw that he had knocked out two of her teeth.

That episode of long ago and this one taking place now seemed to merge, so that for a few seconds I almost believed I was a small child, trying to stand in the way of the thickset man with his fists raised and his face in an ugly snarl, crying out for him to stop. And, sure enough, I heard my voice saying, 'No! Stop!'

Hayden's fist was coming towards me. I thought: I must leave this man; I must never see him again. He's dangerous for me. There were tears in his eyes: how strange that he was already suffering for what he was about to do. Even as I tried to duck away, putting my hands up in front of my face, I thought: He's such an unhappy man. I have never met anyone so unhappy. More terrifying to me than anything he was about to do was the sudden fear that I loved him. That I was in love with him. Oh, head over heels.

One fist caught me violently on the ribs and the other on the side of my head. I staggered back, crashing into the surface, spinning a coffee cup to the floor where I heard it break. My knees were folding under me and I tried to stop myself falling, but then he gripped me around the throat and was shaking me. I couldn't breathe or cry out. My side hurt. The pain throbbed from my throat into my eyes and now I could see colours, dark flowers of blue and green and red opening their petals. My head banged on the floor. Milk in my hair and shards of china on my left calf. I could feel the trickle of blood. I could see Hayden's face looming over me, mouth half open in a cry of grief, as if he was about to kiss me, bite me. Passion is close to hate. I thought: Am I going to die?

Then his hand loosened its grip and his face softened, creased, broke up. The colours faded back to normal day, and I could breathe again, although each breath was sharply painful. I lay quite still. Hayden was bent over the sink, as if he was about to be sick. He was breathing very heavily and occasional groans broke from him.

'That's it, then.' My voice was a croak. It hurt to speak, hurt to swallow. I put a hand up and touched my neck, which was puffy and sore. There was a bump on my head and the blood on my leg tickled, like a fly crawling along my skin. Even picturing myself scrambling to my feet was too much of an effort. I closed my eyes and felt for the edges of my dressing-gown, making sure I was decently covered. I didn't want Hayden to see my nakedness.

'I told you I was no good. I told you.'

'Go now.'

'I want to be with you. You're all I want. Now I know.'

'Go.'

'I can't leave you like this.'

'If you don't leave this minute, I'm going to call the police.'

I heard him walk out of the kitchen, and a few minutes later, I heard him leave the flat. The door clicked shut. Now he would be walking down the road. I knew the expression on his face.

I opened my eyes. I turned my head, first one way and then the other. I flexed my legs. Nothing was wrong with me, except that my ribs ached and my throat ached and I felt a bit sick. Soon I would get up and have a shower, bathe my face. In a minute. Not just yet.

I woke, and for a moment I couldn't think where I was. The floor was hard under my body and my back was sore. How long had I slept? I sat up cautiously, feeling pain knife through my ribs. Milk and pieces of china spread all over the floor. I manoeuvred myself onto all fours and gradually levered myself into a standing position. Everything felt slightly askew. I went into the bathroom and turned on the taps, then looked at myself in the mirror above the basin. My face seemed much smaller than usual, as if it had somehow shrunk. My hair stood up in spikes. And on my neck there was a large brown-blue bruise that seemed to deepen as I stared at it. I touched it with my fingers, feeling the soft puffiness of the skin. Everyone would know.

I climbed into the bath and lay there for more than an hour, turning on the hot tap every few minutes. The tips of my fingers crinkled and steam filled the room. I only got out when the water turned tepid, and then I simply went and lay on my duvet, my arm across my eyes to keep out the light.

It was afternoon when I finally got into a pair of shorts and a T-shirt. I wrapped a cotton scarf around my neck – I wasn't going out but I didn't want to see myself in the mirror. On my way to the kitchen to make myself something to eat, I saw that a folded piece of lined paper had been pushed through the door. I picked it up and opened it. 'Bonnie,' it read, in hasty, lopsided handwriting, scrawled with a blunt pencil. 'There are some things I would like to tell you that I should have told you before. Please let me see you. Please. Sorry. So very very sorry. H'

I crumpled it into a ball and threw it into the bin. Then I retrieved it and straightened it out, staring at the words until they blurred.

The phone rang, startling me. I pushed Hayden's note into my pocket as if somebody was watching me. It was Guy.

'Are you all right? You sound as if you've got a cold. Are you losing your voice?'

'A bit.'

'I was just calling to say I'll be a little late for the rehearsal.'

'Rehearsal.'

'I've been caught up. I'll be there as soon as I can.'

'I don't think I can make it today, Guy.'

'It's at your flat. In half an hour.'

Of course it was. I looked around me in despair. It was

as if burglars had broken in and turned a building site into a bombsite, with me at the centre of the explosion.

'It's all a bit of a mess,' I rasped.

'No one minds that,' Guy said heartily. He lived in an immaculate house, everything in its proper place. I think he liked other people's chaos. I stooped down and picked up a piece of the broken cup. 'But you'll be there to let me in.'

'I'll be there.'

As soon as I put the phone down I started clearing up the kitchen, mopping the milk with a cloth I kept having to squeeze into the sink, and gathering up all the broken china. It's amazing how far china travels when it's smashed. My feet were bleeding now as well as my leg. But then I suddenly grasped that I was concentrating on the wrong task: the mess of the flat didn't matter, the mess of myself did. No one could see me like this.

I hurried into the bedroom. The shorts would do, but not the T-shirt. I had to find something high-necked. I pulled clothes out of boxes until I found a Victorian blouse that I must have got in a vintage shop years ago. I couldn't remember ever having worn it before – it wasn't really my style. I pulled it on carefully, wincing as it brushed against my neck, then stood back from the mirror to examine myself. I looked like a girl who'd been through her mother's dressing-up box. More to the point, the bruise showed above the collar. It seemed to be spreading higher and higher.

I went into the bathroom and opened my sponge bag, where I kept what small amount of makeup I owned. There was some old foundation cream in there and I unbuttoned the shirt to smear it liberally over my neck and up to my jaw. It was darker than I'd expected. I must have bought it when I was tanned, except I was never tanned. I had a milky skin against which the bruise flared vividly. I rubbed in more. Now the bruise was almost obscured, but my neck was a browny orange that ended abruptly at my jaw line, like a tidemark. Above it, my face was whiter than ever. I rubbed some of the cream into it and smoothed it in, making sure it went into my hairline. Then I looked at myself carefully.

My neck and face were almost the same colour, which was an odd kind of bronze. I rummaged in the sponge bag, but there was nothing very useful in it, so I went back into the bedroom and found the box of toiletries I'd been going to throw away. There was a stick of very pale makeup that I vaguely recalled had been used in a school production of *Grease*. I used that to whiten the bronze. Now my face looked thickly tan-coloured and slightly streaky; if I ran a nail along my skin, a thick line of paler skin emerged. I completed the effect by covering the whole lot in *Grease* face powder. I put on some mascara, because my eyes seemed small and sunken in my matt, pasted face.

To complete the effect, I dabbed gloss on my lips and sprayed some perfume an aunt had once given me down my cleavage, onto my bloody feet and into the air of the room. There. I buttoned up the shirt and wrapped the scarf round my neck.

I had about five minutes. I put a plaster on my leg, laid newspaper over the kitchen floor to soak up the last of the milk and protect people from the broken china, swept anything that was on the table into an empty box that I pushed against the wall, then took Hayden's note and put it in my underwear drawer. I was picking up damp towels when the doorbell rang. It was Joakim.

'Hello, Bonnie,' he said, and blushed. 'You look very pretty today. Have you caught the sun?'

After

'Hello, Bonnie.'

When Joakim appeared at my door, carrying a guitar case, smiling, it felt as though he had stumbled on me in a car crash, surrounded by crushed metal, broken glass, covered with blood, and he simply hadn't noticed. I let him in and wondered if I had forgotten about a rehearsal. Then I thought he might have come to tell me in person that he had to drop out of the performance. What a relief that would have been. Then we really couldn't have continued.

But he wasn't pulling out. He told me he thought we needed another song, something people could dance to, but he wanted to try it out on me before he sprang it on the others. He had the sheet music with him and I had barely closed my door before he had got the guitar out and was strumming the chords for me. At any other time I would have been caught up with his enthusiasm. I got out my own guitar and played along with him but it was like watching someone on television being enthusiastic. I hardly felt I was in the same room.

What I was trying to tell myself was: It's over. Or, at least, it's as over as it ever will be. Finally it made sense. Neal had put himself at terrible risk for me and so, in her own peculiar way, had Sonia. In fact, she had done it a second time, when she had come back to the scene to save me from my hopeless self. There was more. The question I hadn't been able to get out of my head ever since I'd realized the truth was whether I should be grateful to Sonia on a whole different level. Had she done what I would have done if I'd had the courage? Had she done what I secretly wanted to do, even if I was unable to admit it to myself? After all, I had let Hayden hit me and apologize and hit me again and still I hadn't left him. What would I have said if I had been told about someone who had behaved as I had? I would probably have described her as weak and pathetic. If it was a friend of mine, would I have had the guts to do something about it, to help her, the way Sonia had helped me?

With the other part of my brain, the automatic part, I played along with Joakim, nodding with him, seeing how the music would work for the group. But I couldn't give myself up to it. There were the old reasons for that. The image of Hayden dead on the floor, which never left me. The process of wrapping him up and lugging him out, like something to dump on a skip. The thought of him there in the dark, cold, deep water. I would never lose that, I knew. But even so, it was over, and I finally knew the truth, and yet it was still nagging at me, spluttering and fizzing inside my head.

It was so easy to picture. When Sonia had told him to lay off me, Hayden would have been startled at first but then he would have become angry, and the guilt he felt, the recognition that he was in the wrong, would have made him angrier still. He would have started shouting, become incoherent and, as words failed him, he would have lashed out. He'd show Sonia – he'd show the self-righteous bitch what drove men to be violent. Except Sonia wasn't like the others. She wouldn't put up with it. She would fight back. Hayden was a coward. His violence was directed against people who wouldn't fight back. There was no doubt in my mind that, in the way Hayden lived his life, he had invited something like this. It was just a question of when he ran into someone like Sonia, rather than someone like me. Hayden and Sonia, an immovable object and an irresistible force.

Joakim was smiling as he watched me play and realized I was accepting his idea, that we really would be playing this funny old bluegrass tune he had downloaded from somewhere or other. I had trouble with one fiddly chord change and he laughed.

'Are you still deferring your university entry?' I asked.

'You mean, now Hayden's dead and no longer an evil influence on me?'

'Something like that.'

'Yeah, I'm still deferring. All my life I've done things just because my parents thought it was the right thing to do. This isn't anything to do with Hayden any longer, it's about what's right for me.'

'Good.'

'I'll never forget him, you know.'

'That's good too,' I said. 'He rated you.'

'Really?'

'Really.'

Joakim hurriedly got his stuff together. I think he had tears in his eyes.

'So you think it'll work?' he asked, snapping his guitar case shut.

'It sounds good,' I said. 'As long as we can write an easy enough part for Amos, we should be all right.'

'It'll be weird doing it without Hayden,' he said. 'You're probably sick of me going on about that.'

'I'm not going to say it's what Hayden would have wanted, because that's the sort of rubbish people say about the dead, but it's probably the right thing to do. We signed up for this. We need to do it.'

The moment I shut the door I felt as if a little explosion had gone off in my head, as if a gremlin had got into my stupid, non-functioning brain and done my thinking for me while my mind had been dealing with Joakim. Sonia and Hayden. Hayden and Sonia. It wasn't any kind of answer or even an idea. But there was something there – something that had been worrying away at me. I tried to think hard. I tried to force myself to remember. What would an intelligent person do in my situation?

First, where was the beer mat? If you're looking for a beer mat, the best place to start is in a pile of beer mats and there it was, the beer mat on which Nat had written his number. I dialled it.

Nat didn't seem especially pleased to hear from me. 'It's been a bloody nightmare,' he said. 'There's this detective, this woman, she doesn't like me. They've talked to me about three times. The same questions. I've only got the same answers.'

'You've got nothing to worry about,' I said. 'You're innocent.'

'How do you know I'm innocent?'

That was a good question. Too good a question.

'You just wouldn't do something like that,' I said feebly. 'You're not the type.'

'That's not much help.'

'Actually, I need help from you,' I said.

'From me?'

'I went to a party with Hayden, just a few days before he died. You were there. Do you remember?'

'Kind of. I wasn't completely at my best.'

'There were old friends of Hayden's. One was called Miriam. Dark hair, big eyes – she was smoking.'

'And?'

'Do you know who she is?'

'No.'

'You were at the party.'

'So were about two hundred other people.'

'Could you find out for me?'

There was a sort of groan. 'Sure, I'll ask around. If I hear anything, I'll call you some time.'

'No,' I said. 'This is really, really, really urgent. What I'd like you to do is phone anyone you know and ask them who this Miriam was. Then you can ring me, or they can ring me. I'll give you my number. Do it now. I'm going to sit by my phone and I want you to ring me back within ten minutes. If you don't, I'll keep annoying you.'

The groan resumed. 'Yeah, yeah, OK, I'll do my best.'

I didn't just sit by the phone. I changed into something smarter, some striped trousers and a pale blue shirt. Serious-looking. I found a jacket and put my purse, a pair of sunglasses and my keys into the pockets. Just as I was wondering if I needed anything else, the phone rang. The voice asked for me by name.

'Who's this?'

'My name's Ross. You don't know me. Nat said you want to find out about Miriam Sylvester.'

'Yes, yes, that's great. Thanks for calling.'

'So what do you want to know about her?'

'I don't want to know anything. I just want to talk to her.'

'All right. You got a pen?'

It was that easy.

On the train I stared out of the window the whole way to Sheffield. I'd handed over a fistful of notes for my return ticket. I wondered if I was being stupid. Should I have done this over the phone? No. It had to be face to face if it was going to be done at all. The last time I'd been on a train out of London it had been with Hayden, an impulsive journey to the seaside just to show we could do it if we wanted to, go anywhere without anyone knowing. Every field, every piece of green had been like a secret message of escape, a sign that we didn't need London, that we were not trapped by our duties and responsibilities. This time it felt different. The countryside was just something to be got through. It was probably at its best in the late-summer sun, but what was the point of it? What did people do there? I saw people playing cricket, tractors, church after empty church. I started to nod off and worried that I might sleep through Sheffield and wake up somewhere far to the north. So I drank a cup of horrible black coffee to keep me conscious.

I got into a taxi at the station and read out the address that the man I had never met had given me over the phone. 'Is it far?' I said.

'No,' said the driver.

As he drove, I looked out of the window. Another place I'd never been before, and because of that the shops and the people seemed just a little bit foreign, a little bit interesting. I knew that if I stayed a day or two the novelty would go and it would look the same as everywhere else. But I wasn't going to stay a day or two. He turned off a shopping street into an area of old red-brick terraced houses on a hill. Some had been gentrified and others hadn't. Number thirty-two, the address I'd been given, was definitely one of the houses that had been. I got out and, once again, paid more than I'd expected. I knocked at the door. God, wouldn't it be stupid if nobody was at home? But the door opened.

'Miriam Sylvester?' I said, although I had immediately recognized the woman I'd talked to on the stairs at the party. Now she was just wearing jeans and a red T-shirt and her face, then exotic with kohl and lipstick, was bare of makeup.

'Yes,' she said, slightly puzzled. 'You must be the woman who rang earlier?'

'Yes, I talked to your, erm, er . . .'

'Partner, Frank, yes,' she said.

Her partner. And I remembered her flirting with Hayden on the stairs. Because that was what women seemed to do around Hayden, like bees around honey.

'We met at a party,' I said. She looked blank. 'You'd heard about me. As far as I remember, you'd heard something about me and my banjo.' She looked less blank but a little more puzzled. This wasn't starting well. Was it possible I'd wasted my time? 'I was there with Hayden Booth.'

'Hayden,' she said, and her expression changed to one of intense engagement. 'Oh, God, Hayden. I read about it in the papers. It's the most terrible thing. At first I couldn't believe it was the same person. Yes, come in, please.'

I'd worried that she might be so freaked out by the thought that I'd come all the way from London to see her that she might not want to talk to me. But it quickly turned out that that was exactly the advantage. I was her first-hand source for the whole Hayden story. She invited me in, sat me down in her kitchen, offered me lunch and, when I turned that down, made me mug after mug of coffee. Being questioned in detail by a virtual stranger about Hayden's death and the police investigation was pretty much the thing in the world that I least wanted, but I thought it prudent to go along with it. So I sat there for more than an hour and answered her questions and listened to her talking about how shocked she was. I calculated that the more I responded to her the more she would have to respond to me.

And so, after she had asked every possible question she could think of, after she had talked about the death of someone else she knew, after she had cried a bit and I had comforted her, after all that, I took a deep breath and asked her the question I had travelled right across England to ask.

Before

Amos and Sonia arrived shortly after Joakim. Amos was wearing a pair of flowery shorts and a clashing T-shirt and looked slightly ridiculous and very happy – happy in a way

I remembered from the past. He kissed me on both cheeks, heartily, and I thought: He's completely over me at last.

He was holding Sonia's hand when I opened the door to them and he didn't let go of it as they entered the flat, so that they had to wind their way through the mess into the kitchen. Sonia was wearing a sleeveless white shift that made her dark hair and eyes seem even darker; her skin was creamy and clean. She glowed with a health that made me feel like a creature who'd been found under a stone, squirming in the sudden unwelcome light. She kissed me too, then held me by my shoulders and said in a quiet voice, so Joakim and Amos wouldn't overhear, 'Are you OK?'

'Me?' I feigned surprise. 'Why do you ask?'

'You look a bit ...'

'What?'

'Tired, maybe.' She narrowed her eyes. 'You haven't been under a sun-lamp, have you?'

'Am I the kind of person who would go under a sun-lamp?' I gave a high, hysterical squeal that was meant to be a laugh. 'Coffee? Joakim, Amos? I'm making a pot. Or would you prefer something cool?'

'Your flat's amazing,' said Joakim, enthusiastically, staring round it.

I saw it for a moment through his eyes. It wasn't just a mess, it was almost surreal. 'You mean a complete tip.'

'My dad would never let me live like this.'

'Quite right too.'

'It's like a statement.'

'Bonnie taking her stand against the bourgeois world,' said Amos. He winked at me. I tried to smile but my face felt stiff and swollen.

Everything was happening at a remove; everything was unreal. Not long ago Hayden had been leaning over me, hand around my throat and an ugly snarl transforming his face into a stranger's, and now here I was, making conversation with people who were behaving as if they knew me.

I drank a cup of coffee, strong and bitter and without milk, then another. My hands were shaking. I wanted to be alone in a cool, shaded wood in autumn. I felt dirty and ashamed.

Neal and Guy arrived together. Guy was wearing a suit and when he took off the grey jacket his shirt was dark with sweat at the armpits and down the back. He rolled up his sleeves and mopped his forehead with a white handkerchief. I opened the windows in every room but it still felt claustrophobically hot.

'There's not really room for us all here,' I said.

'And Hayden hasn't arrived yet.'

'No,' I said. My voice was like dry leaves scraping against each other, and I could feel a flush prickling across my face, under the camouflage. 'Perhaps we should start without him. You know what he's like.' Did that sound natural? Didn't anyone see? Couldn't anyone tell?

'Who the hell does he think he is?' grumbled Amos, and Joakim gave him a dirty look.

'Let's assume he won't be here,' said Neal, in a quiet voice that sent a small shudder of dread through me. He was looking at me appraisingly. I felt his eyes on my face, my throat, and all at once I was sure he could see right through me – through the makeup and the scarf and the stupid, stupid frilly shirt, through all my futile pretence and all my transparent lies.

'Shall we start by clearing the living room a bit?' said Sonia. 'We can pull everything back against the walls.'

Everyone started picking up chairs, moving boxes. I saw Sonia shifting pieces of china that seemed to have made their way in here from the kitchen. I was starting to feel sick, but if I could just get through the next couple of hours, it would be all right. Guy was talking about some terrible accident there had been in the early hours of the morning on the M6, a whole family killed. Sonia was issuing instructions to everyone and miraculously giving the room a kind of order. Amos kept bumping his shins and cursing. I thought of the note from Hayden, now lying in my underwear drawer. What was it he needed to say to me and why was I even thinking of going round to hear him out? If I went, I could tell him that I never wanted to see or hear from him again and he had to pull out of the group. But if I did, I'd see his face, ravaged with guilt, and he would speak words of passion and torment and I might – No, no, I wouldn't. Of course I wouldn't. Never again. Not ever. I hated him. A man who hit women, a man who left women without a backward glance. I hated him. I did.

'Bonnie?' It was Sonia. She put a hand on the small of my back, a light but comforting touch. 'You look miles away.'

'Sorry. I haven't been much help.'

'Shall I get you something for your throat before we start?'

'My throat?' Unwittingly, I put a hand to my neck, which felt sore to the touch. Was it showing? I imagined the colours staining through the makeup I had plastered over it, my mark of shame.

'Milk and honey to soothe it or something?'

'That's nice of you, but I'm fine. It sounds worse than it is. Anyway, I don't think I've got honey and I've just used up the last of the milk.'

'Shall we start, then?'

We began with 'Leaving On Your Mind'. My fingers knew what to do even though my mind was a jumble of thoughts and feelings. Sonia sang and sounded so powerfully sad that everyone in the room seemed taken over by the emotion, even Amos in his bright summer clothes. I saw him gazing at Sonia, her arms at her sides, palms facing forward, and head tipped slightly back.

'We can't,' I said, as the last note faded. 'We can't play this at a wedding. It's a lament.'

'We've been through this before,' said Amos.

'But Sonia's never sung it like that. It's going to make everyone cry.'

'That's good,' said Joakim.

'What? Everyone crying at a wedding?'

'People always cry at weddings, in films anyway. It's not a proper success unless everyone's bawling their eyes out.'

'They don't cry because they're thinking of it coming to an end,' said Guy. 'They cry because they're happy.'

'No, they cry because they're filled with strong emotion,' Neal said. 'You can't call it happiness or sadness.'

'It's too late,' said Sonia, with her usual practicality. 'It's virtually the only one we all know properly.'

'You're probably right,' I said. 'I don't know what Danielle's going to think, though.'

'Who cares what she thinks?' said Joakim, who had never

met Danielle, of course, but seemed to have taken a dislike to her on principle.

'It is her wedding,' said Sonia, mildly. 'What's next?'

At that moment, the phone rang. Everyone looked at me.

'Are you going to get it?' Guy said eventually.

'They'll give up in a moment.'

It stopped and for a brief moment there was silence. Then my mobile, which was on the window-sill, started ringing instead. I went over and turned it off without looking to see who was calling, because I knew. 'You decide what to play,' I said to Sonia. 'I'll be back in a moment.'

I went into the bathroom and closed the door, locking it. Then I turned to face myself in the mirror. If you looked carefully, it was possible to make out the bruise above the shirt. The makeup had rubbed off slightly, so that the collar had a grubby, orange-brown stain on it. But, more than anything, I just looked odd. If I had met myself walking down the street I would have thought there was something wrong with me, askew. I blinked and a single small tear ran down my cheek, leaving a snail trail behind it of half-cleared skin. With a forefinger, I gently rubbed my face back to a uniform colour. I wanted to splash myself with ice-cold water, but I couldn't do that, so I just stood there and gazed at myself hopelessly.

I went into the kitchen and poured myself a glass of water. I could hear them all talking next door and knew I should join them, but I couldn't bring myself to go back in and pretend to be me. Neal came looking for me. He walked over to where I stood, took the glass out of my hand and put it on the table.

'This can't go on.'

'I don't understand.'

We both spoke in hushed voices, scared of being over-heard.

He lifted off the scarf. 'This.'

'Don't touch me.'

'Don't worry, I won't. I'll leave that to your precious Hayden.'

'I don't want to talk about it.'

'I don't get it, Bonnie. You're a strong woman. Tough, even. Until this happened, I'd have said you wouldn't let anyone mess with you.'

'I didn't let him.'

'Look at yourself.'

'Don't look at me, please don't.'

'You look dreadful. Your neck is one great bruise and you can hardly move your face.'

'Only because it's caked in makeup.'

'Don't make a joke of it. You're a victim of abuse.'

'That's not true.'

'What are you going to do?'

'Why is that your business?'

'I'm not going to stand by and let him do this to you.'

'He'll never do it again.'

'So you're going to leave him?'

I turned away. 'This is for me to sort out, not you.'

'I'm not doing it out of concern or kindness,' he hissed. He leaned towards me and I shrank back. 'And I'm not going to stand by. I'm going to go and tell him to lay off. You hear?'

'Hear what?' Amos stood in the doorway. He looked amused.

'Nothing,' I said.

'Nothing at all,' Neal echoed.

'Well, whatever this great nothing is, take a break from it and come and rehearse. Everyone's waiting for you. You look as though you've caught the sun, Bonnie,' he added, as I passed him. 'You should be careful, with a pale skin like yours.'

After

When I got off the train at King's Cross it was late evening and the sky was a glaring purple; the air was heavy. It looked as though the weather was going to break in a great downfall. I didn't go straight home. I needed to think and clear my head, so I walked past all the new flats and offices of curved glass, the swathes of land that were being cleared for redevelopment, and down to the canal. London seemed to drop away. The water was a dark, murky brown, the colour of stewed tea, and ripples blew across it. I felt the first drops of rain on my face and shivered, suddenly cold in my thin clothes. I was tired, jittery with too much caffeine and hollow from lack of food. But my mind was agitated.

I walked along the towpath. There was a barge with tubs of flowers on the deck and, in the cabin, I could see a middle-aged woman in spectacles reading a newspaper. A runner jogged past me, puffing. Bits of rubbish bobbed in the water. A gust of wind shook more raindrops onto my arms and cheeks and the sky darkened. A storm was coming.

Before

I made it through the rehearsal, nodding when people spoke, twisting my mouth into an approximation of a smile, uttering words that no one else seemed to find strange. And then at last people were leaving, pushing guitars into cases, gathering up sheet music, talking about the next time. Sonia was the first to go, Neal the last. I steered him out of the door, ignoring his baleful and beseeching glances, and shut it behind him with a sigh of relief. Then I went and stood under my third shower of the day, cold, of course, but that was welcome because I was clammy from head to foot and felt as grimy as if I had stood in the hot stew of traffic all day. I tipped my head back and let the jets of water hit my face, run over my shoulders, stream over my belly. I could hear the phone ringing. I very carefully massaged my neck, rubbing away all the orange paste there. I washed my hair again, then sat on the floor of the shower, shaved my legs and clipped my finger- and toenails.

I felt better, and when I stood in front of the mirror, I didn't look too bad. The bruise was swollen and it was visible, but it wasn't the dramatic blue-black flowering I had been expecting, rather a dirty yellow. My ribs hurt sharply but I could carry myself straight. I looked depleted but not worryingly so. I pulled on an oversized shirt, made myself a cup of herbal tea and put on a Joni Mitchell CD. I sat on the sofa, still pushed to the edge of the room, and closed my eyes. The phone rang once more but I ignored it. I let the music fill my head.

All my life I had prided myself on being strong and independent. Tough, that was the word Neal had used today, bitterly, and that was the word Hayden had used, admiringly, as if it aroused him, in the past. I had grown up in a household in which my father tyrannized my mother and I had made a pledge to myself that it would never happen to me. Sometimes being strong meant being cool; being independent meant holding myself back from involvement. Amos used to complain that there was always something withholding about me, and perhaps he was right; perhaps that was why in the end we had gone our separate ways. I didn't know; it didn't matter any more because that was over and Amos loved Sonia, and our relationship faded even as I thought about it. I could barely remember what we had been like together, and now when I saw Amos I felt faintly surprised that once we had felt passionate desire for each other. How was that possible?

But Hayden had outmanoeuvred me. Where I was independent, he was detached; where I was anxious about intimacy, he was phobic. I wanted to be free, but he wanted to be freer – and for him freedom meant losing all anchors and rudders and being carried off by whatever wind took him. An ill wind had blown him into my life and an ill wind was blowing him out of it. And I saw, lying on my sofa and listening to Joni Mitchell singing about love and disillusion, that with him I had taken on the unfamiliar role of the more committed and more loving one, the one who got hurt, the one who was left.

He had hit me, twice. What I wanted, what I was waiting to feel, was anger, the welcome fire of it, to burn away every other emotion, leaving no room for pity or for regret. I remembered his face twisted in a vicious snarl and his fists falling towards me, and then I remembered his face wiped clean by love for me.

Joni Mitchell came to an end. I stood up and went into the bedroom, retrieved his note to read again, although I knew what it said: 'There are some things I would like to tell you that I should have told you before. Please let me see you. Please. Sorry. So very very sorry. H'. I stared at it, as if there was a secret code to be deciphered. The sun was low in the sky and its light rippled like water on the ceiling. The day was drifting into evening. The phone rang once more, and after it had stopped, the flat was full of ominous silence.

At last I stood up. I put on clothes – pale blue jeans torn at the knees, a T-shirt, a thin grey jacket. I left the house, feeling the warm evening air on my face, high summer in its breath.

Lightning cracked the sky ahead of me and I counted to eleven before the thunder rumbled. Eleven miles – did that mean eleven miles out or eleven miles up? As I left the canal basin and walked up Camden Road, fat drops were falling, bursting on the pavement like small bombs, and people were running for shelter. I didn't bother trying to keep dry. I walked steadily up the road, feeling the rain splash on my head. Soon the separate drops seemed to have merged and the water was coming down like a sheet. I might as well have jumped into a river. Or a reservoir, I thought, and shivered violently, remembering again what I knew I would never forget. My shoes squelched and my hair dripped. My heart pounded with rage.

I didn't have any battery left on my mobile, so I went back to the flat, peeled off my wet clothes, towelled myself dry, pulled on jeans and a shirt. Then I rang from the landline.

'I need to see you. Yes, now. Are you at home? Alone? Good. Stay there. I'm coming round now.'

Sonia opened the door before I even had time to ring the bell. Her hair was pulled tightly back into a ponytail and there were dark shadows under her eyes, a stretched quality to her skin. She stepped aside and I entered. I didn't usually meet Sonia at her flat; instead she came to mine or we saw each other in pubs and cafés and other people's houses. And nowadays, of course, she seemed to spend most of her time at Amos's. It wasn't surprising – she rented a depressing basement flat a few minutes' walk from mine, which felt damp and underground. It had always puzzled me that Sonia, who was so in control of her life, so practical and careful with money, thrifty even in the old-fashioned sense, shouldn't by now have moved up the property ladder.

'Something to drink?'

'No.'

I sat at her kitchen table and folded my hands tightly together. Sonia sat opposite me.

'Horrible weather. I couldn't bring myself to go out in it. I've been getting ready for the new term. Just a few days left.'

For once I didn't gabble. I didn't even speak. Not yet.

'I don't know what to say, Bonnie. There's nothing I can do to make it better. It was an accident. You know that. Nevertheless, I killed Hayden. And I misled you. I'm sorry. There's nothing else for me to say except I'm very sorry. Sorry for what I did and sorry for your loss.'

I looked at her, waited. I felt the silence grow dense around us. When at last I spoke, it was slowly. I could almost taste each separate word. 'Things have been going round and round in my head,' I said. 'I keep seeing his face, his dead, beautiful face. I remember how it felt to touch him. I guess it's the same for you, the images that won't fade. That's not what I was thinking about this time, though. When I finally knew it wasn't Neal, and he knew it wasn't me – before we knew it was you, though – we all compared crime scenes. There was the one he found and disrupted, and then the disordered one that I found, disordered by him, as I later discovered.'

'Your point being?'

'My point being that the one you left was the one he found. But he found an ordered scene – nothing out of place, just Hayden dead on the floor. He messed it up so that it looked like a struggle or an accident, a robbery gone wrong or something. He probably didn't know exactly what he was trying to do, he just wanted to make it look like something it wasn't.'

'Bonnie,' said Sonia, softly, 'dear Bonnie, you'll go mad, turning it all over and over in your head. Let it go.'

'No. Listen. Nothing was thrown around or broken at that stage. But you said it was. You did, Sonia. I can hear your words in my head. I've been going over and over them. You said you went to tell him to lay off me and it all turned ugly, and he lashed out and things got broken and you picked up the nearest object to hand. That's what you *said*.'

'And that's what happened. He came on to me and I panicked and – well, that's how it all went wrong.'

'Yet everything was in place when Neal arrived a few minutes later. He arrived at an orderly scene – a scene where no struggle had taken place.'

'Perhaps he got it wrong, perhaps I did. For God's sake, Bonnie, I was in a state of shock. A man was dead. Maybe I didn't remember everything clearly.'

'That doesn't sound like you, Sonia.'

'I'm sorry if I didn't behave with total calm and logic. I don't think any of us did.'

'No,' I said. 'You left the flat in good order. You killed him, certainly you did, but not the way you described.'

'I don't know what you're trying to say.'

'That was the other funny thing,' I said. 'Once you realized I'd done it to protect Neal, and Neal had done it to protect me, you knew we'd protect you. Why didn't you tell us? You're a logical person, Sonia. It was the logical thing to do.'

'I wasn't thinking logically,' Sonia said.

'You always think logically,' I said. 'That set me wondering. I tried to work out whether there was any connection between you and Hayden apart from me and that crap about going to see him because he'd knocked me around.'

'Bonnie, how can you say that?'

'And I did. Do you remember that party we all went to after we'd played at that post-exam party?'

She didn't reply.

'Of course you do. You and Amos and me and Neal and Hayden went. There was a woman there who used to know you. She's called Miriam Sylvester.'

'Miriam Sylvester?' Sonia said the name slowly, separating it out into its syllables. She shook her head. 'No,' she said.

'Oh, come, Sonia. Surely you remember. You taught together, after all, in your last job.'

'Oh, her. Yes, I do remember. It was hearing her name out of context that threw me.'

'I went to see her today.'

She got up and started to fill the kettle, speaking with her back to me. 'Why? Was she a friend of Hayden's?'

'Yes. We talked about him. She was upset. Well, women loved Hayden, didn't they, for all his faults? Except you.'

'I wasn't so fond of him,' said Sonia. 'A bully who beat up his girlfriend.'

'You didn't know that, though, did you?'

'Sorry?'

'I don't think you actually knew he hit me until after he'd died. I don't think you realized we were together at all.'

'Of course I knew. I told you. That's why I went round there.'

'You told me you went round there to warn him against ever being violent only after you discovered from me that he'd hit me. When it was a convenient excuse for you to grab onto. You didn't know before. That wasn't why you went round there, was it? Answer me. Tell me what I already know.'

'Answer what? You're not making sense.' Her voice was icy.

'I remembered meeting Miriam Sylvester at the party and I remembered that she didn't seem to like you very much. So I took the train up to Sheffield to ask her about it. She's got nothing against your teaching.'

Sonia put the kettle down without switching it on. She came and sat down. Her eyes looked very dark and her face very white.

'You suddenly had to leave your school and come to London.'

'I left,' she said. 'So?'

'She told me about a boy called Robbie, who died, and the whole school raised money for a charity in his name.'

'Get on with what you're saying, then,' she said, so calm. Her hands were quite steady.

'You stole the charity money.'

'That's not true.'

'Money raised because a thirteen-year-old boy died and the school wanted to do something in his memory. They had sponsored silences and went on three-legged walks and washed cars. And you used it for a down-payment on rather a nice flat.'

'Miriam Sylvester has given you a complete misrepresentation of what happened.'

'No wonder you live in this grotty dump and have no money. You're still paying off your debt, aren't you?'

I had to hand it to her. She was still utterly composed.

'Bonnie,' she said. 'Think about it. What she told you doesn't make sense. There was a dispute about the use of some school funds. It turned ugly. Anyone who actually stole money like that would be arrested and sent to prison. You're making a terrible mistake. You've been under such stress, I know that.'

'Oh, save it, Sonia. You've lied to me enough. Miriam explained all this. They didn't want to bring the police in and drag the school through a tribunal and get all the disastrous publicity. Miriam told me about the admission you signed, about paying the money back, about how you left. Are you still going to brazen it out?'

'I think you should go.'

'You had contempt for someone like Hayden. He wasn't a saint, but he would never have done something like that.'

'You really did have a crush on him, didn't you?'

I could feel my rage and my grief rise, almost blocking my throat, so that it was hard to speak, and when I did my voice sounded unfamiliar – low and hoarse in my ears. 'What if I did? What if I had a crush on him? What if I loved him, wanted him, couldn't keep away from him? What if I feel I'll go mad with missing him? It's not about that, it's not about my feelings and it's not about whether Hayden was a good man or not, whether he behaved badly. No – it's about a life that's been stolen. A life, Sonia. A whole life taken away.'

I stopped. The air throbbed around me. 'Are you going to tell me what happened?' I asked more quietly. 'What Hayden said to you?'

'Nothing happened.'

'OK. I'll tell you, then, as much as I know. It's obvious enough now. Miriam told Hayden about you, and he must have told you. I'm sure it wasn't blackmail. Hayden couldn't be bothered with something like that. But he'd mention it just to take you down a peg or two. Hayden didn't care for hypocrites.'

'That's enough!' At last her voice had a crack in it.

'That was bad enough for you, but you knew it would get worse. He wouldn't be able to resist talking about it. He would probably have told me, wouldn't he, for a start? And then no more deputy-headship, no more moral high ground, no Amos, no way out of this nasty little flat. So what did you do? Maybe you went round to tell him it wasn't true and that he mustn't tell anyone.'

'This is all a fantasy.'

'If you did, he would have laughed. Stuck-up Sonia, trying to cover her tracks. He'd have found it funny. Or perhaps you knew all along you were going to kill him. That's what I think. The more I think about it, the more certain I am that you knew in advance you were going to kill him. He was a threat to you and your precious plans. You came to that rehearsal knowing, didn't you? You were efficient and nice; you cleared up my flat for me; you sang "Leaving On Your Mind" more beautifully than you'd ever sung it before; you did everything impeccably. And all the time you knew what you were going to do. Then you left before anyone else and you went to his flat and you picked up the vase and cracked him over the head with it. Not manslaughter. Murder. Cold-blooded murder. You're a killer.'

Sonia's face was deathly pale, except for red spots on her cheekbones. 'If I were you, I'd stop right now.'

'Or what?'

'Or I'll go to the police and tell them I was your accomplice in taking away Hayden's body.'

'That's fine,' I said, 'absolutely fine by me. I don't care. It would be a relief to my conscience, actually – you know, that strange little voice in the head that torments you when you've done wrong. You tell them what I did and I'll tell them what you did.'

'They wouldn't believe you. It's all conjecture.'

'Try it and see.'

'Even if you're right, Neal and you and I destroyed the evidence.'

I sat back and folded my arms against my chest. I felt hard and desolate. 'You're right,' I said. 'But there's still Miriam Sylvester and the document you signed.'

'So what's the point of all this?'

'You leave the school at once. You leave the teaching profession and never return. And you leave Amos.'

There was a deep silence.

'That's a lot of leavings,' she said at last.

I almost smiled. It was like watching a great, indomitable, unshakeable performer. 'You still don't get it, do you? Have you ever heard of contrition or guilt? You killed someone. You planned it in advance and then you went and did it.

357

The fact that I happened to know him and care about him isn't the point now. You didn't kill him to protect me or out of self-defence or by accident. You planned it and you did it because you didn't want your nasty, ugly little secret to be discovered. You put that above a life. So, no, that's not a lot of leavings, Sonia.'

'Is there anything else you have to say?' She was white-faced and her mouth was thin and fierce, but she remained in control of herself. What would make her crumble?

'Yes. Yes, there is. First of all, if it ever looks like the police are about to charge anyone else, I'll tell them everything, without a blink of hesitation. And, second, I'll be watching you, don't think that I won't. If you don't stick to my conditions, I'll know. I won't let it go.'

'Right. Now, you can make your own way out, I think.'

'You have to say you agree to my conditions before I leave.'

I saw her jaw clench and unclench and her nostrils flare slightly. Then she said, in a stony voice, 'All right. I agree.'

'Right.' I got up from the chair. 'Goodbye, then.'

'Goodbye.' Then she added, 'I only did what you should have done. What you didn't dare to do.'

For a moment, I saw what it would be like to kill someone out of hot, futile rage. I felt the pressure build in me like a gale until it throbbed behind my eyes and filled my throat and clenched my hands into fists. 'You disgust me,' I said. 'Hayden was worth a hundred of you. A thousand.'

I turned away and walked out of Sonia's kitchen. As I closed the door behind me, I heard a violent screaming and then a terrible sound of breaking glass, of objects crashing against surfaces. The screaming went on, like an animal sprung in a trap. I stood there for a few moments, listening to the woman who had once been my dearest friend howling like a creature in agony. Then I walked away.

Before

I took my time, walking up the road to Liza's flat slowly, as if in a dream. People flowed past me and they seemed to belong to a different world, one full of purpose and certainty, of rules to keep and places to get to. The sun had sunk beneath the horizon and in the mysterious half-light it was cool. I shivered in my thin jacket. Summer was disappearing; soon it would be autumn.

How much can a person change? How much can you trust them to change? How much should you be ruled by the head, and how much by the heart? If you want so very, very badly to feel someone's arms around you again, to feel their breath in your hair and hear their voice whispering your name, is it wrong to give in to it?

Each step I took towards Hayden was taking me nearer a decision. For a moment I came to a halt, standing under a knobbled plane tree. To love and be loved, desire and be desired – but to be weak and in someone's power, to be hurt again, betrayed again, left again.

Obviously we musicians didn't get to go to the wedding itself. Thank the Lord. While Danielle and Jed were making their sacred vows in a church in the Strand in front of their nearest and dearest, we were carrying our equipment down into the basement of a hotel in Holborn while other people hauled tables and carried piles of plates and arranged vases of flowers.

We weren't the merriest of bands. A couple of days earlier, late in the evening, I had heard a sound at my door that was barely even a knock. It sounded more as if someone was desperately fumbling and clawing at the door. I'd opened it to find Amos in tears. 'Sonia's left me,' he said.

I led him inside and sat him on the sofa and put a tumbler of whisky into his trembling hands. He gulped at it as if he was desperately thirsty. He spoke in a series of sobs. 'She left me, just like that,' he said.

'I'm sorry,' I said.

'She's moving on,' he said. 'Literally moving on. She's leaving town, leaving her job. She's going to get a job somewhere else. She wouldn't even tell me where she was going.' He rubbed his eyes with his hands. 'Aren't you going to say anything?'

'I don't know what to say,' I said, with rare truthfulness.

'Did you know about this?' he said. 'Did you know she was going to throw everything away, leave everything?'

But it was really a rhetorical question because for an hour

or more Amos talked and cried and talked more. I wanted to tell him to stop. I wanted to say that I wasn't the person he should be saying these things to. I could have asked him why he was so eager to demonstrate to me the strength of his feelings for another woman but, for what it was worth, I think I knew the answer to that. Amos liked to be in control and this had just happened. It hadn't been part of his master plan. I couldn't think of the right question to ask and I didn't care that much. There was nothing Amos could tell me, so in the end it was easier just to sit back and look sympathetic and keep him topped up with whisky and let him talk.

Finally, when he stood up, a bit unsteadily, to go, he said, 'You know what this means, don't you?'

'What?'

'We can't play now.'

I told him very firmly that we had promised to play. I was going through with it and so was he. When the rest of the band were told about Sonia, they reacted more calmly. Guy started to say something sarcastic and bitter but the different events and conflicts had knocked the fight out of him and he muttered something about how he'd do his best and try not to let me down. Joakim barely shrugged. 'I guess why she's done this isn't any of my business,' he said.

'It sort of is,' I said, 'because, without Sonia, you and I are going to have to do most of the singing.'

So the two of us got together and sorted out the vocals in a quick session. Joakim had a wispy, indie-band voice but it would probably appeal to any teenage girls at the wedding. I wasn't sure about my own. I wasn't exactly Bessie Smith, who I wanted to be in all sorts of ways, but I could hold a note and I was used to singing in front of classes to demonstrate how things should go.

When I told Neal, he seemed worried at first and then suspicious. 'Is she losing it?' he said. 'Is she suddenly going to make a confession to clear her conscience?'

'Definitely not,' I said. 'She's not like that.'

Neal looked thoughtful. 'Is there something I should know?' he asked.

'No,' I said, again truthfully. There were things he didn't know, and nothing he should know. But I felt I couldn't leave it at that. 'It was probably inevitable. I don't think we could stay together with something like that hanging over us. It's probably good that she moved – she'll be with new people in a new job.'

'But she left Amos,' said Neal.

'It's probably a lucky escape for both of them,' I said.

'That's a bit harsh.'

'Allow me some bitterness,' I said.

A hotel official directed us to a makeshift stage at the end of the hall. As we set up, I felt we were like people on the morning after a night where we had got terribly drunk and said too much to each other and done things, some of which we couldn't quite remember and others of which we were ashamed. And now, after it all, we were a bit hungover, a bit the worse for wear, and we didn't quite want to catch each other's eye. Oh, and we were nervous about performing in front of a crowd of strangers.

Gradually people began to drift in from the ceremony and look for their places on the tables. I thought they'd be curious about us but they scarcely noticed us. I had a sense of what it was like to be one of the invisible people, those who take your coat or hand you your food or clear up after you. Finally Danielle and Jed came in like a pair of celebrities you don't quite recognize, greeted with whoops and clicks from mobile-phone cameras. They processed around the filling tables, hugging and kissing cheeks. Then Danielle caught sight of us, gave a shriek and, with her huge cream dress billowing around her, ran over to us with the bridegroom in tow.

'Omigod, omigod, omigod,' she said, and enfolded me. 'This is just the most incredible day. I was so nervous. I thought I was going to forget my own name. I can't even remember if I did. I can't remember a single word I said. We're probably not even married. This is Jed. Jed, Bonnie. Bonnie, Jed. Doesn't he look fantastic?'

Jed was tall with a mop of blond hair. He was wearing a grey morning suit with a very flowery waistcoat. He surveyed us with an expression that was slightly disbelieving.

'This is so brilliant of you, Bonnie,' said Danielle, 'after all you've gone through. It's the most awful thing. I can't believe what it must have been like for you. Everyone here can't stop talking about it.' I couldn't bear to say anything so I just nodded. 'When we get back from – well, I'm not meant to say where we're going – we must have a proper talk about it all. I want to have a really good talk.' She stopped and looked at us all. 'Is that what you're wearing?'

We were wearing our alt-country get-up, which was almost exactly what we normally wore: jeans and shirts. I also had on some cowboy boots I'd found at the bottom of one of my packing cases. 'It goes with the music,' I said.

'Brilliant,' she said. 'Is your singer here yet?'

'Sonia can't make it,' I said.

'Omigod,' said Danielle. 'Is anything wrong?'

'She's unavoidably detained,' I said, 'but we'll see what we can do.'

'Good, good,' said Danielle, as if she'd had the first inkling that something might go wrong with her perfect day. 'I've fixed you up with something to eat. If you talk to Sergio, the sweet man in the purple jacket over there, he'll sort you out. We're going to have some speeches after we've eaten and then you can strike up. I'm so looking forward to hearing you and having a bit of a dance.'

Sergio steered us out of the main room and into a sort of store area to one side with cardboard boxes and a picnic table on which there were some pieces of chicken, a bottle of wine and a carton of fruit juice. Joakim and Neal ate heartily while the rest of us sipped our drinks and didn't speak. Guy was drinking orange juice but I stuck to wine. If I was going to sing to this lot, I needed it.

The speeches were perfect. Jed's best friend told stories that fell completely flat about getting drunk and about previous girlfriends. You could hear the wind blowing outside and crickets chirping. Then Danielle's father read out a speech that was too long even though it turned out that a page had gone missing, which rendered quite a lot of what remained meaningless. By the time he toasted the bride and groom, it would have been hard for anything not to be an improvement. Danielle seized the microphone and told the crowd they were in for a huge treat, that one of her oldest friends was a musician and had got a band together especially for the occasion and that they had been practising the entire summer and overcome lots and lots of obstacles and could everyone just put their hands together for Bonnie Graham and her band.

We slunk onto the stage slightly shamefacedly, except Guy. I glimpsed him taking his place behind the drums and had the feeling that, in his imagination, he had become John Bonham going out to beat the skins for Led Zeppelin, *circa* 1972. I just hoped he wouldn't try to sound like John Bonham. I rather wished I was wearing sunglasses, like Roy Orbison, but it was too late for that now. I sat at the keyboard, tapped the microphone and muttered congratulations to Danielle and . . . First there was a tiny pause because I forgot Jed's name and then, when I remembered it but before I said it, there was a howl of feedback from one of the guitars and people in the crowd winced and put hands to their ears. Neal looked at me apologetically. 'A bit of rock-and-roll,' he muttered.

'Sorry about that,' I said to the audience. 'This is for Danielle and Jed.'

And we began 'It Had To Be You'. It was like an out-of-body experience. I watched Danielle and Jed step tentatively out onto the open space, put their arms around each other and start to dance. I was listening to myself. My voice sounded fragile but that was OK. It's a fragile song. Joakim was fine, of course. Guy was all right. Neal wasn't very good. Amos was bloody awful, with wrong notes all over the place. He had a glassy look in his eyes as if he was about to faint. The song came to an end and there was a fair amount of applause.

Joakim stepped forward to the microphone. 'This is a song that is not necessarily appropriate to a wedding,' he said. 'In fact, it's completely inappropriate. But we like it.'

As I sang the first line, basically informing the man that since he clearly wants to walk out, he might as well do it straight away, I saw disbelief pass across the crowd like a Mexican wave. There was a look of deep concern, maybe even of horror, on some faces. Others were grinning. There was nothing to be done. I couldn't give up and try another so I concentrated on singing, and as I did, something completely unexpected happened. I suddenly felt the song in a way I hadn't during all the weeks of rehearsing it. All the pain in the music about partings, about making yourself say goodbye, about recognizing the space that exists between you and someone you were once close to, got me right in my chest. I didn't sing it with a sob in my voice like Patsy Cline does, but I felt myself choking up. I was making a sad song even sadder. When I finished, there was hardly more than a ripple of applause, more a stunned silence, though whether this was because people were moved or appalled or embarrassed I didn't want to think.

I got up and strapped on my banjo, Joakim picked up his fiddle and I instructed the crowd that it was time for people to start dancing. We began playing 'Nashville Blues', the first song we had ever played as a group, and instantly I could feel a whoosh of relief in the room, and there was a rush onto the dance-floor, if only because there was a mass attempt to pretend that the previous five minutes hadn't happened. It's a song that depends on handing the tune between the banjo, the guitar and the fiddle in a sort of friendly competition, and once we saw how people were responding, we extended it, like badminton players keeping a shuttlecock in the air. At one point I looked across at Neal and he grinned at me. Even Amos seemed a bit more lively. For just a moment I had a feeling of what it was meant to be like, of what really good music could do for you, the wounds it could heal, the suggestion it could give of something better. I knew that we weren't playing really good music – or, at least, we weren't playing all that well – but we were doing OK and we were doing it together.

The unity that music gave us was an illusion. I'd lied to Amos. In a different way I'd lied to Neal. Guy felt I'd helped to lead his son astray. What about Joakim? Had I led him astray? And then there were the people who weren't there, the spaces and absences, the faces I would never see again.

But the crowd didn't seem to mind, and when we came to a messy close, there was not just applause but cheers and whistles and whoops. We went into another, even more raucous, instrumental and the dancing became positively tumultuous. Then we played a rare happy Hank Williams song that you can dance to, and we finished with another Patsy Cline song, but a happy one. Except it wasn't the end. When we finished and thanked the audience, Jed leaped up on stage, grabbed the microphone and boisterously asked everyone whether they wanted any more. It turned out that they did. We didn't have any more so we just did 'Nashville Blues' again, but went on for longer, and some of the crowd even started making some strange attempt at a bluegrass dance. When we finished there was a roar of acclamation. We had discovered one of the secrets of life, which is to make people think you're better than you really are.

As I stepped down from the stage, Danielle appeared in front of me and threw her arms around me. Her hair smelled of roses. 'You did a wonderful thing for me,' she said. 'Thank you.'

What would I have given to go back in time and for her not to ask me? Or for her to ask me and for me to say no? Anything. Everything. 'You're welcome,' I said.

I went over to the bar. I was trembling and needed another drink to calm me down. I would have liked vodka or whisky but there was only champagne. It was so stingy and bubbly that it was hard for me to drink it as quickly as I needed to. It took me several gulps to drain the glass.

'That was very good,' said a voice beside me.

I turned to look, and the face was so unexpected and out of context that at first I didn't recognize it. Then I did. It was Joy Wallis. The detective.

'What are you doing here?'

'I wanted to talk to you,' she said, 'and, although it's unorthodox I know, I thought it would be fun to see you at work. And it was.'

'Thank you.'

'What actually is a jambalaya?' she said.

'I'm not sure,' I said. 'I only played the song. It's something you do on the bayou.'

'Is it something you eat?' said Joy. 'Or something you dance to?'

'I thought it was something you go to. Like a party.'

Joy looked around. 'Is this a sort of jambalaya?'

'I'm sorry,' I said. 'What did you want to ask me?'

'Not ask you,' said Joy. 'Tell you. I felt a bit guilty. Maybe we were a bit hard on you.'

'I'm just sorry I couldn't be more help,' I said. 'How's it going?'

'It's not really going. I'm moving on to a different inquiry.'

'I noticed all the media attention had died away. How quickly stories cease to matter. Is it being wound up?'

'Murder inquiries are never wound up,' said Joy. 'Scaled down a bit. I think the boss is starting to think that a drugs deal went wrong somewhere. The car left in the airport, the mysterious woman who drove it there. Your friend knew some unpleasant people. And he was a bit careless with money.'

'That's true,' I said. I was about to say goodbye when I felt a hand on my shoulder and looked round. It was Liza, dressed in a very red, very short dress, with lipstick to match. 'You're back,' I said. 'I didn't know.'

She gave me a hug. 'I was always going to be back,' she said. 'I only just got here in time. I wasn't going to miss seeing you. That was fantastic. I can't believe you got that all together. I heard what happened to your musician. What a terrible, terrible thing.'

'Yes,' I said, willing her to shut up.

'You have to tell me all about it.'

'Another time.'

'Of course.'

'This is my friend Liza,' I said. 'Liza, this is Detective Inspector Wallis.'

Liza gave a theatrical gasp. 'Am I interrupting something important?'

'It's fine.' I turned to Joy. 'Liza was there when Danielle dragooned me into doing this. How was abroad, Liza?'

'Completely mind-blowing,' she said. 'Life-changing. I'm going to invite you round and tell you about it in complete detail. And the flat looks great. The plants are in better shape than they were when I left.'

'Good,' I said.

Liza looked at Joy. 'I'm sorry,' she said. 'You probably have important things to talk about.' She hovered expectantly, but when I didn't contradict her, said, 'Right, I'm going to circulate.' She started to move away, then stopped and turned around. 'Oh, one thing, Bonnie. This is probably stupid, but do you have any idea what happened to my rug?'

Before

On the other side of the road, I saw Neal. He was walking swiftly towards the Underground station, his arms around some kind of bag. His face was strained and wretched and I felt a moment of tenderness and contrition, yet I shrank behind the tree so that he wouldn't see me. I watched him as he dwindled into the distance before setting off again.

I turned down the little dogleg lane and the noise of the cars and lorries dropped away. It was dark and suddenly quiet. I went round the bend, past the small garage that was closed now, only the sign advertising MOTs and bodywork repairs flapping idly in the wind, and at last I was there. A light shone from the living-room window.

I was going to tell him. I really was going to tell him. Wasn't I? Yet my flesh ached for his touch and my heart longed for his smile. Just to see him again, just to stand in his arms one more time and feel his breath on my hair, to hear him whisper my name. My love.

The door was open. I stepped inside.

EXCLUSIVE NICCI FRENCH SHORT STORY!

Last year Nicci French teamed up with Alibi, the only TV channel dedicated to crime, to bring you a competition to write the first line of a short story. We asked you to write the first sentence of a story that would set the scene for a chilling tale.

We received hundreds of entries and it was very hard to pick just one winner. In the end the sentence that inspired Nicci French the most was:

Planning a murder can be very therapeutic.

**Congratulations go to Sandra Gill
for writing the winning line.**

Turn over to read the resulting short story by Nicci French...

www.theperfectalibi.co.uk

Alibi's shows range from hit US crime drama *Castle* and the cutting edge crime teams of *Waking The Dead* to the more traditional investigations of *New Tricks*, *Taggart* and classic sleuths like *Miss Marple*.

Until Death

By Nicci French

Planning a murder can be very therapeutic. Where some people count to ten or write in their diary or go out to the garden shed, Gary Boyle dreamt up strategies for a murder. Obviously, it wasn't just any murder. Or rather, it wasn't just any murder of just *anybody*. It was his wife, Suzanne. It hadn't always been so. In the first years after they were married, he hadn't thought of murder at all. Looking back, he couldn't quite be sure when it had all begun. One possibility was a wedding they had gone to, two or three years into their own marriage. The bride was a friend of Suzanne's. Of course she was. Suzanne was always meeting friends. Lunch with a friend. A drink with a friend. A friend coming round for dinner. Sometimes they would come in pairs. Gary didn't have many friends and even with the few he had, there always seemed to be something wrong with them. His friends were boring, apparently, or talked too much about football or put their feet on the furniture. At this wedding, Gary had gone to the buffet to get them both a drink and as he returned with two glasses of white wine, he saw Suzanne talking to a man called Rob. Rob was the third of the eleven people that Suzanne had told Gary that she'd slept with. Eleven was the official figure, although the real number was probably higher, maybe much higher. Women always round the figure down, men round up, they say. As Gary looked at the pair, he saw that Suzanne was laughing at something Rob had said, with an expression that he had never quite seen before. Suddenly she was a more attractive Suzanne than the one he had married.

He had taken the two drinks and walked outside, feeling slightly foolish. He had quickly drunk one of them, so he could put the glass down and begin on the second. He thought of Suzanne cleaning the windows. Why couldn't they get a window cleaner? But no, Suzanne said it was a waste of money. He thought of her up the ladder, leaning across to get at the corner. People fell off ladders all the time. The problem was that they often died, but they often didn't. He imagined himself in prison and a quadriplegic Suzanne. Or even worse, himself not in prison and at her beck and call. Of course, a quadriplegic Suzanne would be easy to kill, even for him. And by then he really would need to kill her. He could imagine her, shouting down the stairs at him, day and night, year after year after year.

Other people looked back on their marriage through photographs or letters or holiday souvenirs. For Gary it was through his murder plans. The dog, for example. She had insisted on the dog. ('If we can't adopt a child . . .' 'Which you know we can't.' '. . . then at least can I have a dog? I need someone I can talk to and take for walks.') It wasn't just a dog but a dog from a refuge, a dog that had been grievously abused in its early life. When clearing up after it, not just clearing up but scrubbing the carpet with disinfectant, Gary began to think of poison. Arsenic. Wasn't that something you gave in small doses, which killed the victim over an extended period? He liked the idea of the extended period, the gradual decline, the suffering. But did arsenic still exist? Was it something you could buy? He typed 'arsenic poisoning' into his computer and as he did so realized he was a man who had typed 'arsenic poisoning' into his computer. They would find that. Even if he got rid of his computer, it would still be out there. Someone would find it. Maybe they already had. Maybe the police had a program that was activated by people searching the web for murder methods.

There was the time they had gone out to a pub by the river with Maggie, another friend of Suzanne's, and her husband, Geoff, who spent almost the entire time on the phone while Gary just looked out at the river. The River Thames was very fast flowing, almost impossible to swim in, he had heard. Someone who was pushed into the Thames might not survive. Suzanne would, though. Gary had been quite a good swimmer as a teenager but Suzanne was better. She would sweep past him with a front crawl that barely made a splash. To drown Suzanne in the Thames, you would have to hit her over the head so hard that the shock of the water wouldn't bring her round. And if you hit her that hard, why bother with the river? Except perhaps to sweep her out to sea.

Gary read an article in the newspaper. A man had murdered his wife just six months after he had married her. He had planned it, hidden her body, faked text messages to her phone. When he was caught, he had lied at every stage, pretending the death had been caused by accident during a sex game. During the trial he had denied everything. The jury had convicted him unanimously. The judge sentenced him to life imprisonment and told him he must serve at least seventeen years in prison. Seventeen years. That wasn't that long. If Gary had murdered Suzanne six months after marrying her, he would be out in six years time. He would be forty-two. His whole life in front of him. And if you just picked up a frying pan in the kitchen and beat her to death, you could claim you acted on impulse. She was nagging me and I just snapped. Five years, and if you got the right judge or the right number of men on the jury, maybe no time at all.

He knew he'd never be able to do it, though. She would see him coming. And if she didn't, he wouldn't be able to lie convincingly about it afterwards. He just wasn't good at that sort of thing. If the presentations he sometimes had to do at work were any guide, then he certainly wouldn't be able to maintain a convincing cover story in the face of police interrogation. But he could plan. Like he did all those times when he or she or both of them had had a couple of drinks too many after dinner and it always seemed to end in an argument and she would go up to bed and he would stay downstairs and watch the TV. He knew that when he got upstairs, she would be asleep and snoring in that unpleasant way that sounded as if she had a bone stuck in her throat. He'd once read an article by someone who'd said that you could never hate someone if you had watched them sleep. That person had clearly never been one of the eleven or more people who had slept with Suzanne. Instead of just getting into the bed beside her and planning her death, he could take his pillow and put it over her face and push down until the struggling had ceased. It might work. 'I woke up and she was stone cold beside me.' What could have happened?

But of course he did just get into the bed beside her and it was the plan and the thought of how easy it would have been that calmed and comforted him, so that it was easy for him to sleep. There was always another day. Another day, another plan.

Neither of them had ever been religious, but the funeral was held in the local church, a stone's throw from their house. It was a grey and drizzly day. Mourners shook their umbrellas in the porch, then left them there in furled rows. Gradually people filled the pews, taking off their thick coats, settling themselves in, squinting at the order of service in the dim light. Some of Gary's friends were there, but most of them were Suzanne's. They sat in groups, bookended by their husbands, and whispered loudly to each other and handed out tissues and peppermints. But when the coffin was carried in, a hush fell. The creak of the pallbearers' shoes could be heard.

The vicar had a bad cold that day. His voice was thick and every so often he gave several short, hard coughs, as if he was embarrassed. He stood in front of the congregation, folded his hands in front of him and looked at their upturned, expectant faces. He felt lousy. After this, he would go home and have soup for lunch and then if he had time, he would have a nap before the next service. He cleared his throat.

'It is always tragic when someone dies young,' he said. 'And perhaps all the more so when it is unexpected. We ask ourselves why: why is a life cut short? What is God's purpose? But instead of thinking about what we have lost, we should celebrate what we have had. A short life can still be a rich one, full of achievement and of love.'

He paused, momentarily thwarted by his utter ignorance of the deceased, whom he had never met.

'Gareth Boyle was a family man. He lived a simple life, but one full of affection and closeness. I know that all of you in this church will have your own memories of him. Particularly his wife, Suzanne.'

Suzanne, sitting in the front pew beside Gary's brother, lifted her head. Her hair had been cut and highlighted the day before and it fell in soft blonde folds round her face. She had bought herself a new black dress for the occasion as well, calf length and with a cinched waist. She sat upright and looked composed. It didn't seem that she would need the tissues that were folded in her bag. In the pew behind her sat Rob, smart in a grey suit and red tie. He had a small plaster on his neck: he must have cut himself shaving. Once, he leaned forward and whispered something in her ear and although she didn't respond, a tiny smile flickered on her lips.

The vicar was drawing to a close.

'What makes a good life?' he was asking.

Five rows down, Sally – the friend Suzanne always had lunch with on Tuesdays – nudged Claire, who went to Pilates classes with Suzanne on Thursday evenings.

'I know it seems a dreadful thing to say,' she whispered, 'but don't you think that Suzanne looks particularly radiant today? I've never seen her looking so lovely. It must be the grief.'

The vicar ground to a halt, blew his nose. The organ wheezed. The coffin was carried slowly out of the church, into the blank afternoon. People felt in their pockets for change to put in the collection tray on the way out and started wriggling into coats and jackets. Suzanne stood and made her way to the end of the pew. Rob rose as well. Putting his hand under her elbow, he escorted her down the aisle like a bride.

Nicci French

author photo © Mark Read

About Nicci and Sean

Nicci Gerrard was born in June 1958 in Worcestershire. After graduating with a first class honours degree in English Literature from Oxford University, she began her first job, working with emotionally disturbed children in Sheffield.

In the early eighties she taught English Literature in Sheffield, London and Los Angeles, but moved into publishing in 1985 with the launch of *Women's Review*, a magazine for women on art, literature and female issues. In 1987 Nicci had a son, Edgar, followed by a daughter, Anna, but by the time she became acting literary editor at the *New Statesman* her marriage had ended. She moved to the *Observer* in 1990, where she was deputy literary editor for five years, and then a feature writer and executive editor. It was while she was at the *New Statesman* that she met Sean French.

Sean French was born in May 1959 in Bristol, to a British father and Swedish mother. He too studied English Literature at Oxford University at the same time as Nicci, also graduating with a first class degree, but their paths didn't cross until 1990. In 1981 he won *Vogue* magazine's Writing Talent Contest, and from 1981 to 1986 he was their theatre critic. During that time he also worked at the *Sunday Times* as their deputy literary editor and television critic, and was the film critic for *Marie Claire* and deputy editor of *New Society*.

Sean and Nicci were married in Hackney in October 1990. Their daughters, Hadley and Molly, were born in 1991 and 1993.

By the mid nineties Sean had had two novels published, *The Imaginary Monkey* and *The Dreamer of Dreams*, as well as numerous non-fiction books, including biographies of Jane Fonda and Brigitte Bardot.

In 1995 Nicci and Sean began work on their first joint novel and adopted the pseudonym of Nicci French. The novel, *The Memory Game*, was published to great acclaim in 1997. *The Safe House*, *Killing Me Softly*, *Beneath the Skin*, *The Red Room*, *Land of the Living*, *Secret Smile*, *Catch Me When I Fall*, *Losing You*, *Until It's Over*, *What to Do When Someone Dies* and *Complicit* have since been added to the Nicci French CV. *The Safe House*, *Beneath the Skin* and *Secret Smile* have all been adapted for TV, and *Killing Me Softly* for the big screen.

But Nicci and Sean also continue to write separately. Nicci still works as a journalist for the *Observer*, covering high-profile trials including those of Fred and Rose West, and Ian Huntley and Maxine Carr. Her novels *Things We Knew Were True*, *Solace*, *The Moment You Were Gone* and *The Winter House* are also published by Penguin. Sean's novel *Start From Here* came out in spring 2004.

Playing Music

My father played the piano. He would come home from work, take off his suit jacket and sit down on the piano stool with an expression of contentment. He didn't usually have sheet music, but would let his fingers wander up and down the keys, picking out old remembered tunes or improvising. He wasn't a great pianist, but he seemed at home there. He sang as well – he used to embarrass me at weddings and carol services by harmonizing merrily, his light, true voice rising above everyone else's ragged chorus. Music seemed to come effortlessly to him, another way of communicating.

To me, however, music has always been a foreign language and the scenes where the band plays together in *Complicit* are not based on anything I have ever experienced. I have a tin ear and fumbling fingers. At school concerts, I was made to mouth the words rather than sing them out loud, so that I did not ruin the general effect. That seems a bit brutal now, but at the time it seemed a matter of common sense – I could hear how out of place my voice sounded. I was embarrassed by it, and I still am.

When I was eleven, I insisted that I wanted to learn the violin and so I had lessons at school once a week and took home the loaned violin to practise with great diligence. I used to love rubbing rosin on the strings and would stand in front of the mirror to see how I looked with the delicate instrument tucked under my chin. I liked carrying it around with me in its case – I imagined people would look at me and see me as a young musician, someone I dearly wanted to be. But oh Lord, I made such a horrible sound – like a tormented cat, like a dying sea lion, like nails run down a chalkboard, like nothing you've ever heard outside of horror movies where a woman screams and screams in the night . . . I played 'The Minstrel Boy' and 'Silent Night' (I didn't get much further than that). My fingers became thick and couldn't find the right place on the strings, and my neck ached. My parents made me move rooms, so I was at the back of the house and less screechingly audible. After a year, my teacher told me that I wasn't really progressing.

About thirty years later, I took up the violin once more (a triumph of hope over bitter experience), in order to learn alongside my daughter. Sean and I had a plan that we could play music together as a family. But with a sense of mortification, I felt history repeat itself. I couldn't hit the right note. Sharper than sharp, flatter than flat. Cracked, split, jarring music rang out once again in my home. My young daughter looked at me with pity and wonder. Our violin teacher asked me to sing a note before playing it, thinking that would make it easier for me – ha! For people like me, singing is like walking naked on to a stage. Or no, it's much worse than that. It's as if I'm revealing something ugly and discordant at the heart of me. Once more, I loosened the bow strings, put the violin away in its case. Never again.

Yet I still dream of playing and of singing. One of Sean's Swedish cousins, who's a professional flautist, told us that when she is in an orchestra, or plays chamber music, the experience of hearing everyone in harmony and of all the parts coming together to create a glorious whole is better than any other feeling in the world, as close to pure happiness as she ever comes. To stand in a choir and sing a requiem, becoming part of the great architecture of sound, to play the violin in a string quartet, must be to lose yourself in something beautiful. I'd love that. Nobody else would love it, though.

I do sing, though. I sing on my bike. Loudly. Badly. Wildly. The 'Queen of the Night Aria' from *The Magic Flute*, 'You're Just in Love' ('I hear singing and there's no one there . . .') from *Call Me Madam*, Bob Dylan and Neil Young songs, 'Oh My Darling, Clementine' and 'There's a Hole in my Bucket', 'O Little Town of Bethlehem', in summer as well as winter. The wind kindly takes my words away.

NICCI GERRARD

Sean: We wrote the first pages of our first novel, *The Memory Game*, in January 1995. I was thirty-five years old. Our youngest child was a year old and our eldest was seven. Now the eldest two have left home, I'm almost fifty and as I look up I can see that Nicci French books occupy about a foot of bookshelf space and consist, I suppose, of about a million words. When I look at the books, I also see some ghosts. Between *Killing Me Softly* and *Beneath the Skin*, we wrote an entire novel that we scrapped completely. A couple more times we've written fifty pages or so when the novel died on us and couldn't be revived.

I worked on *The Memory Game* in an attic room in Kentish Town. My contribution to the one you're now holding was mostly done in a shed in a garden in Suffolk, a county I had previously only visited to catch ferries to Sweden, where many of my family live. By curious coincidence, our second novel, *The Safe House*, was about a woman who moves, disastrously as it turns out, to the coast of Essex. By the end of the novel she has fled back to the safety of Stoke Newington. Two years after the novel was published, we had moved to a village just half an hour's drive further into East Anglia.

'My contribution to the one you're now holding was mostly done in a shed in a garden'

I sometimes look at that daunting line of spines on the shelf and wonder how we've developed over eleven books and fifteen years. We must have, but really it's for other people to say. When I think about the books, it's not so much their subject matter that I remember but the books as part of our lives as a couple and a family. A lot of it is to do with walks we've taken together: on the Isle of Sheppey on New Year's Day while preparing to start *The Memory Game*, the drive on which we had the sudden idea that became *Killing Me Softly*, the cottage in Sweden where we wrote the first section of *Land of the Living*, the December day we walked on Mersea Island with two of our children and a dog, the very day and place on which *Losing You* was to be set.

We delivered the typescript of *The Memory Game* in July 1995. A week or so later we were phoned in Sweden by our agent, and close friend, Pat

Kavanagh (who died suddenly and much too soon in 2008). She liked the book and was sure it would be published. Nicci and I went for a walk that evening, one of those Swedish summer evenings where the golden twilight seems to last until the sun comes up, and we talked about what this meant for us and how our life might change.

'bad luck comes when you're least expecting it, ambushing you'

It did change, but not entirely in the way we had anticipated. Our first book had been conceived as a sort of experiment – was it possible for the two of us to write together in a single voice? And it had been written in secret. Now we found ourselves as one writer with the freedom to go in to strange places. What if you suddenly fell in love, abandoned your life, all for someone you didn't know? What if you woke in the dark, restrained, with no memory of how you had got there? And then you escaped and nobody believed you? What if your child went missing? What if – as in this book – you kept stumbling on murders that had nothing in common, except for you? What if . . .? What if . . .? One of the things we've done, maybe, is to turn questions into stories.

Nicci: Cyril Connolly famously wrote that the enemy of promise is the pram in the hall – or in our case, buggy in the hall, Moses basket in the living room, potties in the bedroom, babygrows draped over every chair, newborn howling in the night, toddler falling down the stairs, homework to be helped with, mess to be cleared up, sleepovers to be survived . . . But Elizabeth Gaskell said that she wrote in a room off the kitchen, child on her lap and the soup on the hob next door. We've gone for the Elizabeth Gaskell model of writing: writing in the midst of domestic chaos and the insistent demands of children, which don't diminish as they grow older, only become more unpredictable.

And perhaps this is one of the subjects of our novels – that life doesn't happen the way you expect. Sean and I often talk about how most of us like to think that we are in control of our lives. If we are very lucky, we have committed relationships and close friendships; maybe we have children; perhaps we have jobs and mortgages and credit cards; we have a doctor and a dentist and insurance policies and some of us pay money into pension funds; we fill in tax forms, sign contracts, pay bills, read the small print . . . But bad luck comes when you're least expecting it, ambushing you. We always write with the knowledge that life can unravel and one of our subjects is what happens then.

'Sean and I have lived a life in which all compartments have collapsed'

Although I sometimes long for days of uninterrupted tranquility, I know that this is how I've chosen to work and to live. The idea of a writer's retreat, where all you have to do all day is think and compose sentences and you can't fritter your time peering into the fridge (many of our novels are obsessed with the contents of fridges, from the bountifully full to the depressingly empty), drinking cups of coffee or tea on the hour, pairing socks, fielding phone calls from school, is enough to give me writer's block. For fifteen years, for eleven novels published and a twelfth written and a thirteenth in progress, Sean and I have lived a life in which all compartments have collapsed (no divisions between life and work, job and marriage, him and me; everything leaking into everything else). We've written on trains and planes and in strange hotel rooms, in corners of the day. We've written to find out what we think about things, to explore shared fears and obsessions. We've written about the strangeness of life, the fragility of happiness, the turbulence that lies just beneath the surface, the randomness of bad luck. We've written books born out of arguments, out of shared experiences. We've been surprised by each other. There are very few rules and very little structure. And it hasn't got easier, neater or more structured with the years. But if it hasn't got easier, nor has it got less interesting, challenging or unnerving. Sometimes writing feels like a form of madness, or at least something designed to send you mad – to go and sit in front of a screen for hour upon hour, dragging words up from a dark place you don't quite understand. You don't do it because you should, you do it because you must. It's been a strange and exhilarating journey we've gone on together; it's been our shared adventure.

THE SAFE HOUSE

You let a traumatized young woman into your home.
And into your heart.
You want to protect her like a member of your own family.
To save her from the darkness that's pursuing her . . .

Samantha Laschen is a doctor specializing in post-traumatic stress disorder. She's moved to the coast to escape her problems and to be alone with her young daughter. But now the police want her to take in Fiona Mackenzie, a girl whose parents have been savagely murdered. Yet by allowing Fiona in, Sam is exposing herself – and her daughter – to risks she couldn't possibly have imagined.

'A superior psychological thriller' *The Times*

'Emotionally acute' *Mail on Sunday*

BENEATH THE SKIN

Someone's watching you.
You don't know who and you don't know why.
But he knows you . . .

Zoë, Jennifer and Nadia are three women with nothing in common except the letters they receive, each one full of intimate details about every aspect of their lives – from the clothes they wear to the way they act when they think they're alone. And if that isn't terrifying enough, the letters also contain a shocking promise: that soon each life will come to a sudden, violent end. Can Zoë, Jennifer and Nadia discover who their tormentor is? And if so, will any of them live long enough to do anything about it?

'A nail-biting, can't-put-it-down read' *Marie Claire*

'Chilling, startling' *Daily Mail*

'Brilliant' *Evening Standard*

The Books

THE MEMORY GAME

You remember an ordinary, idyllic childhood.
Then one day you discover that your memory is deceitful.
And possibly deadly . . .

When a skeleton is unearthed, Jane Martello is shocked to learn it's that of her childhood friend, Natalie, who went missing twenty-five years ago. Encouraged by a therapist to recover lost memories, Jane hopes to find out what really took place when she was a child – and what happened to Natalie. But in learning the truth about her and Natalie's pasts, is Jane putting her own future at terrible risk?

'Electrifying' *Harpers & Queen*

KILLING ME SOFTLY

You have it all: the boyfriend, the friends, the career.
Then you meet a stranger and, on impulse, you sacrifice everything.
You're in passionate love.
And grave danger . . .

Alice Loudon couldn't resist abandoning her old, safe life for a wild affair. And in Adam Tallis, a rugged mountaineer with a murky past, she finds a man who can teach her things about herself that she never even suspected. But sexual obsession has its dark side – and so does Adam. Soon both are threatening all that Alice has left. First her sanity. Then her life.

'Compulsive, sexy, scary' *Elle*

'Cancel all appointments and unplug the phone. Once started you will do nothing until you finish this thriller' *Harpers & Queen*

'A real frightener' *Guardian*

THE RED ROOM

**The man who almost killed you has been accused of murder.
And you hold the key to his future . . .**

After psychologist Kit Quinn is brutally attacked by a prisoner, she is determined to get straight back to work. When the police want her help in linking the man who attacked her to a series of murders, she refuses to simply accept the obvious. But the closer her investigation takes her to the truth behind the savage crimes, the nearer Kit gets to the dark heart of her own terror.

'Gripping, chilling, moving' *Observer*

'Absorbing, highly addictive' *Evening Standard*

'French is excellent at building up suspense and elegantly exploiting all our worst fears' *Daily Mail*

SECRET SMILE

**You have an affair.
You finish it.
You think it's over.
You're dead wrong . . .**

Miranda Cotton thinks she's put boyfriend Brendan out of her life for good. But two weeks later, he's intimately involved with her sister. Soon what began as an embarrassment becomes threatening – then even more terrifying than a girl's worst nightmare. Because this time Brendan will stop at nothing to be part of Miranda's life – even if it means taking it from her . . .

'Creepy, genuinely gripping' *Heat*

'A must read' *Cosmopolitan*

'Nicci French at the top of her game' *Woman & Home*

CATCH ME WHEN I FALL

**You're a whirlwind. You're a success. You live life on the edge.
But who'll catch you when you fall?**

Holly Krauss lives life in the fast lane. A successful young
businesswoman with a stable home life, she is loved and admired by all
who meet her. But that's only one side of Holly. The other sees her take
regular walks on the wild side – where she makes ever more reckless
mistakes.

And when those mistakes start mounting up, the two sides of Holly blur
together and her life quickly spirals out of control. She thinks she's being
stalked, someone is demanding money from her – threats lurk around
every corner and those closest to Holly are running out of patience.

But is she alone responsible for what's happening? Are her fears just the
paranoia of an illness – or intimations of very real danger? And if she can
no longer rely on her own judgement, who can she trust to catch her when
she falls?

LOSING YOU

**What is worse than your child going missing?
Your child going missing and nobody believing you . . .**

Nina Landry has given up city life for the isolated community of Sandling
Island, lying off the bleak east coast of England. At night the wind howls.
Sometimes they are cut off by the incoming tide. For Nina though it is
home. It is safe.

But when Nina's teenage daughter Charlie fails to return from a sleepover
on the day they're due to go on holiday, the island becomes a different
place altogether. A place of secrets and suspicions. Where no one –
friends, neighbours or the police – believes Nina's instinctive fear that her
daughter is in terrible danger. Alone, she undergoes a frantic search for
Charlie. And as day turns to night, she begins to doubt not just whether
they'll leave the island for their holiday – but whether they will ever leave
it again.

LAND OF THE LIVING

You wake in the dark, gagged and bound.
He says he will kill you – just like all the rest.

Abbie Devereaux is being held against her will. She doesn't know where she is or how she got there. She's so terrified she can barely remember her own name – and she's sure of just one thing: that she will survive this nightmare. But even if she does make it back to the land of the living, Abbie knows that he'll still be out there, looking for her.

And next time, there may be no escape.

'Shocking, uncomfortable, exhilarating' *Independent on Sunday*

'Dark, gripping' *Heat*

UNTIL IT'S OVER

Dead. Unlucky.

Young and athletic, London cycle courier Astrid Bell is bad luck – for other people. First Astrid's neighbour Peggy Farrell accidentally knocks her off her bike – and not long after is found bludgeoned to death in an alley. Then a few days later, Astrid is asked to pick up a package from a wealthy woman called Ingrid de Soto, only to find the client murdered in the hall of her luxurious home.

For the police it's more than coincidence. For Astrid and her six housemates it's the beginning of a nightmare: suspicious glances, bitter accusations, fallings out and a growing fear that the worst is yet to come . . .

Because if it's true that bad luck comes in threes – who will be the next to die?

WHAT TO DO WHEN SOMEONE DIES

Ellie Faulkner's world has been destroyed. Her husband Greg died in a car crash – and he wasn't alone. In the passenger seat was the body of Milena Livingstone – a woman Ellie's never heard of.

But Ellie refuses to leap to the obvious conclusion, despite the whispers and suspicions of those around her. Maybe it's the grief, but Ellie has to find out who this woman was – and prove Greg wasn't having an affair.

And soon she is chillingly certain their deaths were no accident. Are Ellie's accusations of murder her way of avoiding the truth about her marriage? Or does an even more sinister discovery await her?

'You'll be hooked from the first page. A compulsive page-turner' *Daily Express*

'Brilliant. A fast-paced, intricately detailed thriller with unexpected twists and turns' *She*

COMPLICIT

Who is more dangerous? An enemy? A friend? Or a lover?

Bonnie Graham is standing in her friend's flat. She is alone, except for the dead body lying in a pool of blood on the floor. What happened? What will she do? And what role has she played in the murderous events?

Bonnie is a music teacher who has spent a long, hot summer in London rehearsing with a band to play at a wedding. It was supposed to be fun, but the band members find the complicated knots of their friendships unravelling as the days themselves unwind. What was meant to be a summer of happiness, love and music turns deadly as lovers betray one another, passions turn murderous and friendship itself becomes a crime.

Everyone tells lies. But is anyone prepared to tell the truth to uncover a murderer?

'Relentlessly addictive ... friendship and betrayal have never been so deadly' *Mirror*

'Razor sharp twists and turns' *Daily Express*

He just wanted a decent book to read ...

Not too much to ask, is it? It was in 1935 when Allen Lane, Managing Director of Bodley Head Publishers, stood on a platform at Exeter railway station looking for something good to read on his journey back to London. His choice was limited to popular magazines and poor-quality paperbacks – the same choice faced every day by the vast majority of readers, few of whom could afford hardbacks. Lane's disappointment and subsequent anger at the range of books generally available led him to found a company – and change the world.

'We believed in the existence in this country of a vast reading public for intelligent books at a low price, and staked everything on it'
Sir Allen Lane, 1902–1970, founder of Penguin Books

The quality paperback had arrived – and not just in bookshops. Lane was adamant that his Penguins should appear in chain stores and tobacconists, and should cost no more than a packet of cigarettes.

Reading habits (and cigarette prices) have changed since 1935, but Penguin still believes in publishing the best books for everybody to enjoy. We still believe that good design costs no more than bad design, and we still believe that quality books published passionately and responsibly make the world a better place.

So wherever you see the little bird – whether it's on a piece of prize-winning literary fiction or a celebrity autobiography, political tour de force or historical masterpiece, a serial-killer thriller, reference book, world classic or a piece of pure escapism – you can bet that it represents the very best that the genre has to offer.

Whatever you like to read – trust Penguin.

read more
www.penguin.co.uk